# Kathryn

## The Bellamy Sisters
## Book 6

## Minerva Spencer

writing as
## S.M. LAVIOLETTE

This is dedicated to my father.

I miss you every day, Dad.

# Chapter One



I refuse to do this!" Miss Letitia Grayson snapped. "It is immoral. It is wrong. And—and it is *disgraceful.*"

Lady Kathryn Bellamy stifled a yawn. "Then don't do it, Letty. Nobody is forcing you."

Letty's smooth brow furrowed. "But if I do not play then will you—"

"If you do not participate, then do not expect an invitation to the Duchess of Chatham's house party," Katie lied. In truth, she had no say whatsoever in who her sister Hyacinth invited to her annual summer house party. Katie doubted that Hy— who delegated everything pertaining to entertainment to one of the duke's secretaries—even knew who was coming. Hy *despised* house parties and usually hid in Chatham Park's dower house, which the duke had renovated for his wife's private use. But the young women surrounding Katie did not know any of that, and they all desperately yearned for one of the most coveted invitations of the year.

Katie knew she should be ashamed of lying and manipulating them, but—as was so often the case—she could not bring herself to care.

"Katie, I—" Letty stopped, chewing her lower lip so roughly it turned a dark red. "I do not know if I can do this."

Miss Julia Tremont and Miss Caroline Shelby snickered at Letty's unease.

The sound of their tittering grated on Katie's nerves, making it difficult to recall why she associated with the two ninnies.

*Because nobody else wants to spend any time around you.*

Katie knew that was true. It should have hurt, but it didn't. Nothing really hurt or mattered to her, and that was the way she liked it.

Letty leaned close to Katie and whispered. "Please, don't make me do this."

"I am not *making* you do anything," Katie said, not bothering to lower her voice.

Letty glared at Katie; her anger mixed with something that looked like desperation. Although this was Letty's third Season, Katie had not spent much time with her until this year. Aside from huge, lovely hazel eyes with lush brown eyelashes and thick chestnut hair, Letty was a rather plain girl. She was almost as tall as Katie's five-feet-nine inches, but—unlike Katie—she did not possess much of a figure.

Letty was also poor and had worn the same two ballgowns all year. Until Katie brought her into her circle of intimates, Letty's less than spectacular appearance and tiny dowry had made her an outlier at *ton* functions. Although she was reserved, she was also funny and sharp-witted when she relaxed. Katie liked her a great deal more than anyone else she had met in several years and hoped the girl would stick to her principles and refuse to play her stupid *kissing game.*

For a moment, as Letty glared twin holes into Katie's head, it seemed as if principle might win over peer pressure.

But then Letty's shoulders sagged. "Fine. I will do it."

Katie's throat became unpleasantly thick at the other girl's words, and she had to swallow several times to clear it. What a disappointment people were. All of them.

She turned her back on Letty's flaming face and eyed Lady Michelle Beaumont and Miss Elinor Fisher. "What about you two?"

"We are both in," Elinor said, speaking for both of them as she usually did. In fact, Katie wasn't sure that she'd ever heard Michelle speak.

"I want to play," Caroline said.

"Me, too," Julia hastily added.

Katie reached into her reticule to bring out a folded piece of paper. "Here is the list."

Elinor snatched the paper, and Michelle leaned close as she unfolded it, Julia and Caroline craning their necks to see. Only Letty did not try to get a look.

"Read it out loud, Elinor," Julia ordered.

"For one point there is Lord Chambers, Mr. Andrew Morecombe—"

"But Mr. Morecombe is *married!*" Letty hissed.

Katie rolled her eyes. "It is only a kiss, Letty. I am not asking you to give birth to the man's child."

All five women goggled at her.

"Have you no shame?" Letty managed, the only one who appeared capable of speech.

"Not much," Katie admitted.

Letty crossed her arms. "I know Elizabeth Morecombe, and she is a lovely person. I would never kiss her husband."

Katie shrugged. "I already told you that you don't have to—"

"I don't care if he *is* married; I will kiss Morecombe," Elinor said.

Katie lifted an eyebrow at the other girl's brazen claim, and Elinor's cheeks blazed with color, but she did not lower her eyes. Katie was impressed. Who would have guessed that Elinor had so much grit?

"Who else is on there?" Caroline demanded, her blue eyes sparkling.

Elinor continued, "Viscount Telford, Baron Fowler"—she cut Katie an exasperated look. "That is hardly fair!"

"Why not?"

"You are friends with Fowler. He will kiss you just to help you win."

Katie gave a genuine laugh. Angus Fowler, the Duke of Chatham's best friend, treated Katie the same way he did a woodlouse—a harmless nuisance to be tolerated but never encouraged. "If you believe Fowler would help me do *anything* you clearly don't know as much as you think you do."

Caroline frowned. "I still don't—"

Elinor's squeal made the rest of them wince. "*Dulverton!*"

Katie gave the little blonde a withering glance. "Perhaps you might screech that a bit louder, Elinor. There are probably a few people at the far end of Berkeley Square who didn't hear you."

Elinor's mouth clamped shut and she glanced around nervously at a cluster of wallflowers not too far away. Several of them were staring at Katie's group with yearning, but she doubted the other women could hear their conversation over the din of the ballroom.

"The Duke of Dulverton?" Letty repeated, taking the list from Elinor's unresisting fingers, as if she needed to confirm the name with her own eyes.

"He is worth ten points, while everyone else is worth only one. Just think, Letty, you could win with only one kiss," Katie said, amused by their dismayed faces.

Letty snorted. "He should be worth a hundred because he never comes to London during—"

"He is here *tonight*," Julia contradicted smugly, looking to Katie for approval.

Katie nodded. "For once, Julia is right." She ignored Julia's huff of outrage and added, "Dulverton arrived just a few minutes before you did."

"A fat lot of good that will do us," Caroline groused. "He hasn't danced a single set. All he's been doing is talking to some old man."

Six pairs of eyes slid toward where the massive, tow-headed duke loomed over a much shorter, rotund, gray-haired man. Katie could not help noticing how the people around the duke were all stealing furtive glances at him, as if Dulverton was a rare mythical beast that had wandered into their midst. Katie supposed an unmarried duke who was not an octogenarian was about as common as a unicorn.

"How will we ever kiss the man if he doesn't dance or talk to any of us?" Julia demanded.

"That is your problem," Katie said. She already had several ideas but had no intention of sharing them because she was going to win this contest.

"But he is so very *ugly*," Caroline whined. "I cannot imagine kissing him, even if I *could* get near enough."

Even from this distance it was clear that Caroline's words, however unkind, were true. Not only did the duke have the hulking body of a common laborer rather than a gentleman of leisure but his nose was a veritable beak, and his jaw, while chiseled and square, jutted far too aggressively to be handsome. He had deeply set eyes and shadows lurked in the harsh angles of his face and beneath his heavy brow. It was a face that would have been more at home on a gothic carving than a peer of the realm.

His golden-brown skin contrasted bizarrely with his hair, which was a pale cornsilk color usually only seen on very young children. The unusual shade might have been appealing had it not been shorn as short as a sheep in June.

Caroline shivered. "He frightens me. Ten points is not enough for kissing him," she said, her words causing nervous laughter.

"You needn't kiss Dulverton nor anyone else in the room," Katie snapped, for some reason annoyed by their girlish twittering. She swept the group with a contemptuous look. "You needn't play at all."

None of them said a word.

But Katie knew they would play. All of them.

And she would win. Not because she was smarter or more desirable, but because winning, no matter how inconsequential the prize, was the only thing that made her feel anything.

# Chapter Two

Gerrit Boon Jaak Van Draak, the fifth Duke of Dulverton, swallowed a mouthful of champagne and then grimaced as the revolting beverage trickled down his throat.

"You will break that glass if you squeeze it much harder, Your Grace," his uncle, Baron Bas van Renesse, teased in a jovial voice.

Gerrit scowled and gestured to a servant who was passing with a tray. "Take this." He thrust the mostly full glass at the wide-eyed lackey. Once the servant had scuttled away, Gerrit glared down at his uncle, a man he'd only met once before tonight. "You said Lady Mariska would be here at ten o'clock. It is now thirty-seven minutes past ten."

A faint smile pulled at the older man's thin lips, as if something about this annoying situation amused him. "When have you ever known a woman to care about time?"

Gerrit's scowl only deepened at the pointless generalization.

"Have patience, Your Grace."

"I have been patient for two years," he reminded his uncle. "I weary of—"

"Ah, there is Lady Palmer," the baron interrupted.

A stout, well-dressed woman of middling years pushed her way through the crowd. She was red-cheeked and flustered, and her apprehensive gaze flickered to van Renesse and then to Gerrit and quickly away again.

Even Gerrit, abysmal when it came to reading other people's expressions, could see the woman was distressed about something.

Lady Palmer dropped into an impressively low curtsy for a woman of her age and girth. "I am terribly sorry to be late, Your Grace, but—"

"Where is Lady Mariska?" Gerrit demanded, raising his voice to speak over her. Meeting people's eyes was something that had never come easily to Gerrit— something about it had always felt almost like a physical touch to him—but his father had insisted the reaction was a weakness, so Gerrit had struggled for years to overcome his aversion.

The woman recoiled at either his harsh tone, pointed glare, or both, and van Renesse clucked his tongue and chuckled nervously. "You will have to forgive His Grace. He has forgotten his manners in his excitement to meet his prospective bride."

*Excitement?* Gerrit's hands clenched into fists at his uncle's fatuous description of his current frame of mind. He opened his mouth to castigate the older man, but Lady Palmer recommenced babbling.

"I beg your pardon, Your Grace, but the heat in the ballroom was so oppressive that Lady Mariska went out to the garden to take some air."

Gerrit's jaw shifted back and forth, and he narrowed his eyes, keeping Lady Palmer pinioned. Why did he think she was lying? "She has only just arrived and is overheated?"

Lady Palmer swallowed hard. "Er… yes?"

"That sounded like a question."

"No, no. She was feeling uncomfortably flushed."

Gerrit snorted and turned to van Renesse. "What a tender bloom you have brought me, Uncle."

Van Renesse quailed beneath Gerrit's scathing tone and then gave another of his annoying chuckles. He reached out to pat Gerrit's arm before recalling how much he hated being touched and hastily withdrew his hand. "Mariska is a modest girl, Your Grace. The very characteristics that will make her such a conformable, obedient wife also render her shy in public. She has only recently left a strict religious environment. This"—he made a gesture to encompass the room around them—"is the sort of sophisticated function that terrifies innocent young women."

Gerrit had to admit there might be some truth to the other man's words. Even though the girl was one-and-twenty—one of his conditions for the marriage—her family had kept her at the convent to ensure her virtue, something they had decided on after the last broken betrothal.

How must this glittering ballroom—overflowing with ogling peers and silk-clad women falling out of their gowns—appear to a girl who'd been cloistered away from the world for most of her life?

As Gerrit looked around him, men and women, one after another, quickly glanced away rather than meet his gaze. He gave a rumble of displeasure. He *hated* being the center of attention and any pity he might have felt for Lady Mariska was speedily dissipating.

"If she is so bloody retiring then why the hell did you suggest meeting here?" Gerrit demanded, turning away from the gawking party guests back to his uncle.

"It was a mistake, Your Grace, and I see that now," his uncle said, his placating tone incensing Gerrit even more.

A sudden unwanted notion struck Gerrit like a punch to the face. "Is Lady Mariska perchance *hiding* in the garden because she is here against her will?"

His uncle swallowed. "Er—"

"Tell me the truth," he snarled before van Renesse commenced spewing lies. "I will not have a repeat of the last fiasco."

"This will be nothing like the last time," van Renesse hastily assured him. "Lady Mariska was very excited to come to London."

"She was excited to come to *London*?" Gerrit repeated, his temper yet again spiking at the older man's evasive words. "I did not ask about her view on foreign travel. How excited is she to become my wife, Uncle?"

Van Renesse eyes slid to Lady Palmer.

"*Fuck!*" Gerrit grated.

Lady Palmer swooned, and his uncle took her arm to steady her. And then the bastard dared to cut Gerrit a chiding look. "Your Grace, that is hardly—"

Gerrit pointed his index finger in the other man's face, stopping less than a quarter of an inch from van Renesse's nose. "Shut. Up."

Lady Palmer gasped at his vicious order, but his uncle pursed his lips, clearly deciding discretion was the better part of valor.

The urge to throttle the smaller man was so strong that Gerrit was almost dizzy at the uncharacteristic swirl of emotions.

He glared down at van Renesse, whose eyes lowered to the floor in silent submission, a gesture that did nothing to calm Gerrit's rapidly growing fury.

Not only had he paid an immoderate sum to both his uncle and the Palmer woman to arrange this betrothal, but he had wasted his time on this journey to London. He despised being in the City at any time of year, but especially during the height of the Season. And to make matters worse, he was currently standing in a bloody ballroom!

The compulsion to stride from the sweltering, crowded ballroom where he was obviously a figure of morbid curiosity was almost overwhelming.

But the clarion call of duty was even stronger.

God damn it! He needed a wife. He needed an heir. Thanks to his idiot ancestors he felt strongly compelled to take a Dutch wife. He was sick and tired of thinking about the subject and did not want to be thinking about it again for another bloody year. And if he left now, that is exactly what would happen.

Reining in his fury and gritting his teeth, he turned to Lady Palmer. "Does Lady Mariska wish for this betrothal, my lady."

She jolted at his question.

"I would have the unvarnished truth," he warned when she hesitated. "And I would have it *now*."

Lady Palmer cleared her throat. "Lady Mariska is young and innocent and inexperienced, Your Grace—"

"I am aware of her age and condition. That is not the question I asked."

"She is not opposed to the match," Lady Palmer hurried on, flinching at whatever she saw on Gerrit's face—likely the murderous rage he was feeling. "At—at least not entirely."

If she had meant her words to be reassuring, they failed spectacularly.

It was all he could do to keep from throwing back his head and howling like the savage beast he so resembled. "Lady Mariska has had almost two years to reject my offer," Gerrit seethed, his voice impressively quiet given the emotions rampaging within him. "Why has she waited until three weeks before our wedding to voice her reservations?" His voice had risen by the time he reached the end of his question, and people around them were gawking.

Gerrit did not give a damn.

"Answer me," he bit out.

"I—I—" Her voice broke off on a sob.

Van Renesse patted her arm while murmuring, "There, there, my dear."

Gerrit briefly squeezed his eyes shut. What a fucking mess.

He cut a scathing look at the crowds around them, his eyes lingering on the clusters of young women who had drifted ever closer since his arrival but now skittered away like frightened rabbits. Any one of them would marry him— regardless of how hideous he looked—and he could have a wife with a brat in her belly by the end of summer.

But *no*. He had to take a Dutch bride.

He gritted his teeth.

Lady Mariska was his *third* betrothed, not including Christina the bitch, his first wife.

He had never even met the other two women as one had died at the age of seven-and-ten and the other had eloped with her music tutor at eight-and-ten. Gerrit was the least superstitious person he knew, but even he could not help feeling that any betrothal to him was doomed to failure.

After the catastrophic debacle of his first marriage—which his father had arranged—Gerrit had added two iron-clad stipulations to their family's longstanding tradition. First, the woman in question must be no younger than one-and-twenty at the time of their marriage.

And second, he wanted a letter from *her*, not her parent or guardian, agreeing to the union and denying any outstanding emotional entanglements.

This current betrothal had progressed with almost suspicious ease. He had written one letter to Lady Mariska—assuring her that he would only marry her if she gave her written consent—and had received a brief missive from her in the affirmative.

An unpleasant sensation began to creep through him like a slow-moving chill. It took him a moment to identify the emotion: It was indecision.

Gerrit loathed feeling uncertain and took every measure to avoid it by arranging his life with such rigid precision that snap decisions were rarely required. In Gerrit's life, there were no *what ifs* or *maybes*. Things just *were*.

Until tonight.

His uncle edged so close that Gerrit flinched away when the other man's elbow brushed against him.

"What do you want?" Gerrit asked irritably. There was enough moon that he could leave for home tonight if he left right now. He could—

"She has come all this way and you have waited all these years. Why not go to Lady Mariska, Your Grace? Talk to her—be… gentle."

Gerrit bristled. "*Be gentle?* What do you take me for, some sort of ravening beast?"

"No, no, no. Of course not. I meant no offence, Your Grace."

Gerrit turned to Lady Palmer, pinning her with a glare. "Is that her concern? That I am a beast?"

"Oh no, Your Grace! Not at all," she warbled, her eyes huge.

"She is not afraid of you," his uncle chimed in.

Gerrit saw nothing on the other man's cherubic face to calm the nausea roiling in his stomach. Why could people not speak honestly and directly? Why were van Renesse's blue eyes—eyes that were so like Gerrit's mother's—flickering about as nervously as a cat's tail?

"He should go to her, shouldn't he, Lady Palmer?" van Renesse prodded.

"Er, yes," the Palmer woman affirmed, once again sounding less than convincing.

"Damnation! I would have the truth from you, ma'am," Gerrit ground out. It made him ill to think of marrying another woman who did not want him, but he should at least speak to her. Shouldn't he? Or would that be badgering her?

"Y-yes," Lady Palmer said. "*Yes*," she repeated, slightly more convincing. "You should speak to her, Your Grace. I left her in the garden in a quiet spot. You can talk privately," she added when Gerrit continued to stare. As much as he disliked meeting other people's eyes, once he *locked* onto them, he found it difficult to break away.

Only when the woman lowered her gaze was Gerrit free to glance at his watch. It was seventeen minutes until eleven o'clock. He had wasted forty-seven minutes at this tedious function. Fifty-one minutes if one counted the time he had spent in the receiving line before gaining entrance to the ballroom.

Damnation.

"Where is she?" he barked.

Lady Palmer—as well as several people clearly eavesdropping on their conversation—jumped. "On a stone bench in the rose garden, Your Grace."

Without another word, Gerrit pivoted on his heel and strode toward the French doors.

"Wait, Your Grace!"

Gritting his teeth, he swung around at his uncle's voice. "What?"

"Should—should I come with you?"

"That would rather defeat the purpose of speaking to her privately, would it not?"

The older man's face flushed at his scathing tone. "Er, yes, I suppose so. What will you say to her, Your Grace?"

"That is between me and Lady Mariska."

***

Katie squirmed, but the arms around her—hard and male—did not loosen.

A bolt of fear shot up her spine. *Run!* a voice in her head shrieked. *Escape!*

Katie thrust her hands between her body and the hard torso trapping her and shoved. Either she pushed harder than she intended, or Mr. Morecombe's grasp had not been as unyielding as she'd believed because his lips—which had been fastened over hers more tightly than a blob of sealing wax on a piece of parchment—broke away and he staggered backward, halted by the stone bench behind him.

He wore a look of astonishment on his handsome face. "Is aught amiss, my lady?"

Katie dragged the back of her gloved, trembling hand over her mouth, like a child wiping something distasteful from its lips.

Morecombe's expression shifted from concerned confusion to mortified pique at the gesture.

"Nothing is the matter," she insisted in a breathless voice. She stole a glance at the nearby foliage, seeking out the prying eyes of her friends. She knew Julia and Caroline had followed them from the ballroom—not believing that Katie would really kiss Morecombe—but she saw no sign of them.

"Just what are you about?" Morecombe demanded, taking a step toward her. "You all but threw yourself at me when we reached the garden and now—"

"And now I have changed my mind," she said, giving him a cool look she was very far from feeling.

His jaw flexed and his nostrils flared. "I do not know what you are playing at, Lady Kathryn, but it is dangerous."

Katie had to agree; this game had not been one of her wiser ideas.

Morecombe glared a moment longer, and the cold, accusing anger in his eyes made her want to hide under a nearby shrub but she forced herself to hold his gaze.

He quickly mastered himself, his face once again a polite mask as he held out his arm. "I shall escort you back to the ballroom, my lady."

"No, thank you." She smoothed the skirt of her gown with a shaking hand. "I will remain outside for a while."

"As you wish." He sounded relieved, rather than offended and the soles of his dancing shoes made a gritty sound as they pivoted on the stone walk and he strode off into the night.

Katie waited until she could no longer hear his steps before heaving a sigh and collapsing on the stone garden bench. Her eyes burned and her vision became blurry. She squeezed her eyelids shut, refusing to shed tears because she did not *deserve* to cry. Her life was perfect. She was healthy, had a family who loved her— even though most of her sisters, and probably their husbands, were beyond frustrated with her by this point—and her brothers-in-law had collectively settled so much money on her that she could marry an impoverished street sweeper if she so chose.

In short, there was nothing for Katie to do other than please herself.

And yet she was incapable of feeling pleasure. Worse, she was miserable all the time.

Unlike her older sisters, there was no sacrifice for her to make. The four of them—Phoebe, Selina, Aurelia, and Hyacinth—had married wealthy men and saved their family from shame and destitution.

True, all of them had fallen in love with their husbands, even Hy, whom nobody—including Hy—would have believed *could* love somebody. But her reserved older sister loved the Duke of Chatham fiercely.

The only two who were still unmarried were Katie and her brother Dauntry. Doddy was the baby of the family and had just turned twenty, so he had an excuse.

Katie, on the other hand, would be three-and-twenty on her next birthday and was currently in her fifth Season. Her *fifth*.

"Are you sure you want another Season?" Hy, whom Katie had lived with for almost five years, had asked this past Christmas while discussing their plans for the New Year.

Katie had wanted to tell Hy the truth—that she wanted to go back to Queen's Bower, their childhood home and live alone—but she'd known that even Hy, her most unconventional sister, would have drawn a line at allowing such a thing.

And so she had agreed to yet another Season.

She might have gone to stay with one of her other sisters, all of whom had invited Katie to live with them. Although as time had passed, their invitations seemed less and less heartfelt.

Katie felt a rush of shame at the thought. All they wanted was for her to be happy, and she could feel their frustration that she only became moodier every year. What on earth would she do next year?

Oh Lord. She could *not* bear a sixth Season. There was—

"There you are! I have been looking all over for you, my lady." A massive shape suddenly emerged from the dimly lighted path and loomed over her.

Katie jolted at the hostile voice and did a double take when she saw who it belonged to.

It was the Duke of Dulverton, the elusive ten-point kiss.

# Chapter Three

Judging by the way Dulverton was glowering at Katie, she would have more luck challenging him to a duel than getting a kiss out of him.

He was even uglier than she'd thought earlier—mesmerizingly so—and Katie found that she could not look away. He was exceptionally tall, but it wasn't his height so much as his large-boned build that one noticed first. His jaw looked as if it were carved from granite and his cheekbones were jutting, prominent slabs beneath eyes she now could see were a frosty gray. His bow-shaped lips might have been attractive if they'd not been compressed into a grim frown.

Katie shook herself, realizing how rudely she'd been gawking. Before she could respond to his abrupt greeting, he barked something in another language. It was not French, which Katie spoke indifferently but understood, and not German, which she did not speak but thought she might recognize.

But regardless of the language, his tone was clear: he had asked her a question and was glowering at her as if she were an idiot for not answering.

Katie opened her mouth to tell him that he had mistaken her for somebody else, but then his harsh features shifted into an even haughtier expression—which she'd not believed possible—and he hurled another incomprehensible series of syllables at her, employing a tone she would not use on a dog, all the while regarding her with a towering, obnoxious superiority that immediately got under her skin.

Heat suffused her body as if she had swallowed a live flame and wrath pulsed through her veins. Katie recognized and dreaded the furious, temperamental emotion that seized control of her, but, as was always the case, she seemed powerless to stop her fury from overwhelming her good sense.

Rather than explain that he had mistaken her identity—as the tiny part of her brain that was still rational suggested—Katie gave him a look of intense loathing and then nodded, as if she agreed with whatever he had just said.

His dark blond eyebrows sank even lower, and an expression of befuddlement colored his harsh features.

For some reason, his perplexity worried her more than anger would have done.

Good God. What had she just agreed to?

*You are behaving like an idiot.*

Katie briefly squeezed her eyes shut. She *was* acting like a fool.

She opened her mouth to tell him the truth when—without asking Katie's permission—he sat down beside her, his massive frame filling the bench.

Katie turned to gawk, lightly brushing against him in the process.

He jerked as if he'd just touched something foul and shoved his massive bulk to the farthest edge of the bench while regarding her with such a look of revulsion that it took her breath away.

Any remorse Katie might have felt over her dishonest behavior fled. What a boorish, priggish, insufferable oaf! Even seated on the same bench he loomed over her, but she refused to allow his sheer bulk to intimidate her, instead sneering and crossing her arms, rudely jostling him in the process.

Once again, he reacted as if Katie had jabbed him with a flaming stick rather than her elbow.

Incensed, she openly examined his face, not caring if he thought her rude.

The light from paper lanterns cast a romantic pinkish-red glow over their intimate rose-encircled bower, but there was nothing romantic about the Duke of Dulverton.

Distinct lines webbed the outside corners of his eerily pale eyes and deep grooves bracketed his stern mouth, making her wonder how old he was. She was close enough to see that his icy gray irises had a thick dark ring around the outer edge, which made them all the more striking. In any other face she might have thought them attractive. But in the Duke of Dulverton's uncompromising visage, they only added to his severity.

The roughhewn angles of his face brought to mind Viking invaders while his high-bridged beaklike nose would not have looked out of place on an ancient Roman coin. His brutally short white-blond hair would probably curl if given half a chance. But Dulverton did not look like the sort of man to tolerate curls.

His posture was taut with tension and his jaw flexed as he eyed her with a mixture of mistrust, impatience, and anger. His bow-shaped lips were pulled down at the corners in a frown that Katie surmised to be his resting expression. One side of the bow, she noticed, was slightly higher than the other. It was a mouth that she could not imagine ever smiling.

Or kissing.

Tonight was only the second time Katie had seen him in the five Seasons she had spent in London. He was notorious for only coming to London when important legislation was under discussion and avoiding *ton* functions while he was in town.

He did not host dinners or attend parties, and only rarely accepted invitations to dine. The only reason she'd known that he would be here tonight at the Earl of Sutton's ball was because last night Chatham had mentioned that the reclusive Dulverton would be attending his first ball in years.

That was what had given Katie the brilliant idea of putting his name on her list. She had not expected any of them to actually get close to him. Yet here he was, within kissing distance.

And never had Katie met a less kissable man.

She lifted her gaze from his lips to his eyes and was rendered breathless. It wasn't so much the color of them, although that was extraordinary, but the intensity in them. Only a moment ago she had thought him coldly distant, but now he was looking at her. *Really* looking as if she were the only other person in existence.

It was… intoxicating.

Katie squirmed beneath his unwavering gaze.

*You had better confess; this is not a man to be trifled with.*

But once again he spoke first, uttering a series of staccato words in a language that meant nothing to her, annoyance writ large across his face.

This time it was not irritation that sparked within her but curiosity, an emotion that was far, far rarer. For the first time in forever—or at least five years—Katie was curious. And the longer she looked at the haughty, ugly man across from her, the more that spark grew, until it fairly blazed within her. Just what was he *doing* sitting on this bench beside her?

His eyebrows drew closer together and then he tilted his head slightly and sniffed the air, just like a hound scenting prey.

It was so silly and unexpected that Katie did something she rarely did these days—at least not genuinely—she smiled.

***

Gerrit had difficulty comprehending other men, but he was especially awkward when it came to understanding women. He could not help thinking that even a normal man or woman would find Lady Mariska's behavior odd.

He sniffed the air for the scent of alcohol. But if she was intoxicated, she gave off no odor.

Suddenly, she smiled at him—a blazing grin—and Gerrit felt as though a hand had reached into his chest and squeezed his lungs. She was breathtaking, and that was not hyperbole; she actually stole his breath.

Van Renesse had told him that Lady Mariska was tiny, slender, and pretty. The man must not be right in the head. Or perhaps his vision was poor. The woman seated beside him was tall, shapely, and, quite frankly, stunning—nothing like his uncle's description.

The irritation he'd been nursing toward the older man ebbed the longer he looked at his prospective bride.

Gerrit was nonplussed by the effect of beauty on his ill temper. Never would he have believed that he was so susceptible to a pretty face. To an exquisite face, he amended.

Now if only he could get the blasted woman to talk to him.

Conversation was not one of his strong suits. In any language. That was why he was willing to allow people like van Renesse and Lady Palmer to conduct his betrothal negotiations for him. If socializing and charming people—specifically women—came easily to him then he would have found his own damned wife and he would not be sitting beside a mute woman in a garden at a ball in a city he despised.

He allowed himself a lingering look at her, not bothering to hide his frank appraisal even though it was crude and ungentlemanly. Hell. How could any man resist looking at her? Her body somehow managed to be both lithe and voluptuous at the same time, the twin globes of her breasts straining her bodice while showcasing the delicate build of her shoulders. Dress styles seemed to have changed while Gerrit was not paying attention. Gone, it appeared, were the straight silhouettes. Lady Mariska's gown was fitted from her shoulders to a waist so tiny his fingers twitched to encircle it.

She shifted irritably and his gaze lifted to hers. The cold fury in her green catlike eyes was almost enough to stifle his erection.

"Tell me the truth, my lady. Did you respond to my letter?" he asked in Dutch, deciding that speaking in her native language might help settle her ruffled feathers. Although what he had done to ruffle them was a mystery.

Lady Mariska cocked her head. Was there something wrong with her hearing? Or her mind?

*You can hardly ask her those questions.*

He scowled. Of course he would not ask her that. But how did one find out such information? Doubtless there were subtle ways, but Gerrit was *not* a subtle man. It was best to begin as he meant to go on. He opened his mouth.

"What language were you just speaking?"

As feminine as she looked, her voice was low, almost gruff, and as appealing as her person.

It was not, however, a Dutch voice.

"You are not Lady Mariska," he said stupidly, lunging to his feet.

The red-haired imposter smiled again as she gracefully stood, her dark pink lips spreading into an impish smirk, which was every bit as brain rattling as her first smile had been. "I *could* be Lady Mariska. If you wanted me to be."

Gerrit's jaw sagged. Nothing in his prior seven-and-thirty years, one-hundred-and-sixty-nine days prepared him for such a response.

# Kathryn

She chuckled throatily at his slack-jawed stupefaction and then closed the distance between them with swift grace, her attractively tilted eyes lowering to his mouth.

Gerrit only realized as her hand warmed his chest through the fabric of his clothing that he had not flinched at her touch.

An unprecedented reaction for an unprecedented situation.

"You have such a stern mouth," she mused.

And then she reached out and *touched* his lower lip with one finger.

This time, his body responded in a familiar way and flinched—a reaction that seized him almost every time he was touched by another person—his muscles seizing as tightly as pins in a tumbler lock as he stared at her in wide-eyed disbelief.

And then she pushed up onto her toes and pressed her lips against his.

# Chapter Four

Katie had no idea why she was behaving like a common strumpet, not that she had ever met a strumpet, common or otherwise, but the urge to bring this disdainful, disagreeable man down a few pegs was impossible to resist.

But not as irresistible as the duke's mouth.

As stern as it appeared, his lips were astonishingly soft and warm.

They were also unmoving. In fact, after he'd flinched, he'd gone utterly still. Katie was reminded of Hy whenever Katie forgot herself and embraced her sister. Hy, too, froze when confronted with human contact. Well, except for her husband and children. It was quite astonishing how physically affectionate Hy was with Chatham and her sons Elliot and Charles when she was so stiff and reserved with everyone else, even her siblings.

The longer the duke stood still and unresponsive, not even his chest moving, unease threaded through her.

*You are assaulting the man.*

Chilled by the thought, she began to pull away. But before she could detach completely, he abrupted reanimated, his arms lashed around her and he drew her body closer, tilted his head, and pressed his mouth against hers.

Katie was only half-aware when his hand slid from her lower back up to her shoulders and pulled her even tighter, his kisses deep and drugging. Desire rippled through her as his far larger body molded itself to hers, hard sinew and muscle closing around her—engulfing her—and his stern lips softened and teased and caressed and enticed.

Katie had always liked kissing and engaged in it as often as possible. Or at least she had done until the past few years when every activity—illicit or otherwise—had become too dull to bother with.

Although she'd contrived this asinine *kissing contest,* never had she dreamed it would actually be pleasurable. But the cold, unsmiling Duke of Dulverton's hot, eager mouth and deft, breath-stealing touches were all the more exciting when contrasted with his icy, disapproving mien.

Katie's hands were still on his chest, trapped between their bodies, so she freed them and explored the fine, soft wool of his coat, which lovingly hugged his muscular back and shoulders. The more she touched him, the hungrier she became, until wave after wave of desire thundered through her body.

He gave an approving growl, his lips and tongue teasing and taunting her in ways that were far more erotic than any other man she had kissed. Even Mr.

Morecombe—a confident, impassioned kisser who'd shattered her composure—could not hold a candle to Dulverton's wits-scattering assault.

But unlike Morecombe, Katie had no desire to get away when the duke's palm slid around the back of her head, tilting her so that he could *consume* her. Instead, Katie's hands met at his nape, and she stroked the brutally cropped hair, which felt like bristly velvet beneath her fingertips.

His chest rumbled and his powerful hips flexed, the action branding her midriff with a long, hard ridge.

Shock and arousal swirled inside her at the feel of his erection, and Katie opened her eyes and looked straight into his. Gone was the supercilious peer; in his place was a hot-eyed lover. The rolling thrust of his hips was rough and raw, but his muscular arms held her with a tenderness that made her feel precious and protected, a combination that left her fairly swooning with desire.

One of his huge hands slid down her back, not stopping until his palm was on her buttocks. He massaged her with a firm, erotic touch that soon had her grinding against him and not caring how shamelessly she was behaving. Nor did she care when his fingers began the slow process of lifting the diaphanous material of her gown and equally fine petticoat, until cool night air caressed her calves.

*He is going to mount you right here in the garden.*

*Good.*

Katie met him thrust for thrust the next time he ground his iron-hard erection against her. Never in her life had she wanted—

"What the devil is going on here, Dulverton?" a furious male voice demanded.

Katie shrieked and staggered back. Her slipper caught on an uneven flagstone, and she would have fallen if Dulverton hadn't clamped onto her upper arm to steady her.

The same man who'd been talking to the duke in the ballroom was about six feet away, his expression thunderous. A young woman and matron stood beside him. They weren't the only spectators; Katie caught the glitter of at least two more sets of eyes peeping over a nearby rosebush.

The duke looked from Katie to the older man, his lips darker, full, and slick as they parted in surprise. The expression made him look far less daunting and more human. Not quite handsome—it was impossible to imagine what it would take to achieve that feat—but appealing in an austere, savage way.

Suddenly the man who'd just been passionately kissing her disappeared completely and in his place was the grim Duke of Dulverton, his eyes hooded and his mouth compressed in the same condemnatory frown that had so incited her just a short time ago.

The older man turned to Katie. "Who are you?"

Before Katie could answer, the young woman began speaking in the same language Dulverton had been using. Although she couldn't understand the words, the woman's tone was hostile and accusatory with an undertone of something else. Something that Katie couldn't quite identify. Relief? Happiness?

The duke spoke over the woman in a quiet voice that somehow managed to resemble the crack of a whip. The woman shut her mouth, her pale cheeks flushing darkly.

The older man and woman began talking at once, their voices quickly rising to a shout to be heard over one another.

Something one of them said appeared to spur the younger woman and she joined in.

The two sets of eyes behind the rose hedge had become four. Elinor, Michelle, Julia and Caroline were no longer bothering to crouch and hide, but openly gawking.

Katie made a furious shooing gesture which they either ignored or did not notice. Who could blame them? This fracas would provide gossip for weeks— months!

"*Genoeg!*" the duke barked.

The other three instantly stopped talking and the duke began to speak, his voice even softer than before. Whatever he was saying caused his audience to gasp, flush, look enraged, or all three in the case of the older woman.

"Katie?"

Katie squeezed her eyes shut at the sound of her sister Hy's voice. *Oh, wonderful. Just what this rapidly developing farce needed: more witnesses.*

She turned to find Hy with Chatham beside her.

*Blast and bugger!*

Hy's expressionless gaze was fixed on Katie while Chatham's keen eyes darted around the assembled people before settling on Dulverton. "What is going on here?"

"This is a private matter and none of your concern, Chatham," Dulverton snapped in the same curt, arrogant tone he'd used on Katie earlier.

So, it wasn't just mere mortals that he treated rudely and dismissively, then.

Unaccustomed to being addressed like a feudal serf, Chatham bristled. "I beg to differ," he said, his tone colder than Katie had ever heard it. "My sister-in-law is somehow involved in your *private matter.*"

"Sister-in-law?" Dulverton's pale eyes slid from Chatham to Katie, and he frowned, as if he had momentarily forgotten her existence.

But he certainly remembered her *now*.

He pinioned her with the full force of his cold, assessing gaze, and Katie found it strangely difficult to breathe.

"We should discuss this matter—whatever it is—in a less public venue." Hy's quiet voice sliced through the taut silence, and Dulverton gave an abrupt nod before turning away.

Katie exhaled shakily, pitifully relieved to be out from under his gaze.

"Allow me to escort you to my library, Your Grace," the Earl of Sutton said, suddenly appearing beside Hy and Chatham

"Not right now," Dulverton barked at Sutton, making him flinch. "I will join you in the library once I have escorted Lady Mariska, Lady Palmer, and Lord van Renesse to their carriage."

Just like everyone else who'd spoken with the duke, Sutton flushed at Dulverton's curt tone.

The earl opened his mouth, probably to issue an equally curt response, but Dulverton was already striding away, leaving Lady Mariska, Lady Palmer, and Lord van Renesse to scurry after him.

Only when his broad back disappeared did Katie notice there weren't just four pairs of eyes beyond the rose hedge, but at least a dozen.

***

"That is *enough*," Gerrit snarled in Dutch at his uncle and Lady Palmer, both of whom had begun nattering at him the moment they left the crowded garden behind them.

The older couple cut him wounded, mulish glances but obeyed and the journey to the Earl of Sutton's foyer took place in blessed silence.

Gerrit dispatched a footman to fetch the carriage while he and his uncle collected the ladies' wraps before escorting them outside to await their conveyance.

Once he had installed the older couple in Lady Palmer's ancient boat of a coach, he turned to his uncle. "You will come to Dulverton House tomorrow morning, and we will discuss what is to be done. Now, wait here while I have a word with Lady Mariska." He closed the coach door before the other man could open his mouth and gestured for Lady Mariska to accompany him to a spot a few feet away.

"I am so sorry, Your Grace," she babbled in Dutch before they'd even stopped walking.

"What for?" he demanded, finding it difficult to believe this groveling wretch was the same woman who had shrilly—and justifiably—chastised Gerrit for embracing the beautiful stranger in the garden.

He felt a deep, powerful pulse of lust at the memory of the woman's lush body and the way it had bucked and ground against him.

*Not the thought you need right now.*

No. It wasn't. Gerrit dragged his thoughts away from the shapely siren in the garden and focused on the woman in front of him. "Your aunt said you were feeling overheated and that is why you were out in the garden. That is not the truth, is it?"

She hung her head. "No, Your Grace."

"What is the truth?"

"I—I did not want to come." Mariska darted an apprehensive look up at him.

"You did not wish to come to the ball?"

There was a long pause, and then, "I did not wish to come to England."

Gerrit's hands fisted. "You never wanted to marry me, did you?" He had to force the words through clenched teeth.

"It is not you, Your Grace, it is—" Her eyes skittered away from his and she chewed on her lower lip. She swallowed again and blurted, "I am in love with somebody else."

So much for tucking her away in a convent. "How long?"

"F-four years."

A full two years before van Renesse had brokered their betrothal.

"Were you pressured to agree to the betrothal?" he asked, even though he already could guess.

"Yes," she whispered, her face wreathed in misery.

"Why did you not tell me so in your letter?"

She blinked up at him. "What letter?"

Gerrit expected to feel anger at the obvious deceit, but instead he felt only weariness.

"This man you wish to marry, is he suitable?"

"He is respectable, and my father and grandfather would not have objected if—"

"If not for the agreement between our families," he finished grimly.

"Yes."

"My uncle will escort—"

"I cannot go back home, Your Grace." Tears trickled down her cheeks. "If I tell them I do not wish to marry you, they will—"

"I will make certain you are not punished, my lady."

"But...*how?*" she wailed.

"My methods are not your concern."

Her eyes widened fearfully.

Gerrit sighed. "I will not seek vengeance from your father." *No matter how much I might want to throttle him.* He removed his handkerchief from his coat pocket and handed it to her. "You have my word."

She took the square of snow-white linen and dabbed at her tears. "Are you sure, Your Grace?"

"I am sure." He shook his head when she tried to give him the handkerchief. "Keep it."

"I am sorry I did not speak sooner. I never meant for you to—"

"Come. I will escort you back to your chaperone's carriage," he said, uninterested in further conversation with her, his thoughts already on the unpleasantness that awaited him in the Earl of Sutton's library.

# Chapter Five

The Earl of Sutton's library was already occupied when Katie, Hy, and Chatham followed their host into the massive room.

Chatham paused just inside the door, his hand resting on Hy's lower back, his brows drawn down as he looked from Letty Grayson and her mother, Mrs. Grayson, to Baron Angus Fowler.

"What are you doing here, Fowler?" Chatham asked his closest friend, who currently resembled a hulking red-haired thundercloud.

The big Scot glared at Letty before turning his scathing green gaze to Katie. "Why don't you ask your sister-in-law, Chatham?"

Chatham's frown deepened at Fowler's hostile retort and looked like he wanted to rebuke his friend, but Hy spoke first.

"What is this about, Katie?"

Katie looked from Letty—whose pale face was pinched with misery—to a very red-eyed Mrs. Grayson, who was anxiously plucking at her handkerchief, and then back to Fowler, who fixed her with a murderous glare. It did not take a genius to understand what must have transpired.

Katie opened her mouth but was unable to find any words.

Thankfully, the Earl of Sutton spoke, "I'm afraid there is no way to make this situation any more palatable." He looked from Letty to Katie, his lips twisting with disgust. "But you might as well sit, Your Graces, as this is likely to take a while and who knows when Dulverton—"

The door flew open and the man in question strode into the room, his eerie, livid eyes flickering from person to person, like bolts of lightning, lingering longest on Katie before he gave their host his attention. "I had hoped to speak to, er—" He broke off and scowled at Katie. "What is your name?"

"Allow me to present Lady Kathryn Bellamy," Sutton said coolly.

"Bellamy?" Dulverton repeated, his nostrils flaring as revulsion flickered across his rough-hewn features. He snorted, but there was no amusement in the sound. "Addiscombe's daughter." The words were flat and emotionless, like a judge delivering a sentence.

Katie gritted her teeth at his superior, contemptuous gaze. It wasn't the first time she'd been judged by her father's tattered reputation, and it would not be the last. But that didn't mean she had to like it.

"She is your sister-in-law, Chatham?" Dulverton asked in the same insolent tone.

"She is," Chatham said icily.

"Where are her parents, the Earl and Countess of Addiscombe?" Dulverton barked, either not recognizing or not caring that he was antagonizing most of the occupants in the room.

"Lady Kathryn lives with us and has done for five years," Chatham said.

Katie was amazed that her brother-in-law could claim her without cursing her name.

"Her parents are dead?" Dulverton asked.

"Both are alive, but my wife and I stand as guardians to Lady Kathryn."

Dulverton's face settled into what was evidently his habitual superior scowl. He gestured toward Fowler and the Graysons. "What are you three doing here?"

Fowler, already seething, seemed to double in size. "I am here because this— this *girl*," he narrowed his eyes at Letty, "chose to make a mockery of me in the garden." His blazing green gaze slid to Katie. "And I know exactly whose idea this asinine *game* was."

"Game?" Dulverton turned from Fowler to Katie, regarding her with such frigid intensity that she actually shivered. His eyes were undeniably beautiful, but they looked inhuman. They also exerted an almost tangible pressure on her, like slabs of flagstone pressing against her chest.

"It is all my fault," she said. "The whole thing was my idea."

"I do not understand. What *thing*?" Dulverton demanded.

Katie looked from face-to-face, hoping for… something. Dulverton managed to look conceited and bewildered at the same time; Hy's expression was unreadable; Chatham's disappointed; the Earl of Sutton disgusted; Mrs. Grayson terrified; Fowler enraged; and Letty alternately accusatory and sick with self-loathing.

There was not a friendly face in the room.

Katie forced herself to meet Dulverton's impatient, inquisitorial gaze. "We were playing a game." Her voice broke and she had to clear her throat twice before she could speak. "A kissing game."

***

Gerrit's temples pounded.

*A kissing game.*

The words burned through the fog of confusion, and he stared at the red-headed seductress—*Lady Kathryn*, he reminded himself—and said, "I beg your pardon?"

25

"Damnation!" Fowler bellowed, causing not only Gerrit, but everyone else in the room, to startle. "It was a bloody game about kissing, Dulverton." The massive baron sprang up from his chair and stalked across the room, not stopping until he was towering over Lady Kathryn. "You have finally done it, haven't you?" he snarled.

Lady Kathryn, to her credit, did not flinch from the raging giant. Only her hands, clenched and white-knuckled, betrayed her agitation. "I am *sorry*, Angus."

"You're *sorry*?" Fowler bellowed.

This time the girl did flinch.

"Lower your voice, Fowler," Gerrit warned as he eased his body between the furious peer and the woman who was likely going to be his wife.

Fowler's eyes threw sparks. "Who the hell do you think you are, Dulverton?"

"You are scaring Lady Kathryn," Gerrit said in a low voice.

Fowler gave an almost hysterical laugh. "Scaring her? Scaring *her*?"

"You are in a gentleman's library, Fowler," the Duchess of Chatham said, her quiet voice more effective than Fowler's shouting. "Not on the deck of one of your ships."

Fowler glared at the duchess and opened his mouth, no doubt to issue a thundering rejoinder, but the Duke of Chatham interceded. "Have done, Angus. Now is not the time."

The baron shook his head. "Fine. I have had enough of this. I will leave you to deal with her, Chatham." He cut Lady Kathryn a scathing look and then turned toward the two women cowering on the settee. "I will call upon you and Miss Grayson tomorrow, Mrs. Grayson."

The older woman nodded while the younger one—her daughter, Gerrit presumed—lowered her gaze, her face turning a splotchy red.

Without another word the baron strode from the room.

The door had scarcely banged shut behind Fowler when Mrs. and Miss Grayson leapt to their feet. "If you would excuse us," Mrs. Grayson whispered, ushering her daughter toward the door.

"Allow me, madam," the Earl of Sutton said, already headed in that direction. He looked from Gerrit to the Duke of Chatham. "I will give the four of you some privacy while I show these ladies to their carriage."

This time, the door closed without a sound.

Gerrit turned to Lady Kathryn. "A kissing game? And yet I do not remember agreeing to play, My Lady."

The girl opened her mouth, but it was Chatham who spoke. "I think an evening to calm our frayed tempers and take stock would be beneficial at this point, Dulverton. If you will pay a visit—"

"I want some answers, Chatham, and I want them *now*." Gerrit glowered at the other man who glowered right back.

The duchess set a staying hand on her husband's arm and Chatham stood down.

Gerrit shifted his attention from the duke to his wife, who—with her rail-thin body, plain face, and bright orange hair—looked nothing at all like her sister. "Describe this game."

Chatham again bristled but the duchess said, "My sister and her friends were playing a game that involved kissing men on a list." Although her voice was emotionless, two spots of color appeared on her cheeks.

It was not the first time Gerrit had found himself the butt of other people's jokes, but it had not happened in years. He did not like the feeling any more now than he had when he'd been a powerless boy at school.

"What list?"

The duchess's mouth tightened as she turned to her sister. "You drew up the list?"

Lady Kathryn gave the duchess a look of pure misery. "Yes."

"Each man was, I presume, worth some point value?" the duchess persisted.

"Good Lord, Hy!" Lady Kathryn burst out, her cheeks the color of ripe cherries. The two women engaged in a silent glaring match. Evidently the duchess won because Lady Kathryn's shapely lips twisted unhappily, and she turned back to Gerrit. "Every man was worth a certain point value. The person who collected the most points won."

"Won what?" Gerrit demanded. "A husband?"

Her green eyes rounded with shock. "No! That was not our plan, at all. Truly," she added at his look of scathing disbelief. "I never imagined any of us would be—"

"What was the prize?" Gerrit persisted, as if that somehow mattered.

"There was no prize," Lady Kathryn insisted, staring at her feet.

She had destroyed his carefully contrived plans for the future for nothing more than a lark? Why did that fact seem to make this asinine game all the more insulting?

Gerrit struggled with the fury that threatened to undo him. Only the memory of Fowler's enraged, ill-mannered display kept his own temper in check.

Chatham cleared his throat. "There is no denying that Lady Kathryn's behavior tonight has been… lacking." He looked from his sister-in-law to Gerrit, his face hardening. "But Sutton assured me that—according to more than one witness—you were not an unwilling participant when it came to kissing."

Gerrit's face heated, and he would have given anything to be able to throw Chatham's words back in his face. But the other man was right. Although Gerrit had been startled for a few seconds after she'd first locked her lips with his, he'd never made any attempt to step away from her. Instead, he'd quickly conquered his usual abhorrence of a stranger's touch and had kissed her with more enthusiasm than he had done in years. Perhaps ever. It had stunned him how quickly kissing—something he had only done with one other woman two decades before—had come back to him.

And then there was the grinding and fondling. Not to mention that he'd lifted her gown up to her knees by the time his uncle had interrupted them. Gerrit could not deny that he would have fucked her right there on that garden bench if they'd not been caught.

His prick gave a happy pulse at the thought.

Realizing the room had gone quiet, he looked up to find three pairs of eyes on him.

"Yes, I am equally to blame," he admitted gruffly.

Chatham was not appeased by Gerrit's admission and pressed on. "By tomorrow there will not be a soul among the *ton* who does not know about this, Dulverton."

Gerrit nodded, faintly nauseated at the thought of the shame even now attaching to his name. He had spent the last twenty years trying to scrub out the stain his first wife had left on his reputation, and all his efforts had apparently been for naught.

"I will present myself at Chatham House on the morrow," he said after an unpleasant silence. Gerrit suddenly recalled the other meeting he had the next day—the one with his uncle and Lady Palmer—and the nausea that had been simmering in his belly swelled. Tomorrow would truly be a day from Hell. "I will come after noon," he added.

"Your Grace?"

Gerrit looked up at Lady Kathryn's voice and met her anxious green eyes. "Yes?"

"There is no need for you to—"

"We will discuss this matter tomorrow," the duchess said, staring hard at her sister. For the second time that evening the sisters engaged in silent combat.

After a long moment Lady Kathryn scowled at her sister and turned back to Gerrit. "I shall see you tomorrow, Your Grace."

Why did her words sound more like a threat than a promise?

# Chapter Six

Neither Chatham nor Hy said a word to Katie on the short carriage ride home. When they did finally speak to her—in the foyer of Chatham House—it was only to say a polite, *goodnight.*

Katie didn't know whether to be relieved or worried that Hy was going to allow her to go to bed without delivering a full-blown raking. But as she trudged up to her chambers, she did know that she would not get a wink of sleep tonight.

Becky Stone, her lady's maid, confidante, and erstwhile childhood playmate was dozing in a chair when Katie entered her chambers.

Becky blinked at the sound of the door shutting and glanced at the clock on the mantel. "You are back early."

Katie tossed her reticule onto her dressing table.

"Oh no," Becky said, pushing up from the chair and hurrying toward her. "I know that look. What is amiss?"

Katie and Becky had been born only three days apart. For most of Katie's life Becky, whose large family mostly worked in service, had been the richer of the two even though Katie was the daughter of the Earl of Addiscombe. Not until Katie's sister Phoebe married the screamingly wealthy Viscount Needham did Katie have a frock that was made just for her rather than one of her sisters' remade dresses.

Five years ago, Katie's mother had forbidden her to engage Becky as her lady's maid. "The girl is a hayseed, Kathryn. You will engage a proper servant."

But after the Countess of Addiscombe had been banished to Bath by Katie's older sisters and their husbands Katie had gone to live with Hy, who had allowed her to choose her own maid. The decision had been an easy one and Becky had been with Katie ever since.

"I am in trouble," Katie confessed as Becky removed the lustrous set of pearls from her neck and laid them in their special velvet-lined box.

"What did you do now, my lady?" Becky asked as she plucked the tiny emerald brilliants from Katie's hair.

Katie stared at her reflection in the mirror, her head spinning.

"What happened, Katie?" Becky asked again.

Katie met Becky's worried gaze. "I don't want to talk about it right now—but I will later, I promise. I need to pay a visit to Andrew." Andrew Derrick—a cousin by marriage—was Katie's closest friend. Before his marriage Andrew had been one of the most notorious bachelors in England for decades. If anyone could tell her about Dulverton it would be Andrew.

"You wish to call on Mr. Derrick?" Becky asked in dismay. "Shouldn't you wait until morning?"

"This cannot wait. I need to see him now," Katie said firmly.

Becky's jaws flexed and she didn't move.

"Please," Katie wheedled. "It's just across the square. You know I won't be in any danger."

"Fine. But you will take me with you."

"Fine," Katie echoed, lacking the energy to argue with her determined servant.

A sleepy footman opened the door at Andrew's house.

"Is your master available?" Katie asked as she hurried inside.

The handsome young man blinked owlishly "Aye, my lady. He's not gone to bed yet. I believe he is in his study."

Katie unfastened her cloak and handed it to Becky.

"What about Mrs. Derrick?" Katie asked as she pulled off her gloves.

"She's out of town, my lady."

Katie was relieved to hear it. She liked Stacia Derrick a great deal, but it would be uncomfortable enough getting the information she wanted out of Andrew without having an audience.

She gave Becky her gloves, "I won't be long. I know the way to the study," she told the footman.

The young man eyed Becky with obvious interest. "I can put the kettle on down in the kitchen."

Becky gave him a repressive smile. "I will wait in the parlor, thank you."

Katie bit back a smirk at the footman's obvious disappointment and hurried up the stairs.

Andrew wasn't in his study, but Katie had a good idea where he might be and took the stairs to the top floor. Outside the nursery, a young maid lolled in a chair beside the door. She leapt to her feet when she saw Katie. "Good evening, my lady."

Katie smiled. "He is in there, I presume?"

The maid giggled. "I have never seen a man who loves his children so much."

"You should meet my other brothers-in-law," Katie muttered. "I cannot believe he makes you sit out here and wait."

"Oh, no, my lady. He told me to go have supper earlier. When I came back I didn't want to interrupt him in case he'd got Miss Cordelia off to sleep. She is teething and miserable. The master is the only one who can stop her crying, poor mite.

Andrew Derrick had a way with females of all ages.

Katie quietly opened the door to the dimly lighted nursery.

"Katie!" Andrew cried loudly, smiling as he stood up from the chair where he'd been rocking his daughter. His bright blue eyes flickered over her ballgown, and he raised his eyebrows.

Katie ignored the question in his gaze and said, "I hope I didn't wake the baby."

"Miss Cordy wasn't sleeping, was she?" he asked the infant in a silly voice. "Nooooo, she wasn't," he crooned. "She's a night owl just like her papa." He kissed Cordelia's nose and the baby gurgled happily. His eyes went ridiculously round, and the stupidest look Katie had ever seen settled on his gorgeous face. "Who loves Papa best, hmm? Who is Papa's darling?"

Katie rolled her eyes, but then Cordelia gave a joyous shriek of laughter and she could understand Andrew's urge to elicit that magical sound.

"She's getting sleepy," he said in the same silly voice, gently rocking the baby as he walked the expanse of the room. "If you give me just a few minutes…"

"Take all the time you need," Katie said. She sank into one of the comfortable chairs and watched as one of the most infamous rakes in England patiently carried his daughter back and forth and back and forth, whispering to her and kissing her and rocking her until she finally drifted off to sleep. And then he tiptoed to the cradle and gently laid her inside it. He covered her to her chin, took one last look, and then motioned to Katie to follow him.

Outside in the corridor, the nursery maid stood when she saw her employer. "You can go in now, Mary. Ring for me if she wakes again and is fussy."

"Of course, sir." The young woman gave Andrew the same fatuous look that every female did, from eight to eighty.

"So," Andrew said as he led Katie to his study, shut the door, and gestured to a chair. "What are you doing running around dressed to the nines at this hour of the night? I hope you brought your maid with you, or Chatham will scold me."

"Yes, yes, yes—of course I brought my maid." Katie flopped into a chair and then winced and reached beneath her. She snorted when she pulled out a baby's rattle and set it on the table next to her. "What do you know about the Duke of Dulverton?"

Andrew gave her a startled look and then barked a laugh. "You mean the Duke of Dullness?"

Katie frowned. Dullness? Good God! The man had not been dull. Rude? Certainly. Arrogant? Undeniably. But dull? The memory of that scorching kiss and the duke's hard, hot length thrusting against her belly slammed into her like a wall of heat. Katie resisted the urge to fan herself.

No. Not dull.

Katie saw that Andrew was looking at her oddly and realized he was waiting for a response.

She hastily smothered her heated recollections and sneered. "Oh, I see. *Dull*-verton. How very clever and droll, Andrew. Are you ten years old?"

"Trust me, the man did not get the name just because it was alliterative; Dulverton *is* dull. The name might have been coined at Eton, but His Grace has only grown into it more fully in the years since." He sat back in his chair and propped his feet on the corner of his desk. "Why the devil are you here"—he twisted to look at the longcase clock— "at half past two in the morning asking about the Duke of Dullness of all people?"

Katie ignored his question. "Is there something wrong with him? I mean, other than your claim that he is dull."

"Wrong with him?" he repeated doubtfully. "Aside from being dull he's also bloody rude. At least he is to me anytime I have the misfortune to encounter him. Which is rarely, thank God. The man hardly ever comes to town and almost never—" He broke off, sat up, and his feet slid off the desk and hit the floor with a *thump*. "Wait, wait, wait just a minute. Chatham mentioned Dulverton was in town this week." His eyes were out on stalks. "Don't tell me the duke offered for you?"

She bristled at his amazement. "And why would that be so shocking, pray?"

"Not because of you, darling, but because I never believed he would marry again."

"*Again?* I didn't know he was married before."

"It was more than twenty years ago and it ended in disaster. He was young—not yet come into his title—seventeen, at most. He hasn't mingled in society ever since, so I suppose any gossip about him being married before simply died down." He snorted. "An unexpected benefit of being such a boring fellow."

"You and I know that gossip is always ready to rise from the dead."

"Perhaps for most people, but the man really is duller than ditchwater."

"Who was his wife?"

"Nobody you would have heard of." A faintly lecherous smile stretched Andrew's gorgeous lips.

"Why are you smirking?" Katie asked.

"I never smirk." His smirk only grew larger.

Katie snorted. "Ah, I see."

"See what?"

"You were her lover."

He tried to look innocent and failed spectacularly.

"Men are such dogs."

"*Tut, tut,* darling. She was the one breaking her vow to Dullnes—er, Dulverton," he corrected at her scowl.

"What was she like?"

"Gorgeous. Promiscuous. All in all, a lovely little piece of fluff."

It was difficult to think of the arrogant, proud man she had met earlier married to a *lovely little piece of fluff.*

"I was not the only man she dallied with," Andrew said, as if that excused his behavior.

"What happened?"

He squinted up at the ceiling. "If I recall correctly, Dulverton had to leave London because his father was dying. It was right in the middle of the Season and the lovely Christina remained in town and ran amok." He brought his gaze back to Katie and smiled. "I was just teasing you when I asked if he'd offered for you. The Dukes of Dulverton don't condescend to marry mere English misses."

"What do you mean?"

"They always take Dutch wives. It's some ancient family tradition dating back to the Glorious Revolution."

The young woman in the garden tonight now made sense. Dulverton must have been meeting her for the first time—and the two older people with her were probably Dutch matchmakers of some sort—and Katie had ruined their plans.

*Not just theirs, but Fowler's and Letty's, as well.*

"What is going on, Katie?"

Katie looked up from her unpleasant thoughts. "You said the marriage was a disaster? What did you mean?"

"Oh, didn't I say? She ran off with another man."

"*What?* Who?"

"Viscount Hendry's youngest son. You won't have met him as he never came back after running off with Christina."

"Are you saying that Dulverton is still married?"

"No, no. He obtained a divorce."

Katie's jaw sagged. "A divorce!"

He looked amused by her reaction. "Hard to imagine old Dullness embroiled in such a scandal, isn't it?"

Actually, Katie had a hard time imagining a woman running away from such an intimidating man. He did not look as if he would allow it. "Tell me the story, Andrew—all of it, please."

"Well, as I said, Dullness—"

"Would you please *stop* calling him that?"

Andrew's eyebrows shot up, and curiosity glinted in his sky-blue eyes, making Katie wish she'd held her tongue.

Thankfully, when he opened his mouth, it wasn't to ask uncomfortable questions. "His father arranged the match, and I gather the two of them met for the first time a week before they married. They'd not been in London very long when Dulverton was called to his father's deathbed. Foolishly, he left his new duchess in London, and she ran wild."

"And you helped her."

"I wasn't her first lover, Katie," Andrew said, looking miffed. "And when I discovered what she wanted I ended our brief association."

"What did she want?"

"Someone foolish enough to run off with her."

"And she found one."

"Yes. She and Hendry were packing their bags when Dulverton returned." He paused and gave her a thoughtful look.

"What?" she asked.

"I probably shouldn't tell you this next part—it's not really for a lady's ears and—"

"I cannot believe that you, of all people, would utter such rubbi—"

"Calm down, darling. I'm going to tell you." He raised his hands in a placating gesture but quickly lowered them again at whatever he saw on Katie's face—likely murderous rage at being told to *calm down*. "Dulverton challenged Hendry to a duel."

"Good Lord! With swords or—"

"It was Hendry's choice and he picked pistols."

"And is Dulverton—"

"He is a crack shot."

"Then why did Hendry choose pistols?"

"Because the duke is also an expert hand with a sword and damned handy with his fives, not to mention outweighing poor Hendry by at least two stone." Andrew frowned and his gaze turned vague. "I was a few years ahead of Dulverton at school, but I recall that he had a devil of a time his first year and got thrashed almost weekly."

"But he is enormous."

"*Now* he is. But he was a late bloomer. Back then, he was a spindly little lad. Not only was he puny and gangly and awkward, but he always had his nose in a book and spent every spare moment studying."

"Then why do you keep calling him *dull?*"

Andrew said, with exaggerated patience, "I meant *dull* in the other sense of the word, darling. Even as a boy he had impossibly dull habits. He was no fun."

"Fun?" she repeated.

"Yes. Fun. You know about fun, don't you?"

"I know about stupid young bucks and their notions of fun," she retorted. "Just get on with your story. What happened at this duel?"

"I'm getting there," he said in a chastising tone.

Katie bit her lip.

"My point in mentioning his younger days was that when he came back to school the second year, he wasn't that much bigger, but he suddenly knew how to fight. Somebody had taught him well over the summer and that was the end of his weekly thrashings. He also joined both the shooting and fencing clubs—and was bloody scary at both." Andrew shrugged. "As far as I know, Dulverton never did make any friends, but everyone left him well alone after the first year." An almost fond smile curled his lips.

"What is it? Why are you looking like that?" Katie asked.

"I was just remembering that duel. I have to admit it was one of the most fascinating things I've ever seen.

"You were actually there?"

"Lord, Katie! You don't think there was a man in the *ton* who missed that, do you?"

"All those men and nobody had the sense to try and stop it?"

He looked at her as if she'd just sprouted a second head.

"Never mind," Katie said. "Men are truly idiots."

Andrew didn't seem to hear her, his thoughts obviously on the past. "Most of us expected Hendry to run for his life, but the man had a sliver of honor after all. Or he might have stayed because Dulverton made such a huge bloo—er, target that Hendry thought he might be lucky. In the end, he did get lucky—at least as far as the duel went—because Dulverton just stood there and let Hendry get the first shot off." Andrew snorted and looked stunned. "Dulverton's a dull duck, but there's no denying the man has ice in his veins. Poor Hendry's hand was shaking so badly that he didn't come close to hitting Dulverton even though the duke faced him head on rather than turning to the side to make a smaller target." He cut Katie a look. "Which is what a man with any sense would do. After Hendry's shot went wide he looked on the brink of fainting away, but again he surprised us and held his ground. And then Dulverton did something nobody expected." He met Katie's gaze and shook his head in wonder.

"What?" she demanded. "What did he do?"

Andrew laughed. "He handed the pistol to his second without even taking a shot."

"And that is… odd?"

"Unprecedented, is more like."

"But surely Dulverton would have faced repercussions if he'd killed the son of a viscount?"

"Lord, Katie. Hendry was in the process of running off with the man's wife. There wasn't a peer in the land who'd have punished Dulverton for killing the man."

"So why didn't he?"

"That is actually the best part of the story. He did Hendry one worse than killing him; he humiliated him. *Twice.* First, he lowered his pistol without shooting. Then he marched up to the man and said, *"Christina is yours, now. That is the only reason I left you alive; so you can take her and be gone.* And then he hopped in his carriage and left."

"I do not understand why you are so amazed. It seems a sensible thing to do to me," Katie said. "Why keep a wife who didn't want him?"

Andrew rolled his eyes. "There speaks a woman."

"A *sensible* woman," she muttered.

Andrew was still caught up in the past and did not appear to hear her. "As far as I know, that is the only time Dulverton did not behave dully."

Katie rolled her eyes. "What happened afterward?"

"Hendry and Christina left soon after. Dulverton's divorce was granted with startling celerity, even for a duke. Even though she was free, Hendry never married her, and she died in childbed a few years later."

"I cannot believe I never heard so much as a whiff about this duel and his divorce."

"It was almost two decades ago."

"That shouldn't matter with such a scandalous tale. Divorces are as rare as hen's teeth and that duel sounds like the stuff of legends.

"Gentlemen do not gossip to ladies about duels." Andrew must have realized what he'd just said because he looked a bit sheepish. "I only told you because it seemed so important. As for not hearing about the divorce, the man has hardly shown his face in a ballroom for decades. That doesn't make for a very interesting gossip. People haven't just forgotten about his divorce, they've forgotten about the man. You've been on the town for five years—have *you* ever heard of any matchmaking mamas scheming to catch Dulverton?"

"Now that you mention it, I haven't," she said. Katie had to admit she'd not thought of the duke herself until she'd put him on her list, more for entertainment value than any real belief that one of them would be in a position to kiss him. The irony of that was not lost on her.

"He is a duke. Why aren't women scheming to marry him?" she asked.

"Because the Dukes of Dulverton only marry Dutch women."

Katie wondered what Andrew would say if she told him that was no longer the case. That Dulverton would be proposing to *her* on the morrow…

The urge to laugh hysterically suddenly struck and she needed to swallow hard. Twice.

"I know you do not want me to say it," Andrew went on, "but the man *is* dull and there is no denying that contributes to the lack of gossip. Dulverton doesn't have friends, and I've only seen him at White's a handful of times. He is a loner and always has been. Aside from that duel he's never made time for anyone or anything other than books and rocks."

"*Rocks?*"

Andrew squinted thoughtfully. "Er, perhaps fossils. Or maybe dirt. I don't know." He gave a dismissive wave of his hand. "Something of that sort. He is a member of the Royal Society, but I doubt he spends much time even with that boring lot." He fixed her with a too piercing look. "You still have not told me why you are so curious about him, Katie."

"Dulverton was at the Sutton ball tonight."

Andrew's eyebrows arched. "Ah. And he piqued your interest?"

Katie shrugged.

"I shouldn't have thought such an ugly fellow would appeal to you. Or is it the title?"

Katie ignored his question.

"You aren't going to tell me why you are so curious about him, are you?"

"No."

He laughed. "You cannot keep any secrets from me, darling. Chatham will tell me." Andrew smirked. "He tells me everything."

"Bully for you," Katie muttered.

"Oh, by the by, Stacia and I won't be going to Chatham Park this summer."

"But you can't miss it, Andrew!"

Hy and Chatham's annual house party was second only to her family's Christmas gatherings as Katie's favorite time of year. And Stacia and Andrew had been regular fixtures every year since their marriage five years ago.

"I'm sorry, my lovely, but we simply have too much to do at Rosewood."

"Oh, I know. But it will not be the same without you and Stacia."

"We'll go again next year, darling."

Of course, if Hy and Chatham and Dulverton had their way tomorrow then Katie would probably be married and tucked away at the duke's remotest country estate by this time next week. Something told her that a man who abhorred the London Season would not be fond of house parties, either.

# Chapter Seven

Katie had hoped that by eating breakfast in her room she could avoid the unpleasant conversation awaiting her.

She should have known better.

She had just finished her pot of hot chocolate and was pondering the wisdom of having a second when Becky entered her chamber, a grim frown on her normally cheerful face. "Her Grace wishes to see you."

"I was just about to ring for more chocolate."

Becky rested her fists on her hips.

Katie groaned. "Please don't look at me like that." The other woman had been behaving sourly ever since Katie had confessed after her visit to Andrew what had transpired at the ball.

"I cannot believe you did such a thing, my lady," she said for the fifth or sixth time.

Katie smiled at her friend. "You can't scold me *and* call me *my lady*, Becks."

"Her Grace wants to see you. Right now," Becky retorted, unmoved by Katie's wheedling.

Katie sighed, swung her legs over the side of the bed, and shoved her feet into her slippers. "Bring me a dressing gown and I will go right now."

"You should wash and dress and—"

"You said *now*, so I am going *now*. My dressing gown, please."

Becky's expression was worth a thousand words. She would probably use all those and more later on, when she learned that Katie would be rejecting Dulverton's offer.

"At least put this on," Becky begged, following Katie to the door with a white lace cap.

Katie grabbed it and yanked it down over her head without bothering to look in the mirror.

"Where is she?" she demanded, swatting Becky's hands away when she attempted to straighten the lace.

"In the library."

Katie strode from the room without another word, stomping past a startled housemaid and footman who were moving plinths so the maid could clean behind them. She felt a stab of envy so strong it made her steps stutter. She knew their lives were not as simple as they seemed to her at that moment, but she would have traded places with them in an instant.

Katie and her sisters had scrubbed, dusted, and washed laundry just like domestics when her family had lived at Queen's Bower. Back then, when she'd worn a plain mobcap rather than one with pretty lace, she had fantasized about a day when she wouldn't have to do maid's work. A day when she could wear beautiful gowns and flirt with handsome men at *ton* balls.

Right now those long-ago days living in a cramped house with her sisters and brother seemed like the fantasy.

It was indeed a case of *be careful what you wish for.*

Katie paused at the library door, took several deep breaths, and then opened it and peered inside, hovering on the threshold when she saw it wasn't the duke and duchess gauntlet she had feared, but only her sister.

Hy was sitting at the desk the duke usually occupied. The massive glossy wood surface was completely bare, so she was staring at nothing. She glanced up at the sound of the door and for a few seconds she looked a thousand miles away. Of all her sisters Katie knew Hy the least, even though she had lived with her these past five years.

Hy was considerate and generous but remained an aloof enigma to Katie. Chatham Park was the size of a small village and Hy and the duke occupied their own wing of the house, which meant that days passed when she only saw her sister at meals. And even then Hy did not speak much. Katie suspected the only person who knew Hy well was her husband.

Hy's vague gaze slowly sharpened. "Thank you for coming, Katie. Have a seat," she said in her strangely inflectionless voice.

Katie threw herself into one of the chairs facing the desk. "If you are going to try and talk me into marrying Dulverton, you might as well save your breath."

Hy stared, her angular face expressionless and her aqua-green eyes—her only claim to beauty—as hard and cold as gemstones.

Katie's courage wavered in the face of her sister's formidable regard, and she lowered her eyes to her fingers, which were fidgeting with the gold braiding on her dressing gown. She stilled her hands and clasped them loosely.

"I saw your list, Katie."

Katie looked up, determined not to shy away this time. But the longer she looked into Hy's eyes, the hotter her face became.

"You think it is amusing to make a game of kissing married men?"

She opened her mouth but then shut it. She had no defense because there was none.

"I'd hoped the stunt you pulled at Christmas five years ago was enough to cure you of your irresponsible behavior."

Katie bristled. "I know locking Andrew and Stacia up in the priest hole for a few days at Wych House was reckless, but you have to admit their happy marriage is worth it."

"The fortunate outcome does not justify you playing with people's lives, Katie. The fact is that you took away their choices."

Katie gritted her teeth. How could a person argue with that logic?

"You've had five Seasons and every year you have become less content and more unpleasant to be around."

Katie gasped and then her lungs seemed to freeze. Hy thought she was *unpleasant?*

*Don't you think you are unpleasant?*

Mortification rolled over her, as heavy and crushing as the wheel of a mailcoach. "If—if you think I am so unpleasant than why did you not send me away?" Katie immediately wished she could rescind the angry retort.

"Send you where? You think I am the only one who thinks you have become unmanageable? The others do not want to take you."

Pain and shock robbed Katie of speech.

"You have become the sort of petulant, self-indulgent person you would have ridiculed and avoided when we lived at Queen's Bower. You do not need to work and pinch pennies. You do not need to worry about losing the roof over your head. And you do not need to marry a wealthy stranger to save your family. You are breathtakingly beautiful, generously dowered, and have the world at your feet and yet you choose to fritter away your time by engaging in cruel, reckless pranks."

Katie could hear her own breathing—more like wheezing—as a tear slid down her cheek. She dashed it away with the back of her hand, but more followed, until her face was streaked with them.

Hy leaned across the desk, a folded white square of linen resting on her palm, the corner embroidered with Hy's initials woven into a duchess's coronet. The handkerchiefs had been gifts from Katie the first year her sister was married.

*Back before you were too bitter and miserable to pick up a needle.*

Katie took the handkerchief with shaking fingers and dried her cheeks, unable to contrive a response to Hy's damning indictment because what *could* she say?

But her sister was not finished.

"The Duke of Dulverton has been humiliated and shamed for no reason other than your selfish whim. He has shied away from society for decades, and now—the first time he's made an appearance at a *ton* event in years—you have made him a figure of ridicule and an object for scandalmongers. You have robbed him of his dignity and privacy. And you have taken away his choices."

Katie's tears fell faster, and it was all she could do not to run from the room to escape her sister's quiet words, which fell like the lash of a whip. "Everyone at that ball—everyone in London—knows he was merely a victim. Dulverton does not need to offer for me."

"You know that is not true. The game might have been your idea, but he will be equally—if not more—to blame."

Katie wanted to argue, but she knew that was the truth.

"You are my sister and I love you, Katie. But I do not respect you and that pains me. There is still time to correct your self-destructive course, but whether you do so is entirely up to you."

"You are talking about me marrying Dulverton," she said dully.

"Neither Chatham nor I will force you to accept Dulverton's offer."

"But that is what you *think* I should do, isn't it?" Katie insisted, the blasted tears still falling. "You think I should pay penance for my—admittedly—cruel action for the rest of my life by marrying the man. And what about him, Hy? Should *he* be forced to suffer by marrying *me*?"

"I will not tell you what to do or say; you must find that answer within yourself. But I will say that it is time you thought not just about what *you* want, but what those around you deserve." And then her quiet sister—who'd spoken more in the last ten minutes than the prior ten years—rose from her chair and strode from library, looking every inch the duchess she was, regardless of her plain morning gown.

Katie stared unseeingly at the elegant room around her, the chilling heaviness in her chest spreading until she was suffused with bleakness. Everything Hy said was true; Katie *was* unpleasant. She did not even like herself; why had she been so shocked to discover that her family no longer wanted to be around her?

But that didn't make the knowledge any less painful. She felt as if her sister had driven a knife into her chest, but the gaping wound poured anguish rather than blood.

Katie had wanted to give Hy an answer—something that might explain why she had been so rootless, miserable, and detached for so long—but the thought of where that conversation would lead was even more painful than her sister's condemnation.

Besides, it didn't matter why she'd thought up that stupid game. It only mattered that she had acted on her impulse and—yes—had taken the choices from three other people. Angus and Letty would have to marry if either of them wanted to show their face again.

And so would Dulverton.

And so would Katie, because she had taken away her own choices, too.

When Dulverton asked her, she would have to say *yes*. She owed him that much, at least.

*But first you must tell him the truth.*

Katie squeezed her eyes shut. *Oh, God.* She could justify not confessing her festering shame to her sister but she would *have* to tell Dulverton. She owed him that much before he yoked himself to her for the rest of their lives.

She gave a watery, miserable laugh. How appropriate was it that she would have to bare her soul—and her greatest humiliation—to a man whose life she had ruined?

A proper punishment, indeed.

***

"Would you care for something to drink, Dulverton?" The Duke of Chatham gestured to a collection of decanters on a small round table.

Gerrit was more tempted to drink than he had been in years. Decades, even. But he had a laughably low tolerance for spirits and behaved like an idiot after just one glass. He suspected he could behave like a fool all on his own today.

"No, thank you," he said abruptly. The meeting with his uncle and Lady Palmer had been ghastly. It had also been expensive. Regardless of the fact that Lady Mariska's emotions were engaged elsewhere, Gerrit had claimed the decision to end their betrothal was his. Jilting a woman was outrageous, but he could weather the storm of familial disapproval far better than poor Lady Mariska.

Not only had he needed to offer recompense to Lady Mariska's family for reneging on the contract, but both van Renesse and Lady Palmer had wanted their palms generously greased before he could get them out of his house.

It was a meeting Gerrit never wanted to relive, and yet here was another miserable encounter even worse than seven-years transportation because the outcome would be a life sentence.

Good God. Would this day never end?

"I wanted to talk to you about Kathryn before you see her," Chatham said.

Gerrit was immediately wary. "Talk about what?"

"My sister-in-law is an impulsive young woman but—"

"Not so young, I think."

Chatham's eyebrows rose at his comment.

"What?" Gerrit demanded.

The other man looked annoyed, but said, "She is no schoolroom chit and will be three-and-twenty on her next birthday."

Gerrit grunted, somewhat surprised she was so young. Despite her immature behavior and youthful appearance, her world-weary expression had been the sort he associated with an older woman.

"I know this is a mess of Kathryn's making, but I refuse to condemn her to an unhappy marriage simply because of one thoughtless act," Chatham said.

Gerrit bristled. "*Condemn her?* Are you saying you oppose an offer from me?" He felt both offended and hopeful. Perhaps he might leave here today without being betrothed to that red-headed hellion.

"I'm not saying that at all," Chatham replied, crushing Gerrit's fragile hope.

He gave an irritable huff. "I would have plain speaking, Chatham. I am not a man who appreciates subtlety." Or understands it, for that matter.

Chatham's mouth twitched. "Of course, Your Grace."

Gerrit squinted. Was the man *smiling?* God only knew what he found amusing in this situation, because Gerrit saw nothing to laugh about, but then he'd frequently been accused of possessing no sense of humor. Not so surprising for a man who'd been stigmatized the *Duke of Dullness* by his contemporaries, a name that had caused him agony when he'd been a boy. But his boyhood was far behind him, and it had been decades since he'd been ashamed of who and what he was. If others saw his inability to chatter like a magpie in social situations as amusing or *dull* that was their concern.

"Here it is in plain speaking, then," Chatham said. "I know it is a longstanding tradition that the Dukes of Dulverton marry women of Dutch descent."

"Correct." It was hardly a secret.

"Marrying Kathryn will break that tradition."

"Correct," Gerrit said testily. Did the man think he was so dull-witted as to not realize that? "What the hell is your point, Chatham?"

The other man's face hardened. "I want your word that you will not bear a grudge against her for breaking that family tradition."

"Bear a grudge?" Gerrit repeated, genuinely confused. "Why would I do such an illogical thing?"

To Gerrit's complete mystification, Chatham laughed. "My wife told me you were not the sort of man to engage in illogical behavior."

"Your wife? How would she know? I only met her for the first time last night."

"I suspect it was just an educated guess."

There was something about Chatham's smirk that told Gerrit he was, yet again, missing some conversational nuance. But he could not bring himself to care about that at the moment. Instead, he dragged the conversation back to the matter at hand. "I will treat Lady Kathryn with the same respect and consideration that I would any woman."

"Thank you. That was my main concern."

"Was there something else you wanted to discuss?" Gerrit prodded when Chatham kept staring at him.

Chatham appeared to shake himself. "No. No, that was it. I will fetch Kathryn."

Gerrit nodded and the other man left the room. He stared at his hands rather than the shelves full of mismatched books that surrounded him. But even though he was not looking at them he could *hear* them jeering at him. His unease at the distracting *noise*—for lack of a better word—was something he felt often whenever he was outside his home. After all, the world was an extremely disorganized and unsymmetrical place.

The duke's library was worse than the Earl of Sutton's ballroom. Perhaps that was because a ballroom was, by its very nature, lacking in symmetry when it was being put to its specified use. A library, on the other hand, was a place for quiet reflection. But there would be none of that in this cacophonous chamber.

Gerrit's gaze slid from his hands—one of which rested on each knee, exactly an inch from his kneecaps—to his exquisitely polished Hessians, his eyes widening with revulsion at the random scatter of blood-red roses on the thick pile beneath his boots. Although he jerked his gaze away immediately, the haphazard rug pattern branded itself on his mind's eye and he had to squeeze his eyes shut until silver sparks on a field of black velvet purged the image from his brain.

"Your Grace?"

Gerrit's well-tutored body unfolded from the chair at the sound of a female voice.

"Your Grace, Lady Kathryn," he said as the two women approached. He frowned at Lady Kathryn's red-rimmed eyes. Did she have a summer cold, or had she been weeping? Gerrit determined to keep a safe distance from her in the event it was the former.

"I will sit in the window seat so that you two may talk privately," the duchess said, her plain, expressionless face far easier for Gerrit to look at than her beautiful sister's, which was positively seething with emotion.

Lady Kathryn gracefully lowered herself onto the settee, and Gerrit flipped up his tails and resumed his own seat. Lady Kathryn gazed at her feet, giving him a moment to study her unobserved. Was she being forced into this? Is that why her eyes were red?

He would be damned before he married another unwilling female.

"Are you here against your will, my lady?"

Her head whipped up and Gerrit's belly clenched when he met her brilliant green eyes, which fairly blazed in the sunlight. The vivid translucent shade brought to mind the emeralds he'd dug in the Wadi Sikai Valley on one of his trips abroad.

*Eyes like emeralds?* Gerrit blinked at the uncharacteristically fatuous thought.

"I am here of my own free will, Your Grace."

So, it would be marriage, then. Gerrit took a deep breath and opened his mouth.

"But there is something you should know that might change your mind about—about what you are about to ask."

*Good God. What now?*

Thankfully, he only thought the words. Aloud, he said, "What do you mean?"

She swallowed. "I am not a virgin."

# Chapter Eight

The face of Gerrit's dead wife rose like the specter she truly was. "How many men?" he snarled.

Lady Kathryn went from mortified to mulish in the blink of an eye. "How many lovers have *you* had?"

He ignored her impertinent question. "How many?" he repeated icily.

She held his gaze for a long moment before wavering and once again lowering her gaze. "One."

"What is his name?"

This time when she looked up, her eyes blazed. "I refuse to tell you about such a—a private matter."

Gerrit's fury licked across his skin like flames, but he kept his voice low and level. "I belong to a number of clubs, Lady Kathryn. Although I do not visit them with any frequency, I would prefer to know who your lover is rather than be forced to wonder and guess at his identity every time I look another man in the face."

"And will you tell me all the names of *your* lovers, as well?"

Gerrit abruptly leaned toward her and was pleased when she recoiled from whatever she saw on his face. "I have taken no lovers from among the *ton* so you will not have to worry about encountering them," he hissed, holding her gaze. "Now. I would have your lover's name, my lady."

"He is nobody you know."

"How can you be so sure of that?"

"Because he is a footman," she retorted, her face a flame.

Nausea rose within him as if he'd been kicked in the ballocks. That he—Gerrit Van Draak—would likely be forced to marry a woman who fucked her servants was so ironic that he almost laughed.

If there was one attitude that he loathed, it was the predatory behavior so many of his peers exhibited toward their social subordinates. And now, evidently, he was going to marry one of that ilk.

"When did you last fornicate with this man?"

Her jaw dropped at the word *fornicate,* but she recovered quickly and fixed him with a look of pure loathing. Was she going to tell him to go to hell? What would Gerrit do if she refused to answer? Would he do the honorable thing and accept another man's castoff? Would he endure a marriage to yet another woman who hated him and bedded every man in sight whenever his back was turned?

# Kathryn

The voice of Gerrit's long-dead father filled his mind, the words coming back to him from almost twenty years ago, the night that Gerrit first learned he was to wed Christina.

*It does not matter that you have never met her. You are like me, Gerrit; you are incapable of that emotion other men call* love. *The sooner you accept that, the sooner you can get on with the business of marriage as it will be—not as others tell you it* should *be. And the sooner Christina is made aware of the situation, the better it will be for both of you. Her duty is to give you an heir. Once she does that, both of you will be free to live your own lives free of one another. It is what I did with your mother, and it will have to be the same with any woman you take to wife. Tell her your intentions in plain words and tell it to her before she can develop unreasonable expectations of you.*

Gerrit experienced a nasty niggling in his belly as he recalled his sire's unpalatable but undeniably accurate advice. Advice that he had rejected at the time, naively hoping he could find happiness with Christina, despite his father's warning.

He knew now, after the disaster of his first marriage, that the old duke had been painfully astute with his advice. Gerrit was far too ugly, awkward, and strange for any woman to love, or even like, so he should take what he could get—hopefully an heir this time—and look for physical pleasure with a woman who was paid to welcome him into her bed.

But even as he opened his mouth to give his prospective wife carte blanche to copulate with whomever she wished, a strange sensation joined the anger simmering inside him and it took him a long moment to identify it. Good God… Was that jealousy he felt?

He was not immune to the unpleasant emotion—he was as human as the next man, despite a common consensus to the contrary—but it was not a feeling he'd experienced since the early days of his first marriage. That had been a natural reaction, albeit short-lived.

But why in the hell would he be jealous of Lady Kathryn Bellamy, a woman he did not know and did not want to marry?

The illogical reaction distracted him for a moment, and he could only stare, too perplexed by his disorganized thoughts to speak. For reasons beyond his ken, the thought of a marriage of convenience rankled, and rankled badly. It made no sense. Less than a day ago he had been resolved to enter that exact sort of union with Lady Mariska. So, why would—

"More than five years have passed, so you needn't fear I am with child."

Gerrit blinked, needing a moment to recall what she meant.

"I am speaking the truth," she said, evidently mistaking his confusion for suspicion.

Five years ago? Chatham had said she was two-and-twenty, which would mean she'd been scarcely more than a girl when she'd bedded her footman. And there had been no other man since?

Why did he find that so hard to believe? After all, she had been the one to mastermind this blasted *kissing contest.*

"Nobody else in five years," he repeated skeptically.

"Yes. That is the truth," she said through gritted teeth.

Gerrit remained silent and stared, which generally served to get most people talking.

It worked this time, too.

***

Dulverton regarded her with cold, reptilian eyes, their iciness all the more noticeable given how very hot Katie's face felt. He dwarfed the chair he sat in, his arrogant fury cloaking his massive shoulders and making him look even bigger and more striking.

Yes, Katie decided that *striking* was a far more accurate word for him than *ugly*, which was too simple. Dulverton's looks *struck* a person like an axe. In fact, she did not have to stretch her imagination at all to imagine his huge hand wielding an axe, stripped to the waist with his near-white hair plaited and hanging down his back, his powerful torso glistening with—

"Lady Kathryn!"

Katie jerked her gaze from his broad chest—garbed in an exquisite coat rather than sweat and the blood of his vanquished foes—to his harsh, austere face. "I beg your pardon, Your Grace?"

His scowl deepened and he cut her a look of such loathing that Katie knew he was going to say something offensive. "I asked if this *footman* is still in your employ?" He regarded Katie as if she were vermin—the same way that *she* would look at *him* if he had confessed to bedding a housemaid. She had always believed there should be a special circle of Hell reserved for masters—or mistresses—who took advantage of their servants and now she had plunked herself right in the middle of that vile cohort.

Katie hated that she'd lied, but she could hardly tell him the truth, could she? Even if she ignored the story Andrew had told her about Dulverton's lethal skills and willingness to duel, the proud set of the duke's jaw and the barely restrained savagery in his frigid gaze persuaded her that the first thing he would do if he encountered her prior lover—Lord Jasper Staines—at one of his clubs was call him out. He might not banish Katie to the Continent as he had his last wife and her lover since her affair had happened *before* their marriage, but he might very well kill or maim Jasper to send a message.

50

By lying about the identity of her lover, Katie had likely saved Jasper's life. Not that the scheming weasel deserved it.

"I would like an answer. *Now*," Dulverton snapped, his abrupt, dictatorial tone setting her back up.

*Rein in your temper! This man will likely be your husband.*

Katie ignored the wise warning. "He is not my footman; he never was. He was a servant at my aunt's house but no longer works for her. So, you needn't tease yourself about ever seeing him again." His look of loathing bit into her like a spur. "Unless you frequently encounter *footmen* at your clubs, that is."

He stared at her with his unnervingly pale eyes, the pupils narrowed to pinpricks of displeasure, his lips compressed into a thin, disapproving line.

Katie did not blame him one bit. But that didn't mean she had to *like* being examined as if she were dung.

"Why are you looking at me that way, Your Grace?" she demanded.

"What else am I supposed to do?" the duke snarled. "Throw a parade to celebrate your woefully catholic taste in rutting with a servant? Award you a medal to—"

"*Enough*, Your Grace!" She crossed her arms, as if that could protect her from his stinging derision. "You have made your point and then some."

His jaw flexed and, to her astonishment, he nodded. "You are correct. I apologize for my incivility."

Katie ignored his apology. "You asked me if I was being forced into this?"

He frowned at the change of subject but nodded.

"I am not, but I *know* you are."

He did not try to deny it.

Katie told herself to be grateful for his honesty no matter how much it stung. "You have done your duty by coming here today and offering for me. I absolve you of any responsibility toward me."

"But I have *not* offered for you," he pointed out pedantically.

"Rest assured that I will tell everyone I rejected your offer. Nobody but the two of us will ever be the wiser and we can go our separate ways.

He rubbed the back of his neck, his gaze distant. A moment later his pale eyes sharpened and he sighed. "Scandal is attached to both our names. The only way to vanquish it is to marry."

She dearly wanted to bring up the last scandal in his life and point out how *that* seemed to have miraculously disappeared. But even she was not that cruel. "It seems extreme to marry a person you loathe merely to avoid damage to one's reputation."

"Perhaps *your* reputation is of no concern to you, but mine is to me, and I daresay your family will care," he said, not denying his loathing for her.

Katie's sisters were hardly sticklers for propriety, but none of them would appreciate having her appalling behavior attached to their names. But was that reason enough to spend the rest of her life shackled to this cold, rude man? Katie tried to imagine bringing Dulverton to her annual family Christmas celebration—the three weeks each year that she lived for—and knew he would hate it. If he even permitted her to go.

No. She could not do it. She might deserve punishment for what she did, but a lifetime was simply too much. "I still think—regardless of the scandal—that the potential for disaster in such a union outweighs any benefit," she said, not ungently.

His eyes narrowed.

"I could never be what you expect in a wife," she babbled on, desperate. "And I am certain you could never make me happy." As usual, Katie had said more than she'd intended.

But if her words hurt him, he did not show it. "Do you even know what I require? Because you have not asked."

"It was my understanding that you required a convent-raised Dutchwoman as your bride."

His eyelids flickered slightly at her snide reply. "What I need is an heir." No surprise there. Before Katie could respond, he continued. "But I do not need one so badly that I'm willing to marry a woman who will make me wonder who fathered my child."

She flinched. "I would never—"

"If we were to marry," he went on, raising his voice to speak over her, "I would expect fidelity until you have produced a son. After that your life is your own as long as you do not bring shame to my name or fill my nursery with bastards."

Katie was too stunned to speak, which was just as well because Dulverton was not finished.

"I have several houses and you may live in any of them except my London house or my estate in Devon. That still leaves five to choose from. We need never see each other again after you have done your duty."

Katie had not expected a declaration on bended knee, but neither had she believed Dulverton would lay out a future so bleak and devoid of not only love but affection and companionship.

Swallowing down the emotions that threatened to choke her, she fixed him with a watery glare. "This is—" She broke off and shook her head, shattered by the brief vision of her future he had just offered. "Why are you persisting with this? I have already confessed my deepest, most mortifying secret." Well, not her *deepest* secret, but Dulverton hardly needed to know the whole of it as there would be no marriage. "I have absolved you of offering for me. I cannot do anything about the scandal I have already caused, but if you are worried that you might be forced to occupy a ballroom with me in the future you should put your mind at rest. I will retire from society, and you shan't have to see my face ever again." Her eyes burned with unshed tears, but she valiantly managed a sneer. "At least not unless you develop a fascination for herding goats in the Outer Hebrides." Katie stood up and all but ran from the room before she broke down and shamed herself.

Somehow, Dulverton was at the door before her, blocking it with his large body.

"What do you *want* from me?" Katie begged, furious at the quaver in her voice. "I have already relieved you of any responsibility to save my honor. I have apologized. Should I grovel?"

"One of my houses overlooks Cula Bay," he said in his characteristically haughty tone.

Katie blinked. "What on earth does that mean? Is it some sort of euphemism for—"

"Cula Bay is in Scotland—the Outer Hebrides, to be precise. I keep a yawl there and take it out on occasion and visit the islands." He cleared his throat and an incongruously delicate pink stain spread over his axe blade-like cheekbones. "It is entirely possible that I might encounter you and your, er, herd of goats."

Her jaw dropped. "Did you just make a *jest*, Your Grace?"

He looked away and rocked back on his heels. The pose reminded her so much of her brother Doddy when he had been a little boy and had done something naughty that Katie suddenly saw the towering man before her from a different angle. Yes, he was stiff and awkward and teeth-grindingly arrogant, but perhaps that was not *all* he was. He had made a joke, and he'd done so in the midst of a wretched situation that he'd had no hand in creating—or at least not much. Somewhere inside him lurked a sense of humor. True, it was probably as wizened and dried up as the turds Doddy's pet squirrel left all over the house, but it was still a sense of humor.

If he possessed one human characteristic, there very well might be more hidden behind his stony façade and frosty gaze. And that meant there might be somebody to hurt.

Katie sighed. "What are you trying to say, Your Grace?"

"Both our lives are effectively ruined, my lady. We might as well spend them together."

It wasn't kindness she saw in his gaze, but neither was it derision or anger. It was the look of a man proposing a cease fire.

"Are—are you certain?" she asked, a hopeful quaver in her voice.

"I am certain. Will you do me the honor of becoming my wife, Lady Kathryn?"

"I—" Her voice broke. Katie cleared her throat, filled her lungs with air, and—for good or for ill—said the words that would change her life forever. "Yes, Your Grace, I will marry you."

# Chapter Nine



*Two Weeks Later*

Katie smiled and nodded at Lord Brimley, the man seated on her right, even though she had no idea what he had been talking about. Evidently a smile and a nod were good enough because Brimley resumed his tedious monologue.

Keeping her smile firmly fixed, Katie stole a furtive glance at her husband of only a few hours. Dulverton sat at the foot of the table on Hy's right. He was not talking to either Hy or the woman on the other side of him, yet another guest at her wedding breakfast whom Katie could not recall meeting before.

Dulverton was solely focused on the food on his plate, which he was methodically demolishing.

Hy, for all that she was the hostess, mirrored Dulverton's actions so completely the two might have been bookends.

The woman on Dulverton's other side laid a hand on Dulverton's shoulder to get his attention and then flinched when he jerked away at her touch. Those around them looked over curiously at the abrupt movement. The duke murmured something to the woman and all conversation ceased as people craned their necks to listen. He must have apologized because her tense posture relaxed, and she began speaking.

Dulverton cocked his head, attentive to what she said, his face wearing a surprisingly polite expression, certainly not one he'd ever given Katie.

Although they'd been civil to each other whenever they'd met these past two weeks, her betrothed had never been what one would call *warm*.

Dulverton suddenly looked in her direction, his pale, keen eyes causing her pulse to pound annoyingly fast, just as it always did. Katie hastily jerked her gaze away, looking instead at the massive ormolu clock perched on the white marble mantelpiece.

*Dear God.* Only five minutes had elapsed since the last time she'd sneaked a peek.

Dulverton's breakfast companion was not the only stranger at the long banquet table; Katie was hard-pressed to recognize even half the people celebrating her nuptials. Hy had asked her if she wanted to wait until their siblings were able to attend to have the wedding, but Katie just wanted to get it over with. Besides, it would be half a year before the Bellamy siblings could all get together.

Doddy was on the Continent visiting their father, Phoebe and Selina were both expecting interesting events within the next six weeks, and Aurelia had gone on a naturalist expedition with her husband and would not return to England until just before Christmas.

Katie could not wait six months to marry. Two weeks spent in the strange netherworld of *scandalously betrothed* had already been far too long.

Thankfully, the Season had officially ended the week before and the younger set had fled for country house parties or Brighton. Most of the guests today were friends of Chatham's rather than Katie's. Not that she had many friends left at this point.

She felt a light touch on her left elbow. "I beg you will excuse me, my lord?" she said, cutting Brimley off in mid-sentence.

He blinked, looking like a stunned carp. "Oh… of course."

Katie turned to find Andrew wearing his characteristic smirk. "Are you bleeding out your right ear?" he asked in a tone more suited to a military parade ground.

"*Hush!* Brimley will hear you."

"No, he won't," Andrew said, making no effort to lower his voice. "Look at him."

Katie turned just enough to look at the other man. Sure enough, Brimley was already engaged in conversation with his other breakfast companion, his voice droning on as if he had never stopped speaking.

"What a windbag," Andrew said, ignoring her chiding scowl. "Who the devil invited him?" He squinted around at the other guests. "Who invited most of these frights? I don't—"

"*Andrew!*"

He stopped talking but looked unabashed.

"It was Aunt Constance who planned everything," she said in a low voice. Aunt Constance was a cousin of Chatham's and not actually related to Katie, but she liked the gentle, soft-spoken woman a great deal. Constance lived at Chatham Park year-round and took care of the hundreds of details that the Duchess of Chatham would normally manage if that duchess wasn't Hyacinth. Although Hy had been married for more than five years, she would never be a great society hostess, or even a mediocre one. But Hy and Chatham seemed to have worked out an agreement because Hy was left to her own devices most of the time. Which was just as well, because her sister's forte was not socializing, as was evidenced by the way she was currently ignoring both her table companions.

"I suppose poor Connie was forced to scrape the bottom of the barrel as everyone has fled town," Andrew said, nodding at the footman to replenish his champagne. Katie was already working on her third glass and briefly pondered having a fourth before coming to her senses and shaking her head.

"Why did you and Dulln—er, Dulverton wait so long to marry?"

Katie gave him a scathing look. "Do not do that again."

Andrew did not ask what she meant. "I won't," he said, looking serious for a few seconds.

"You call two weeks *long?*" she asked.

"It is when the marriage is one of exigency." He grinned. "Just consider poor Fowler. He was caught in parson's mousetrap a mere three days after the infamous Night of Kissing."

Katie suffered a well-deserved guilty pang at the mention of the big Scotsman's hasty marriage. "I think Fowler wanted to get married quickly so that he would have an excuse to leave town and avoid *my* wedding."

"That might be true. He is not your greatest admirer right now," Andrew added with a chuckle.

That was putting it mildly. Fowler had had a special message for Katie when he'd come to hand deliver his wedding invitations to Chatham, Hy, and Katie. He had waited until the duke and duchess had stepped out of the room before cornering Katie and snarling, "If you have any decency at all then you will find yourself too busy to attend."

Katie had been stung. "Why did you bring me an invitation if you didn't want me to come?"

"Mrs. Grayson felt compelled to invite you as Chatham and the Duchess will be there."

Katie had counted Angus Fowler among her closest friends for more than five years. Indeed, she had grown to think of him as an older brother. And now she had forced him into marriage with one woman when she knew he had already lost his heart to another.

"I am truly sorry, Angus," she said quietly while he'd paced Chatham's drawing room, refusing to look at her.

"You can show your contrition by avoiding my wedding."

"Of course, I will do what you want and send my regrets to Mrs. Grayson."

He'd spun on his heel and glared at her through eyes that were almost the same color as her own. She had seen not just fury and thwarted desire in Angus's gaze, but grief and loss. "You take pride in doing the unexpected, no matter how much devastation you leave in your wake. I hope to God you have learned something this time after wrecking three lives."

"Three lives? There are four people getting married, Angus."

"You don't expect any sympathy from me?"

Katie bit her lip, but the words had slipped out anyhow. "I do not think your life is wrecked. I think Letty will make you a wonderful wife. Far better than Elizabeth Jennings. Not that you would have ever come up to scratch and made Lizzy an offer given that you could scarcely speak three words to her—"

"How dare you even say her name?" Angus thundered.

Katie had shut her mouth then and kept it shut while Angus had ranted and raged about the loss of Lizzy.

While Katie mourned the loss of his friendship, she could not feel terrible about saving him from a marriage with Lizzy Jennings, a sweet girl with scarcely two thoughts to rub together. Angus was a clever man, and he deserved a wife who would be his companion and not just a pretty ornament on his arm. If he was even half as smart as Katie hoped he was, he would stop dwelling on Lizzy and recognize Letty's value sooner rather than later.

"Katie?"

She looked up to find Andrew watching her, a notch of concern between his eyes.

"Is something wrong?"

"I am fine," she said, drinking the rest of her champagne and wishing she had asked for more.

"Angus will forgive you, Katie." Andrew patted her hand. "He won't come around quickly, but he'll come around. I very much liked the little I saw of Fowler's wife."

"Letty is a wonderful person, but Angus can't see beyond Lizzy Jennings."

Andrew laughed. "Oh, Angus never would have asked Lizzy to marry him. Hell, he could hardly ask her to dance with him."

"That is what I said to him."

"I'm sure he enjoyed that observation."

"He said that he was on the verge of proposing and I believe him. I haven't seen him that way about a woman before."

"Ah, but that's because you've not known him very long. You should have seen how wrecked he was by Selina five years ago. Trust me, Katie, he never would have come up to scratch with Lizzy Jennings if he'd been left to his own devices. He was attracted by the idea of her, but his heart was not touched. I think not so deep-down

Fowler knows that and wishes to keep it that way by falling for unattainable women. In any event, do not fret, my dear. He'll forgive you."

"Letty is both intelligent *and* kind. He is a fortunate man."

*And you just forced her into a marriage with a man who will never love her.*

"I am sure Angus will recognize her value," Andrew replied absently, his speculative gaze on Dulverton, who was still giving all his attention to his food. "As for you and your new husband…" Andrew's smile looked a bit forced. "Well, I'm sure it will all work out for the best," he added lamely.

"More champagne, Your Grace?"

Katie startled at the sound of her new title. "Yes, please," she said to the waiting footman after a moment. "Pour me another glass."

***

Gerrit was bloody exhausted by the time the harrowing wedding breakfast came to an end.

Chatham's speech had been blessedly brief. But after the duke had come his cousin and former heir, Andrew Derrick.

Gerrit had not been able to decipher the thrust of several of Derrick's obscure comments but—judging by all the laughter aimed in Gerrit's direction—they must have had something to do with Gerrit. In general, he was not bothered about being the subject of mockery. Indeed, taunting was something he had lived with all his life and learned to tolerate. However, it seemed the outside of enough that he was forced to endure such abuse at his own wedding breakfast—and from Derrick in particular—but Gerrit gritted his teeth and bore it.

His new wife scowled at most of what Derrick said, so perhaps Gerrit was not the only one at the table without a sense of humor.

Four more people spoke after Derrick, but Gerrit stopped listening, his thoughts on the more pleasant subject of Briarly, where he and his new wife would be retiring for the summer. He missed his home with an almost tangible ache. He'd had to—

"Your Grace?"

Gerrit looked up to find Chatham staring at him. "Yes?" he barked.

Chatham raised his eyebrows and gave Gerrit a meaningful look. Although what it meant, he wasn't sure. Unless… Good God! Did the man expect him to make a speech?

Before Gerrit could do something rash like shout, *not bloody likely!* the Duchess of Chatham stood and drew the attention away from him.

The tall, pale woman blandly regarded the guests, as if she had only just now noticed them and quietly murmured, "Let us retire to the drawing room."

After a moment of stunned surprise, people stood and began leaving the room.

The duchess turned her opaque gaze on Gerrit. "Nobody will expect the bride and groom to stay much longer, Your Grace."

Gerrit gave her a genuinely grateful look. "Thank you for organizing this celebration."

She merely nodded and turned away, a woman of admirably few words.

When he entered the drawing room he found his wife beside Andrew Derrick, listening to something he was saying.

Gerrit did not bother to wait for the man to stop speaking. Instead, he raised his voice and talked over him. "Are you ready to leave, Your Grace?"

His wife's face flushed at his rudeness, but Derrick chuckled.

"Eager to get your new wife alone, are you Dulln—er Dulverton?"

Gerrit had planned to continue ignoring Derrick, but the irritating cad had made that impossible, so he lifted his gaze to Derrick's laughing blue eyes and said, "Yes."

Derrick blinked, either at Gerrit's brevity or perhaps he could see the animus in Gerrit's gaze. He did not hate Derrick for his endless jests and digs over the years, nor even for being one of the many men who had fucked Christina. No, what he truly loathed him for was lacking the tact and decency to absent himself from Gerrit's bloody wedding.

"Er, just so," Derrick said in his hail-fellow-well-met voice. He kissed Kathryn on the cheek. "Do not forget to write." He cut Gerrit an unreadable look. "Take care of my little sister, Dulverton." This time his annoying smirk was nowhere in evidence. Instead, there was a hard edge to his voice before he strolled across the room to join another cluster of people.

"*Sister?*" he repeated.

Kathryn gave him an odd look. Gerrit suspected he would be getting many such looks from her in the years to come.

"Well?" he prodded irritably.

"He is Chatham's cousin, so I consider him family."

Gerrit contemplated telling her that she was welcome to write Derrick ten times a day if she chose, but she had better not ask the man to visit.

He decided that was a conversation for when they were alone.

He held out his arm. "Come, let us take our leave."

She lightly laid her hand on his proffered sleeve.

Gerrit knew it was only his imagination, but for a moment it felt as if her palm burned through his coat and into his skin like a brand.

*****

Katie's brand-new husband stared broodingly out the window during the five-minute drive to Dulverton House. She could not blame him for being annoyed. She had wanted to slap Andrew for his deliberate slip with Dulverton's wretched nickname. And everyone called *her* immature.

Katie pulled her attention from Dulverton and looked out the window as the carriage rolled to a halt. The entire staff appeared to have lined themselves up outside of Dulverton House.

"Goodness," Katie said, shaking off her sour mood. "Have they just been standing there all this time?"

Dulverton looked at her as if she were an imbecile. "I sent one of my servants from Chatham's house twenty minutes ago to alert them of our imminent arrival."

Katie felt like an idiot. Perhaps that last glass of champagne had been ill advised, after all.

Servants clad in coffee-brown livery with gold lacing had approached the carriage, but the duke opened the door, hopped out, and put down the steps himself before handing her out.

Four footmen flanked the carriage, each tall and handsome with auburn hair and light blue eyes. It was tradition in most aristocratic households to engage handsome, physically similar footmen, but never had Katie seen four men who looked so alike.

A tall, bone-thin man who could only be the butler bowed low. "It is a pleasure to meet you, Your Grace. I am Willow." He turned to the older woman beside him. "This is Mrs. Kent, your housekeeper."

"Welcome to Dulverton House, Your Grace," Mrs. Kent said, dropping a low curtsey.

And so it went on down the line, all the way to Billy Pickle, the boot black.

The procedure took so long that Katie was sober by the time Dulverton led her through the cavernous foyer and up the staircase.

"I believe your maid is in your chambers," the duke said as they ascended the stairs. "Would you care to rest for a few hours before dinner, or perhaps take a tour of the house?"

If Katie crawled into her bed at this point, she might not be able to crawl back out of it. "I only need a few minutes to refresh myself and then I'd like to see the house."

"I will send Mrs. Kent up to you in three-quarters of an hour, if that is sufficient?"

She'd thought Dulverton would want to show his wife his own house. How foolish of her. "That will be fine."

He stopped in front of a massive set of double doors and opened the one on the right. "I will see you at dinner," he said, and then bowed.

Katie watched him walk a short distance down the hall—which seemed oddly empty, now that she was looking around—and disappear through an identical set of double doors that must lead to the master's chambers. But then Katie noticed that all the rooms appeared to have grand double doors, even those at the end of the corridor, which would usually lead to a servant staircase.

Katie shrugged aside the thought and shut the door, leaning up against it. So, that was it, then. She was married. And to a man who exhibited about as much emotion as the slabs of wood that comprised his many doors.

"My lady—er, Your Grace?"

Katie looked up at the sound of Becky's voice and heaved a sigh of relief. "I am glad to see a friendly face, Becks."

Becky's eyebrows shot up. "Were the servants not friendly to you?"

"I misspoke—I should have said a friendly *familiar* face."

Becky nodded, looking distracted.

"Is something amiss?" Katie asked as she stripped off the mint-green gloves that matched her wedding gown.

"No, no, nothing is wrong. In fact, everything is grand." Becky gave an uncharacteristically giddy laugh. "It is just—well, I have quite risen in the world, is all."

"Risen? Oh, you mean you're higher up the table?" Katie handed Becky her the gloves before reaching for her hatpin.

"Yes, indeed. I am quite a grand personage now, Your Grace."

"Must you call me that when we are alone?" Katie asked as she followed her maid into a truly cavernous and empty dressing room. But there was no reason to unpack her trunks as they would only stay one night.

"It wouldn't do for me to call you anything else," Becky said primly, taking Katie's arm, leading her toward the dressing table, and shoving her down on the bench.

"I don't see why you can't call me by my name when you are perfectly comfortable scolding me and pushing me about."

Becky ignored her grousing. "I'd better tidy your hair. It's gone quite wild in this humidity," she added beneath her breath, her hands already busy.

"Don't take me apart too much," Katie said, lifting a hand to her mouth and nibbling a fingernail. "Mrs. Kent will be here in a little over half an hour to show me the house."

"No chewing," Becky barked.

Katie dropped her hand, turned her gaze toward the mirror, and looked at Becky rather than her own tired face. "Any handsome footmen, grooms, or underbutlers that catch your eye?"

Becky pursed her lips. "I'm sure I wouldn't know."

"It's perfectly fine for you to have a life of your own, Becky. Just because you are my maid does not mean you need to be a vestal virgin."

Becky barked a startled laugh and gave Katie's shoulders a gentle push. "The things you say."

Katie smiled wearily. "One of us should at least choose her own husband."

The humor drained from Becky's face and her hands stilled. "This is your bed, Your Grace, and nobody made it but you."

"It takes two people to kiss," Katie snapped.

"His Grace is a man!"

"What is that supposed to mean?"

"It means there isn't a man in London who would say *no* to kissing you when you all but flung yourself at him."

"You are supposed to be on my side," Katie reminded her.

"Part of being on your side is pointing out when you are in the wrong, Katie. His Grace might have kissed you back that night, but *you* were the one who conceived of that wretched game."

Katie scowled. "Fine. I am in the wrong and everything is my fault. I will accept that. Can we not speak of it again? Or at least not for a week—or perhaps a month? After all, I will be paying penance for the remainder of my life."

Becky shook her head and nimbly unwound Katie's hair, brushing it to a shine before sweeping it up into an elegant French twist, all without speaking.

Good. Because silence was better than incessant berating. Hy's cutting words had rung in Katie's head over and over again, no matter how hard she had tried to forget them. The last thing she needed was Becky adding to the mental din.

"Mrs. Kent said that His Grace's last wife did not occupy the mistress's chambers but stayed in rooms all the way at the other side of the house," Becky offered, evidently deciding not to punish Katie with silence. "She said the last woman to use *these* rooms was His Grace's mother."

Katie glanced around at the rather faded pink bed hangings and heavy velvet drapes. "It does look a bit dated." She suddenly recalled what Andrew had said about Dulverton's last wife and how she had taken many lovers. Had she brought other men into the duke's own house? That might account for her not taking an adjoining room.

She felt a bit ill thinking about that. After her brief *affaire* with Jasper and five Seasons, she hardly expected *ton* marriages to be faithful. But surely it would be egregious to entertain other men under your husband's roof? And if Dulverton had been telling the truth about never having a *ton* lover—and the man had no reason to lie—did that mean he had been faithful to his wife? Or did it mean he'd kept mistresses? Katie suspected it was the latter. Aristocratic men were hardly known for their abstemious ways, after all.

"His Grace's valet, Mr. Court, is quite… odd."

"Odd how?"

Becky placed the last pin in Katie's hair and stepped back to admire her work. "I could barely get a word out of him."

Just like his master. "Is that unusual?" she asked.

"Indeed, it is, if we are ever to coordinate your and His Grace's schedules and preferences. Not only that, but Mrs. Kent said Mr. Court doesn't eat in the servant hall but takes his meals in his room."

"Nobody else eats in their room?"

Becky gave her an amused look. "Who do you think has to bring his meals up?"

"Oh," Katie said, feeling rather foolish. "Another servant. They don't care to do that, I take it?"

Becky laughed. "Not in general. Besides, why would somebody want to eat alone?"

Katie could think of plenty of reasons but kept that to herself.

"Mrs. Kent says Mr. Court has been with the master since he was just a lad and that he even went to university with him."

"Which one did he attend?"

"I don't know," Becky said in a tone that made it clear such information was of no interest to her. She smiled sweetly. "He is your husband. Why don't you ask *him*, Your Grace?"

Katie ignored her pert response.

"Mrs. Kent says His Grace is almost eight-and-thirty," Becky went on. "He was born when his father was two-and-forty and his mother only eight-and-ten. His mother was the last duke's second wife."

"I have learned more about Dulverton in the last thirty seconds than I have in the past two weeks," Katie said drily.

Becky gave her a lofty look. "It is part of my duty as your dresser to gather information, Your Grace."

"Ah, so you've been elevated to *dresser* as I've been raised to duchess, have you? You and Mrs. Kent seem to have become bosom friends in such a short time."

There was a polite knock on the door and Becky hastened to open it.

It was Mrs. Kent, who curtsied to Katie. "His Grace said you would like a tour of Dulverton House, Your Grace."

"Indeed, I would," Katie lied. She had little interest in a house they would be leaving first thing tomorrow. Still, touring the house was better than enduring another scold from her maid or sitting in her room dreading the bridal evening ahead.

"I will begin the tour on this floor, if that suits you?" Mrs. Kent said as they left Katie's chambers.

"I place myself in your hands, Mrs. Kent. Have you been at Dulverton House long?"

"All my working life," Mrs. Kent said proudly. "His Grace's father hired me when I was just a girl. A very kind master he was." She paused and then said in a confiding tone, "If I may be so bold, His Grace is very much like his father, both in appearance and disposition."

Dulverton was a kind master? Given the rude, abrupt, haughty way he behaved with his contemporaries, that seemed an unlikely claim. Well, at least the woman was a loyal servant.

Mrs. Kent opened the door to the suite of rooms at the end of the corridor. "This is the Blue Suite."

The rooms beyond the door had clearly not been decorated by the same person who'd done the rest of the house. It was excessively feminine, and the word *bower* came to mind. The bed was a massive four-poster with powder-blue hangings and every inch of the floor was covered in carpets incorporating the same shade.

It was pretty, although a bit too cloying for Katie's taste. Above the fireplace hung a portrait of a beautiful blonde woman seated on a gilt, throne-like chair holding a pug in her lap. Her hair was dressed high with a cluster of blond ringlets cascading over one shoulder, the middle part effectively showcasing her wide-spaced, round blue eyes, which were stunning. Judging by the recent era of clothing, this had to be Dulverton's first wife.

"These chambers belonged to His Grace's first wife, Your Grace," Mrs. Kent said in a hushed tone, as if the information was somehow profane. Which she supposed it was given that Christina Van Draak had eloped with another man. Katie was rather surprised the portrait had not been tucked away in an attic.

"If Your Grace would prefer to use these chambers—"

"I will stay where I am, thank you," Katie hastily said, not wishing to occupy such a fussy room even for one night.

They visited several other rather sterile suites before moving to the floor below. There was a large drawing room that was part of an enfilade of four rooms which included a magnificent music room, complete with a gilded harp and one of the largest pianos Katie had ever seen. When the doors were all open the four rooms would form a generously sized ballroom.

"Do you play, Your Grace?" Mrs. Kent said as Katie lightly stroked the glossy piano case.

"Indifferently. Certainly not well enough to deserve an instrument like this one. Did His Grace's first wife play?"

"No, not that I ever heard. This was a gift from His Grace's grandfather to his wife, who I am told could have performed professionally, if not for her elevated status."

"And what about His Grace's mother? Does she play?"

"Er, as to that, I could not say."

"The dowager does not come to London?" Katie knew she should be asking her husband these questions, but Dulverton was about as approachable as a medieval castle with arrows bristling in all its embrasures.

"Not since I have worked here, Your Grace."

Good Lord! Dulverton's mother had *never* visited London?

"When was the last time a ball was held at Dulverton House?"

# Kathryn

"Oh, good gracious me," Mr. Kent said, her gaze going vague. "That would have been two decades ago, when the old duke was still alive. It was the betrothal ball for—" She broke off when she realized what she'd been about to say.

Katie smiled. "It is fine to mention my husband's former marriage, Mrs. Kent. I will not be offended."

The older woman bowed her head, hesitated, and then seemed unable to keep the next words from pouring out. "If you will pardon my curiosity, will Your Graces be coming to London next Season?" She smiled uncertainly. "It is just—well, we *do* so enjoy having family in residence."

"I really couldn't say. You would have to ask my husband," Katie admitted, sorry to take the hopeful look off the other woman's face.

Mrs. Kent nodded, her shoulders sagging slightly as she guided Katie out of the grand, unused room.

A few moments later the housekeeper opened another set of double doors. "This is the library."

Katie's lips curved into a smile as she entered the cavernous book-lined room, inhaling the familiar scent of beeswax, leather, and wood deeply into her lungs. Chatham had magnificent libraries at both Chatham House and Chatham Park, but those weren't *hers*. This library belonged to Katie. Well, at least as much as anything of the duke's belonged to her.

"His Grace is very fond of this room," Mrs. Kent said. "He spends almost as much time here as he does in his study."

Her words warmed Katie. A love of libraries and books was an excellent sign, wasn't it? Dulverton could not be *too* horrible if he loved books.

Cheered by the thought Katie strolled toward one of the shelves, her smile slowly fading the closer she came to the books. "My goodness," she murmured, her gaze flitting from book to book and shelf to shelf. All the spines were bottle green— the exact same binding style for every single book. She glanced at the next shelf and saw it was the same. As was the next and the next. Hundreds—no, thousands—of identical book spines.

She turned to the housekeeper. "Is this a new library?"

"No, no, it is quite ancient."

"I have never seen *all* the books in a private library bound the same way."

"His Grace's father had all the books rebound when he inherited, and His Grace has bound all his acquisitions in the exact same style."

Stunned and vaguely unnerved, Katie slid a book from the shelf and turned it in her hands, her mind on the three cases of books that were among her things. They were bound in all sorts of styles and colors. Would they also be rebound in dark green leather and absorbed into her husband's collection?

Something about that thought left her uneasy and she hastily replaced the book on the shelf. Suddenly the room was not so cozy and comforting after all, but eerily remote and unwelcoming.

Much like her husband.

Katie headed for the door, suddenly desperate to get out. As she sped from the room she noticed the odd placement of the furniture, which was upholstered in the same dark green leather as the books. Each piece was exactly the same—large wing chairs, there were no settees—and positioned in four separate seating areas.

Identical clocks sat on the identical mantelpieces above massive fireplaces at either end of the room. Large mirrors in plain gilt frames hung above each. Katie spun around, this time looking at the walls rather than the books. The mirrors were the only things on the wall. There wasn't much wall space that wasn't covered in books, but what there was, was bare.

"Why are there no paintings?"

"Er, His Grace does not care for paintings in the library."

Katie laughed but then saw the other woman was not laughing with her. "Whyever not?" When the other woman hesitated Katie added, "You may always speak plainly with me, Mrs. Kent. As you probably know, Dulverton and I are not well acquainted." She smiled faintly at the understatement. Katie did not doubt for a moment that every servant in London, not just the duke's, had heard about *The Night of the Kissing Game*—as some wag had dubbed it—and its resultant marriages.

Mrs. Kent cleared her throat. "His Grace—like his father—has very particular tastes when it comes to certain things."

"Things like paintings?" Katie urged when Mrs. Kent ground to a halt.

"More than just paintings. He requires order and cannot tolerate clutter."

Katie raised her eyebrows. "Paintings are clutter?"

Mrs. Kent inhaled deeply and then let both her breath and the words out in a rush. "His Grace requires symmetry. And when that is not possible, he prefers there be… nothing."

"So, if there aren't two identical paintings, then nothing?"

"No, no. They do not need to be *identical*, but—" She broke off and chewed her lip. "I believe His Grace does not wish for more items on the walls given that there are already so many books."

"There is not much art in the hallway and there are no books out there."

Mrs. Kent looked flustered. "I, er—"

"Never mind," Katie said, feeling like a bully for interrogating the poor woman.

Mrs. Kent's forehead was deeply furrowed, as if she was worried that she'd said something wrong.

Katie wanted to reassure her but discovered she had no reassurance to spare. What on earth had she gotten herself into?

"You may continue the tour, Mrs. Kent," Katie said, needing to get out of the room, not that the stark corridors would be any better.

Once they'd left the library, Mrs. Kent led Katie back the same way they'd come—or at least she tried to.

"Where does that lead?" Katie pointed to the only set of double doors the housekeeper had not opened.

"That is His Grace's study."

Katie suddenly had a burning, irresistible desire to see what her husband's personal sanctuary looked like.

"Oh, you mustn't, Your Grace," Mrs. Kent cried, trotting after Katie. "His Grace does not care for—"

Katie ignored her and briefly knocked on the door before opening it and stepping into a dark-paneled room.

Dulverton sat at a desk that looked to be in the center of the room—and likely was in the *exact* center based on what she had just learned from Mrs. Kent.

He shot to his feet, his eyebrows drawing low over his pale eyes, which immediately slid toward the housekeeper. "Is something—"

"Do not scold Mrs. Kent," Katie said in a breezier tone than she was feeling. "She tried to stop me from entering but I was curious. What are those?" she asked and strode toward the longest wall of the study which had four large sash windows—equidistant—with sections of wall between each. There were dozens of identically sized and spaced shadow boxes mounted on the walls. She peered into the boxes, which were about two inches square. Each box held a tiny fossil and there was little variation between them. Indeed, some looked identical to others.

"Why do you have so many that are all the same?" she asked, reaching the end of one row, and starting on the one beneath it.

"They are not all the same." Dulverton's voice came from right beside Katie and she flinched. He certainly moved like a cat.

She turned to him and smiled up into his heavy-lidded eyes. "They look all the same to me."

"Did you need something, Your Grace?" he asked coolly.

"No, I didn't need anything. I was just taking the tour." She cocked her head. "Am I not permitted to come in here… Gerrit?" She'd seen his Christian name for the first time today, on the register.

His jaws worked and his nostrils flared, but he didn't speak.

"You look displeased, Your Grace. Am I not supposed to use your name, either?"

He turned slowly, until he was facing Mrs. Kent, whose jaw was sagging so low it was in danger of falling off.

"I will complete the tour, Mrs. Kent. You may go."

The woman's mouth snapped shut and she dropped a curtsey. "Of course, Your Grace."

Only when they were alone did Dulverton turn back to her, meeting her gaze with eyes that were not dead and cold, but blazed like white fire. "You do not like to do what is expected, do you?"

His question startled a laugh out of her. "I could say the same thing about you—I certainly didn't expect *that* question."

"This is my private domain," he said coldly, unmoved by her gentle raillery. "There is no reason for you to be in here."

Katie's eyebrows shot up. "I just wanted to look."

"And now you have."

Her flaming hot face felt exactly as it used to do whenever her mother slapped her, a punishment the countess had used freely.

"And am I allowed the same right?"

He frowned. "What do you mean?"

"May I refuse you admittance to *my* private domain?"

She hadn't thought it possible for his eyes to grow colder, but they did. "I have no interest whatsoever in your sitting room."

The quiet words were like a slap. Katie opened her mouth to demand if the same could be said for her bedroom, but thankfully he spoke before she could utter such foolishness.

"Come," he said, gesturing to the door. "I will finish the—"

"I will show myself the rest of the house," she retorted sharply, pleased when his tanned cheeks darkened at her snappish response. If he wanted to be rude and abrupt? Well, two could play at that game.

She thought he might insist—as if he didn't trust her to roam his house unaccompanied—but he inclined his head. "As you wish, Your Grace."

Katie did not enjoy snubbing him as much as she'd hoped. And so, she needled him a little more, "Before I leave, perhaps you might tell me if there any other doors I am not allowed to open?"

"You may open any door you please."

*Except this one.*

A suffocating wave of weariness suddenly swamped her as she glared at her husband of less than six hours. This was her new life and thus far it was even more bleak and joyless than she had feared.

Overwhelmed by the grim vision of her future, she strode toward the door, desperate to get out of this place where she was not wanted.

The duke was there before her. Rather than let her out, he paused and said, "One more thing."

Katie gave him a wary look.

"If you must use my Christian name, you should know it is pronounced *heh-REET*, not *GAH-ret*."

And then he opened the door and waited silently for Katie to leave.

# Chapter Ten

Gerrit glanced at the clock and gritted his teeth. It was now four minutes past eight.

He looked from the clock face to the two footmen who waited along with him. "Avery, will you please go and inform Her Grace that—"

The door opened and his wife breezed into the room. "I am sorry I'm late," she announced, not sounding sorry in the least.

Willow came in behind her, and Gerrit knew his butler had probably been hovering outside the room wringing his hands. The old man's gaze flickered anxiously from Gerrit to the duchess.

"You may serve now," Gerrit said.

"Very good, Your Grace," Willow said, soundlessly closing the door behind him.

Avery hastened to pull out Kathryn's chair at the foot of the table. Rather than be seated, however, she stood staring from her seat to Gerrit's. "What is your name?" she asked the hovering footman.

"Avery, Your Grace."

"Avery, would you please move my place setting closer to His Grace?"

Avery darted a look at Gerrit.

So did Kathryn.

Gerrit gnashed his teeth. If he did not assert himself now, she would run roughshod over him. He had trained countless dogs and more than a few horses over the years. Surely, he could train one small woman.

"Leave the place setting where it is," he said, and then turned to Thomas, who was watching the proceedings with wide-eyed awe. "Help Avery remove all the table leaves."

The servants jolted into action, and Gerrit seethed at the food for gossip they were currently providing. He knew he should allow her to sit at his right or left hand, but he'd be damned before he'd endure an entire meal feeling nauseatingly off-center.

Kathryn's eyes drilled into him, a twisted smile on her lovely face. Gerrit was no fool; she viewed his countermanding of her request as shots fired across her bow. Her openly antagonistic expression told him she was more than willing to engage in a pitched battle.

So was Gerrit.

# Kathryn

The difference between them was that he would win.

***

After the leaves had been removed and the food served, Katie's plan had been to completely ignore her husband and eat in silence. But a few surreptitious glances across the table—now shortened to a laughably small four-person size in the massive dining room—told her that *heh-REET* was delighted to dine in silence and was enjoying the peace and quiet.

Well, she could not have that, could she?

"What time are we leaving in the morning, Your Grace?" she asked, even though Becky had already told her they would be off at first light.

He looked up from his poached sole. "At first light."

"Ah."

He turned back to his plate.

"How long will it take to get to our destination?"

He looked up again, locking eyes with her as he set down his fork, finished chewing his mouthful of food, wiped his stern mouth with his napkin, and said, "The trip takes fourteen hours."

Katie frowned. "That is longer than I thought. Where will we break our journey?"

"The moon is full so we will travel straight through."

"Lord! That sounds like misery. What is the hurry, Dulverton?"

Knots rippled up and down his jaw as he glowered across at her. "Leave us," he barked, never taking his gaze from her.

The footmen scuttled from the room.

Once the door had shut behind them, Dulverton said, "This will not serve, Kathryn."

A flutter of excitement erupted in her belly at the sound of her name on his tongue. It had been years since anyone had called her by anything other than her nickname. Only her parents had ever used *Kathryn* and then, usually, it had been when she'd misbehaved and was going to be punished. Her father—when nagged by her mother—had employed the time-honored *bend over the desk and endure a series of swats* method of correction. Katie and her sisters had laughed uproariously at the earl's ineffectual smacks with a switch.

Their mother, on the other hand, delivered a constant series of pinches and slaps that left bruises all over one's arms. But worse than that, were her punitive silences that dragged on for days. It had been at least five years since Katie had endured chastisements from either of her parents, but the unpleasant feeling of not measuring up had not changed.

She wondered what sort of punishments Dulverton favored.

The realization that yet another person possessed the authority to control and discipline her was like the jab of a red-hot poker to her already tender sensibilities and her temper—already hanging by a thread--snapped. "What will not serve, Your Grace?" she retorted with a sneer. "Me having the audacity to ask questions?"

"Your combativeness will not serve."

She opened her mouth, but he lifted a hand. To her shock, the words froze on her tongue.

"I can see that it is in your nature to challenge authority." He sat back in his chair and regarded her coldly. "But that will not serve, either."

"I suppose *you* are the authority."

"Correct."

Katie's vision blurred, not with tears, but with outraged frustration. "So, now we come to the crux of the matter. You are domineering, controlling, and overbearing and I will have no choice in—in *anything* having to do with my own life."

"If by domineering, controlling, and overbearing you mean there is only one master in this marriage and I am he, then *yes,* you are correct. You can either accept the way it will be, or you can futilely rail against my authority. Rest assured that I will win in the end."

Katie didn't open her mouth, not because she feared him—which made her an even bigger fool—but because she would rant and rave which would only make her look like a child having a tantrum. The infuriating truth was that the rage boiling inside her like an overfull pot was all her doing. Her last act of free will had been swearing to honor and obey him. The moment the vicar had declared them man and wife, Katie became Dulverton's chattel, just like his houses, his bloody fossils, and every other possession. Becky had been right; Katie had made her bed and now she would have to lie in it.

Thwarted, she sat back in her chair, her hands shaking so badly she hid them on her lap.

He regarded her sternly for a long moment, as if to assure himself that she had submitted to his bullying, and then said, "I daresay you have noticed that I have what are considered *odd humors*?" Katie did not trust herself to open her mouth, so she just glared. Either he didn't really expect an answer or took her hostile look as a *yes,* because he continued. "I require structure in my life if I am to function efficiently and see to my myriad duties. Capricious actions that upset the order I have imposed on my home and surroundings are not acceptable. Do you understand what I am saying, Kathryn?"

She flinched under the weight of his opaque gaze but refused to look away. "I am not sure I do, Your Grace. You had better explain precisely what you mean so I do not run afoul of your expectations again."

Dulverton nodded without hesitation and Katie suspected he'd not noticed the heavy sarcasm in her tone. "Very well. I am talking about any disorderly behavior. Dinner is at eight. And that means *eight*. Not four minutes after eight. *Eight*. Numerous servants have worked diligently to prepare and deliver a meal precisely at that time. Common courtesy compels one to respect that and arrive—"

"Common courtesy?" Katie laughed.

"Why is that so amusing?"

"You bark at your servants as if they were medieval serfs. Of course, you barked at Chatham the same way and he is a duke, so at least you do not discriminate on the basis of social standing. In any event, getting a lecture from you about common courtesy is the height of irony."

He leaned forward in his chair, and Katie flinched back in hers. "I lack a honeyed tongue, is that what you are saying?"

"I am saying you have a tongue like a thistle bush."

He nodded slowly, the gesture oddly menacing. "Many people believe a honeyed speech *is* courtesy. Those same people—often the men and women of our class—frequently prey on those weaker than them, their servants for example. But as long as they keep a pleasant tone and smile sweetly, they are dubbed courteous."

Katie face heated at the accusatory glitter in his eyes; even an idiot would understand the point he was making. Namely, that a woman who'd bedded a family servant was in no position to talk about courtesy. Not for the first time did Katie regret that she'd begun their marriage on a lie. Especially given how that lie robbed her of the right to defend herself.

When she did not speak, he continued. "I believe actions are almost always more important than words. My servants, tenants, and others who rely on me need never be concerned that I will dishonor their daughters, nor will I sack them without cause or force them to live and labor in squalor or dangerous conditions. I offer generous compensation and a decent, healthy environment in which to work. *That*, Kathryn, is what I consider courtesy."

"I could not agree more with most of what you said, Your Grace. But I fail to see how it applies to me." She eyed him sourly. "Unless you consider me just another of your servants."

"I certainly do not."

"I am relieved to—"

"My servants fulfill their obligations without engaging in endless conflict merely for conflict's sake."

Katie's mouth snapped shut.

"As my wife and my duchess, you occupy a singular role and have unique duties. One of those is to not publicly embarrass me or yourself. It is also your duty to not undermine my authority in front of my subordinates. If you wish to dispute a matter with me, Kathryn, I ask that you do so in private."

Katie hated him in that moment. Not just for his lofty, autocratic manner, but because she *had* behaved badly in front of their servants. She'd hurled his Christian name at him—without ever having his leave to use it in the first place—in front of their housekeeper, and she'd deliberately come late to dinner. There was no doubt in her mind that her arguments and childish tantrums and rebellion were providing grist for the thriving below stairs rumor mill.

And she knew, not too deep down, that she had overstepped by accusing him of discourtesy. Yes, he was abrupt—even rude—but Dulverton was right about one thing: Jasper had been as honey-tongued as a man could be and he had been rotten to the core.

As she held Dulverton's cold gaze, she resolved to pay more attention to his actions and less to his awkward manner, no matter how much it might irk her to do so.

"I agree that arriving late for dinner is not just discourteous to you, but those who labored over it. But do you not extend latitude for events beyond one's control that might account for tardiness?"

"Are you saying that is why you were late tonight? Due to circumstances beyond your control."

Instead of lying or arguing, she said, "And that is all? I should not argue with you in front of servants or be late for meals?"

He gave her a pained look.

"I do not wish to run afoul of any *rules*, Your Grace."

"It is far more likely that you want to know what rules are in place so that you can go about breaking them."

Katie gave a startled laugh; her new husband had certainly taken her measure uncomfortably quickly.

***

A sharp but not unpleasant sensation squeezed Gerrit's chest at the sound of her throaty chuckle. Laughter was something he had little experience with, and he could not recall the last time he'd found humor in anything. He had not believed he was missing anything in his life, but an odd sense of yearning seeped through him, making him wish that he could laugh with her.

*Foolishness.*

Gerrit's new wife did not have the faux, tinkling laugh one heard so often at society events. Rather, it was a discordant squawk that made his lips twitch up at the corners.

"Are you smiling?" Kathryn asked, eyeing him with unnerving keenness.

"No."

And then she laughed again, damn it.

"I think you are."

Gerrit ignored her teasing and pondered the worrisome realization that she had intentionally flouted the dinner rule and yet he was fighting a smile. What the devil was wrong with him? Gerrit rarely found things amusing. Indeed, his lack of a sense of humor was one of the things that seemed to forever separate him from normal people.

So why was he tempted to smile?

"In future," she said, pulling him from his uncomfortable introspection, "I will always be at the dinner table at eight o'clock, unless I am physically unable."

"We eat at six o'clock when we are at Briarly."

Her smile dimmed, and Gerrit suspected his abrupt reply was responsible. What else should he have said? Damnation! This sort of awkwardness was why he despised socializing.

"Briarly is the name of your estate?" she asked, and then drained a third of her wine in one swallow. It had not escaped Gerrit's notice that she'd had four glasses of champagne at the wedding breakfast. Was his new wife a dipsomaniac?

He saw she was looking at him quizzically and recalled she had asked him a question. "Correct."

Her dark auburn eyebrows rose incrementally, as if she was waiting for him to say more. When he did not, those fascinating lips of hers twisted into a taunting smirk. "Well, you needn't bore on about it."

Gerrit frowned. Was that sarcasm?

"Where is Briarly?" she asked after a moment.

"How is it that you do not know these details already? I told all this to my man, Court, so that he could pass it along to your dresser—her name is Stone, I believe."

"Yes, Rebecca Stone."

Why was she telling him her servant's Christian name?

"And is that how you prefer to communicate?" she asked. "Through my maid and your valet?"

"What is the point in me seeking you out to share such mundane information?" he asked, genuinely confused.

"Mundane? You consider the subject of where we are going to live *mundane?* Besides," she went on, "we barely have anything to talk about as it is, so I think the last thing we should do is pass along the few opportunities we have for conversation to our servants."

She had a point. "Briarly is five miles from Lyme Regis."

"I thought your country seat was Spenwood."

"It is."

She raised her eyebrows at him yet again.

Gerrit wracked his brains; what more did she want?

She gave a huff of annoyance. "You do not return there in the summer?"

"I visit Spenwood at the start of the season."

"Shooting season?"

*What the devil else would it be?* Thankfully, Gerrit did not speak that aloud. "Correct."

"How long do you stay?"

"Six weeks." Six *long* weeks of living with his mother, during which time he spent every moment out of doors either shooting or seeing to estate matters. Gerrit did not want to think about this year's visit—and he certainly didn't want to *talk* about it—until he was forced to do so. He reached for his fork.

"Are we coming to London next Season?"

He set down his fork. "I do not come to London for the *Season,* I come for the Session and to do my duty." The sooner she realized there would be no endless rounds of vapid parties and balls, the better.

She turned her wine glass around and around and around, her gaze fixed on the patterns the foot made on the snowy damask. "But you will come for some part of the year?"

"Correct."

"*You* will come, but I will not?"

"I have not given the matter any thought." Gerrit experienced an unpleasant niggle at his not entirely truthful response. Kathryn was not only extremely beautiful, she was also wild to a fault. The last thing he wanted was to watch her ensorcel one man after another during the whirl of a London Season. Distasteful memories of Christina rose up in his head, and he felt his face settle into a scowl.

He thrust the unwanted reminders of his first marriage to the back of his mind and looked at his wife. Kathryn was not waiting for any answer from him. Instead, she was staring at her wine glass, lost in thought, which meant Gerrit could gorge unremarked on her lovely face.

Hers was a classical beauty made all the more stunningly vibrant by masses of burnished copper hair. The features on her heart-shaped face were finely drawn and delicate, from her large green eyes that tilted up at the outside corners like a cat to her perfect Cupid's bow of a mouth.

They had socialized several times since their betrothal and Gerrit had discovered—to his growing unease—that he could not look at anyone else when she was in the same room. The urge to stare was even more powerful now that they were married, and she belonged to him.

*She is mine, utterly and completely.*

Gerrit's mind was appalled by the potent throb of ownership that gripped him at the primitive thought, but his body rejoiced and thrummed with anticipation. Again and again, he tried to pry his gaze from her but could not. Christina had loathed and derided his tendency to fixate on whatever fascinated him. On one memorable occasion, she had hurled both invective and a half-eaten dish of raspberry fool at his head because she thought he had looked at her too long.

He was no longer an infatuated seventeen-year-old and had become adept at controlling his curiosity. At least he'd believed he had. But his new wife mesmerized him almost beyond bearing and the wall of detachment he had built brick by painstaking brick between himself and the rest of the world had begun to crumble where she was concerned.

The dark smudges beneath her huge green eyes did nothing to dim her loveliness. In fact, he thought they made her look even more beautiful, not to mention fragile and helpless, two things she most emphatically was not.

Now that he was no longer hostile—or at least not much—about the asinine kissing game that had forced their marriage, he marveled at what sort of mind would conceive of such a thing. He also burned with curiosity to know who else had been on that bloody list and how many of them she had kissed that night.

Christ, he was an idiot.

Gerrit pulled his uncharacteristically meandering thoughts back to her question about bringing her to London with him.

*You have to bring her with you. She is too enticing to leave alone in the country. You'll come back to find her with another man's babe in her belly.*

The thought ignited an unwanted possessive burning in his chest. It wasn't jealousy, he assured himself. It was simple practicality. He'd already had one wife who'd fucked everything in breeches. He wasn't going to let that happen again. Until she was breeding, he needed to keep her close enough to keep an eye on her.

"You will come with me to London," he abruptly announced. *Where I shall keep you on a short bloody leash.*

Her eyes glittered like the emeralds they so resembled, and the nostrils of her pert nose flared, making him worry for a moment that he'd spoken that second part aloud.

Her mulish, offended expression was not difficult to decipher. Gerrit realized that he might have couched that more diplomatically. Well, it was too late now. Besides, the sooner she knew who held the whip hand and accepted their respective positions in this marriage—Gerrit to give the orders and Kathryn to obey them— the better it would be for both of them.

"And what if I do not wish to go with you?" she asked coolly.

Irritation and an unexpected pang of distress stabbed at him. Gerrit grabbed hold of the irritation but suppressed the pain, viciously driving the pitiful emotion back into whatever crack in his consciousness it had crawled out of.

Echoing the chill in her tone he said, "If you are not breeding by the time I go to London then you will accompany me, regardless of what you *wish.*"

Her plump coral lips parted, and an angry red flush crept from the exposed swells of her breasts up her chest and throat.

Gerrit's cock, which had gone soft at her rejection awoke with a vengeance. Why was she blushing? Was she imagining him putting a child inside her? He bloody well was and had been for two long weeks.

Or was she merely furious at his high-handed behavior?

He did not care. Frankly, it was rewarding to get a reaction from her that was not jaded ennui or supercilious mockery.

"If you are enceinte when I come to London," he went on, savoring her sharp inhalation and what it did to her bodice, "then we shall revisit the matter."

Still breathing fast, she opened her mouth but then closed it.

Gerrit felt a pang of disappointment at her submission. He had eagerly anticipated one of her tart retorts or cutting set downs. Well, it had been a long day, and likely she was tired. He was bloody exhausted.

Again, he reached for his fork. This time, she didn't distract him with a question. Indeed, she didn't say another word for the remainder of the meal.

She waved away the footman's offer of dessert and abruptly stood. "I will leave you to your port, Your Grace." She strode from the dining room before he could inform her that he did not engage in the after-dinner ritual unless he was in company.

Bemused, Gerrit stared at the door she had just stormed through. While he was pleased that he was no longer furious as he'd been at the beginning of dinner nor as irritated as he'd been after she had insisted on playing ducks and drakes with the table arrangement, he could not help feeling as if something important had occurred during the meal that he had missed, entirely.

# Chapter Eleven

Katie sat mute while Becky brushed out her hair and babbled happily, a flush on her plump cheeks as she shared the servant hall gossip, too distracted by her exciting new life to notice Katie's grim, uncharacteristic silence.

Dinner had been a miserable disaster.

And the day was not over yet.

More specifically, the *night* was not over.

How could she have ever believed that she could bear being married to such a dictatorial, rigid, passionless man?

"—and you would have laughed, Katie if you'd heard how condescendingly he talked to me."

Katie snapped out of her self-absorption. "Dulverton was pompous toward you? What did he—"

"Of course it was not His Grace." Becky cut her a chiding look as her hands split Katie's hair into three sections. "I daresay the duke does not even know I exist." Her maid's tone implied she was quite happy to continue to escape Dulverton's notice.

"Then who was pompous?"

"His Grace's man, Mr. Court. I am convinced he is the most arrogant, haughty man I have ever met."

Not unlike his master. "What did he do?"

"He said there are new trunks for all your clothing."

"But mine aren't even two years old."

"I told him that. He said His Grace did not care to have unmatched trunks visible on the luggage coach."

Katie stared.

"That is *exactly* the look I gave Mr. Court," Becky said, her fingers deftly plaiting. "Not just trunks, but your valises as well," she went on, tying a green ribbon around the end of the thick braid. "When I thanked him for his suggestion and said our luggage was just fine, he gave me the most odiously snubbing look and said the sooner I learned that His Grace didn't give *suggestions* to his servants, the better it would be for me."

Katie could see the other woman wanted her to refuse the new luggage and take a stand, but the memory of her husband's behavior at dinner was exceedingly fresh in her mind. She could just imagine what would happen if her own trunks were strapped to the coach tomorrow. She was just too exhausted to argue. And really, what did it matter to her which trunks were used?

"Repack everything in the new luggage."

Her old friend's jaw sagged. "But—"

"Just do it," Katie said wearily, standing up and turning away from the mirror and facing Becky. "And if this—what was the valet's name again?"

"Court."

"If Court gives you any other suggestions when it comes to insignificant organizational matters either immediately comply or, if you absolutely find that you cannot do so, bring the issue to me and I will tell you what to do. This marriage is—" She broke off, having no earthly idea how to complete that sentence.

To her relief, Becky seemed to understand and gave Katie an uncertain smile. "I understand. I will do as you ask, Your Grace."

Katie stood still as Becky placed one of her new lace-trimmed sleeping caps on her head and tied it in a bow beneath her chin. "There," Becky said, nervously twitching the lace before meeting Katie's gaze. "You look lovely."

She squeezed Becky's hand to make sure she knew that Katie was not angry. At least not at her. "Thank you. I shan't need you again tonight."

"Of course, Your Grace." Becky's flushed cheeks told Katie that her maid's thoughts were also on Katie's night ahead and she hastened from the room.

Katie had just kicked off her slippers and was preparing to remove her dressing gown when there was a light tap on the door.

"Yes?"

The door opened and one of the housemaids peeped inside. "I beg your pardon, Your Grace. But His Grace wished you to know he was in library."

"Er, thank you—what is your name?"

"I'm Polly, Your Grace."

"Thank you, Polly."

The girl curtsied and closed the door.

What was that all about? Had she broken one of his many rules by coming to bed? What would they do in the library if she went? Bicker, most likely. Or Dulverton would hurl orders and Katie would be expected to jump to obey them.

No thank you. She'd had enough of that already.

Katie changed her mind about getting into bed and pulled her dressing gown tightly around her and slumped into a chair, closing her eyes.

The door to the room in her mind where she'd long ago locked up memories of her month with Jasper suddenly sprang open and the past came pouring out. She had been so vigilant at blocking him from her thoughts, but her defenses had been worn down, not just by the day's events, but by her pointless, rudderless life these last five years.

The last memory to escape its cell was the worst of the lot. Like a leviathan it had lurked in the murky recesses of her mind, biding its time, and waiting to strike.

"Oh, God," she whispered, squeezing her eyes shut until she saw stars. No. She could not—would not—remember that day. Not tonight of all nights. Instead, her thoughts moved to the first time they'd been together. Well, it had been *her* first time, not Jasper's of course. The act itself had hurt, but Jasper had held her and kissed her and promised her the next time he would show her how pleasurable it could be.

And there had been a next time. And it had been better. Although in truth she had not really understood what all the fuss was about. But Katie had loved the too brief time afterward far more than the hurried, sweaty couplings. Jasper held her and soothed her and together they'd made plans for their future. He promised they would marry as soon as he spoke to Katie's father. Jasper was older than her by twelve years and had already traveled the great cities of Europe, but he told her they would take a bridal journey to the Continent.

"I cannot wait to see all those cities and wonderful sights through your eyes, my darling," he had told her more than once.

The last time they'd lain together, he'd told her that his grandmother, the Countess of Grimsby had summoned him. Lady Grimsby had long intimated that she would leave the bulk of her vast personal estate to Jasper when she died, and he was eager to keep her good opinion. He promised Katie he would be gone no longer than a week—ten days at most.

"I would have needed to tell her about you before we could marry. She is a very old lady and extremely sensitive to perceived snubs so this could not come at a better time. When I return, I will tell my father of our betrothal and he will host a celebration ball."

Katie had been so overjoyed it had been difficult to keep the news to herself while she'd waited. Over and over, she'd considered telling her Aunt Agnes, but she had kept her secret to herself.

Which turned out to be a very good decision.

A week crept past, and then another. Katie did not become concerned until three weeks had gone by. She'd known something was dreadfully wrong by the time six weeks passed. She'd spent night after night wondering if she should approach Jasper's father and ask if his son had been injured or called away somewhere else. But the Marquess of Lindhurst was an intimidating, distant man and she'd not been able to work up the nerve.

By the time two months had gone by Katie knew that Jasper had abandoned her. By then she'd made another, even more terrifying discovery and had fallen into a melancholic abyss.

And then—at ten weeks and one day—a coach with Lady Grimsby's escutcheon arrived at the Marquess of Lindhurst's house.

Jasper had returned.

Katie had been jubilant and humbled. How could she have ever doubted him? He was here and everything was not lost, after all.

But less than an hour after his homecoming the news had swept the village: Lord Jasper had brought his new wife home with him.

The sound of the connecting door opening jarred Katie from her reverie. She blinked up at Dulverton, her mind still mired in the past. He was dressed in his evening clothes, his cold eyes and austere features all the more jarring when contrasted with her memory of Jasper's handsome, laughing face.

"I waited for you in the library," he said.

Katie got to her feet and pulled her dressing gown closed. "By the time you sent the servant I'd already changed for bed. I did not realize you expected me." She paused but then could not resist adding, "I only received orders for dinner, not the rest of the evening."

His lips tightened. "You prefer to retire early?" he asked, evidently deciding to ignore her provocative comment.

"I do not prefer it. I just did not know what else to do."

"What do you usually do after dinner?"

"The same thing everyone else does."

"Enlighten me."

"I go to a ball or the theater or some other function."

"What do you do when you are in the country?"

"Accompany my sister-and-brother-in-law when they go to various functions. Or they often entertain at Chatham Park." She didn't tell him that she often took over the hostess duties for Hy.

"Do you do anything other than attend balls, parties, the theater, or other entertainments?" His tone was even but there was a faintly supercilious twist to his lips.

"Of course I do other things," she snapped.

"Such as?"

"I read." Foolishly, she pointed to the novel on her nightstand. She had been attempting to read *Waverly* for weeks but only managed a page or two most nights before she snuffed the candle and proceeded to stare into the darkness.

"You read," he repeated flatly. "Is that all?"

Katie's mind stubbornly remained blank, which, illogically, just made her angrier at Dulverton. "I am useless. Is that what you were attempting to ascertain, Your Grace?"

He opened his mouth.

"I am a creature of frivolity, and my head is full of fluff and—" Katie broke off with a yelp when he closed the distance between them in four long strides. She took a step back, forgetting the chair, and stumbled. He caught her, just as he had that night in the garden, and held her upper arms. Rather than release her, he loomed over her, and Katie had to crane her neck to see him.

The muscles of his face worked beneath his darkly tanned skin, his wintry eyes slid to her mouth, and the nostrils of his prominent, high-bridged nose flared. Heat blasted off his body like a blacksmith's forge. For a moment Katie thought he was going to kiss her. Instead, he firmly put her at arm's length, and she could not decide whether she was relieved or disappointed.

"I do not care for balls, the theater, dinner parties, and the like," he said.

Katie snorted. "Really? You shock me."

He ignored her sniping and said, "You will have to find other ways to occupy your time in the country." He cast a dismissive glance at the copy of *Waverly* on her bedside table. "As you are such a great reader you will need to tell my secretary what books you want, and he will purchase them for you."

"Thank you for your kind offer," she said acidly. "But I can purchase my own books."

"He will also see that the tomes are appropriately bound before they are delivered," he went on, as if she hadn't spoken.

"Appropriately bound?" she laughed rudely. "Too bad you can't do the same thing to me so that I fit in."

"Who says I can't?" His eyes glittered darkly.

Katie felt a stirring of alarm and something else, too. Something she had no word for. Something that left her hot and confused. "I b-beg your pardon?" she asked uncertainly.

He merely stared, the hard curve of his mouth not just stern, but… wicked?

No, that could not be.

Could it?

She shook herself, furious at feeling so wrong-footed. "You needn't worry about me polluting your library. I will purchase my own books and keep them—"

"Must you dispute every order I give you?"

"Must you give orders every time you speak to me?"

His lips parted but then he closed his mouth. It was the first sign of uncertainty she had ever seen him exhibit. A nerve jumped in his temple as he stared down at her. "You are tired," he finally said. "I will leave you to your rest. Goodnight." He turned to go, and Katie's hand—as if it had suddenly grown a mind of its own—shot out and closed around an arm that was as hard as a tree trunk.

Dulverton stiffened and glared down at her fingers.

Katie jerked her hand back, scalded by his disdain. As much as she would have liked to chuck him out her bedroom window, she did *not* want their wedding night hanging over her head for yet another day. "Are—are—will you come to me later?" she asked, loathing her breathy voice.

"No. You have had a long day, and we are leaving very early in the morning."

"I would rather not wait." Katie could not believe the words coming out of her mouth.

Either could Dulverton, who looked visibly startled.

"What?" she demanded, goaded by the look of *whatever* she saw on his face. "I want to get this over with." Katie bit her tongue, wishing she had phrased that more diplomatically. "I just meant—"

"I see," he said icily. Some emotion—Katie did not know what—flickered in his gaze, reminding her that he was not, after all, made of stone.

"I'm sorry, Your Grace. I did not mean that the way—"

"Get on the bed."

Katie flinched at his curt command.

"Do you wish me to stay?" he asked sharply, his face hard and unyielding. "Or shall I leave?"

"No, stay," she blurted, for once entranced rather than irked by his autocratic behavior.

"Then get on the bed," he snapped, his eyes stormy. "The sooner you do; the sooner we can *get this over with.*"

# Chapter Twelve

Dulverton held her gaze until Katie backed toward the bed and stumbled up the three steps to the high mattress, perching on the edge to watch.

He turned away from the bed and strode to one of the two identical chairs that faced the fireplace and sat, his huge body dwarfing the delicate piece of furniture.

Moving with graceful economy he pulled off one Hessian and then the next, setting his boots neatly beside the leg of the chair before standing and unbuttoning his coat and tugging off his cravat. Once he'd neatly folded both garments and set them on the chair, he pivoted toward the bed and caught her staring. "Lie down."

Katie clumsily swung her feet onto the mattress and stretched out on her back, twitching her nightgown so that she was modestly covered.

Still clothed in stockings, pantaloons, shirt, and waistcoat, Dulverton climbed onto the bed, kneeling high as he stared down at her. "Lift your skirts." His eyes sent a chill shivering through her.

Katie jolted at his abrupt command and glanced at the candles on the bedside table. "Aren't you going to snuff—"

"No. Lift your nightgown," he repeated.

She slowly raised the hem up to her knees.

He closed his hands over her ankles and opened her legs.

"What are you doing?" She pulled her thighs back together—or trying to—but his hands were like hot, unyielding shackles.

Dulverton frowned. "How is it that you do not know what I am doing? You said you fornicated with your aunt's footman."

Katie gritted her teeth at the word *fornicated*. "I know about—about *coitus*. I just do not understand how you are going about it." Face flaming, Katie cut a pointed look at the front of his pantaloons, where the stretchy weave of the fabric did nothing to hide the long, thick ridge of his arousal. "You are still clothed, Your Grace."

His eyelids drooped and one corner of his stern mouth twitched. On anyone else, Katie would not have noticed such a slight change of expression, but on Dulverton it was the equivalent of a face-splitting grin.

"Do you find something funny, Your Grace?"

"No."

Katie saw nothing to indicate amusement in his opaque gaze; she must have been mistaken. Of course she had. The Duke of Dulverton didn't know how to smile. Certainly not when—

"I am going to spread your legs" His voice was quieter, almost gentle, and nothing like his normally cool, clipped tone. Katie looked down the length of her body to where his warm, strong fingers stroked the thin skin of her ankles. There was something about the ropy blue veins on the back of his hands that made her pulse pound.

She knew he was waiting for some response from her, so she nodded.

Dulverton moved her feet until they were shoulder-width apart and this time Katie did not struggle against him. Her heart *thud thud thudded* like a blacksmith's hammer against her ribs as he caressed up her calves, the slightly roughened pads of his fingers leaving goose pimples in their wake.

"Lift your gown higher."

The air was suddenly thinner, and even breathing through her mouth Katie could not fill her lungs. This was not what she remembered with Jasper. He had never looked at her the way Dulverton was looking at her—as if he wanted to consume her—nor had he—

"Kathryn."

The sound of her name pulled her from her daze, and she reached with shaky fingers for the fine muslin and lifted it higher. His pupils flared to life and an expression of such hungry anticipation settled on his harsh features that Katie could not bring herself to care how exposed she was.

He made a low rumbling sound of approval. "You are perfect." His praise played havoc with her already thundering heart and made the muscles in her sex clench and send shivers of pleasure through her body.

Dulverton lowered to his elbows, his face close enough to her mound that she felt his hot breath on her skin.

"Wh-what are you doing?" she asked shrilly.

"I am readying you."

Katie made a mortifying squeaking sound when he gently parted her netherlips, his eyelids lowering as he studied her.

"You are so wet," he marveled, briefly looking at her face before lowering his blazing gaze.

She opened her mouth to say something—because… shouldn't she? Shouldn't she tell him to stop messing about down there?

# Kathryn

Katie was still working up her nerve when he suddenly lowered his head and closed his lips around the source of her pleasure.

"Oh, Dulverton," Katie mumbled in a croaky voice as her suddenly boneless elbows slid out from under her, and her eyes rolled back in her head.

***

Gerrit heard his name and then nothing except a great deal of moaning and gasping.

As shocked as Kathryn had first appeared, she had not told him to stop. His cock throbbed with possessive pleasure at the knowledge that Kathryn's footman lover had not done this one thing for her. At least in this way, Gerrit would be her first.

Encouraged by the noises she was making, he slid his arms around her silky thighs and spread her wider, settling more comfortably so he could relax and enjoy himself. Her needy whimpers quickly turned to earthy groans and her hips bucked as she chased his tongue. Gerrit was tempted to give her what she needed, but sex was one of the few times he engaged in physical contact with another person, and he was in no hurry to end the rare pleasure.

The sight of his proud, combative wife turning into his writhing, begging bed-slave made his own aching need an exquisite agony. But Gerrit could wait. Waiting would only make his release that much sweeter.

Feeling her muscles tense and tighten, Gerrit paused his tonguing, smirking at her frustrated exclamation. The view up her soft, curvaceous body was sensational, and his mouth watered at the sight of her erect nipples thrusting against the thin fabric of her nightgown.

*I should have stripped her bare.*

Indeed, he should have. But this was only their first night together, so there was no rush. She was his now and he could explore her body as often and as thoroughly as he pleased.

*She is only yours until she provides you with an heir…*

Gerrit shoved away the unwanted thought and resumed teasing her greedy little bud, working her until she thrashed in his arms, but never giving her quite enough to push her over the edge. When she tried to grab his hair, the tips of her slender fingers scrabbled on his shorn locks before she was able to get a good grip and drag his mouth to precisely where she wanted him.

Amused, Gerrit decided to torment her a little more and slid a finger inside her.

She groaned, her body clenching at the invasion.

As he proceeded to tease her with both his tongue and hand Gerrit could not recall when he had last enjoyed himself so much.

He was in no hurry to put an end to his pleasure.

***

Katie could not think straight. Every time she clawed her way to the edge of bliss and teetered on the edge Dulverton would simply wander off, dropping her back down to earth.

*"Please!"* she all but wept.

Rather than show mercy, his lips and tongue disappeared altogether. "Relax for me, Kathryn." Hearing his voice sent a shock through her. She had not forgotten who she was with, of course, but it was still staggering that the passionate lover between her thighs was the same disagreeable man from dinner.

A large hot palm caressed one of her thighs while a second finger eased in beside the first.

Katie stiffened at the uncomfortable stretch.

*"Shhhh,"* he soothed. "So tight," he said, his warmly approving tone causing an involuntary clenching in her sex. Katie desperately hoped that Dulverton didn't notice her body's mortifying reaction to even the tiniest bit of praise.

"Ah, you like that," he said.

*So much for hoping.*

"I like that, too," he said, stroking her faster and deeper. His lust-black eyes pinned her, and the corner of his mouth kicked up the tiniest amount before he said, "You are a such a good girl, Kathryn."

To her shame an even more powerful bolt of arousal coursed through her body.

"Very nice," he muttered smugly, and then his soft, hot lips closed around her bud.

Katie's eyes fluttered shut as sensation seized her. If Dulverton stopped again and left her hanging, then Katie would—

She cried out, her thoughts swept away when his thrusting fingers stroked something exquisitely sensitive inside her, sending her hurtling over the edge. Waves of bliss rolled through her in brutal spasms until she was wrung out and limp. Everything was pleasantly fuzzy and her limbs were far too heavy to move. She felt drunk, but much happier than the handful of times she had over-imbibed while playing stupid parlor games at the house parties that used to fill up her summers.

Katie drifted back to herself; she knew she should at least push her nightgown back down and stop lolling about, but she couldn't make herself care.

*You will be deeply humiliated when you recall how you eagerly you moaned and begged and shoved Dulverton's head between your spread thighs.*

For once, Katie easily ignored the voice. Instead of worrying about later, she relished the moment. She especially relished her new husband's earthy, enthusiastic lovemaking. If *readying her* meant rendering her boneless then he had exceeded his goal.

*What about the pitiful, wanton way you responded to his praise? Are you really so desperate? So needy? So easily won?*

The niggling voice found a toehold and a tendril of unease snaked through her post-climax haze. Was she really so needy for approval? Could she truly be—

"Are you still awake?" a deep voice rumbled.

Her eyes opened a crack. Dulverton had risen up high on his knees and was staring down at her. Perhaps she *was* asleep, although even in her dreams she would never have believed he could look so passionate and almost feral. His lips were slick and red, and his eyes were predatory, sensual slits as he unhooked his fall, yanked open the buttons, and then shoved his snug pantaloons down his thighs.

Katie's breath caught when he exposed his thick, ruddy shaft and wrapped a huge hand around it. He unashamedly stroked himself, his broad palm slicking the fat red crown, squeezing clear drops from the slit with sensual deliberation.

It was a more riveting show than any she'd ever seen at Drury Lane.

When he gleamed with wetness, he lowered his torso over hers until they were almost nose to nose.

"Look at me," he said when she closed her eyes against his blazing intensity.

Only when she submitted to his searching gaze did he position himself at her entrance and push inside her.

Even with all the *readying* he'd engaged in, Katie's eyes watered as he slid into her inch by inch. She had either forgotten how uncomfortable this part could be or Dulverton was a great deal larger than Jasper. Either way, she was certain she could not bear even a fraction of an inch more when he bumped something inside her and caused a bone-deep ache of pleasure edged with pain.

Dulverton's eyelids fluttered as he kept her full, waiting for her body to accommodate him.

She felt unaccountably shy staring into his eyes but could not look away. How odd it was to be so intimate with a stranger.

He raised up on his arms and looked between their bodies as he slowly pulled almost all the way out and then plunged back in to the hilt. Again and again, he entered her with deep, powerful thrusts and then languidly withdrew, watching what he did for several moments before lifting his eyes to hers. "You look beautiful taking me, Kathryn."

Inevitably, her inner muscles spasmed, earning a low animal growl of approval.

"So good," he hissed, an undeniably smug expression spreading across his austere face as he braced himself on one forearm and reached between their bodies to stroke her.

This time, he did not make Katie beg or wait, and all too soon her climax overtook her.

Dulverton thrusted a half-dozen times before pinning her to the mattress with his hips, his powerful body spasming with the force of his release until his shoulders finally sagged, and he went still.

Katie knew the moment awareness overtook him and for the second time that night her body acted with a will all its own and her legs wrapped around his hips when he began to withdraw, her heels digging into his impossibly hard buttocks to keep him exactly where he was.

For a moment she thought he might give in to her urging, but then he pushed up on his arms leaving her with the choice of clinging like a monkey or releasing him. She missed the heat and comforting weight of his big body immediately. The warm contentment she'd been feeling only moments before drained away as he left the bed without meeting her gaze.

With his back to the bed, he slipped on his coat, draped his neckcloth over his shoulder, and picked up his boots. Before Katie realized what he was doing he'd snuffed the candles and threw the room into blackness.

"I have changed our traveling plans." His disembodied voice came from beside the bed. "We will make the journey in two days, rather than one."

Had he changed his plans because of what she had said at dinner?

Before she could think of a response the connecting door opened and a shaft of light slanted across her husband's torso, leaving his face in shadow. "Good night, Kathryn."

"Good night… *heh-Reet,*" she said, her mind reeling at the suddenness of it all.

He paused a moment, and Katie—who fully expected him to correct her pronunciation—felt strangely deflated when he merely stepped into the other room and silently shut the door behind him.

She stared up at the darkness above her bed, erotic images from the past hour running through her mind's eye. Dulverton's passionate, competent lovemaking was unlike anything she had ever imagined. How could such a cold man be so hot in the bedchamber?

Her warm recollections froze when she came to his abrupt departure. He should have stayed with her and held her and—and—

*And what? Engaged in the sort of post-coital banter you enjoyed with Jasper?*

She squeezed her eyes shut at the return of her disparaging inner voice and tried to picture Dulverton laughing and lounging beside her, but her imagination failed her. Katie wanted to be angry at him for leaving the way he had, but really, what did she expect? They hardly knew each other. It might sting that he'd wanted to flee so quickly, but it was likely for the best given their brief, argumentative history.

Rather than feel abandoned, she should be grateful that the night hadn't been a complete disaster. Quite the opposite, in fact. For two long weeks she had made every effort to avoid wondering what sort of lover Dulverton would be. But not so deep down she had envisioned a cold, indifferent man who mounted her in darkness and stayed only long enough to spill his seed.

He *had* run off almost immediately after his climax, but not until he'd seen to her pleasure.

Twice.

Thanks to her five Seasons in London, Katie knew plenty about what went on in *ton* bedrooms as opposed to what went on between aristocratic men and their mistresses. There were a great many marriages like her mother and father's— although few others were so acrimonious—and numerous women gratefully looked away when their husbands went elsewhere to feed their carnal appetites.

For years Katie had known that only a man desperate for money or family connections—or somebody trapped, like Dulverton—would marry a woman who was no longer a maiden. It was acceptable for *ton* women to take lovers after marriage, but a woman who went to her marital bed anything other than a virgin was considered a whore.

Was that how Dulverton thought of her—a whore? Is that why he had just treated her the way he had tonight?

Uncertainty rose within her, threatening to overwhelm the pleasurable afterglow from their coupling.

On the heels of that uncertainty was hot anger—at herself—for caring what Dulverton, or anyone else, thought about her. He had known she was not a virgin before he'd made his offer; there was no point in flogging herself all over again.

Katie rolled onto her side and winced at the soreness in her hips, her face heating in the darkness as she recalled her body's worrisome reaction to Dulverton's vulgar commands and encouraging words. Why would it arouse her to be called his *good girl?* She was a woman, after all, not a child. She yawned and decided that she did not want to examine the matter too closely. She could worry about that later. Much later.

Instead, she would be grateful that Dulverton was a skilled, considerate lover and bedding him would certainly be no chore. It was more than she had ever dared to hope.

*And it is certainly more than you deserve.*

Yes, it was. If Katie were to get what she deserved... Well, that would be grim, indeed.

# Chapter Thirteen

ulverton's cortege left the following morning at first light.

Katie had traveled with Hy and Chatham times beyond counting and was accustomed to ducal pomp, but she'd never experienced anything as grand as this journey.

"Four lovely black coaches all with four identical black horses," Becky murmured, all but bouncing on her seat in excitement, her cornflower-blue eyes glued to the window as they rolled away from Dulverton House. "*Four*," she repeated before turning to Katie. "And Mrs. Kent said that two more coaches loaded with trunks already went to Briarly last week. Have you ever seen the like?"

"Four. Amazing." Katie yawned and rubbed her eyelids and then winced; it felt as if somebody had sprinkled sand beneath them. Although it had scarcely been eleven o'clock when Dulverton left her chambers, she had tossed and turned until well after two. When Becky had roused her at six o'clock that morning, Katie felt as if she'd only just closed her eyes.

"Here, Your Grace." Becky held out a small flask wrapped in a knitted cozy.

"What is it?" Katie reached for it.

"Hot chocolate. I thought you might want it as you did not break your fast." The words were chiding. Katie had begged another half hour of sleep in lieu of eating.

"You think of everything, Becks." Katie wrapped both hands around the warm wool and lifted it to her mouth, drinking greedily. "Ah," she sighed after several mouthfuls of satiny hot chocolate had slid down her throat. "Thank you, thank you, thank you."

Becky clucked her tongue.

Katie gave a tired chuckle. "I am sorry. I meant to say *thank you, Stone*."

Becky rewarded her with a prim smile and then turned to watch as London slid away. "I am glad to escape this nasty heat."

Katie gave a noncommittal grunt and took another greedy gulp of chocolate.

"Jeremy says the master usually stays at Briarly all the way up to shooting season, which is when he goes to Spenwood."

"Who is Jeremy?"

Becky pointed to one of the red-headed servants in livery riding beside the coach. "He is the one of the gingers—the handsomer one."

"Aren't they identical twins?"

"Yes."

"Then one cannot be *more* handsome than the other, Becks, er, Stone," she corrected at Becky's scowl.

Katie enjoyed the last of the chocolate in peaceful silence before screwing on the cap and handing it back to Becky, who tucked it into a large hamper beside her feet.

Katie yawned, shifted her bottom on the plush leather until she was more comfortable and briefly considered removing her ankle boots. After a moment, she dismissed the notion. Her oh-so-proper maid would object if she sat in an un-duchess-like manner and Katie was too tired to argue right now. "What is the other twin's name?" she asked.

"Jacob."

"How… alliterative."

"Don't be clever with me," Becky snapped, briefly forgetting Katie's elevated status.

"Alliterative just means that both names start with J's. Remember that rhyme we learned when we were little? *Peter Piper picked a peck of pickled peppers?*"

Becky grunted but looked appeased.

Although they'd been playmates as children—indeed all the Bellamy offspring had socialized with the children from the village—Becky had left school and gone into service when she turned ten. The months that followed Becky's departure had been the loneliest in Katie's life up until then. Not only had she lost Becky, but her other friends from the village—Dora, Meg, and Sharon—also left school to begin working.

Their lives had diverged, and Katie had seen them infrequently in the years that followed. She'd often envied Becky and wished that she, too, could go into service. Not because she had a burning desire to do backbreaking labor from dawn to dusk, but because it would have gotten her away from her mother.

Even though Katie had been the youngest—and therefore least important—of five daughters the countess's expectations had still been onerous. Her brother Dauntry and their oldest sister Aurelia had drawn the majority of their mother's oppressive attention, but the countess had not spared the rest of them the sharp lash of her tongue.

Thankfully, the countess had been banished to Bath five years earlier after misbehaving at the annual family Christmas house party. But that hadn't stopped her from writing letters, one every two weeks for the past five years and weekly letters since the night of Katie's ill-conceived kissing contest.

For a change, Katie had been amused as the countess had swung between disgust and delight—disgust at Katie's reprehensible behavior, but delight that she'd landed such a matrimonial prize—in letters that often ran to four pages.

A significant portion of the last two letters had been unsubtle hints that Katie needed her mother's guidance in the early months of her marriage.

Katie had laughed out loud at the thought of inviting the countess to live with her. As if she didn't have enough problems!

Speaking of problems, Dulverton—mounted on a magnificent black horse that looked exactly like all his other black horses—trotted up beside Jeremy and the two men exchanged a few words before the servant nodded and urged his mount into a gallop that took him out of sight.

Dulverton had an excellent seat, his big body more suited to the black riding breeches and black clawhammer than it was to evening clothes. He looked even more massive and implacable than usual. He and the massive black horse moved as one, making it easy to imagine him with furs draped across his bare chest and his pale hair long, rather than cropped, and streaming behind him like a Viking marauder.

Her gaze lingered on his magnificently thewed thigh flexing beneath the tight leather of his breeches. How was it that he looked even bigger today than he had felt lying on top of her last night?

Dulverton turned toward the coach and caught her ogling, his pupils pinpricks and his irises shockingly pale in the bright light of day.

Katie wanted to look away, but that would be letting him win, wouldn't it? Instead, she stared right back at him, her pulse pounding harder the longer he held her pinioned by his impassive gaze. An image of him from last night, when he had looked anything *but* emotionless, flickered through her mind's eye.

He turned away abruptly, and she exhaled shakily, as if a boulder had suddenly been lifted off her chest.

Katie had experienced attraction before, of course, but this raw, enthralling lust was unlike anything she had ever felt. She had certainly not been seized with crippling desire for Jasper. She had enjoyed flirting with him at parties and assemblies and dancing with him far more than she had ever liked the physical aspect of their relationship.

The sorry truth was that Katie had only capitulated to Jasper's incessant pressure for physical intimacy because she had sensed his attention slipping the longer she denied him her body.

In hindsight it was obvious that all he'd ever wanted was to bed her. But Katie had been a sheltered seventeen-year-old country girl who'd been so lonely for her brother and sisters, and so desperate for affection of any sort, that Jasper had barely needed to exert himself to get her on her back.

The hatred she'd borne Jasper for so many years no longer burned like a bonfire but still roiled beneath the surface like molten rock. Katie looked forward to the day when it would cool completely, and she would be able to think of him with as much emotion as she did any other stranger.

In any event, her affair with Jasper had not prepared her in the least for whatever she now felt for Dulverton. The duke was an entirely different animal than her glib, selfish erstwhile lover. Based on his behavior in her bed last night, Dulverton desired her. And yet today he was no different than he'd been since that fateful night in the Earl of Sutton's garden. Clearly he had no interest in her outside of the bedchamber. That should not be any surprise given the offer he'd made her; all he wanted was an heir.

Katie needed to throttle any emotional attachment that threatened to develop after last night. Dulverton liked sex, even with the woman who had trapped him into marriage. That is all there was to it and only a self-deluding fool would hope for more.

"I brought this for you, Your Grace." Becky held out a familiar tapestry bag.

Katie frowned. "I don't want that."

"Needlework will give you a way to pass the time. You can hardly stare out the window for eleven hours."

*Oh, yes, I can. I do it all the time.*

"I brought a book," Katie said, giving the bag a look of loathing. Needlework had been the only way in which she had ever pleased her mother and just looking at a tambour or embroidery silks made her feel ugly, useless, and lower than a worm.

*"I suppose I should be grateful that you possess at least* one *accomplishment,"* the countess had often said, her cold, critical gaze burning twin holes into Katie, as if she could see every lazy or wicked thought she'd ever had.

Katie still did needlework when she was forced to—for example when one of her sisters asked her for something—but she took no joy from it anymore.

Becky sighed and lowered the bag. "You do the loveliest work I have ever seen, Kat. I have never met anyone who can bring flowers and birds to life the way you can. I don't understand why you suddenly took it in such dislike."

Katie didn't even try to explain. Mrs. Stone, Becky's mother, was a loving, kind woman. Even though she had been forced by financial exigency to send Becky out to work at such a young age, she had never withheld love to bend her daughter to her will.

She turned away from Becky's importuning look and stared out the window, her brooding gaze again and again returning to her husband's distant, unreadable profile.

***

By the end of the first day of traveling—which was three hours longer than the six hours Gerrit had allotted due to heavy rain—he was relieved that he had decided to break the journey into two days.

Even though he made frequent stops to allow Kathryn to stretch her legs and take sustenance, she looked exhausted by the time they reached the inn he favored.

"Take your mistress up to her chambers and I will send a meal to her private parlor," he'd instructed Kathryn's maid the moment he'd seen the dark smudges beneath his wife's eyes.

It was a sign of how tired she was that Kathryn meekly obeyed.

Gerrit ate his own meal in the public room and spent the night in his own room half-hard for her. But even an insensitive oaf like him knew she needed her rest far more than he needed a rut.

The following morning, he delayed their departure by an hour to allow her more sleep—an impromptu change to the schedule that made him itch as if he were covered with lice—but she still looked fatigued when they set out. And by the time they reached Briarly, just after dusk, Gerrit could see that she could scarcely keep her eyes open. Even though the trip had taken twice as long, he knew that he had still pushed her too hard and should have taken three days.

Guilt and relief vied inside him the closer they got to Briarly. Surely it had been better to spend fewer days traveling? Lord. He'd never given so much thought to a simple bloody carriage ride.

The sound of hooves approaching pulled him from his thoughts. It was Jeremy, whom he'd sent ahead an hour ago to alert the servants that their master and mistress were on the way.

He was surprised the man had ridden back to meet them. As Jeremy came closer, Gerrit felt a stirring of alarm at the grim expression on his normally gregarious servant's face. "Is aught amiss?"

"The Dowager Duchess is at Briarly."

"My *mother* is here?" What a stupid question. What other dowager duchess would the man be talking about?

"Yes, Your Grace."

Blast and damnation! What on earth was she up to? She had never come to Briarly before—at least not in his lifetime and only once when the old duke had been alive. Briarly had always been his father's sanctuary, the only place he could be sure to avoid his wife's distracting presence. Indeed, Gerrit had not seen his parents in the same room—or in the same house or even in the same part of the country—since he was nine years old.

Why was she here *now*, for God's sake?

He was seized by an irrational urge to wheel his horse around and ride hell-bent for leather back to London.

The uncharacteristically reckless thought sobered him. He was behaving like a child. If the dowager was here, he would simply need to send her back home. Immediately.

Gerrit's thoughts had just begun to settle when the brightly lit entrance to Briarly came into view. There, standing on the flagstone in front of the house, torches blazing behind her, was the woman who'd so disordered his mind.

"Your Grace?" Jeremy said, his face wreathed in confusion.

Gerrit only then realized that he'd stopped Centurion a good thirty feet away from the entrance to Briarly. From his mother.

Feeling leaden, he urged his mount into a trot and reached the coach just as Jacob handed Kathryn out of the carriage.

He dismounted and was on the verge of offering his wife his arm when his mother hurried toward them, hands flapping and her typically gauzy, untidy garment fluttering around her as she reached not for Gerrit—she knew better—but his wife.

"Welcome! Welcome!" she chirped. "Oh, look at you!" His mother rarely spoke if she could exclaim. She reached for his wife's face, cupping it in her small pale hands. Gerrit flinched in sympathy although Kathryn looked more surprised than alarmed. "You are so lovely!" the dowager twittered in the breathless voice that irritated Gerrit almost beyond bearing. And then she gave one of her brainless, tinkling laughs and stood on her toes. "I am too short to reach your cheek, my dear. You will have to meet me halfway."

Kathryn smiled. "Of course, Your Grace."

"Oh, I do hope you will call me Mama!" his mother insisted, kissing both Kathryn's cheeks. "If you do not wish to call me that, then please, please, please call me Betje!"

"Thank you, Betje. Please call me Katie."

His mother looked delighted. "We are going to be the best of friends, aren't we, Katie?"

Inexplicably, Kathryn laughed, the sound genuine. "Yes, I believe we are."

The dowager clapped her hands in delight.

Gerrit could not help noticing how soothing his wife's low-pitched voice and throaty chuckle was in comparison to his mother's high-pitched twittering and giggling.

He tamped down his irritation and closed the distance between them, holding out his hand before his mother could fling her small body into his arms.

The dowager turned away from Kathryn with obvious reluctance, her smile becoming guarded when she met Gerrit's gaze. She held out a hand with a tentativeness that both irked and pained him. As always, his mother elicited a flood of confusing, unwanted emotions in his breast simply by existing.

Gerrit bowed over her small, cold hand and released her with more haste than courtesy. "What a surprise to see you here, Your Grace."

She flinched at his chilly greeting, her foolish smile faltering. "I wanted to welcome my new daughter into our family." She paused, her smile turning a bit sour, the expression accentuating the lines that bracketed her mouth and making her look her age. "As I received no invitation to the wedding."

Gerrit had no intention of discussing his decision not to invite her, certainly not in front of Kathryn and all his servants.

"But I am delighted to be here now," she hastily added, reading his thoughts clearly enough. She held out her hand to Kathryn. "Come, come. It is too late to meet all the servants tonight. I will show you to your chambers. I'm sure you would adore a tray in your room after you've had a chance to wash the dust off, wouldn't you? Don't you just abhor traveling? I have always—"

Her voice faded away as she disappeared into the house, towing Kathryn behind her.

A throat cleared behind him, and Gerrit turned to find Cranston, his butler, waiting for him. "Er, welcome home, Your Grace."

"Tell me the worst of it, Cranston," he ordered, and then felt a pang of remorse when the old man jolted.

"As you instructed in your letter, I had the Rose suite prepared. But when Her Grace arrived, she instructed me to have the master and mistress chambers stripped, aired, and new hangings and carpets installed."

Gerrit gritted his teeth to keep from howling. After all, it was hardly his butler's job to argue with his mother. "How long has she been here?"

"Ten days, Your Grace."

She must have come directly from Spenwood after he'd sent a messenger informing her of his impending marriage. Gerrit could almost imagine the struggle that would have gone on in her flighty head as she'd considered disobeying him and traveling to London to attend the wedding. He tried to be grateful he had, at least, been spared that unpleasant drama.

"I wanted to write to you, Your Grace," Cranston said in a shaky voice. "But Her Grace commanded me to keep her arrival a secret. Er, she wanted it to be a surprise."

Gerrit met Cranston's watery blue eyes, and the older man winced.

"None of this is your fault. I know you could hardly disobey a direct order."

Cranston's erect shoulders sagged with relief. "Thank you, Your Grace."

"You said she wanted the master and mistress chambers prepared. What did she do with all my father's things?"

"I had it all carefully packed and moved to the Yellow Suite." He paused and added, "I suggested to Her Grace you would not wish to have your possessions transferred to the master suite, but she was most adamant and—"

"She overrode you," he finished for the other man, pleased when his anger at his mother did not bleed into his voice.

"Just so, Your Grace," the older man murmured. "I—I attempted to dissuade Her Grace from moving your things, but—"

"I can imagine," Gerrit interrupted, not wanting to hear the gory details of what his mother had managed to effect in ten entire days. His feet felt rooted to the gravel drive, and he could not make them move—at least not in the direction of the house and whatever horror awaited him there.

"Go inside," he told the older man. "I will be in shortly."

Cranston hesitated, his face a mask of remorse that even Gerrit could read.

"You have done nothing wrong, Cranston."

The older man did not look convinced but inclined his head. "Will you have your usual tea in the library?"

"Yes, in the library in an hour—" He broke off. "Unless she—"

"Her Grace did not touch the library," Cranston hastily assured him.

Well, that was something, at least. Gerrit told himself to be grateful for small favors and then turned in the direction of the dower house that was just on the other side of the small, ancient cluster of trees known locally as *Echo Forest*. It was late, but Amelia would have heard he was arriving today and would still be awake. He mounted Centurion and urged the big horse into a gallop, directing him toward the tight cluster of trees across the park.

There was nothing like a conversation with Amelia St. Clare to soothe his ragged nerves.

***

"—the prettiest color! And what clever embroidery this is all along the hem. I haven't seen work of this quality since I was a very young girl. Did you do this?" the dowager asked a stupefied Becky.

Becky blinked. "Er, no, Your Grace, that gown is from——"

"Oh, and this is *lovely*! I just adore green but cannot wear it without looking like a corpse." The dowager thrust aside the gown in question and continued rooting through Katie's garments.

Katie met Becky's stunned gaze as Betje enthusiastically riffled through the contents of the trunk Becky had opened.

How was it possible that this tiny, flighty, loquacious woman was the mother of a man who hadn't uttered as many words in the last two weeks as Betje had in the past two minutes?

As she watched the other woman taking such obvious joy from pretty things, she couldn't help thinking of her own mother. If the Countess of Addiscombe had ever shown such unfettered excitement for anything in her life, she certainly had not seen it.

Katie had been morbidly fascinated by her husband's normally impassive face, which had exhibited a veritable storm of emotions—none of them good—at the sight of his mother. She had the distinct impression that the dowager was not supposed to be at Briarly.

Betje suddenly looked up from the trunk. "Oh, dear! Look at how badly I'm behaving. Just like a naughty child rooting through your things. No wonder Gerrit is so horrified to find me here. What must you think of me, Katie?" She fluttered toward Katie and dropped onto the settee beside her, her small body shoving up against Katie just like a friendly kitten.

"I think you are delightful, Betje," she answered truthfully, looking down into a pair of warm sky-blue eyes that were so very, very different from Dulverton's. In fact, other than their fair hair—although her husband's was a white, rather than golden blond—Katie could see no resemblance at all between the two.

"I could not resist snooping as you have such pretty things." Betje's girlish gurgle of laughter should have sounded incongruous, but Katie found it irresistible. "I can already see that you are kind as well as lovely," the dowager said, patting Katie's hand. "I cannot tell you how delighted I was when I heard Gerrit was not marrying the girl my brother selected for him."

"Your brother?"

"My brother is Bas van Renesse. He and Lady Palmer have been scheming to foist one of the de Heeckeren girls on poor Gerrit for years." Her face puckered into a scowl. "I despised their mother when I was a girl."

Only now did Katie hear the other woman's faint accent, reminding her of the tradition of taking Dutch brides.

"You do not mind that I am not Dutch?" Katie asked.

Betje gave one of her charming burbles of laughter. "Goodness, no! I am delighted. Just delighted. Gerrit is already so stuffy that the last thing he needs is a terrified, obedient, convent-bred Dutch wife."

Katie gave a startled laugh. "But aren't *you* Dutch?"

"Yes, yes, I certainly am." She nodded vigorously.

"If you will excuse me for saying so, you do not seem, er, *stuffy*."

Betje laughed. "No, no, no. Not at all. My father had to chide me to within an inch of my life to stifle my exuberance when he brought me to England all those years ago to meet Boon for the first time."

"Boon?"

"Gerrit's father."

"What an unusual name."

"It is quite common back home. Poor Boon." Betje clucked her tongue. "The two of us were married all right and tight before he discovered the unfortunate truth about my gregarious nature." She laughed again, but Katie did not think it was amusement she saw in her Delft-blue eyes. "Ah, well." Betje suddenly leapt up. "Why am I rabbiting on so when you must be parched and exhausted? I must ring for tea. I am such a scatterbrain that I should have already—" A tap on the door interrupted her chatter. "Come in," the dowager called, evidently forgetting it was Katie's room.

A maid entered bearing a heavily laden tray.

Betje clapped her hands. "Look at that. Cranston knew what you would want before I could even tell him." She lowered her voice and said in a confiding tone, "Fortunately for your comfort, Cranston is very wise."

Katie wanted to remind the woman that *she* had been the one to suggest the tray when they had arrived, but the faint smirk on the maid's face stopped her. There were strange currents in the house, and she suspected the duke's mother was at the root. Dulverton certainly hadn't expected her. Or at least he hadn't told Katie that she would be here.

"I will leave you to relax," Betje said once she'd overseen the placement of the tray.

"Won't you stay and take tea with me?" Katie asked. "There are two cups and—"

"No, no, I mustn't. You will need your rest and Gerrit will want to speak to me," she added, more to herself as she fluttered toward the door.

"Will there be anything else, Your Grace?" the pretty, dark-haired maid asked Katie, her eyes sliding curiously to the trunks that were scattered about.

"No, thank you. That will be all—what is your name?"

"Nora, Your Grace."

"Thank you, Nora."

Once the door had closed, Katie turned to Becky, who was waiting for her with wide eyes.

"Have you ever heard the like?" Becky marveled, shaking her head in wonder as she moved toward the tray and began to prepare the tea.

"She is certainly an original," Katie said, pulling the pins from her hair and letting the heavy tresses fall with a groan of relief.

"She seems nothing like His Grace." Becky put two lumps of sugar and some milk in a cup before handing it over to Katie.

Katie gave a mirthless laugh. "No, she is not. Take tea with me," she ordered, prepared for an argument. But to her surprise, Becky merely nodded and fixed herself a cup.

Katie massaged her aching scalp as she inspected her chambers. "This is very pretty," she murmured, her eyes lingering on a lovely painting of a meadow that looked so realistic she could almost smell the wildflowers.

"How odd that His Grace has never occupied the master's chambers," Becky said, taking a sip of tea before setting down her cup and saucer and returning to the trunk she'd been unpacking before Betje interrupted her.

Katie had been surprised to hear that, too. She knew Dulverton's father had been dead for at least twenty years. Had Betje made the decision to move her son's things to the master's chambers, or had he? Something told her it had been the former.

She wandered the generous suite with her cup and saucer, examining what were surely new blue silk hangings and a lovely blue and cream Aubusson rug. Floor-to-ceiling windows ran along the north side of the room, and she pushed aside the heavy cobalt blue drapes to gaze out at the moonlit landscape. Her room overlooked a parterre garden which was magnificent even at night. Beyond that was a deer park that was bordered by a rather magical-looking wood.

Movement caught her eye, and she squinted. A man on horseback emerged from the woods and galloped toward the house. Katie recognized her husband long before she could see his face.

Where in the world had he gone at this time of night?

Or, more likely, *who* had he gone to see?

# Chapter Fourteen

Gerrit rode through the moonlit night heedless of the beauty around him. All the pleasure he usually took in returning to Briarly had been shattered by his mother's presence. Not even Amelia's soothing influence—a balm to his nerves, which had been rubbed raw after barely five minutes in his mother's company—could completely suppress his agitation.

But running to Amelia to snivel rather than entering his own house and facing whatever carnage his mother had wrought had simply put off the inevitable. Briarly had always been his refuge from the outside world and now his mother, a woman he'd run away from at only nine years of age, had invaded it.

Even worse had been Amelia's reaction to his anger.

"She is your mother, Gerrit. She has every right to visit your home and meet your wife."

Gerrit had been rendered speechless by her words.

Amelia had smiled faintly at his shock. "I know what you are thinking, but—"

"That is not difficult," he retorted. "My butler knows what I am thinking. Hell. I'm sure all my servants know—down to the youngest scullery maid. What surprises me is that you do not agree that her presence here is"—he scrambled for words to adequately describe the chaos the dowager brought in her wake but failed to find them.

"It is upsetting to you, I know that. But—" She stopped and pursed her lips.

"But what?"

"But you are eight-and-thirty, Gerrit. It is past time to forgive your mother. *Long* past time."

"Forgive her? I do not know what you mean, Amelia. I do not bear her any ill will. I simply do not care for her presence, which, you must admit, has always been disruptive.

Amelia had merely raised her eyebrows at his claim.

"Fine," he'd admitted, his face heating slightly under her quiet regard. "I am still *displeased* by her horrific behavior."

"Horrific behavior?"

He scowled. "You know what I mean. Do not make me say it."

"You cannot forgive your mother taking a lover and yet you forgave your father for his relationship with me."

"Good God, Amelia," Gerrit sputtered. "What you had with Father was something else entirely. You are a gentlewoman and were his intellectual equal. You could discuss paleontology with him as articulately as anyone who belongs to the Royal Society."

"That's as may be, but never fool yourself that I was not, first and foremost, your father's mistress."

Gerrit cringed to hear her speak the words aloud. "I know that," he snapped, his face ridiculously hot.

"And yet you have allowed the interests I shared with Dulverton to make you believe I was something more."

"How can you denigrate how important you were to him, Amelia? Your attachment was both profound and of long-standing. Whereas *she*—" Gerrit became tongue-tied, unable to give voice to the tangled emotions in his head.

"*She* is your mother. And she deserves some respect from you. I am glad she has come all this way to welcome your new wife. You should be, as well."

That had been her final word on the subject, and it had left him confused and despairing. He had known Amelia for three decades and, tonight, for the first time, he had found himself in deep disagreement with her.

But then again, they had never before spoken of his relationship to his mother. That was one of the other reasons he found her company so soothing; she never complicated their friendship by introducing uncomfortable subjects. The time he spent with Amelia focused on his recent finds, or journal articles, or other matters relating to fossils. They were usually of such like minds on most important subjects that Gerrit rarely needed to articulate his thoughts because she already knew.

But tonight the rare, precious rapport they had always shared was absent. And the reason for that was his mother. She did what she always did and contaminated everything around her.

Gerrit's jaws were clenched tight as he slid from his horse and tossed the reins to one of the grooms without a word.

His feet instinctively took him toward the suite of rooms he had occupied for all the years he'd lived at Briarly. Just as he was about to open the door, he recalled that his mother had had the audacity to move his possessions to his father's room. His *father's* room. That is what the master's chambers had always been in his mind. There had been times when Gerrit had—yes, illogically—gone to the master's chambers and felt a sense of peace merely being in the same room with his father's belongings. He had not done it often, but it had been a small thing that had brought him peace.

And the dowager had robbed him of it.

Scowling, he pivoted on his heel and strode toward his new chambers.

And then came to a halt at the appalling, unsettling sight that met his gaze when he turned the corner. There were paintings. Not just one or two, but a dozen of them littering the walls of the corridor between the main staircase and the master suite. No, not a dozen—he rapidly counted—*thirteen*. She didn't even have the decency to clutter the walls with an even number.

Symmetry, that critical design found throughout the natural world, had utterly evaded his mother.

He strode past the visual chaos, keeping his gaze on the soothing geometric pattern of the same carpet runner that had lined the corridors of Briarly since his boyhood. At least she'd not replaced *that* yet. Although given enough time, she would disrupt everything if he did not put a stop to her meddling.

He flung open the door to his room and paused on the threshold.

His valet, Court, was in the process of removing a medium-sized landscape from the wall across from the bed. "Ah, Your Grace. I had hoped to be finished with this before you returned." He set down the gilt frame, taking care not to damage it. "Jeremy and Jacob have taken one load and will return shortly for these."

*These* were a stack of variously sized frames—*seven* of them—that were now leaning against the wall. Gerrit glanced around at the disorder in the room and swallowed hard against the bile that rose in his throat, as if he were on the bridge of a ship in bad weather. He hated that this sort of disarray affected him so strongly, but it was a fact of life and the best way for him to manage it was to take himself elsewhere until everything had been put in order.

"Shall I move your possessions back to your old room, sir?"

Gerrit's gaze slid to the connecting door. He could hear the sound of movement on the other side where his wife was likely preparing for bed. If he moved back to his old chambers, he would undoubtedly be more comfortable, but he would also have to traipse down the main corridor to Kathryn's room.

"No. I will stay here. His gaze yet again slid toward the connecting door. "Her Grace is settling in?"

"I believe so," Court said, and then paused, his lips compressing and a faintly disapproving look flickering across his bland features.

"Speak, Court," Gerrit said, dread swelling in his belly at his servant's expression.

"I informed Her Grace's dresser about the artwork in the duchess's chambers and requested a convenient time to have it removed. She indicated her mistress would not be pleased."

"I will speak with the duchess myself. Do not send anyone to change anything until I give the order."

"Very good, sir. The library is untouched, Your Grace," Court added when Gerrit stood frozen in place.

He gave an abrupt nod. "Fetch me when all is settled here."

"Of course, Your Grace."

Gerrit turned away from the mess and then paused when he recalled what awaited him outside the nightmare room.

Court's voice came from behind him. "I will make sure the corridor has been seen to before you return, Your Grace."

Gerrit nodded, left the room, and then hovered in the corridor. He was tempted to take the servant stairs—a place he knew his mother would not have thought to wreak havoc by festooning the blank walls with bric-a-brac—but there were so many maids and footmen bustling about right now that he would likely get in the way.

He used the main hallways and stairs, keeping his eyes on the carpet until he reached the serene safety of the library and could breathe normally again.

A glance at the longcase clock told him it was just after ten. He had brought a good deal of correspondence with him from London and should sit down and work on it while he had the time. But his thoughts were as willful as a basket full of kittens, and he knew it would be impossible to concentrate on business matters just now.

Instead, his mind wandered to his wife's suite of rooms, which lay roughly above his head.

Kathryn would be tired, not only from the journey, but because Gerrit had abandoned her in the care of his yammering mother.

He should allow her to rest tonight, probably for two days after that grueling journey. Maybe even longer after how vigorously he had taken her on their wedding night.

Not for the first time did Gerrit grow hard at the memory of that night and her lovely body and enthusiastic response to him.

He scowled and shifted his erect cock before crossing the room to the shadowboxes that filled one wall. It was a much larger collection than the one in his London study. Usually looking at the exquisite fossils calmed him. Not tonight. Instead, his ungovernable thoughts kept veering back to his wedding night.

Gerrit had not intended to use her like she was his mistress, but she was so beautiful that she stole not only his breath, but also his wits. And of course there was her defiant, challenging behavior and impertinent tongue, both of which brought out the beast in him and stoked his already dominant nature.

His prick throbbed at the memory of her reaction to a bit of praise and vulgar pillow talk. It had stunned him to discover that her jaded sophistication was merely a mask—albeit thick and polished—and Gerrit never would have guessed that she needed reassurance and bolstering. His new wife was a snarling, spitting alley cat during the day, but in bed she became a sweet, purring kitten after only a little petting.

Although he regretted his lack of finesse on his wedding night, he did not regret the actual acts. Gerrit refused to go to her like a burglar in the night, sliding between the sheets in the darkness and taking his release, impregnation his only goal.

*Perhaps she'd prefer a swift, expedient fucking? After all, you promised her a marriage of convenience, not one of passion.*

Gerrit didn't care. Yes, he had treated her more like a mistress than an earl's daughter, but her open and eager carnality convinced him that she'd enjoyed herself. Why should he curtail his own pleasure—and hers as well—just because they had been forced to marry?

He glanced at the clock again. It was three minutes later than the last time.

*Damnation.*

He banished his delectable wife from his thoughts, sat down at his desk, and pulled the stack of correspondence toward him. Work would settle his rampant thoughts. At least it always had in the past.

***

Katie had extinguished all the candles and given up on Dulverton coming to her when the connecting door opened. She studied him from beneath lowered lashes as he paused on the threshold, a monolithic black figure limned by the faint light behind him. He tilted his head to the side and she realized he was trying to discern if she was sleeping.

Katie suspected that if she remained still, he would leave.

Although she was tired, she had thought constantly of their wedding night, reliving it over and over again. She might not like him, but she wanted him physically. At least her body did.

She paused at that thought. No, that wasn't accurate; she wanted more than just physical pleasure from him. Dulverton the man intrigued her and made her feel alive as nothing and nobody else had done for years.

"I am awake."

He closed the door, throwing the room into complete darkness. There was a faint rustle of cloth before the edge of the mattress dipped and the blankets lifted and hot, hard flesh pressed along her right side. A hand, the skin slightly rough but warm, settled on her midriff and lightly caressed over the fine muslin of her nightgown.

Katie was so excited she could scarcely breathe as his mouth lowered over one of her breasts and he suckled her nipple through the thin material. Rather than blunt the sensation, the cloth barrier somehow enhanced her pleasure.

Being under sensual assault with candles blazing had been wits-destroying, but something about the anonymity of utter darkness made her feel as if all the nerves in her body had migrated to the outside of her skin.

Without his piercing gaze to strip her to the bone, she was unencumbered by self-consciousness. Instead of having to worry about what she looked like, she gave herself up to his expert seduction.

"Lift your bottom," he murmured, hardly pausing his kissing as he pushed her nightgown up over her thighs, hips, and waist until the fabric was bunched above her breasts. "Now your arms." Katie complied and he removed the nightgown, tugging off her sleeping cap in the process.

A gentle but insistent knee nudged between her thighs, spreading her legs as his hot silky mouth sucked her nipples until they were hard, needy peaks. Katie closed her eyes and arched her back as he slid his hand over her belly and between her legs, easily breaching her shamefully slick body with one thick finger.

The low, almost inaudible grunt he gave as he sank deep inside her was the single most arousing sound Katie had ever heard. And *she* had done that to him. Or at least her body had. Raw need incited her to boldness, and she raised her hips to encourage his wicked hand.

A shudder passed through his big frame as his arm began to move and he worked her with slow, deliberate strokes. Katie decided that being *readied* by her husband was as wonderful as the main event.

The only sounds in the room were of heavy breathing and an embarrassing wet sound as he pumped her, easing a second finger in. Every muscle in her body clenched when he used his thumb to tease her bud, his other hand working her harder, deeper, and faster.

*Please don't let him tease me endlessly.*

But it seemed that Dulverton had other plans tonight and his stroking didn't falter as Katie lifted her hips and met him thrust for thrust, exploding when the sensation became too much to contain. Spasms of intense bliss seized her again and again, until her limbs were suffused with languor.

Dulverton stilled his stroking, but his thumb—oh, his wicked, wonderful thumb—pressed against the base of her pearl in such a way that a second powerful blast of pleasure lifted her hips off the bed.

And then he began to withdraw.

"No—" she murmured, tightening her inner muscles. But it was too late, and her body clenched around nothing.

"*Shhh.*" The sound was hot on her temple as his broad torso lowered over hers and he held his weight on one elbow, using his free hand to guide himself.

Katie opened wider for him without being asked, a moan slipping from between her clenched teeth when his thick length thrust inside her, not stopping until he'd buried himself to the root.

He gave a soft grunt of pleasure as the echoes of her orgasm massaged his rigid shaft, remaining motionless as her climax ebbed. Only when she was limp and boneless did he begin to move, his taut hips pumping slowly and deeply, filling her utterly with each erotic caress. He gave a slight twist of his hips when he withdrew and soon the friction caused a familiar tightening sensation to build.

Katie reached for him without thinking, and his body jolted when her hands landed on the tightly meshed muscles of his waist.

She jerked her hands away. "I'm sorry," she whispered, the passion that had been building within her instantly flagging.

"Touch me."

When she hesitated, he thrust deep and kept her pinned and filled. "Touch me, Kathryn," he hissed into the darkness.

She was far more tentative his time, but he didn't pull away, so Katie caressed from his waist up the flaring muscles of his back to his ridiculously broad shoulders, earning a low purr of encouragement. Emboldened, she stroked downward, not stopping until her hands lightly grazed his firm, smooth globes of his buttocks.

"Yes, like that," he growled. "Everywhere—harder," he ordered as he raised his hips, the action pushing his hard buttocks against her palms.

She gripped the taut muscles tighter and a shudder wracked his body as he resumed his pumping. The sensation of being joined with him was as exciting as it had been that first night, but even more arousing was the barely leashed savagery of thrusts. Even in the darkness she could feel his control fraying. The knowledge that it was *her* bringing about this metamorphosis sent her flying over the edge into yet another climax just as Dulverton gave a primitive roar, the ferocity of his release shocking for a man who rarely exhibited any emotion.

She curled her legs around his muscular thighs to hold him inside her, locking her arms around his broad back. It felt like every muscle in his body spasmed, his shaft swelling with each jerk as he spent deep inside her.

When it was over, he slumped, the entire weight of his torso all but crushing her. But Katie didn't so much as twitch. Scarcely a minute passed before he roused himself.

Reluctantly, Katie released him, her legs and arms sliding away as he raised himself up and rolled to the side. For a moment she thought he might rest, but the mattress shifted, and the blanket, rather than hot male body, settled over her.

She didn't hear another sound until the connecting door opened, throwing the same slanting light into her room. He stood poised on the threshold. "Good night, Kathryn."

"Good night, Dulverton," she said, but he had already shut the door, leaving her once again in darkness, wondering if she had just woken from a fever dream.

# Chapter Fifteen

Katie was disappointed when she went down to breakfast the following morning and discovered that Dulverton had eaten hours earlier and left on estate business.

"And the dowager? Has she already come down?" she asked the footman, a man she did not recognize.

"Her Grace takes a tray in her room, Your Grace."

Katie was amused by the sheer number of *your graces* around. What a recipe for confusion.

She was relieved that she would not need to face Betje first thing in the morning. She liked the sweet, garrulous woman, but a little of her chatter went a long way—especially before Katie had ingested the requisite amount of coffee.

She took a little from each of the various chafing dishes and sat at the table, telling herself that she was glad Dulverton was not there. After all, it wasn't as if they would have anything to say to one another. And if he *did* say anything it would be to find fault with something she was doing. Or where she was sitting or what she was wearing or—

Katie gritted her teeth against the flood of resentment and pushed her eggs around on her plate. She was not really hungry but was in no hurry to leave the room and get on with her day. After all, what on earth was she supposed to do at Briarly? The house ran like clockwork and Katie would likely muck everything up if she interfered.

She could ask Dulverton about her duties—aside from the obvious one, of course—but her husband had evidently fled at dawn. Doubtless Betje would have some suggestions, but did she really want to listen to a woman who got on Dulverton's nerves so badly?

Katie chewed and stared moodily out the window at the beautiful garden, mulling over the matter and dawdling over her breakfast for a quarter of an hour before she could stand the tedium no longer.

The footman she'd spoken to earlier hastened toward the door when she stood.

"What is your name?" Katie asked.

"Thomas, Your Grace."

"Where is the library, Thomas?"

"The first set of carved double doors to the right of the stairs, Your Grace."

Katie passed at least four housemaids on her way to the library. Each one dropped a low curtsey and then quickly scuttled away. Given how early Dulverton had left the house they were probably not accustomed to seeing their employers wandering about at this time of day.

Her mother would have thrown a tantrum if her eyes had been blighted by the sight of a servant working. The Countess of Addiscombe was not alone in that opinion; many aristocrats felt servants should neither be seen nor heard unless one summoned them.

She hoped Dulverton did not live by the countess's code. She could accept his need for order and symmetry—although it was annoying—but she refused to behave as if servants were dumb animals or pieces of furniture. And she would give Dulverton her opinion in no uncertain terms if he thought to impose such behavior on her.

Katie was so caught up in mentally drafting the dressing down she would deliver to her husband that she almost passed the library. She reached for the handle but then paused and rapped her knuckles on the slick surface, just in case.

When no sound came from within, she opened the door and sucked in a breath. The library in London had been grand, but this was truly magnificent and rose up two stories with a mezzanine level that wrapped all the way around the capacious room.

Just like the rest of the house, there were two of everything, except… Katie squinted across to where four identical tables sat, two chairs at each. Even from this distance she could see there were chess sets on them. Or chess *games*, rather, as the pieces were not set up in the starting position.

The usual mix of nostalgia and revulsion flooded her at the sight of the familiar pieces. Normally, she would bolt in the opposite direction to avoid being dragooned into a game. But she was alone, so she allowed her curiosity to draw her closer, interested despite herself.

Katie's family had been as poor as church mice when she'd been a girl and they'd had to make their own entertainment, which had meant lots of chess, draughts, charades, dictionary, and a dozen other games—everything but cards, which her mother did not allow in her house.

In a family filled with talented, clever sisters, Katie had excelled at only two things: needlework and chess.

When one of her sisters wanted pretty embroidery on a gown or help sewing a new dress, they had come to Katie.

As for chess, Katie had often pitted herself against all four sisters—and Doddy, too, when he was old enough to play—at once. And she *always* won.

Until she met Jasper.

As Katie stared at the chessboards, memories of that summer with Jasper flooded her. Her aunt had been so delighted that Katie received so many invitations to the Marquess of Lindhurst's—Jasper's father—house. Not just for the small, informal dances the marchioness gave every two weeks for her unmarried twin daughters—Jasper's youngest siblings—but also several times a week to take tea with the girls, who were the same age as Katie.

What Aunt Agnes hadn't known was that Katie spent part of every visit alone in Lord Jasper's company. She'd been terribly flattered that he'd singled her out on those magical afternoons, walking with her in the gardens, always choosing her for charades, and then one fateful afternoon when rain had kept them all inside playing three games of chess with her in the magnificent library.

During the first game he had surreptitiously caressed her hand while smiling warmly into her eyes.

After she'd won, he'd laughingly chided her for distracting him and demanded a chance to redeem himself.

There'd been no caresses during the second game.

And by the time Katie had won the third game, his eyes, usually a bright sky blue, had taken on an arctic edge.

Jasper had not thrown a tantrum as Doddy had done on occasion when he lost. No, his reaction had been far more subtle and punitive.

That very night Jasper had chosen to lead every other girl except Katie onto the dance floor. The other men in the neighborhood—all of whom idolized the older and more sophisticated Lord Jasper—had followed his lead, leaving Katie a wallflower.

Katie had been frantic by the time supper came, finding it harder and harder to breathe. Her keen-eyed aunt had been furious. "Why is Lord Jasper giving you the cut direct? You see how the others are all following his lead. What have you done, Kathryn?" She'd sounded so much like her sister, the Countess of Addiscombe, that Katie had frozen just as she always did whenever her mother rebuked her.

"I've d-done nothing, Aunt Agnes!"

But that had been a lie. She knew exactly what she'd done.

Not even the wallflowers had wanted to sit beside her after supper, and Katie was almost lost to despair by the time Jasper asked her to dance the very last set.

He'd smiled coolly down at her, a worrying glitter in his eyes. Only by biting her tongue so hard it bled had Katie been able to keep from shaming herself and begging his forgiveness for thrashing him at chess. As green as she'd been she'd still known not to expose his weakness in such a way.

Instead, she had simpered and flattered and prayed it would be enough to appease him.

For ten days there were no invitations from the marchioness. By the time Jasper called at her aunt's house on the eleventh day and asked her to go for a drive in his curricle, Katie had been so desperate to please him that she'd almost wept with gratitude when he'd driven them to a small hunting cabin on his father's estate and relieved Katie of her virginity.

Katie shoved away the nauseating memory and turned to study the four games. Two were likely to end in a draw and white should win the other two.

She felt something cool and smooth in her hand and was stunned to see her fingers curled around a black bishop. She dropped the piece as if it was a live coal. Thankfully it landed harmlessly on carpet rather than shattering on the hard wood floor.

Once she'd put the piece back, she stepped away from the tables.

Katie could just imagine how Gerrit—who'd looked thunderous when she'd merely *looked* at his shadowboxes in London—would react if she actually touched any of his possessions.

Of course, the boards might be the dowager's.

Katie smiled at the thought of the flighty woman playing chess.

No, these would be her husband's games, and something told her that Jasper's long-ago punishment would pale in comparison to Dulverton's if she moved so much as one piece. She shivered at the thought and put her hands behind her back, not trusting them.

An irrational but irresistible urge to get away from the boards seized her. By the time she reached the double doors she was almost running. She flung open the door and almost collided with the dowager.

"Goodness!" the older woman squeaked, taking a hasty step back. "What is wrong, my dear? You look like the devil was on your heels."

Even if she could have spoken, Katie had no rational explanation for the terror that had just gripped her.

The dowager took Katie's arm. "Come and sit down for a mo—"

"No," Katie said in a far-too loud voice, pulling away as Betje led her back into the library, or at least tried to. "I—I'm fine." She forced a smile. "Truly, I am fine."

The dowager's somber expression looked incongruous with her frivolous pink crepe gown. "I am sorry I did not come join you at breakfast, my dear." She pursed her lips. "I told Dove to wake me early this morning but—" She broke off and fluttered her hands. "Well, you know how it can be with servants one has had all one's life. They wish to coddle and protect one, even from one's own commands."

"Yes, I do know how they can be."

The dowager suddenly smiled. "Today is a special day." Her smile spread until it was an infectious grin.

"Er, it is?"

"It is your first in your new home!" Her smile dimmed. "I understand my son has gone out to his dig."

"His dig?"

"He did not tell you about the dig?"

"No." Because that would require actually talking to Katie rather than issuing commands.

"Oh, Gerrit," Betje muttered under her breath. She shook herself and met Katie's gaze. "I was hoping we could wait to have our talk, but I can see that won't be possible."

"Our talk?" Katie repeated, beginning to sound like a parrot.

"Come, my dear. My chambers are much more comfortable than standing about here in the corridor." She glanced at the bare walls but did not comment as she led Katie back toward the part of the house referred to as the *family wing*, one of the four rectangular blocks that extended off the main portion of the building.

The dowager chattered the entire way, flitting from subject to subject like the butterfly she so resembled. Yet again Katie marveled that this woman was related to Dulverton. The dowager was the antithesis of her son. While he skewered a person with his intent, stone-cold gaze, the dowager's eyes never rested on any single object for more than a few seconds. And while Dulverton rarely spoke more than two or three words together, his mother hardly stopped chattering.

Betje's chambers were as fluffy and bright as the woman herself. Indeed, the sheer amount of pink—carpets, wall hangings, drapes, silk-covered settees—was a bit hard on the eyes.

The duchess waved a hand to the room. "I had this chamber done when the drapers came to refurbish the master and mistress suites," Betje said. "Do you like it?"

"Oh, yes. Very much," she lied. "They must have worked fast," she added.

"I told them it was an emergency. And it was, it was." She pulled a face, as if she'd just smelled something foul. "It was all brown, brown, brown, brown, brown!" Betje gestured to the pink-on-pink silk settee. "Please, won't you sit?"

"You mentioned a dig?" Katie reminded the other woman once they were both seated.

"Er, yes, I did. Were you aware that my son is one of the foremost authorities on fossils in England?" she asked, bristling with pride.

"No, I was not," Katie admitted. But that would explain all the fossils. So, that was what her husband did all day, every day.

Her brother Doddy had been wild about fossils. And because Katie and Doddy—separated by only two years—had been all but joined at the hip when they'd been younger, Katie had gone on fossil hunts with him. They hadn't found much, but they'd had great fun digging until their mother had put an end to it, insisting Katie's time would be better spent learning how to behave like a lady.

What had ever happened to Doddy's rather pitiful fossil collection? Did he still hunt for fossils? Katie hardly knew her little brother anymore, seeing him only briefly once or twice a year.

"It is a hobby he learned from his father," Betje went on. "Boon was also well-respected in the field, as was *his* father."

"And where does he go to do this digging?"

"He has an encampment right here on the estate."

"Encampment? Do you mean he has someplace else that he will stay?"

"It is a commodious tent, and I believe it is equipped for overnight stays, but I cannot imagine Gerrit will use it with you here." Betje's brow furrowed. "Or at least I hope not," she added, more to herself. "But that is what I wished to talk to you about."

"His encampment?"

"No, no, not that, but rather how you might, er, accommodate yourself to my son."

A spike of irritation stabbed her at the other woman's words. How much more *accommodation* could there possibly be? Dulverton already controlled every facet of her life.

"I know the circumstances that spurred your betrothal, my dear."

"I should think all of Britain is aware your son was forced to marry me."

"*Tsk, tsk.*" The dowager scooted closer on the settee and patted Katie's hands, which were clenched in her lap. "You must not sound so bitter."

"Trapping one's husband in a kissing contest is hardly something to take pride in."

Betje chortled delightedly. "Oh, now you are giving me a severe look. But I must say it warmed my heart to think of my son marrying a woman with such daring."

"Not to mention such a stupid woman."

Again, the dowager laughed. "There is no denying your behavior was a bit wild and reckless," Betje said, squeezing Katie's hands as if to take any sting out of her words. "But that is not always a bad thing."

Katie gave the other woman a look of disbelief, earning another laugh.

"You think I am a bit crazy, don't you?" Thankfully, Betje went on rather than wait for a response. "You will have observed that my son is neither of those things."

"Yes, I have noticed," Katie said dryly.

"In many ways Gerrit is very much like Dulverton. Er, I mean the last duke," Betje amended.

"I suppose that is quite normal with fathers and sons," Katie said when the dowager appeared to fall into a distracted reverie.

"What's that, my dear?" Betje said after a moment.

"I just said that it seems natural for sons to be like their fathers." Although she dearly hoped that Doddy was nothing like their profligate, gambling father.

"Oh yes. Just so," Betje said with a nervous laugh, her pale skin coloring for some reason as she gave Katie a strange, almost evasive, look. "Er, yes, Gerrit does get his looks from Boon's side of the family. But I was referring more to their rather stringent requirements when it comes to their surroundings and such." She gave one of her titters of laughter, but this time Katie heard no amusement in the sound. "I sometimes wonder if Gerrit inherited anything from me at all."

Katie could understand that.

"Gerrit was not happy to discover me here last night. I knew he would not like it. He forbade me to come to the wedding ceremony."

Katie felt intensely uncomfortable. "My sister Hyacinth—er, the Duchess of Chatham—was the only family I had at the wedding and that is because I lived with her and her husband for the last five years. But I didn't invite any of my other siblings. His Grace probably did not want to make you come all the way to London for such a small affair."

The dowager smiled sadly. "You are kind to try and make me feel better, but the reason Gerrit did not invite me is because he does not care to be around me. You mustn't feel bad for me, my dear. I'm afraid I brought it all on myself."

Katie suspected that was at least partially true. She'd only been married to Dulverton a few days, but she already knew the duke required a certain sort of order in his surroundings. Why would Betje have thought it was a good idea to change things so drastically at Briarly?

But Katie did not want to make assumptions, so she said, "Are you talking about rearranging the house?"

"No, not for what I've done to Briarly, although I know that by trying to make the house more comfortable for you, I have angered him." She frowned, and the expression made her look like an angry, fluffy little bird. "But I don't care anymore. For years I have let him slowly turn into Boon. But it must stop *now*, before he is lost forever."

"What are you talking about?"

"I am talking about how Gerrit has become a cold, isolated, and lonely man. You must not allow him to go on the way he has, Kathryn. You are his wife, and it falls to *you* to challenge him."

"Challenge him?" she repeated, utterly mystified.

Betje nodded. "Yes. Gerrit needs to have his rigid expectations challenged—or at least questioned. It was a failure on my part that I never did so with Boon. He told me how things would be, and I capitulated utterly. Like Boon, Gerrit is wealthy, powerful, and accustomed to being obeyed. In short, Gerrit is the master of his world. But he has forgotten this is *your* world, too. It is not right that Gerrit should have everything his way. And I think it is not good for him. He is so rigid, so very closed off from others." The older woman's blue eyes were vague, as if she was looking at something not in the room. "I should have never given in to all Boon's demands," she said in a voice that was a dry husk of her normal ebullient tone. "But Boon was so much older and so very wise and dignified that I thought he knew best. I thought he—" She broke off and stared at her hands, which were clasped together so tightly the knuckles were white. "I have to tell you something and it is shameful and embarrassing. But you must know. You must have a chance to do better," she whispered, more to herself. She met Katie's curious gaze. "I was younger than you when I married Boon—only seventeen—and he was a few years older than Gerrit."

Katie could easily imagine Betje at seventeen. She was still a beautiful woman; she must have been a breathtakingly lovely girl.

Betje twisted her fingers and sank her teeth into her lower lip, her gaze once again distant. "I was Boon's second wife. His first had died long before, when he was a young man. He waited almost twenty years before seeking a bride." She suddenly gave a gurgle of laughter, her pale eyes filled with nostalgia and mischief, giving Katie some idea of what she had looked like all those years ago. "I had six older sisters. One after another they hoped to be Boon's bride. But one after another they were forced to marry elsewhere as the time to wed came and went and still Boon did not marry. Finally, my grandfather—a terrifying old man not accustomed to having his will thwarted—told me I would accompany him to

England." Her gaze slid to Katie. "He brought me here without telling Boon we were coming. My grandfather quickly discovered that Boon was not a boy to be ordered about. Instead, he appealed to Boon's honor by pointing out the agreement between our families could not be fulfilled if Boon did not take me to wife as the next oldest granddaughter was barely two years of age."

"Did you wish to marry?" Katie asked.

"Oh, yes!" Betje answered without hesitation. "Boon was not a handsome man, but he was very dignified and commanding. I was so ready to fall in love with him," she said softly, a fond smile on her face. "By marrying him I would do what all my sisters had failed to achieve and become a duchess." Betje's smile faded. "He was very reserved during our brief courtship, but I was sure he would become warmer once we married. With so many married sisters I knew what happened in the marriage bed." She looked sheepish for raising such a subject. "I hoped that physical intimacy would bring about the same sort of emotional intimacy that my sisters enjoyed with their husbands. I was young and very romantic." A bleakness settled over her. "Boon put paid to my dreams on our wedding night."

Katie realized that she had been holding her breath and exhaled, a sense of impending doom filling her as she waited for Betje to continue.

"He was very gentle and kind—in his reserved way—and made sure I did not suffer that first time. When it was over, he told me how our wedded life was to be. My duties were to be few." She gave a bitter bark of laughter. "In truth, I had only one."

Katie knew what Betje would say before she even said it.

"He did not need me to serve as his hostess as he rarely entertained at Spenwood. I was not required to accompany him to London because he had no interest in *ton* socializing. In almost every way I was superfluous when it came to his life. My only responsibility was to provide him with an heir. Once I had, my duty to him would be at an end and we would live separate lives." She looked down at her hands. "My wedding night, which I'd dreamed about for so long, ended in despair."

They sat in uncomfortable silence.

Katie looked at the dowager's bowed blonde head and knew she could not hold her tongue. "Gerrit had a similar conversation with me, although it took place before we married."

Betje looked stricken. "I cannot say I am surprised, although I was hoping it would not be so. And is that what you want, my dear?"

"What do you mean?"

"I mean is that the sort of marriage *you* want? One in name only."

"It hardly matters what I want. Dulverton made his expectations clear before we married, and I agreed. It would be unfair to him if I changed my mind now. Besides—" Katie broke off, at the last moment recalling just who she was talking to.

"Yes?" Betje prodded. "Please, Katie—tell me the truth. I know this conversation is appallingly blunt, but I fear what will happen if we spare both our blushes."

"I'm not sure your son wants any other sort of marriage. Based on our first few days as man and wife, I'm not sure he even believes any other union is possible."

"Oh, he does, Katie! I am sure he does," Betje said, her eyes almost feverish with something that looked like hope.

"What makes you say that?" Katie asked.

"He might not look like me, but he is at least half mine. There is no reason for him to be like Boon—" She broke off, her eyes sliding away from Katie for a moment. Something that looked like shame flickered across her pretty face. "I love Gerrit and I want him to be happy. He won't be happy if he continues on this way. I want to help you fight for Gerrit—and for your marriage."

Katie felt almost scorched by the emotion rolling off the other woman. What made Betje believe such a travesty of a marriage could be saved? Especially since she had not managed to save her own to Gerrit's father?

*Doing something is better than doing nothing.*

Katie met the other woman's desperate, pleading gaze. "What would you have me do?"

# Chapter Sixteen

Gerrit handed the reins to his groom and strode toward the house, his mind still back at the dig. It had been months since he'd had a chance to immerse himself in his work, but that did not mean the project came to a halt in his absence. Gerrit was fortunate to have a man like James Jessop to oversee matters whenever his ducal duties took him to London or one of his other estates.

"Ah, there you are, Gerrit." His mother stood standing on the landing, as if she had been waiting for him.

"Did you need something, Your Grace?" he asked, unable to entirely keep his irritation from his voice. He was tired and dirty and wanted a bath.

"I wish to speak to you."

Gerrit made a *get on with it* gesture.

"Not here in the corridor," she said, for once not dithering but giving him a direct look that he did not like. "In the library."

He wanted to tell her he did not have time but could see by her determined expression that would only postpone the inevitable.

Neither of them spoke until Gerrit was seated behind his desk and his mother perched on a chair across from him. All the furniture in the library had been built for Gerrit's father—who had been only an inch shorter than Gerrit's own six feet and three inches—and so only the toes of her slippers grazed the floor.

"I know you did not want me to come to Briarly, but I refuse to be a stranger to my own daughter-in-law. Especially as I fear that she will soon be banished to Spenwood to live with me."

He blinked at this frontal assault. "I beg your pardon?"

"You will do as your father did. As you did with Christina."

He flinched at the sound of his dead wife's name. "I fail to see what concern any of—"

"It is my concern because I am your *mother* and you are my son. You are my only child. I care about your happiness and—"

"If you care so much about my happiness then why did you come to Briarly and immediately disrupt—"

"Did you learn nothing at all from your first marriage?" she demanded, talking over him in an overly loud voice.

Her words were like kerosine on a bonfire. "Have a care, madam," Gerrit said coldly. "For you know not of what you speak."

"I know *exactly* what I am talking about because Boon told me what advice he would give you regarding your marriage. He told me how you could never love a woman and should not even try. I begged him not to doom your marriage as he had done to ours, but he refused and because of that, Christina ran and—"

Gerrit slammed his hand down on the desk, the loud *thwack* making his mother jump. "You know *not* of what you speak."

"Then tell me why a man with your obvious intelligence would behave the same—"

"I scarcely needed to employ my father's advice with Christina given that she was already pregnant when she came to our marriage bed."

His mother's eyes bulged. "Wh-what?"

"She was three months pregnant on our wedding night." The words were like bile on his tongue, even after all these years.

"I—I am so sorry. I had no idea. What happened to the baby?"

"She had a miscarriage." Gerrit put both hands on his desk and pushed himself up. "We are finished here." When she did not move, he strode toward the door, adding, "At least I am."

"Gerrit!"

He squeezed his eyes briefly shut but swung around to face her. "What?" he bit out, not caring how rude he sounded.

"This marriage is a second chance for you—Katie is not Christina—" Her eyes widened. "Unless... Dear God. Is she also—"

"Kathryn is not pregnant," he snapped, inexplicably irritated that his mother was already calling his wife by her pet name.

"Then this is a fresh chance for you. A chance to have a real marriage, not the disaster that Boon and I shared. I know what he always told you, Gerrit, but you are *not* him. You are lovable and I know that you have love to give. Just because Boon was not capable of—"

"You know *nothing* about me, madam. Just the same way you knew nothing about my father."

She flinched as if he had struck her. "So what are your plans, then? To install your own mistress here at Briarly as Boon did with his whore?"

"Don't you *dare* use that word when referring to Amelia. Not when *you*—"

"I am your mother!" the dowager shouted hoarsely, her voice echoing in the cavernous room. "*She* is not, as much as you obviously wish that were so. Half of you came from *me*, Gerrit. Me, not her, for all that you give her the respect of a parent. And yes, I know you went to see that—that *whore*—yes, I will call her what she is—last night mere moments after your arrival."

"You are hardly without blame when it comes to the subject of whoring, madam." Gerrit saw her hand coming and could have dodged it easily, but he relished her loss of control and was darkly amused by the look of horror on her face after the loud *slap* filled the room.

She reached for him with both hands but jerked her them back when he recoiled. "Oh, dear God! Gerrit, I did not mean to hurt you, I am so—"

"You do not possess the power to hurt me, Your Grace," he assured her, unmoved by the tears sliding down her face.

Remarkably, she stood her ground. "I gave up on Boon on our wedding night—after he made it clear that he wanted nothing from me save an heir—"

"You would paint yourself as blameless even though you brought your lover with you to England? Even though he lives openly at Spenwood and has done for decades?"

"I will not deny the truth of your words, but neither will I continue to apologize. For years I have allowed my shame to keep me quiet, but no longer. I refuse to sit by and watch as you destroy your chance for—"

She broke off with a startled yelp when Gerrit closed the distance between them, not stopping until they were so close they were almost touching. "If you meddle in my marriage, I will have you put away somewhere you can never interfere in my life again."

Gerrit did not think she looked more shocked than he felt that such a vile, cruel threat had issued from his mouth.

"You would not," she said, her voice quavering with uncertainty.

No, he wouldn't. But she did not need to know that. Instead, he said, "Do not test my patience, Your Grace. You will find it is non-existent where you are concerned."

She swallowed convulsively, for a moment looking like a cornered animal. But then, just as he was turning away, another expression slid over her normally soft, almost indistinct features. It took Gerrit a moment to recognize it because he'd never seen such a look on his mother's face before. It was resolution.

Her shoulders stiffened and she seemed to grow a several inches in stature. "You must do what you feel best, Gerrit. But if you want to lock me away then you will have to bodily carry me out of this house. Until that time, I will stay and fight for your future, whether you want me to or not."

He stared dazedly as she stormed from the room.

She should have appeared laughable—her slight form as insubstantial as a child and garbed in one of her silly, fussy pink gowns—but for the first time that Gerrit could remember, the dowager looked like somebody who deserved respect.

***

Katie pushed her poached sole from one side of her plate to the other—the dowager's determinedly cheerful voice a constant hum in the background—and waited for the meal to end.

The table was just as long as it had been in London, but Katie had not bothered to insist on shortening it. When she entered the room at three minutes to six, she had been amused to see David Sessions—her husband's steward—and knew that Dulverton must have invited him to balance the table. Both the steward and the dowager valiantly attempted to maintain a flow of conversation without much help from either Katie or the duke.

Katie was exhausted, for all that she had done very little other than tour the house with Betje for a few hours. Sometimes it seemed like doing nothing was more exhausting than dancing until dusk.

Once the last plate had been cleared, the dowager glanced at Katie and gave her an encouraging look, reminding her that *she* was the mistress of Briarly. At least for now.

Katie stood. "We shall retire to the drawing room and leave you gentlemen to your port."

"I hope you will join us afterward?" the dowager piped up.

Dulverton frowned. "I will work in the library, and I am sure Mr. Sessions has better ways to spend his evening."

The steward's face reddened at his employer's rudeness.

Undaunted, the dowager smiled cheerily at her son. "Then we shall join *you* in the library, my dear."

Dulverton's lips tightened and for one moment Katie thought he might actually forbid them to invade his sanctum. But even he was not so obnoxious. "As you wish, madam."

The moment the door shut behind them the duchess turned to one of the footmen. "Will you please tell Dove that I want my needlework brought to the library."

"Of course, Your Grace."

"Oh—and tell her to fetch Her Grace's basket as well."

Katie opened her mouth to tell him not to bother, but the man was halfway up the stairs.

"Won't it be lovely to have somebody to chat with while we are so virtuously employed?" Betje asked, taking her arm, and guiding her toward the library.

Needlework.

Katie forced a smile. "Yes, it will be lovely."

**An hour later…**

"Oh, Katie! How clever and quick you are at this," Betje twittered happily. "Why, it looks beautiful now that you have put it to rights. I'm afraid I have never been much of a hand when it comes to such delicate work. Indeed, it seems a terrible shame that—" The dowager broke off and pulled her lips between her teeth before saying, "No, no. I couldn't ask that of you."

Katie bit back a groan. "Would you like me to finish it for you, Betje?"

The older woman clapped her hands. "Oh, would you?"

"It would be my pleasure," she lied, unable to resist sliding a look beneath her lashes from the chirping, chattering dowager to her dour, glowering son.

Earlier Dulverton had marched into the library as if he were entering a gladiatorial ring, offering Katie and Betje the most minimal of greetings before striding resolutely to his desk.

When the dowager had suggested the three of them play a game of widow whist, he had given his mother a look of horror and tonelessly, but firmly, rejected her offer before settling down at his desk.

For the most part he ignored them, but from time to time he would glance up at his mother's louder expostulations or laughter and regard her with a furrowed brow, looking both perplexed and irritated.

Exactly the sort of look he was giving the dowager right now.

"—and there is one of my gowns," the dowager happily chattered, blissfully unaware she was the focus of her son's scowl, "that is the most delightful shade of pink. Not *pink* pink, you understand, but more of a rose pink. Although not a common sort of rose, but one that is less of a pinkish-red and more of a… well, a pinkish pink perhaps. Quite my favorite shade of—"

Katie caught her lower lip to keep from laughing at Dulverton's revolted expression as his mother rabbited on. The woman could talk, but as she rarely required a response Katie found her company quite soothing.

Obviously, her son did not feel the same way.

Katie set down her tambour to root through the dowager's hideously untidy needlework bag, searching for more periwinkle blue floss to finish the hydrangea she had mostly unpicked. Never in her life had she seen needlework as poor as the dowager's. Not even her sister Hy—who'd viewed needlework as a worse punishment than being stretched on the rack—had produced such dreadful work. How could a woman Betje's age be so very bad at it? And why would she persist in a hobby when the result was so atrocious?

Now that Katie had volunteered to finish the work, she would have to unpick the rest of the flowers, and also the vase itself. Indeed, she'd have to start afresh. As she untangled a ball of thread, she reflected that this was the first time she had picked up a needle since last October when she had reluctantly agreed to embroider several handkerchiefs Phoebe had begged her to make for Needham for Christmas.

"Your monograms are even lovelier than Stacia's," Phoebe had said. "But please never tell her I said so."

Katie did not think her work was nicer than Andrew's wife's exquisite illuminated letters, but she was a good deal faster.

"—and then Dove did the cleverest whitework around the puffed sleeves. Although I suppose one must call it *pinkwork* as it was done with pink floss on pink muslin. Regardless, it resulted in the *most* delightful border on my second favorite morning gown. No, my third favorite, now that I think more on the matter and—"

Smirking to herself, Katie found the color of floss she needed but had to untangle it from a half dozen others. Indeed, every single thread in the dowager's basket was snarled and knotted. It was rather an achievement to have created such utter chaos.

"What a mess my basket is!" Betje tittered as Katie painstakingly untangled the blue floss. "I cannot seem to keep it tidy, no matter how hard I try. And now that my vision has become so poor it is *such* a dreadful chore."

Katie could see where this was leading. "Would you like me to organize it for you?"

"Oh, would you?" Betje clapped her hands—one of her favorite ways to express happiness. "I would be excessively grateful. Dove usually sets it all to rights but grumbles and wears the most cross expression while doing so."

Katie imagined that she, too, would be cross after untangling such messes for forty odd years.

"It would be my pleasure," she said, not entirely lying this time. She hated to admit it but having something to think about—even something like tangled threads or needlework—was better than endlessly pondering Dulverton and their marriage.

She had tried several times to think about Betje's advice from earlier that day about how Katie could pierce Dulverton's wall of reserve, but most of her suggestions—insisting that he bring her to his dig, asking him to take her to the theater in Lyme Regis, or thrusting her company on him during the morning rides he apparently took most days, to name but a few—had sounded like recipes for disaster to Katie. She failed to see how forcing him to be around her would do anything but alienate him more.

Katie would need to ponder the matter, but not now. She glanced at the clock, wondering what time she could respectably retire and prepare for her nightly visit from her lord and master.

An unmistakable frisson of anticipation caused her thighs to clench at the thought of another night with him. She bit her lower lip, profoundly grateful the contents of her head were private.

Betje had not suggested it, of course, but perhaps Katie might ask Dulverton to stay longer tonight rather than leave the moment they'd finished coupling. Was there some rule that said they could only do it once per night?

*You are a whore!*

Katie scowled at the voice—her mother's, of course—and hastily shoved the matter from her mind and turned back to the basket, laying out the snarled contents on the coffee table.

Betje yawned. "*Do* forgive me, my dear."

Katie merely smiled.

"I don't know *why* I'm so tired." The dowager babbled for a few more minutes before yawning a second time.

Katie could not help thinking it sounded feigned.

"How rude I am, dear Katie. Would you mind terribly if I retired for the night? I'm afraid I am not accustomed to rising so early."

Katie looked from the threads she'd just spread out everywhere. "No, of course not. I will accompany you if you wait a moment until I put all this—"

"No, no, no. *You* don't need to go to bed. It is far too early for you." She nodded to the contents of the basket. "I am so grateful to you, my dear." The dowager got to her feet. "Good night, Gerrit," she called to her son, who got to his feet, still holding his quill in one hand, an openly impatient expression on his face.

"Good night, my dear," the dowager said as she leaned down and kissed Katie's cheek.

"Good night, Betje."

Katie was rather surprised when Dulverton left his desk long enough to open the door for his mother before immediately striding back to resume his work.

At first the library seemed oppressively quiet. But at some point, she sank into the near-fugue state that took over her mind when she engaged in what had once been her favorite hobby.

"*Kathryn?*" The way Dulverton said her name made her think it wasn't the first time.

She glanced at the mess of threads—which she had loosened and was carefully untangling—and looked up to find her husband only a few feet away. "I'm sorry. I was off in my own world."

"It is kind of you to set that to rights for her."

"I don't mind."

For a change, he did not look impatient or arrogant, but thoughtful, his gaze resting on the tangled threads in her hands.

"Did you say something to me?" she prodded when it seemed he would just stare.

"It is time for bed."

Her breathing hitched, not just at his words, but at the unmistakable flare of heat that warmed his cold eyes.

"Er, just let me put all this back into the basket."

"Would it not be easier to leave it out until you have finished?"

"Yes, it would. But"—she gestured to the mess— "it is unsightly." She didn't feel it was necessary to point out just how much he disliked clutter.

"Leave it for tonight. I will not work in here until tomorrow evening. You can finish it then."

She was about to tell him that she would probably work on it tomorrow because…what else did she have to do. But instead, she merely nodded. After all, it was the first time he had indicated a willingness to spend time with her, even if they didn't actually converse while they were in the same room.

He held out his hand and she set hers in his large warm palm and allowed him to help her to her feet. They did not speak as they made their way to their rooms.

He stopped at her door, opened it, and said, "I will come to you in half an hour."

For once, Becky was not bustling around Katie's chambers. Rather than ring for her, Katie removed her jewelry and began to undress, gazing around as she did so. Jeremy and Jacob had removed the landscapes from her bedchamber, but they had found places for them in her private sitting room, which was not at all as spartan as her bedchamber.

Among the many suggestions Betje had made was that Katie should resist Dulverton's reordering of her private space. That seemed needlessly combative, especially as it was not a matter she cared enough about. Just the thought of confronting her cold-eyed husband about his decorating requirements, not to mention demanding that he discharge his mistress—Betje's most outrageous suggestion—left her feeling exhausted. Katie was tired of arguing and rebelling; she needed time to rest and recoup and then—maybe—she might take some of Betje's suggestions.

Katie had unbuttoned two of the six buttons on the back of her gown and was twisting it around so that she could reach the rest when the door opened and Becky bustled into the room.

"Oh, I am sorry, Your Grace!"

"I undressed myself for years, Becky, it is hardly a catastrophe if I have to do so again on occasion."

Becky clucked her tongue and speedily and efficiently stripped Katie down to her chemise.

"Where were you?" Katie asked as her maid pulled the pins from her hair.

"Oh. Er, Mr. Court was showing me his special method for laundering bed linen."

Katie blinked. "What?"

But Becky had gone into the dressing room to fetch a nightgown and didn't hear her.

"Does the duke not employ washerwomen?" she asked when Becky came out a moment later, bustling around her and refusing to meet Katie's eyes. "Are you blushing?"

"Of course not! I just hurried to get up here and am a bit winded." Becky yanked the chemise over Katie's head.

"Ow! You caught my ear."

"I beg your pardon," Becky said, not sounding particularly contrite.

Katie caught a brief glance at Becky's even redder face before her maid dropped her nightgown over her head.

"You should have waited until I put your gown on to unpin your hair. It is a mare's nest."

"You are exaggerating; it's only a foal's nest. So, tell me about this laundry you were doing."

"'Tis naught," Becky muttered, her color deepening. "Just that His Grace is somewhat particular about his bed linens. Mr. Court said he is especially sensitive to textures. And as he—" she worried her lower lip. "As he, er..."

"Are you trying to say *comes to my bed?*"

"Just so, Miss Saucebox," Becky snapped, her face fiery, now.

Katie laughed.

"Oh, you go ahead and laugh, you."

"I beg your pardon, Becky. I was just teasing a little." Katie then spoiled her apology by laughing again.

Becky ignored her. "Mr. Court recommended I employ his method on your bedding."

"An excellent notion."

"His Grace does not care to sleep on bedding two nights running," Becky added, still studiously avoiding Katie's gaze.

"Goodness. That sounds like a great deal of work."

"Oh, I shan't need to do it all myself. Mr. Court just wanted to show me so that I would be able to keep a close eye on the laundry woman, who is heavy-handed with the starch if she is not kept in check."

"Engage more help if you need it, Becky. I don't want you run off your feet. Or getting nasty, chapped hands from doing endless washing."

Becky finished combing out the tangles and plaited Katie's hair into a thick rope. "Mr. Court is very knowledgeable about a great many things. I—I was wrong about him being standoffish. He is merely reserved and a man of few words."

Katie made a noncommittal noise.

"I am extremely fortunate that he is here to advise me," Becky added when Katie didn't speak, her tone a bit defiant.

Katie was bemused by her friend's attraction to her husband's valet. Court was the sort of man it would be easy to overlook. He was tall and lanky with dark hair shorn close to his head, hooded eyes, and unexceptional features. It fascinated her that Becky had become so enamored of such a dull-looking man.

Katie blinked at the thought. Hadn't Andrew called Dulverton *dull?* And Katie did not see how that nickname could ever fit her husband. Perhaps dullness, like beauty, was in the eye of the beholder?

"The Duke of Chatham keeps an under valet to manage his laundry," she added, sounding defensive.

Katie was amused. "Does he? I did not realize my brother-in-law was such a stickler. I look forward to having softer bedding and garments," she added soothingly when she saw Becky was looking a bit ruffled.

Becky gave a low *hmph* and tied the ribbons of Katie's cap beneath her chin.

"That's too tight," Katie demurred, taking the ties from Becky's fingers. "Well, don't work all night on my laundry. With Court," a teasing imp made her add.

"No, no, of course not." Color flooded to her friend's face yet again, and Becky opened her mouth, but then shut it and regally inclined her head. "If that is all, Your Grace."

"Yes, that is all for tonight." On impulse, she seized the smaller woman and gave her a loud kiss on the cheek. "Thank you, Becks."

"Oh, leave off, you," Beck sputtered, scrubbing a hand over her wet cheek and giving Katie a playful shove.

Naturally, Dulverton chose that moment to open the connecting door, pausing on the threshold and regarding them with such a look of startlement on his severe features that Katie laughed harder.

Becky, however, looked mortified and dropped a curtsey low enough for a king before scurrying from the room.

***

Just when Gerrit did not believe his wife could look any more beautiful, he discovered he was wrong. He had no idea what she and her dresser were up to that had caused such mirth, but the laughter illuminated her lovely face in such a way that his chest actually *hurt* looking at her. Even her staid nightgown, tightly plaited hair, and the ugly, matronly nightcap could not dim her allure.

"I beg your pardon, Dulverton," she said, tucking away her smile as if it was something dirty.

Her apology rankled, even though engaging in such mirth with a servant was undignified. Gerrit shut the door and entered the room. "You needn't apologize to me for being happy, Kathryn."

The last traces of her good humor fled. "Duly noted, Your Grace."

"I would prefer your hair be unbound when I come to you. And I do not care to see you in a nightcap."

She seemed to swell in size and even Gerrit could recognize the signs of an impending tantrum. "Please," he added.

She hesitated a long moment before her hands went to the laces of her cap. Once she removed it, she carelessly tossed it onto the bench at the end of the bed.

Gerrit gritted his teeth and turned his back until the garment was hidden from view, his eyes on his wife as she pulled the thick auburn rope over her shoulder and untied the bit of ribbon. When she would have thrown it down with the cap, he wordlessly plucked it from her fingers and slid it into the pocket of his banyan, his thumb absently caressing the smooth strip of silk.

She raised her eyebrows but did not comment.

Gerrit watched in fascination as she unraveled the strands and her hair, the color of banked coals, sprang to life.

"Curls," he said, and then wished he could snatch the stupid word back.

She gave him a rueful look. "Yes. A great many of them." The curls quickly built into a thick froth as she carded her fingers through the bright auburn spirals that fell to the middle of her back.

The compulsion to feel it was too strong to resist and Gerrit took a fistful. Kathryn stiffened but did not move away when he raised the curls to his nose and inhaled, pleased that he could smell the scent of woman rather than heavy perfume.

Her chest was rising and falling faster as she watched him, desire blazing in her eyes. When she tipped her head back and parted her lips, he lowered his mouth over hers. It was the first time they'd kissed since that night in the garden, and her body went pleasingly pliant against his, the press of her full, soft breasts pushing against his banyan.

Savage bolts of pleasure shot from his groin to every part of his body, speeding his heart and fogging his brain. He slid his fingers into her hair and cupped the back of her head, tilting her so that he could feast on her sweetness, and she *was* sweet, he was not imagining it. Caramel and the faint hint of raspberries. Gerrit normally had no taste for dessert, but he was enjoying it tonight.

He slipped his free hand between the front edges of her dressing gown and splayed his fingers over the ripe globes of her buttocks before pulling her close enough that his erection was pressed firmly against the gentle swell of her belly.

He was pleasurably surprised when her hands cupped his hips until she was mirroring his actions, her long, delicate fingers turning into claws as she dug into the muscles of his arse.

Gerrit deepened his kiss, fucking into her with slow, thorough sweeps of his tongue, his actions illustrative of what he would soon be doing to her. His hips rolled, pulsing his sensitive shaft against her soft body. An answering shudder wracked her tall, slender frame and she ground herself against him, jerky with need.

He steeled himself and pulled away, her lips chasing his until he set her at arm's length. "I want this off," he said in a gravelly voice, pushing her dressing gown off her shoulders and for once not caring that it pooled untidily on the floor.

He fumbled with the buttons on her nightgown, unfastening just enough to pull the garment over her head.

"Dulverton," she said, staying his hands before he could lift the garment over her head.

Gerrit looked up from her nightgown to find her staring up at him, her lips swollen from his kisses, her pupils huge black pools.

"What is it?" he asked, his voice rough with need.

"May I—may I remove your robe?"

Gerrit felt positively woozy. When had a woman ever wanted to look at *him*? Even his mistresses—whom he had paid ridiculously well—had never been in any hurry to uncover his brutish body. He jerked a nod. "Yes."

The syllable was barely out of his mouth before her fingers tore at the sash. Gerrit shrugged the garment off his shoulders, not caring when it fell to the floor.

It seemed it was a night for firsts.

His prick was heavy and swollen and he wouldn't have believed it could harden any more, but when she gawked at him, her tongue peeking from between her coral pink lips, his balls clenched, and a hot bead of pre-ejaculate slid down his throbbing shaft.

"Oh," she mumbled, the soft sound just about undoing him.

"Arms up. Now, Kathryn," he ordered when she continued to stare at his prick, his voice even harsher. He'd be spilling on their bare feet if he didn't get inside her soon.

She wordlessly obeyed and Gerrit dropped the fine muslin to join the pile, his jaw dropping as he reveled in her perfection. It was the first time he'd seen her completely nude, and the sight wiped every thought from his head.

He could not say how long they both stared at one another without touching, but it was long enough that the cool air caused her pale, flawless skin to grow goose pimples.

Gerrit wrenched his gaze away from her mouthwatering breasts, caught up her hand, led her to the bed, and yanked back the bedding. "Get in," he ordered gruffly, shamelessly gorging on her plump arse as she mounted the two steps that led to the high mattress.

He climbed in with more haste than grace and lowered his torso over hers, unable to resist one more taste of her sweet lips. She opened to him, welcoming his tongue into her wet heat with a low, encouraging moan, her arms snaking around his neck and holding him close.

He'd intended the kiss to be a brief one, but she rippled beneath him like human silk, her hips lifting as she offered herself to him.

Gerrit took up her gauntlet, kissing her so deeply and without reserve that for one strange moment it was hard to tell where he left off and she began.

Only the dull, painful ache in his balls finally penetrated the fog of lust that had built between them. He pulled back to give her a chance to breathe. "Are you cold?"

"I'm burning up," she said, her voice barely a whisper.

Gerrit slid a hand down her flat belly, and she spread her legs for him without being told, her submissive response squeezing his balls and sending more moisture running down his shaft.

Gerrit wasn't the only one who was wet. Even before he slid a finger inside her body, he could feel the slick heat coating her soft thighs. He worked her with slow, deep caresses, taking his time and preparing her properly.

She shivered and rocked her hips, so responsive to his touch that it was a pleasure to tease orgasms from her. There was also a perverse sort of pleasure to be had from denying himself release until he was so bloody hard that he ached to fuck her.

Gerrit imposed control over his eager body, suddenly recalling how much she'd enjoyed his vulgar praise the night before he leaned closer and murmured, "So wet and tight for me."

The way she shuddered and writhed told him he'd not mistaken the matter, and he smiled to himself as her pussy squeezed his fingers.

"Be a good girl and take one more for me," he said a moment later, easing a second finger into her silky sheath.

She clenched around him and squirmed delightfully, her face so red it looked sunburned. It amused him how much her body enjoyed his words and yet her mind still rebelled. Making her blush and cry out and shake with need was becoming something of a mania with him.

Gerrit strummed her bud with his thumb while he worked her, teasing her toward fulfillment but stopping just at the edge.

She ground her hips, trying for more friction. "Please," she gasped.

"Please, what?" He was bloody impressed by how cool he sounded when he was teetering on the edge of exploding.

"I want—I want—"

"What do you want?" he asked, wanting to hear a bit of naughty talk himself.

Sharp, white teeth sank into her lower lip while her hips rolled beneath his fingers. Just when he'd given up hoping that she would voice her demands, she said, "I want you inside me when I—*you know.*"

Gerrit was amused by her unwillingness to say the word *orgasm*. She might have fucked a servant five years before, but it was clear her experience was not extensive.

"You will get what you want," he promised, sucking her nipples to hard points, until her breathing was ragged, and she could not stop writhing. "But only when I decide to give it to you."

She narrowed her eyes up at him, anger and arousal vying for ascendance in her gaze. He knew she was pondering some insolent response in that clever head of hers. But she must have thought better of it because she kept her tongue behind her teeth. Gerrit had no idea why he liked making her wait for her pleasure, but there was no denying it heightened his own arousal to a nearly unbearable level.

He gently withdrew his fingers and lined up his cock, savoring the sight of his blunt crown breaching her slick pink flesh. She was so tight that his eyes threatened to roll back in their sockets as he sank deep inside her.

*Control.*

Gerrit gathered up the tattered remnants of his self-control and fell into a slow, steady rhythm before reaching between their bodies to stroke her. Her eyes drifted shut and her lips parted, an expectant expression settling on her lovely face.

He'd scarcely commenced his erotic caresses when she gasped, his only warning before her climax tore through her. He remained still and deep within her as her sheath squeezed him over and over, tormenting him until he thought he would explode.

Only when the final, faint wave of pleasure rippled through her did he move his hips, needing only a few hard thrusts before he found his release.

A powerful lethargy seized him even before the last spasm. He didn't so much decide to close his eyes and take a moment to rest as his body decided for him.

***

When Dulverton suddenly collapsed on top of Katie it pressed the air from her lungs and she experienced a moment of panic. She quickly discovered that of course she could still draw breath with his weight on her. Just not *much* breath.

Being surrounded by his heavy, hot body was so lovely that Katie did not want to move and risk waking him, so she held her position—her arms wrapped around the broad muscles of his back and her legs curled around his thighs. Her lips twitched into a smile when she realized that his breathing had become even and deep. The stiff and stern Duke of Dulverton had fallen asleep. On top of her. Inside her.

It felt wickedly decadent to lie beneath him, pinioned by his softening shaft, trapped beneath the massive, yet somehow vulnerable, weight of his sleeping body. She shifted as minutely as she could, stopping when she reached a position that allowed her to enjoy his considerable weight and still breathe. She was desperately tempted to slide her hands back down to his bottom, which she yearned to explore in more detail, but she suspected he would wake if she began groping him, no matter how stealthily. Of course, she could still never fall asleep like this. Not in a thousand years could she…

Katie woke in utter darkness, needing several seconds to recall that she was at Briarly in her bed. The evening came back to her in a rush—Dulverton making love to her and then falling asleep while on top of her.

And inside her.

She patted the mattress around her, confirming what she had already guessed: he was gone. He must have extinguished the candles when he left.

Only the ache in her thighs remained.

Once again, another night had gone by without them having a chance to converse—nothing serious, just the sort of chatter she had engaged in with Jasper.

*Clearly, Dulverton is* not *Jasper.*

And Katie was glad of that fact. But surely lovers spoke to each other? How would they ever get to know each other if they never talked? They seemed most at ease with each other in the bedchamber. If they could not talk here, then where?

Katie closed her eyes, too tired to think about the tangled mess that was her marriage.

It was better that he'd gone while she slept, that way there would be no awkward leave-taking.

That is what Katie told herself.

# Chapter Seventeen

The next four days at Briarly followed the pattern of the first one: Katie woke late and sated from a night of passion, broke her fast alone, spent the afternoon learning housekeeping matters, exploring the extensive gardens, visiting the massive succession houses and selecting flowers—which were allowed in the dining room provided there were two arrangements and they were exactly the same—eating dinner with her husband, Betje, and David Sessions, spending a few hours on needlework in the library, and then receiving her husband in her bed.

Every night she tried to initiate conversation with her husband and every night she failed. Dulverton never responded beyond a curt *yes* or *no* and Katie took the coward's way out and did not try to keep him in her bed again.

She also spent some time answering the veritable flood of letters she received from her family. To the countess she penned her third polite but adamant rejection of her offer to visit. To her sisters—all except Hy, who was still angry at her because marrying Dulverton was evidently not penance enough for her stickler of a sister— she sent short, cheerful missives about Briarly, deliberately omitting any mention of her marital situation.

Katie spent most of each day with the dowager, who advised her to rest for a week and commence morning calls the following Wednesday. "People will understand if you take a week to settle in, but you really cannot wait much longer. Although given Gerrit's insistence on privacy—and the fact that he long ago trained the neighbors to expect little in the way of socializing from him—you might be able to get away with two weeks. But that is the limit."

Yes, Katie knew exactly how it was to be a duchess in a rural setting. After all, she had lived with her sister Hy for five years. Every year it was the same when they'd retired to Chatham Park for the summer and autumn. Poor Hy was forced to make the social rounds before she could retire from center stage and leave the planning of dinners, house parties, the annual ball, and the public day to her husband's well-trained secretary.

The only thing that changed on Katie's fifth day at Briarly was that it was a Sunday and, for the first time, Dulverton was in the breakfast room when she went downstairs.

He stood when she entered. "Good morning, Your Grace."

He only called her *Kathryn* when they were alone. She called him *Dulverton* all the time. Maybe that was something she could change tonight? She could call him *Heh-REET*. Would he notice? And if he did, would he care?

Her husband was looking at her curiously, making her realize she'd never responded. "Good morning, Dulverton." She nodded at Thomas to pour her a cup of coffee. Once she'd filled a plate with fruit, toast, and a ramekin with a coddled egg, Dulverton closed the newspaper he was reading and set it aside.

"Please do not stop reading on my account," she said.

"I was finished." He glanced at the clock.

Katie was instantly on edge. "I was told we would not leave until a quarter to eleven." She sounded resentful to her own ears.

But Dulverton didn't appear to notice. "Correct," he said, as curt as ever. He glanced at the footman. "Please go and see if the dowager plans to join us this morning."

"At once, Your Grace."

"You have not ridden since coming to Briarly," Dulverton said once they were alone.

Katie looked up, surprised he'd initiated a conversation. Had he done so in the past? Only to chastise her, she thought.

"I have been occupied exploring and gaining my bearings." She didn't mention the other reason—that she'd hardly felt confident enough to enter her husband's stables and demand a mount without his permission—because she was revolted by her own timidity. The last thing Dulverton needed to know was how much his displeasure terrified her.

The duke's austere face was neither approving nor disapproving.

Katie experienced one of the bizarre flashbacks to the night before and hastily lowered her gaze, as if somehow Dulverton might see that she was imagining his face—more specifically, the expression on it—when he was looming above her and moving inside her. His eyes rarely left hers, unless it was to inspect her body with a hungry avidity that sent thrills through her. He left the candles burning, sometimes lighting even more, evidently comfortable in her bedchamber now that there was nothing on the walls to offend his sensibilities.

Plenty of expressions flickered across his normally impassive face when he was in her bed: raw carnality, sensual satisfaction, and masculine possessiveness, and so forth. One of her favorite expressions was the one he wore for the few seconds when he achieved release, when bliss transformed him.

Now he was looking at her as if she was a stranger, and not a very interesting one. He was certainly a stranger to her and seemed determined to remain that way. Betje was deluded to think he wanted more. And Katie was deluded for hoping Betje was right. The best thing she could do is—

"I purchased a mount for you," Dulverton said, the words pulling her from her unhappy thoughts.

"You bought me a horse?" she said stupidly.

"Yes."

"Oh. Well, thank you."

His piercing gaze slid away and then he cleared his throat. "After church we will go for a ride."

She felt a twinge of irritation at his dictatorial manner but swallowed it down. After all, she wanted to go riding. She was accustomed to going most mornings in the country and had missed it greatly. "I would like that."

He grunted. "Finish your meal."

Again, she gritted her teeth but obeyed him without causing a fuss.

A moment later he spoke again. "My mother says she will accompany you on morning calls next week."

"Correct." The word slipped out before she could stop herself.

If Dulverton noticed the mocking echo of his own favorite word, he gave no sign of it. "Two of the neighboring gentry are widowers, so you will not want to leave cards with them. Both have estates touching Briarly so I will make the necessary gesture," he said, shocking her with his unprecedented garrulousness.

Before she could come up with a response, Thomas entered. "Her Grace begs your pardon, but she will not be attending the service this morning."

Katie found it passing strange that Betje would ignore an opportunity to get out of the house. She was a woman who enjoyed company and had mentioned her active social life at Spenwood with longing.

If Dulverton found his mother's decision unusual, he did not show it. Instead, he looked at the clock.

Katie glanced at her half-full cup of coffee with regret and tossed her napkin onto the table and stood. "I am ready."

Whatever talkative muse had seized Dulverton at the breakfast table deserted him in the carriage and they made the short journey to the church in silence.

The vicarage sat just on the edge of the village of Colton, which was comprised of a few dozen cottages, a quaint inn called the Sleeping Boar, a smithy, a post office, and a tiny mercantile shop. Katie assumed the town had had no reason to grow any larger given its proximity to Lyme Regis.

The carriage deposited them outside the vicarage at one minute before the hour and most of the pews were full as they made their way to the front of the small church.

Katie was not surprised when Dulverton led her to a private box. It was elegantly appointed with red velvet cushions on the wooden seats, the walls of the box ending just above Katie's chin. The top edge had a narrow strip of stained glass that was framed by intricately carved wood. The slight amount of concealment that was afforded by the high walls of the box was not quite enough to ameliorate the feeling of being watched, so it was only after the service began that she was able to relax and sneak surreptitious glances at her surroundings.

The church was as elegant and snug as a little jewel box and was obviously lovingly cared for. The intricate arched stained-glass windows, she saw by one of the brass plaques, had been donated by a Duke of Dulverton in 1701.

There were six private boxes, two large ones on either side of the aisle and two smaller boxes behind each of those. The two boxes behind Katie and Dulverton were filled by large families.

The large box across the aisle was every bit as lovely and ornate as Dulverton's, but it was empty and only one of the smaller boxes behind it was occupied. A modestly garbed woman who looked to be the same age as Betje sat alone.

The woman caught Katie staring and smiled at her. She felt flustered but her lips naturally curved upward before she hastily turned away. After that encounter, she kept her attention on the vicar until the service was over.

It seemed to Katie that the entire congregation was lingering when she and Dulverton exited the church. Her husband stopped in front of the vicar and two women and turned to Katie. "This is the Reverend Adam Nicholson, Mrs. Nicholson, and his sister, Miss Dorcas Nicholson. Reverend, this is my wife."

"It is a pleasure to meet you," Katie said, smiling at the trio as they bowed and curtsied.

"The pleasure is ours, Your Grace," the vicar said. "And may I offer you both my sincere congratulations."

"Thank you," Dulverton said stiffly.

"It is always such a delight to see faces in the private boxes," the vicar went on.

"And this summer they will *all* have occupants," his wife chimed in. "It will be the first time in two years that Lady Grimsby will be with us."

Katie stiffened at a name she had not heard in five years. Jasper's grandmother lived *here*? How did she not know that?

"Is aught amiss Your Grace?" the vicar asked, a notch of concern between his eyes.

"No, no, just a goose walking across my grave. The, er, Countess of Grimsby lives here?" she asked faintly.

"She only spends a portion of each summer here," the vicar said. "And these past two years not even that. She has been on the Continent with Lord Jasper, her grandson, and his wife—who was very ill and unfortunately died. We've recently heard her ladyship will arrive at the end of the month."

Jasper's wife was dead?

"Do you know the countess?" Miss Nicholson asked politely.

"Er, no, we have never met," Katie said.

The vicar turned to the duke and started talking about something else.

Katie blocked out the man's voice, her thoughts on Jasper's grandmother. Or Jasper, rather. Would he be accompanying his grandmother?

Good God. That would be a disaster! She was finding it difficult to get enough air. What were the chances she would move right next door to Jasper's grandmother?

When Katie had first gone to London, she'd been terrified every day for a month that she would encounter Jasper. Thankfully, he had taken his new wife off on a Grand Tour and she'd neither seen him nor even heard any gossip about him in almost five blissful years.

If the countess rarely came to her estate for more than a brief visit it was unlikely that she would bring her grandson with her. Wasn't it?

Out of the corner of her eye Katie saw the woman who'd been in the private box. Rather than stop and speak to the vicar or Dulverton, she slipped past without a word. Mrs. Nicholson followed the woman's progress with narrowed eyes, her lips tightly pursed and her cheeks a fiery pink.

What on earth was that about?

Katie didn't have a chance to think about Jasper or the mysterious woman as the next twenty minutes were consumed with nonstop introductions to at least forty people who had waited to meet her and greet the duke.

Not until she was back in the carriage with Dulverton did she recall the woman. "Who was the woman in the private box across the aisle?"

Dulverton's jaw flexed and he said, after a pause, "That was Mrs. St. Clare, one of my tenants."

Katie wanted to ask why a mere tenant had a private box, which were usually reserved for neighborhood gentry, but his expression was even more forbidding than usual, so she held her tongue and tried to think of anything other than the possibility of Jasper showing up on her doorstep this summer.

Less than ten minutes later Dulverton was handing her out of the coach. "Will an hour be enough time to change into your riding clothing?"

"A quarter of an hour will be plenty of time."

His eyebrows rose, but after a brief hesitation he nodded and said, "Very well," before turning away to say something to one of the grooms.

Becky was not in Katie's room when she reached it, so she rang the bell. She'd just removed her spencer when her maid arrived, no longer garbed in her church finery.

"You must have hurried back," Katie said as Becky helped her out of her gown. "I'll want the dark green habit as I'm going riding," she added.

Becky nodded. "We didn't have to face the neighborhood gauntlet that you did after the service." She disappeared into the dressing room with Katie's gown.

Katie sat and removed her earrings.

Becky returned and laid the habit out on the bed. "It is a pretty little church, isn't it?"

"Yes, it is."

"Mr. Court said that His Grace's grandfather purchased the windows."

"Oh, you rode with him to church?"

"Yes, along with Mr. and Mrs. Cranston."

Katie smiled at her friend's red face and defensive tone; clearly Mr. Court was a sensitive subject.

A glance in the mirror showed Katie that her own face was more than a little flushed with excitement. She was delighted to be going riding—it had been more than a week.

*You're more delighted about who you are going riding* with.

That was true, too.

It seemed that Becky wasn't the only woman in the house who'd lost her sense over a reserved, haughty, unfathomable man.

# Chapter Eighteen

Gerrit did not honestly expect his wife to be ready in a quarter of an hour and was surprised when she arrived with three minutes to spare.

"You did not think I could do it, did you?" she asked, smirking up at him and slapping her whip against her palm.

He felt a rare twinge of amusement at her challenging look. "No."

She laughed and Gerrit tried not to enjoy the sound too much.

Burrell, his stable master, led Kathryn's new mount into the courtyard, and Gerrit took the animal's reins and presented the horse to his wife. "This is Robin, Your Grace."

Kathryn's eyes glowed as she approached the chestnut. "He is exquisite," she cooed, offering her slender gloved hand to the fidgeting gelding.

Gerrit felt a burst of pleasure at her approval—almost enough to override his unease at having a chestnut horse in his stables. Like his father, grandfather, and great-grandfather before him, Gerrit had always purchased Friesians and always in their traditional color of black. But when he'd approached Burrell about a mount for Kathryn, the stablemaster had mentioned seeing a rare chestnut Friesian at the breeder Gerrit favored. Gerrit had known upon sight that this was the horse for Kathryn. Not only was Robin extraordinarily beautiful, but the gelding had a sweet temperament with a touch of mischief in his eyes. Perfect for his mistress.

It was just a shame the breeder had not had *two* chestnuts. He decided the pang of discomfort he felt owning just one chestnut was easily offset by his wife's obvious pleasure. Of course that was a thought that *also* left him feeling uneasy. Since when did he care so much about her likes or dislikes?

Kathryn stroked and fussed over the animal and cut Gerrit a shy look. "I love him. Thank you. He has the most unusual reddish chestnut coat I have ever seen."

Gerrit thought so, too. Indeed, with her standing beside the animal he was amazed at how similar in color the gelding's long, rippling mane was to her lovely hair.

"The breeder said he has only ever seen two chestnut Friesians in all his years. Most are black, although you will see the occasional bay or gray."

Her brilliant green eyes turned to him, softer than he'd ever seen them before. "Well, he certainly is lovely. Thank you," she said again.

Any unease at having a sole chestnut horse in his stables—or wanting to please his wife—drained away at her obvious happiness at his gift.

"Come. I will help you mount," he said, the strange emotions in his chest making him sound abrupt and causing her to flinch, her glorious eyes shuttering.

*Damnation.* Would he ever learn how to speak to her without uttering commands or snarling?

Gerrit slid his hands around her slender waist and easily lifted her into the saddle. While she fastened her train he lengthened the stirrup. "How is that?" he asked, looking up and meeting her now-cool gaze.

"Perhaps one more."

He lowered the stirrup by another notch.

"That is good," she said before he could ask.

He mounted Centurion and they rode in silence as they left the courtyard. Gerrit knew that he would need to be the one to speak first after he'd been so curt back at the stables.

Christ but he hated small talk.

He glanced at her. "Your seat is excellent."

He'd not meant to sound condescending but judging by her slight smirk and the way her cool green gaze flickered over him he'd obviously failed.

Heat pooled in Gerrit's groin—not a desirable reaction when one was astride a horse—as she studied him with a lingering thoroughness.

"As is yours," she finally said, and then turned to face forward.

He snorted softly and adjusted himself. He deserved that.

Gerrit tried to think of something to say but his mind was infuriatingly blank.

After several moments of silence Katheryn saved him the bother by saying, "My sister is excessively fond of riding, and Chatham's cousin, Andrew Derrick"— she cut him a quick, not so polished look— "breeds hunters and often brings them to Chatham Park for the three of us to ride." She suddenly chuckled. "Chatham has threatened to submit a bill to Andrew for all the free training."

"Do you hunt?" he asked.

"Not as much as I would like, but—" She broke off.

"But?" he prodded.

She paused, but then said, "Chatham is generous, but I scarcely wanted to keep a string of hunters at his expense."

Gerrit thought her impulse did her credit. "I will see you are well mounted when we go to Spenwood."

"I did not mean to suggest—"

"You are my wife, Kathryn," he said, once again sounding curt. Gerrit sighed. He needed to do better. "If hunting is something you enjoy then it would be my pleasure to mount you."

Her delicate throat flexed, and a faint flush spread across her cheeks. "Thank you."

Bloody hell but conversation was exhausting.

"Is it far to the water?" she asked.

"It takes half an hour."

"Is that where we are going?"

"I thought today I would show you some of the estate. Specifically, there are a series of paths that will take you in a loop back to Briarly and make for a pleasant ride."

"I would like that. Do I need to take a groom with me?"

He cut her a glance. "I would prefer it."

"Even on your land?"

Gerrit frowned. What was she trying to say?

"I would rather ride alone—at least on the estate. I did so at Chatham Park and also at Wych House."

Gerrit pondered her request. His father had permitted Amelia to ride without a groom. He supposed there was no danger on his own land. At least not until she was with child. He would reconsider the matter at that point.

He turned to find her waiting for him. "You may ride alone provided you exercise care."

Her smile was blinding. "Thank you, Dulverton. I will be careful."

He hastily turned away, his heart pounding uncomfortably hard. What on earth was the matter with him today?

"My family's home is in Hampshire, and we were only half a day from the coast, but we only went one time, when I was very little."

Gerrit slid a look at her and saw that she was facing forward. Was she expecting a response from him?

"I see," he said.

It must have been an adequate answer because she went on, "We went to visit with my father's younger sister, Lady Fitzroy."

"Er, did you enjoy it?" he asked, genuinely curious.

She turned to him. "I did, very much."

Gerrit could not look away. "I will take you to the beach."

Once again, she smiled. "I would like that."

He had no idea of what to say, so they rode in silence until they reached a fork in the path, and he led them to the left.

"Where does the other path lead?"

"It goes through Echo Forest to Briarly's Dower House."

"I did not know there was one. Is it occupied?"

"Yes."

She flinched at his harsh tone, the open, happy expression on her face dimming.

"Mrs. St. Clare lives there."

"Oh, the lady from the private box at church."

"Correct." Gerrit was not ashamed of Amelia, but he did not relish explaining her presence to his new wife. Especially not with his mother here. Once the dowager went home—soon, he hoped—Gerrit would attempt to explain his father's arrangement with—

"What is that child doing?" Kathryn pointed to the pasture off to the right where he could see a blond head in the tall grass. "The poor thing is sobbing her heart out." She reined in and awkwardly slid down from her horse.

"Kathryn, wait." Gerrit quickly dismounted. "I will go see what is amiss. You stay—"

But she was already hurrying through the grass, leaving Gerrit to hold the horses.

***

"Why, what is the matter?" Katie asked, dropping to her haunches when the child— a tow-headed little girl—stared up at her with big pale blue eyes.

"Bobby and Davy weft me," she said, her chin quivering.

"How dreadful of them. Are they your brothers?"

She nodded, lower lip thrust out.

"Brothers *can* be awful," Katie said. "What is your name?"

"Susan."

"That's a pretty name. Where do you live?"

Susan pointed in the general direction of the path.

Katie held out a hand. "Why don't you come with me, and I will take you home."

Susan shook her head.

"I'll let you ride on Robin. That's my horse—the pretty copper one." She pointed to Dulverton, who was leading the horses in their direction.

Susan's eyes grew even larger. "I can wide on her?"

Katie bit back a grin at the girl's adorable inability to say her r's and l's. "Robin is actually a boy horse, but yes, you may ride him. Just think of how your brothers will envy you."

That was all the encouragement Susan needed.

Katie took her hand and led her toward Dulverton. "Her name is Susan, and she says she lives just around the curve. Her older brothers abandoned her. I told her we would take her home and she could ride Robin."

"I know who she is and where she lives." He looked down at the child, who gazed up at him, placidly chewing on her finger and clearly not afraid.

Katie smiled at the little girl. "Susan, this is the Duke of—"

But Susan dropped a creditable curtsey. "Good day, Your Gwace."

Katie should not have been surprised; after all, Susan's father must be Dulverton's tenant.

"You should not be out here alone," Dulverton said crisply. "I will speak to your brothers."

Susan nodded solemnly and then pointed to Robin.

"No, you will ride with me." He turned to Katie. "It would be too difficult for you to ride with her on that saddle. "Let me help you up."

"I thought I'd lead Robin with her on his back."

"It is too far to walk." His big hands closed around Katie's waist, and he lifted her into the saddle with ease, making her feel like a waif—when she most certainly was not—before turning to the little girl. "Come here, Susan."

The child went to him eagerly and chortled happily when he lifted her into the saddle. Only after he'd swung up behind her did Katie realize they might be father and daughter. Not just their pale hair and light eyes, but also their strong, almost blunt, features.

Bemused, she stole glimpses at the pair, more and more uneasy. By the time a small cottage came into view, Katie was feeling grim.

Outside the house a woman was talking to two boys. Judging by the way she was waving her finger at them they were getting a scolding.

All three turned at the sound of the horses.

"Susan!" the woman cried out, running toward them.

Susan laughed with delight and waved. "I'm widing! I'm widing!"

The duke dismounted before lifting down the little girl, who ran to her mother and was swiftly caught in a crushing embrace. "You had me worried half to death!"

Susan's lower lip once again shoved out, the glory of the horse ride forgotten. "Davy and Bobby *weft* me, Mama."

"I know they did, dearest." The woman wrenched her gaze from her child, her cheeks flushing a fetching cherry red when she turned to the duke. She hastily lowered Susan and dipped a low curtsey.

"Thank you for bringing her back, Your Grace."

Dulverton ignored her thanks and turned a glare on the two boys, who hastily doffed their caps. "Did you abandon your sister by Mr. Roman's pasture?"

The older one—perhaps ten or eleven—cut a nervous glance at his mother before nodded. "Aye, Your Grace. But she was followin' us even though we told her not to."

"That's as may be, but her safety should always be your first concern. Mr. Roman's bull is in that field and Susan might have wandered into it."

Both boys suddenly looked horrified, as did their mother.

"Do not leave her alone like that again," Dulverton chided.

"Aye, Your Grace."

"Thank you, Your Grace," the woman said again, nervously pushing back a silky lock of dark blonde hair that had come loose. Her gaze slid to Katie.

Dulverton either did not see her curious look or chose to ignore it.

When it became clear that her husband would make no introduction Katie said, "How do you do?" She had aimed for amusingly wry but landed somewhere between confrontational and arrogant.

The other woman looked startled but dropped a curtsey. "Anna Wilson, Your Grace. Would—would you care for some cider, Your Graces?" Mrs. Wilson asked, cutting a look between the two of them.

"Not today," Dulverton said curtly.

The crushed look on the other woman's face made Katie feel guilty for her earlier aggression. She forced a smile and said, "Perhaps another time, Mrs. Wilson."

Her answer—as polite as it was—made the other woman's cheeks flame and her mortified gaze slid to the duke.

He ignored her and mounted his horse, dipping his chin slightly before leading his horse back to the path.

"Is Mrs. Wilson the wife of one of your tenant farmers?" Katie asked when Dulverton made no effort to speak.

"She is a tenant, but the cottage does not have a farm."

"What does her husband do?"

Dulverton's lips tightened. "She does not have a husband."

"She is young to be a widow."

His eyes narrowed at either her expression or tone or both, but he did not speak.

Katie's mind bounced the beautiful woman and her three handsome tow-headed young children to the attractive cottage to the fact that the duke knew the children well enough to deliver a fatherly chastisement. Was that because they *were* his children?

She looked at her husband; his haughty profile was to her. He had told her he did not take lovers from among the *ton*. Did that mean he kept one on his own property? How convenient that would be for him!

Seething, Katie turned away from Dulverton, struggling to understand the emotions roiling inside her. She identified disappointment, anger, despair, and something else. Something that felt suspiciously like jealousy.

Good God. She hoped not. She didn't love Dulverton. She didn't even *like* him. But she loved what they did in her bed every night. Could she really be so shallow that she would feel jealousy for a man who clearly felt nothing for her except lust?

If that was true, then she was even more foolish than she had believed possible. She had entered this marriage with the knowledge that her husband thought so little of her that he did not care if she took lovers. All he cared about was an heir and that she did not bring shame on his family name as his first wife had.

The duke's voice interrupted her frantic musing. "No, not that way," he said as Katie guided Robin toward the right-hand fork in the path. "We will keep to the left."

"What is to the right?" She asked the question more to keep her thoughts from spiraling out of control rather than a desire to converse.

"That leads to the Morris farm."

"Who is Morris?"

"Morris works the largest of my tenant farms."

"You are not going to introduce me to the Morrises?"

He blinked. "I had not thought to do so."

"Why not?"

"There hardly seems to be any point."

"There is no point in the mistress of Briarly meeting her tenants?" Katie could not help thinking of Hy, Selina, Phoebe, and Aurelia who all knew their dependents by name.

"You will not spend much time at Briarly in the future, so it—"

"So, where *will* I live, then? Or do I have no choice in the matter?" she demanded, the tension inside her boiling over.

He opened his mouth, but then closed it, his indecisive expression looking strange on his stern, determined features.

"I suppose you will want me to live at Spenwood with your mother?"

He regarded her steadily. Normally, Katie found it difficult to meet his gaze, but not today.

"I told you there are several other estates besides Spenwood and Briarly for you to—"

"What if I wish to spend my summers at Briarly?"

"That would not be wise."

"Why not?"

"You know why."

"You mean it will inconvenience you to have your wife in the same place where you keep your mistress?"

His face, which had worn a faintly perplexed expression, hardened at her words. "I mean that you and I can never be in each other's company for ten minutes without arguing."

So, no denial about his mistress, then.

Fuming, now, she glared at him. "*Never?*" she repeated scoffingly. "We have been married exactly a week and this is only the second or third time we have actually been alone together."

He raised an eyebrow at her.

"Other than *that*," she hissed. How dare he allude to their time in bed! Especially now that she knew he kept a mistress on hand. Just when did he have time to *service* poor Anna Wilson. Not that three children didn't speak of a great deal of *servicing* going on at some point.

Katie thrust the vile thought from her head and said, "We are having a discussion right now, not an argument."

"We are disagreeing, as we always do," he said firmly. "We are also off the point."

"I'm sorry, what *was* the point, pray?"

"Your question about living at Briarly."

"Ah yes," she snapped. "And me living at Briarly is not permissible, I take it."

Dulverton gave a pained sigh. "When my visits to your chambers are no longer necessary then why on earth would we live in the same house and expose ourselves to such disharmony if there is no reason?" He looked genuinely perplexed.

His words were worse than a slap. Actually, they were like a slap, a kick, *and* being spat upon. "No reason? We are *married*." Only after the words left her mouth did she realize she was shouting. Not only that, but her claim was hardly compelling. After all, her parents were married and lived in different countries to avoid each other. Plenty of married people lived separate lives.

*And you agreed to exactly that.*

That was true; she had. All Dulverton wanted was her womb. Yet here Katie was, begging to live in the same house with him. She was pathetic.

His eyebrows had descended, and he was staring at her as if he'd never seen her before. "Yes, we are married. But what does—"

"Never mind. I misspoke. You are correct."

He hesitated only a fraction of a second before nodding, accepting her admission with a calm arrogance that made her hands itch to shove him off his horse.

Katie smiled at him, although it was not a nice smile, and said, "There is no reason for you to introduce me to *your* people."

Again, he nodded.

*There is no need for you to put yourself out, dear husband, because I am perfectly capable of introducing myself if and when I decide to meet them.*

She did not speak another word for the rest of the ride, not that he seemed to care.

When she returned to her chambers to change out of her riding clothes, she discovered that her flux had commenced.

So, she was not with child and would not be expected to remove herself from Briarly and her husband's presence just yet.

Katie hated the burst of joyous relief she felt at the thought. What was wrong with her? Why would she want to foist herself on a man who clearly did not want her?

"Because you are an idiot who believed Betje when she said there was a chance for this marriage," she whispered as she stared at her reflection in the mirror.

Becky's head popped out of the dressing room. "I beg your pardon, Your Grace?"

"I didn't say anything," Katie lied, resuming her staring match with herself when Becky disappeared.

She had at least another month with Dulverton, and would spend that time proving to Betje that her optimistic hopes were horribly misplaced.

*You can use that time to extinguish your own unfortunate attraction for Dulverton, while you are at it.*

Yes. Yes, she could. And she would.

With any luck, she would be with child by the end of the next month and would never have to see her husband's face again.

# Chapter Nineteen

Naturally, Dulverton did not come to Katie's bed for the next five nights, which meant she saw even less of him than she had before.

Now there was only dinner—always in the company of at least his mother and the steward, and once with the vicar, his wife, and sister-in-law—and later in the library they would sit and work independently while the dowager chattered.

Betje had taken to staying for the first hour—gradually down to three-quarters of an hour and then half-an-hour until Katie wondered if she would soon stop coming at all—before claiming exhaustion and leaving them alone. It was obviously her sweet, although misguided, attempt to throw Katie and Dulverton into each other's company.

Katie did not think she was imagining the increasingly desperate tone Betje's chatter took on as she realized that Katie and Dulverton were every bit as aloof with one another as they'd been that first night. Indeed, Katie had even less to say to her husband after their first and only ride together. She had been relieved that her courses prevented him from visiting her the night she had learned about his mistress.

Even now, after five entire days, she was not looking forward to having him in her bed again.

*Liar.*

Oh, very well. She *did* like the time they spent in bed, but it was tearing her apart. It was simply too difficult to use him—or his body, rather—for nothing more than sexual satisfaction. How on earth did men detach themselves emotionally from their mistresses? Or did they? Perhaps Dulverton really was capable of love—as Betje believed—but for Anna Wilson rather than Katie?

The thought made her too ill to ponder.

Evidently, Mr. Court had come to Becky that morning to inquire whether the duchess was over her *indisposition*. Katie could hardly ask her servant to lie on her behalf, but that did not mean she had any intention of allowing matters to continue the way they had been. No, tonight was the beginning of a new phase in their marriage.

Betje had suggested that Katie challenge Dulverton, and so she would do exactly that. Although she doubted the other woman had meant that Katie should—

"—do you not think, Katie? *Katie?*"

Her head jerked up at the dowager's question. "I beg your pardon, Mama. I was just trying to decide what to do with this section," Katie lied.

Betje scooted closer on the settee and cocked her head, resembling a little pink bird. "What about a peony? They are quite my favorite."

"A pink one?" Katie suggested with a faint smile.

The older woman laughed. "You know me so well already, my dear."

Katie had begun calling her *Mama* two days earlier. It had been an impulse of the moment, after they had paid several rather tedious calls together and, instead of lamenting the boring visits, the dowager had smiled and bounced on the plush leather seat in her son's coach, looking like a child on Christmas morning. "Just spending time with you makes even bitter old Baroness Hellier worth visiting."

The words had been like a flaming arrow that pierced the constant gray fog that seemed to surround her since encountering Anna Wilson and arguing with Dulverton—sorry, *discussing*—about why he did not want her at Briarly. Her eyes had burned as she'd taken the older woman's hand. When had anyone last said something so lovely to her?  "Thank you," she'd said, her voice choked. "That was quite the nicest thing anyone has said to me in a long time, Betje—would you mind terribly if I called you Mama?"

"Oh, I should adore it above all things, my dear! I am so delighted to finally have a daughter. It seems I've been waiting all my life for you, Katie."

Katie *had* shed a tear at that point.

"You will be finished with this piece before I leave," the dowager said now, pulling her from her pleasant reminiscence.

"Leave?" Katie said sharply. "What do you mean?"

"I'm sorry, my dear, I meant to tell you this morning after I received word from home, but the time never seemed right. I must return to Spenwood on the morrow."

"*Tomorrow?*"

Betje's huge blue eyes flickered toward where Dulverton sat silently working on whatever it was that kept him so busy every night. She lowered her voice. "One of the servants who came with me from home—from Utrecht, that is—has fallen ill at Spenwood and I must return immediately."

"Of course you must. I am so very sorry." In more ways than one. Without her mother-in-law at Briarly, life would be lonely. And grim. "I—I will miss you greatly."

Betje patted her hand. "And I you. I regret that I won't be here when the Countess of Grimsby finally returns from the Continent."

Katie stiffened at the sound of Jasper's grandmother's name.

"The woman is a tartar, but her society is impossible to ignore," Betje went on. "Elm Hall is one of her smaller estates and she does not come here often, but I gather she has decided to—" she broke off and waved a dismissive hand. "But why am I am babbling about that right now? I just wanted you to know that I regret I won't be by your side to offer support when you finally meet the dragon."

The last thing Katie wanted to think about just then was Jasper's grandmother. "I will miss your company, Mama," she said, meaning it.

The dowager cut a glance at Dulverton before leaning close and whispering, "I should have made better use of our time, my dear."

Katie stole a look at Dulverton, as well. But his head was bent, and his brow was furrowed in thought. "What do you mean?" she whispered.

"I don't know," Betje admitted. "I just wish I had tried… something. But I want you to remember that you are mistress here, Katie. If you stand aside now, you will always be on the edges of Gerrit's life. *Always*."

Katie jabbed her needle into linen, her eyes blurring slightly. She'd thought about riding out to the Morris farm during one of her daily rides—the only way she could think of to stake her claim as duchess—but every day she'd come up with a reason not to. Because she was a coward. "Sometimes…sometimes a person has no choice in the matter," Katie whispered. "Sometimes a person is pushed aside."

Betje set her small hand on Katie's forearm. "Fight for your marriage," she hissed in a voice throbbing with intensity. "*You* must be the one to push. And keep pushing until you get what you want. And what both of you *need*."

But Katie had no response because she did not want to lie to the other woman. Pushing for what she wanted was not something she knew how to do. At least not with a man who could not wait until she was gone from his life. Not for the first time did she see Anna Wilson's beautiful face—and those of her lovely children—in her mind's eye.

When she didn't answer Betje said, "There is love in my son, Katie. And I believe you are the one who can bring it out of him."

Like the coward she was, Katie reached into her needlework basket and took out the card wrapped with shades of floss. "Help me choose the pink you want for the new peony, Mama."

***

Gerrit paused on the threshold to his wife's bedchamber and squinted into the darkness. Had Court misunderstood Kathryn's maid message? Why was the room in complete—

"I am awake. Come in." Her voice floated toward him like a chill wind portending an ice storm.

"Why is the room in darkness?" he asked, making his way slowly toward her bed, which was nothing but a huge shadow in the faint light from the half-moon shining through a gap in the drapes.

"Because I prefer it that way."

He opened his mouth to remind her that he most certainly did *not* prefer it this way.

But she was not finished. "I would rather we commenced this part of our life the way we mean to go on."

"What are you saying?"

"I'm saying there is no point in us behaving like lovers when we are nothing more than… associates."

"Associates." Gerrit could honestly say he had not been so flummoxed since…well, since that night in the garden when a beautiful stranger had kissed him. "What do you mean?" He wanted to kick himself for sounding like a damned imbecile. It was perfectly obvious what she meant. But Gerrit wanted to hear her say the words.

"I agreed to bear your children. I did not agree to s-service you in the bedchamber the way a mistress would do."

Gerrit was grateful it was dark because he was certain the expression on his face was not one he wanted to share. He heard the rustling of sheets.

"I am ready."

Bitter, vicious fury spread through his body.

*Not to mention the stabbing pain of rejection*, an unwanted mental voice chimed in.

Bloody unbelievable. The one thing Gerrit had to offer his wife—his skill in the bedchamber—she did not want.

So be it. If she wanted cold, calculated *servicing*, he would bloody well give it to her.

He shrugged off his banyan and flung it away, not caring where it landed or if he could find it again afterward, and clumsily climbed up onto the bed.

His hands shook as he shoved her nightgown up to her waist.

She spread her thighs for him, but when he reached for her sex—to ready her—she flinched and tried to pull her legs closed. "Please don't. Just…do it."

Gerrit gritted his teeth so hard it was a miracle they didn't shatter. He lowered to one elbow, his movements jerky with anger, and took his cock in his hand. It was as hard as ever, evidently not sharing his brain's distaste for what was about to happen.

Not since his very first time with the mistress his father had engaged for him when Gerrit had been fifteen had he mounted a woman so selfishly and taken his release.

# Kathryn

But if that was what Kathryn wanted? Then, by God, he would give it to her.

***

Katie felt the rage radiating off Dulverton in the darkness. Indeed, it amazed her how easily she could read the language of his body even though she could not see him. She kept waiting for him to say something—preferably *no*—but something told her she would be waiting a long, long time.

She bit her lip to keep from making any sound when he dragged his slick crown against her soaked, swollen sex. He jolted—as if surprised to discover how wet she was after issuing such a cold declaration—and Katie silently cursed her eager body. But it wanted what it wanted without any care for what her heart or mind preferred.

So did her hips, which tilted to take him deeper, a shudder rippling through her at the exquisite stretch. Rather than pause to allow her time to adjust, as he normally did, he worked her with thrusts so relentless and savage that each one drove her up the bed. Being penetrated—just the notion of having his body inside hers—was always enough to make her hungry for him, but tonight the pleasure that usually coiled inside her until she could no longer contain it was slow to build. And when—scant seconds later—Dulverton's pounding grew faster and wilder, Katie knew that this time, unlike all the others, he would not ensure that she reached her climax before him.

He plunged uncomfortably deep, and his big body froze, his thick shaft swelling deliciously and *almost* pushing her toward the edge.

Katie tightened her inner muscles around him until she was close, so close, so—

But then his body stiffened again, not with arousal, but with awareness—he *knew* she was on the brink of release—and he abruptly withdrew, leaving her shockingly empty.

Katie clenched her hands, frustration suffusing her as he slid off the mattress. This was not going the way she had planned—had hoped. He'd not resisted or insisted. He'd just… accepted.

She opened her mouth to tell him that she had been wrong—that she'd not meant what she'd said earlier—but the words stuck in her throat like burrs.

"Goodnight, Kathryn." He opened the door and disappeared into his room, leaving her alone with only doubt and need for company.

# Chapter Twenty

Gerrit looked up at the sound of the knock, but the door opened without a response from him, and his mother entered, dressed in her traveling clothes. Pink, of course.

He grimaced. It was barely six o'clock. Gerrit had not believed she would be awake and ready to leave so early or he would have left the house even earlier. He sighed and got to his feet. "What can I do for you, Your Grace?"

Rather than take a seat, she strode to the front of his desk. "I will only take a moment of your time, Gerrit."

He raised his eyebrows, willing her to get on with it.

"I wish I did not have to leave right now, but—"

Gerrit sneered. "But your lover needs you."

Her gaze briefly flickered ceilingward—as if she were seeking divine assistance—and then she sighed heavily, looked him directly in the eyes, and said, "You need to give your marriage a chance, Gerrit. You need to give Katie—"

"It astounds me that you believe I want your advice about my marriage. Or anything else, for that matter."

"You can insult me, Gerrit, but it does not erase the fact that you are slowly killing off the delicate shoot that is your future happiness. I know about your mistress in Lyme. I know you plan on following in Boon's footsteps just as you have done in every other—"

"You are keeping my horses standing, madam. It is time you were off. Past time."

"You cannot make me stop loving you, Gerrit."

"I do not *want* your love," he seethed. "I never have and—"

"That is not true. You were an affectionate, loving little boy—so sweet and you doted on me—"

"Before I walked in on you *fucking* a servant!" For a moment it looked as though she would slap him as she had done the last time. Indeed, he wanted her to do it; he wanted to see self-loathing settle on her frivolous features.

But her fisted hands stayed firmly at her sides. "We are talking about you, not—"

"No. *You* are talking about me. My marriage—my life—is none of your concern."

"You have a second chance. A chance to be happy and—"

"I am happy." Or at least he had been until last night and his wife had made a good start to destroying everything. But he was hardly going to tell his mother that.

"Do not ignore this opportunity for happiness, Gerrit. Make an effort to know Katie—to be her friend and her lover. The road you are choosing to travel—Boon's road—only ends in unhap—"

"Your carriage awaits you, madam." Gerrit walked past her and stopped at the door, which he opened.

She heaved a sigh and walked heavily toward him. When she came abreast of him, she stopped.

Gerrit deliberately looked away.

After a moment, she walked past him out of the room.

He shut the door with a definitive snap, his hands shaking. That was his mother, all over again, driving him half-mad with her emotional demands and incessant meddling. Thank God she was leaving. Now the household could finally settle down to some semblance of normalcy.

A memory of last night, of the *new regime* in his wife's bedroom, struck him like a sharp punch to the groin.

Gerrit scowled and dropped into his chair. Christ. How was he supposed to do without their nights together?

***

Rather than miss Betje less as time went on, Katie found she yearned for her flighty, cheerful mother-in-law more with each day that passed.

The dowager's last words echoed in her thoughts, as well. *Please love my son, Katie. His soul is suffering, and he needs love so very desperately.*

Did he? Because he did not seem to be a man who was suffering to Katie. Indeed, in the five days and four nights since she had instituted their new *regime* in the bedchamber, Dulverton had not changed a jot. He still ignored her at dinner and in the library at night and disappeared all day, every day. And he still visited her every night and executed his duty, generally taking less than five minutes to achieve his release. Which was more than she could say for her own satisfaction. That was something she had to see to herself, to her intense mortification.

Those delicious nights with her husband had been the only good part of her marriage. And she had been the one to destroy it. Katie couldn't believe she'd been so misguided as to believe that Dulverton would argue with her when she'd told him their couplings should no longer be filled with passion. She'd been stupid to think

165

her demand would start a discussion between them. A *normal* man would ask why she would make such a ridiculous demand. Not Dulverton.

*Quit blaming him for your asinine idea. Apologize and tell him you've changed your mind.*

No. She couldn't. Whenever she envisioned eating her pride and crawling to Dulverton on hands and knees—metaphorically speaking—images of the lovely Anne Wilson and her equally lovely children flooded her head.

And those images seeded her brain like a fertile field, producing a crop of bitter jealousy.

No, she would not apologize and beg. She could not.

And she knew that he wouldn't either.

Which meant that what they had right now was all they would ever have in their marriage. It was what they had both bargained for, after all, and it was time that Katie learned to live with it.

"Your Grace?"

Katie turned at the sound of Becky's voice and saw her maid holding up one of her favorite morning gowns. She shook her head. "I think I'll go for a ride," she said, not wanting to sit plying her needle alone in the drawing room. She smiled at her friend. "Today I'll introduce myself to some of my tenants."

Becky grinned. "That is a grand idea."

Twenty minutes later Katie was garbed in her peacock blue habit and cantering away from Briarly. Excitement filled her as she reached the fork in the path. The righthand path was the one she'd taken with Dulverton—and she already knew it led to his mistress—so she took the left fork toward an ancient preserve called Echo Forest. The word *forest* was only a trifle aggrandizing. Although the collection of trees was not extensive, the species that lived in the area were the massive sorts of yews one thought of when reading Arthurian tales.

Riding into the wood, there was an immediate hush and the temperature dropped sharply, the latticed canopy overhead holding in the moisture and filtering the light.

It was as though she'd stepped into another world. Although the path itself was well-trammeled, massive yews, lush ferns, and thick bracken ruled beyond its edges, trees and plants jostling with each other for the scarce beams of sunlight that found their way to the forest floor.

A sense of calm settled over her, all the more noticeable for being so unusual— so rare these days. Indeed, when was the last time she had truly felt at peace? Could it really be since she'd lived at Queen's Bower? Five long years. While her siblings had got on with their lives, Katie had calcified into a rigid lump of discontent, accreting layer upon unhappy layer of reserve until she'd isolated herself inside a shell too thick to crack.

She laughed at the dramatic metaphor. It must be the rarified forest air that was leading her to such fanciful thinking.

The sun beckoned not far ahead, a bright light at the end of a cool, crepuscular tunnel. Even Robin seemed to feel the difference in the air, his step hastening as if he was emerging from equine torpor. Katie blinked against the brightness of the day, shading her eyes with one hand.

The first thing she saw was a lovely Elizabethan Era house just ahead. It was composed of white plaster, exposed dark beams, and a charming thatched roof. The only jarring element was the structured, manicured, and—yes—symmetrical hedges that surrounded it, the very antithesis of the sort of natural garden that would have suited the manor. Did her husband impose his need for order even upon his tenants? For this house was, she was certain, part of the estate. Who lived in such a—

The arched front door opened, and Mrs. St. Clare emerged. "Good afternoon, Your Grace."

"I apologize if I was gawking at your house, but it is simply so delightful."

The woman smiled and came toward her. "Thank you. I think it delightful, too. I am Mrs. Amelia St. Clare."

"Ah, so this is the Dower House," Katie said, absently patting Robin's neck.

The other woman's cheeks stained a delicate pink. "Yes, it is." She hesitated before saying, "That is a lovely horse—the color is so unusual. If I'm not mistaken, he is a Friesian."

"You are correct, he is a Friesian. He is a gift from my husband."

Mrs. St. Clare's eyebrows shot up. "Is he indeed?"

Katie thought the comment was rather odd, but just smiled.

"Would it be terribly forward if I invited you in for a cup of tea?"

"I should love to join you," she said, more interested in the woman herself than food or drink.

Mrs. St. Clare beamed. "Let me just summon my—ah, there he is," she said as a man in the garb of a groom came from around the side of the house. "Come and take Her Grace's mount, Lake. She will be staying for tea."

Katie dismounted with the servant's assistance before following her hostess into the cool, dim interior of the house which, strangely, reminded her a bit of the ancient woods she'd just ridden through.

The sitting room was decorated in soothing shades of green and brown, just like Echo Forest. It took Katie a moment to realize why it felt so familiar: because everything in the room was in pairs—from the paintings on the walls to the chairs and tables. It was almost exactly like the sitting room at Briarly, although much smaller.

How…interesting.

Katie could not help wondering why she and Betje had not called on Mrs. St. Clare during their flurry of visits.

Mrs. St. Clare spoke briefly to a female servant before taking the seat across from Katie. Up close Katie could see that her hostess's face was deeply lined, her tanned complexion that of a person who'd spent a good deal of time out of doors. She was not beautiful, but handsome in a dignified way that aged far better than mere *pretty*.

"How are you enjoying Briarly, Your Grace?"

"The grounds are delightful, and the house is the perfect for the two of us."

"You are from Hampshire, originally, so we are neighbors."

"I'm from Hampshire, but my family's home is close to one hundred miles away." Katie smiled kindly. "So, perhaps very distant neighbors."

"Yes, yes, of course. I just meant—" An unreadable expression flickered across the other woman's face, and she sighed. "I'm sorry, but I find that I cannot engage in polite chit-chat.

Katie was not sure what to say to such a bizarre announcement. If she'd not wanted company, then why had she invited Katie to tea?

Mrs. St. Clare's narrow face darkened as if Katie had spoken aloud. "I have been trying to contrive an excuse to see you since you arrived at Briarly." She smiled ruefully, but there was something else behind it. Shame? "I—I am pleased that you came by today.

"I am sorry I did not visit before now, especially given that you are so very close. My mother-in-law and I have been paying calls and we should—"

Mrs. St. Clare laughed, although it sounded more like hysteria than amusement. "The dowager would never have called on me, Your Grace."

"I am sure she would have done so eventu—"

"I was her husband's mistress."

The words tumbled out in such a rush that Katie had to play them over in her head before their meaning hit home. Her mind immediately lurched to another duke's mistress who also lived in a cottage on the estate, although not nearly so grand.

How convenient for the Dukes of Dulverton!

An echo of Mrs. Clare's hysterical laughter bubbled up inside her. "I see," she said in a high-pitched voice.

"I am terribly sorry, Your Grace. I—I should have conveyed that in a less shocking manner."

"I cannot think of a way that would make such information any less shocking." Katie felt shrewish when Mrs. St. Clare's cheeks darkened but could not bring herself to apologize.

Rather than look offended, Mrs. St. Clare gave her a self-deprecating smile. "I thought I had come to terms with my position in life more than forty years ago, but I find that every decade or so it...chafes."

Thankfully, the door opened just then, and a maid deposited a tea tray.

Katie's mind raced as Mrs. St. Clare fussed with the tea. She should leave. Immediately. To sit here with this woman was deeply disloyal to Betje.

And yet she burned with curiosity. Mrs. St. Clare obviously wished to say something to her. Why else would she force such an unorthodox meeting?

"How do you take your tea, Your Grace?"

"Black, please," Katie said.

Such was the soothing miracle of making tea that by the time the older woman handed Katie her cup and saucer she looked almost serene when she spoke. "Gerrit told me the dowager returned to Spenwood several days ago."

The sound of her husband's Christian name—a name she did not feel welcome to use—made Katie want to fling the cup and saucer at Mrs. St. Clare. Thankfully, she kept that impulse in check and took a sip of tea, her stomach roiling with jealousy, not only because this woman could casually refer to Dulverton by his name, but also because he appeared to visit her and talk to her.

"You are wondering why he would confide such a thing in me," Mrs. St. Clare said.

Katie was actually wondering if Anna Wilson and Mrs. St. Clare sat in this room and enjoyed tea with one another while reminiscing about their lovers. Did Mrs. St. Clare have children, as well? Only pride kept Katie from asking.

"Nothing my husband does surprises me," she said coolly. "Because I don't know enough about him to guess what he would or would not do."

Rather than look startled or embarrassed at such an intimate confession, Mrs. St. Clare nodded. "Yes, Gerrit is a very private person."

"Yet he confides in *you*."

"I have known him since he was a little boy." She smiled, but the expression was strained. "In many ways, I stood as a mother to him."

Considering that he could not abide the presence of his own mother, that seemed like an obnoxious claim. Katie set down her cup and saucer with a clatter. "Perhaps you might tell me why you wished to speak to me, Mrs. St. Clare."

"You are angry now—on behalf of the dowager, which does you credit as she certainly deserves your loyalty."

Katie gritted her teeth; when would she learn not to broadcast her every emotion to the world?

"But this isn't about the dowager or me," Mrs. St. Clare went on. "This is about her son, whom I love a great deal. Did you know that Gerrit—I beg you will excuse my familiarity, but I will call him that to avoid confusion between him and his father, the man I will always think of as Dulverton. Did you know that Gerrit spent all his school holidays here at Briarly from the time he was nine years of age?"

"*All* of them?"

"Yes, every single one."

Katie thought back to what the dowager had said about not having visited Briarly for more than twenty years. Had Betje meant she had not seen her son in that long?

"Why would he have done that? More to the point, why did the duke allow it?" Katie asked.

Mrs. St. Clare hesitated. "I believe Gerrit should tell you that."

"My husband does not confide anything in me. If there is something you want me to know, you will have to do the telling."

The other woman looked genuinely torn. "I—I do not wish to be indelicate—"

Katie gave a bitter laugh. "It is rather late for that, Mrs. St. Clare."

Anger flashed in the woman's cool gray eyes, and Katie thought Mrs. St. Clare might ask her to leave. But after a moment, she said, "When he was ten Gerrit walked in on his mother and her lover."

Katie's jaw sagged. Here was a part of the story that Betje had never told her. "Where was this?"

"Spenwood."

Katie could scarcely believe her ears. The dowager had brought her lover under the same roof as her son? Suddenly the old duke's behavior—keeping Mrs. St. Clare in the Briarly dower house—did not seem so egregious.

"Gerrit ran away from Spenwood and made his way all the way to Briarly on his own," Mrs. St. Clare went on.

"Good Lord! That is hundreds and hundreds of miles."

"Yes, it took him almost a month to get here and by then the duchess had come to Briarly and both she and the duke were frantic. His Grace sent Runners and a dozen servants to comb all possible routes." Mrs. St. Clare's lips twitched. "Only when Gerrit finally arrived did we learn what happened. He'd climbed into a wagon full of vegetable marrows and fallen asleep, not waking until the carter went to unload. The man knew by Gerrit's clothing he was not an impoverished urchin and tried to get the truth out of him, but Gerrit would not reveal his identity. Instead, he demanded to be put to work for his passage." Mrs. St. Clare chuckled fondly. "And so that is what the carter did, expecting Gerrit to capitulate after the first hour of hard labor. It actually took more than a week."

Katie felt a reluctant twinge of amusement. Why wasn't she surprised that he'd been stubborn even at such a tender age. "What finally convinced him to confess his identity?"

"He read in a newspaper that the Duke of Dulverton's excavation had ceased due to a family emergency. Clever boy that he was, he knew why and promptly told the carter who he was. The poor man could hardly spirit him to Briarly fast enough." Her smile faded. "When Gerrit arrived, he took his punishment like the stoic he is. But when it came to returning to his mother, he told Dulverton he would run away again. He was emphatic that he would not go back to Spenwood." Mrs. St. Clare sighed. "And so, he did not see his mother for seven years."

"Seven years! That is dreadful."

"I agree. I pleaded with Dulverton to bring about a rapprochement between Gerrit and the duchess. To his credit, he tried to convince Gerrit to forgive his mother, but the few efforts he made ended in disaster and so he made fewer attempts as the years went by. Gerrit voluntarily went to Spenwood when he began to learn estate management from his father, but he was already a man by then—ten-and-seven—and the breach appeared unbridgeable."

"How could Dulverton forgive his father but not his mother?" she asked before she could consider to whom she was speaking.

Mrs. St. Clare's jaw flexed, and her face once again flushed. "It does not seem fair, does it?" she asked, a faintly mocking expression on her face.

Katie's question might have been crass, but that did not make it any less true and she refused to apologize. Not only had her husband forgiven his father for his infidelity, but he also seemed to have embraced Mrs. St. Clare as a mother figure. Or at least he cared for her enough to confide in her and visit her.

"Dulverton and I only disagreed six times in all the years we were together, and Gerrit was the subject of our disputes four of those times. Dulverton gave me a fair hearing, but he was unshakeable in some of his beliefs." She stopped and cocked her head, "Have you seen the portrait of him at Briarly—one that was painted when he was a very young man?"

"I have seen it," Katie said. Like his son, the last duke had not been a handsome man. Her husband had inherited his father's Vikingesque features and pale eyes, but—based on the portrait—Gerrit was much taller than his sire. "But why do you ask?"

"I want you to know what he looked like because what I am about to tell you will sound a bit… cruel, otherwise, and I do not want you to think too badly of the last duke. You see, Dulverton believed it was important that Gerrit understand that his awkward personality combined with his less than handsome appearance meant that he was not appealing to the opposite sex—" Mrs. St. Clare broke off at Katie's huff of irritation, and she smiled. This time, the expression reached her eyes. "Do you disagree with that assessment, Your Grace?"

Katie did not want to share anything with this woman—who was Betje's enemy—but this subject was too important for her to allow it to slide by unaddressed. "It is true that Dulverton is not handsome by *ton* standards, but that does not mean he is not appealing. Indeed, it is difficult for a woman to look at any other man when he is in the vicinity."

Mrs. St. Clare's smile grew. "Is that so?"

Katie scowled, her face no doubt fiery. "Fine. It is difficult for *me* to look at anyone else. Go on with what you were saying before I interrupted," she rudely ordered.

Still smiling, Mrs. Clare said, "Incidentally, I feel as you do about Gerrit. Unfortunately, Dulverton managed to convince Gerrit that he was too ugly and disagreeable to win any woman's affection." Mrs. St. Clare gave Katie a pained and unhappy look. "In short, he convinced Gerrit that he was unlovable."

Katie could not help comparing Mrs. St. Clare's words with what Betje had told her about Gerrit's father. It seemed the old duke hadn't been satisfied with condemning his own marriage to failure, he'd had to stifle any chance of happiness for his son, as well.

Again, she could not resist prying. "Was the last duke happy with you?"

Mrs. St. Clare opened her mouth, hesitated, and then said, "I believe he was."

"If *he* could find happiness with a woman who cared for him then why didn't he think his son could?" Katie persisted.

"That is an excellent question. And I'm ashamed to say I never thought to employ such an argument with Dulverton." She gave Katie a sheepish look. "The last duke was an intimidating man. I—I loved him, but there was a wall of reserve around him that even I was never allowed to breach." She turned to look at her tightly clasped hands. "I see now that in many ways I was a coward. Not once did I tell Dulverton that I loved him."

Katie felt a sharp pang of sympathy for the other woman. If the old duke was even a fraction as intimidating as his son, she could understand why Mrs. St. Clare had been cowardly.

After a long moment of silence, Mrs. St. Clare looked up and met Katie's gaze. "I'm afraid Gerrit's first wife—and their awful marriage—only convinced him that his father had been right about his unlovable nature. And now there is you, Your Grace."

"What about me?" Katie asked warily.

"I heard about you long before I met you."

Katie arched a brow, refusing to look away in shame. "Anyone who cared to read a newspaper in the past few months has heard about me."

"I'm not talking about newspaper gossips. I heard about you from Allison Kent."

"Kent?" Katie could think of only one person with that name. "The housekeeper at Dulverton House?"

"Yes. Allison and I have been dear friends since we were girls. She is the only person who did not turn away from me when Dulverton moved me into this house. Allison Kent's maiden name was St. Clare, and I was married to her older brother. He was an officer in the navy and died after we had been married less than six months. I was with child at the time and returned home to live with my father." She cleared her throat. "I lost the baby and afterward I remained with my father, keeping house for him, and assisting him with his work. That is how I met Dulverton. My father was something of an expert on fossils. By extension, I learned a great deal. When my father died, I continued to work for some of his associates, but—" She broke off and gave Katie a bitter look. "The work of a woman, you see, is not as valuable as that of a man, regardless of the fact that I had nearly a decade of experience. Dulverton, unlike many others, continued to bring me work. Between what my husband and father left me I had enough money for a comfortable, if not luxurious, life." Her cheeks darkened. "I suppose that makes what happened between me and Dulverton all the more sinful. Most women who become mistresses are forced into that life. I chose it eagerly and willingly."

Katie suspected her own face was a similar shade of red. But as embarrassing as listening to such a story was, she was positively riveted. The gently born, well-spoken, educated woman across from her was the last thing she would ever expect from a mistress. Is this what her husband had found in Anna Wilson?

"Of course I knew Dulverton could never marry me," Mrs. St. Clare went on. "When he became betrothed to his second wife—Gerrit's mother—I told him I could not, in good conscience, see him any longer." She gave Katie a wry look. "Clearly I changed my mind. His Grace could be very persuasive when he put his mind to it, and I missed him dreadfully after only a few months" She shrugged. "Our arrangement lasted forty-three years."

Katie was stunned. For some reason, she'd always believed men traded out their mistresses for younger, prettier ones every few years. What Mrs. St. Clare and the last duke had shared sounded like marriage. More like marriage than what poor Betje had been offered.

"But I have digressed," Mrs. St. Clare said. "I was talking about Mrs. Kent. We have been correspondents for more than half a century. It was she who told me about you—and what she said made me optimistic for this marriage."

Katie gave a surprised laugh. "I was only there a night; I cannot imagine what she might have said that would make you feel optimistic."

Mrs. St. Clare smiled. "It does not take long to see that you are intelligent, curious, and full of life."

"That is—that is kind," she said, more uncomfortable with praise than she was with censure. And what did that say about her?

"Allison also said you were not afraid to challenge Gerrit."

Katie gave an unladylike snort. "I feel compelled to point out that a month in Dulverton's company has made me accept that his determination to get his way is far more formidable than mine."

Mrs. St. Clare leaned forward so suddenly she jostled the tea service. "No, no, no! You must not give up, Your Grace."

Katie felt scorched by the passionate, imploring fire in her eyes. "I—what are you saying? That I should bicker with him about where paintings are hung or insist my books remain as they are? I do not care enough about such matters to fight about them."

"I do not mean that you should bicker about incidentals. What I mean is that Gerrit's insistence on order obfuscates what he truly dreads."

"You are saying that he does not really care about order and symmetry?"

"I believe that a certain degree of order is essential for Gerrit's peace of mind, but for a long time Gerrit has used his requirements to keep his emotions—and any emotional attachments—at bay. And now he is using them to keep *you* at bay. Dulverton was wrong about Gerrit not being lovable and able to love. Very wrong." Mrs. St. Clare looked as if she was struggling with something. "I have spent a great deal of time with both men over the years, and I know that Gerrit yearns for something Dulverton never wanted: a happy marriage."

"That was not what he said to me when he proposed," Katie blurted.

Rather than look shocked, Mrs. St. Clare merely nodded. "No, I'm sure he is still adhering to his father's disastrous advice," she murmured, more to herself. "Somehow you need to crack the shell he has so painstakingly built around himself—around his heart."

Katie blinked at the other woman's words. Words which were almost identical to the thoughts she had been having about herself earlier. She *had* held herself aloof from the world—from her friends and family, even—all because she had been hurt. Is that what Dulverton was doing?

"And you think I can do this how?" Katie asked.

"I do not know. Somehow, he needs to be shaken from his—his, I don't know what to call it. A rut, perhaps? Although that seems so mundane. Whatever it is that keeps him imprisoned inside himself, he needs to be set free to love."

"*Love?* He can scarcely tolerate the sight of me, Mrs. St. Clare. We spend as little time as possible in each other's company—and that is not by my design but by his. He disappears at dawn and is away until dinner. He spends an hour or two sitting in the same room with me after the evening meal, not out of choice, but because his mother all but bludgeoned him into it. When he spends a day at home he is sequestered with his steward, secretary, or bailiff. In short, he avoids me as if I were a dunning agent. He is merely biding his time with me until I am—am breeding and then he can set me aside and go on about his life." Her face flamed at her admission.

"That is the illusion he presents, but the reality is quite something else. Indeed, the horse you rode here today is proof of how he feels about you."

"*What?*"

Mrs. St. Clare looked amused by her surprise. "Surely you have noticed all his other horses are black, my dear?"

Katie blinked. "Er—"

"The Dukes of Dulverton have only ever had black Friesians. Until now. Until you. He changed his ways because he knew how charming you would look mounted on a chestnut horse. He *changed* for you."

Katie could only shake her head. "You are deluding yourself, Mrs. St. Clare." She gave a confused half-laugh. "And you are not the only—" Guilt for almost betraying Betje made her stop.

"Yes?" Mrs. St. Clare said.

"And you are not the only one," Katie finally said, deciding the subject was too important to keep such information to herself. "The dowager labors under a similar misapprehension."

Mrs. St. Clare looked pleased. "It does not surprise me in the least that the dowager believes as I do. I knew when she arrived here that she must have a plan in mind."

"Yes, well her *plan* has not worked, so both of you are wrong. She is determined that if we are thrown together enough, we will magically fall into each other's arms. To that end, she has done everything in her power to put us in the same room at the same time. It has come to naught."

Suddenly Mrs. St. Clare fluffed up like an angry hen. "Have you made any effort to scaling the walls he has built around himself?"

"I *tried* to converse with him—to become acquainted—and he slapped down my every effort."

"When was this?"

"During the early days of our marriage."

"Oh, you tried for days."

Katie bristled at her derision. "Just how long do you think I should keep putting myself forward only to be ignored or scolded or shoved away?"

"You are *married*. Marriage is for *life*, Your Grace. Surely a few months of effort—yes, and swallowing some rejection—is not too much to ask for a future with your husband?"

Katie's face heated. "You have no idea what—"

"Do you know about his first wife?"

She blinked at the sudden change of subject. "Er, you mean how she eloped?"

"I can see you have heard the stories."

"A few."

"I did not mean the elopement so much as the behavior leading up to it. Gerrit had no chance with Christina. They were doomed before they ever wed for a number of reasons, not the least of which was that Christina was an extremely frivolous woman who was interested in nothing but balls and parties and society. But you are different."

"I don't see why you think—"

"What do you have to lose if you try and fail, Your Grace?"

"What?" Katie asked rudely, confused by the zigging and zagging in the conversation.

"What do you have to lose if you try to salvage your marriage—if you continue to try and get to know Gerrit? Is it your pride you are worried about?"

"It is more than just pride, it's—"

"What could be more important than not only your own future happiness, but that of your husband and—one day—your children?"

Dulverton's icy gray gaze rose up in her mind's eye. The same look he had given her every single time they had been anywhere but in bed, a sort of irritated weariness, as if she were nothing but a ninny and a bore and a trial.

"Allison said one other thing about you in her letter," Mrs. St. Clare went on when Katie did not answer her question. "She said she caught a glimpse of something on your face, something simmering beneath your smooth sophistication. She saw pain."

"That is hardly surprising as everyone in the world has experienced pain at some point."

"She said this was no ordinary pain."

"Goodness! Mrs. Kent is wasted as a housekeeper. She should purchase a crystal ball and make her fortune having her palm crossed with silver."

"Somebody hurt you and you have tucked yourself away—just as Gerrit has done."

"You are even more skilled than Mrs. Kent. She, after all, spent several hours in my company while you"—Katie snapped her teeth shut and cast a pointed look at the clock as she stood—"why look at the time. How rude of me to have overstayed my half-hour."

Mrs. St. Clare raised her hands in a placating manner. "Please, I have managed this badly. Do not leave yet. Especially not angry. I just wanted to help—"

"You do not have the slightest notion of what it is like living with Dulverton," Katie snapped. "It is like trying to squeeze emotion from a brick."

"I know *exactly* what it is like, and I have been able to break through Gerrit's reserve, so I know it can be done. I know he can be warm and confiding and caring."

Katie gritted her teeth, not with anger this time, but with jealousy. She wanted to fling hurtful words at the other woman, to point out the immorality of being proud of not only taking another woman's husband, but her son, too. But her anger was seasoned with a fierce yearning to know how she had pierced Gerrit's seemingly impenetrable shell of reserve.

"How do I get through when there is not so much as a crack in his veneer?" she asked, not caring about the desperate quaver in her voice.

"Never give in when you should stand firm. Do not let him put you at arm's length. I can see you are attracted to him. Do not allow your pride to stand in the way of showing just how much you want to get to know him. Do not let him treat you as he did his mother. Somehow, you must shake him from his—his complacency and seize his attention. And then keep it. The time to claim your marriage and your husband is *now*, Your Grace. Not after you've given him a child. Do not wait even another day. Demonstrate that you are a force to be reckoned with. That you are formidable, and he needs to respect you."

Katie shook her head, her eyes burning with unshed tears and frustration. What did she need to say to make this stubborn woman—and Betje—understand just how little power she had in her marriage?

"Can't you see?" she demanded, her voice breaking. "There is nothing I can do that will—" She stopped and stared at the woman across from her, surprise blooming in her chest. Surprise and maybe something else; maybe… hope.

*No. That is a terrible idea—terrible. Don't you ever learn?* her mother's voice demanded in her head.

"What is it, Your Grace? What are you thinking?" Mrs. St. Clare asked.

"There is nothing I can do," Katie finished, her voice barely a whisper.

But that was a lie. There was *one* way Katie could show Dulverton just how formidable she was. But she wasn't sure that respect would be his reaction. In fact, it was just as likely to drive him away forever.

# Chapter Twenty-One

Gerrit stared at the chessboards, the only parts of his body not frozen in shock his eyes, which bounced from table to table to table. He looked again, hoping he would see something else.

But he saw the same thing again.

Somebody had moved pieces on all four boards.

*Somebody.*

For almost thirty years Gerrit had tested himself by playing multiple games and not once had anyone touched the pieces. Not his father, who had—quite remarkably—disliked the game, not even his flibbertigibbet of a mother—even though she had been in the same house with him for weeks, and never had any servant disturbed so much as one piece.

There was only one person who would dare.

The door to the library opened and Kathryn swept in, carrying the tapestry bag that had become ubiquitous every evening for the past weeks.

Evenings were spent trying to ignore his mother and wife, even though his ears extended as if on stalks each and every time he heard the low, soothing murmur of Kathryn's voice in response to his mother's grating falsetto.

How pathetic was he to enjoy those few hours a night in proximity with a wife who no longer wanted the one thing Gerrit had to offer a woman? And wouldn't she mock him if she ever discovered how he had abbreviated conversations with his steward or secretary just so he could get to the library a few minutes early to be near her?

*And this is how she repays you.*

Kathryn's eyes darted to the boards and then back before she settled in her usual chair and began rooting about in her bag.

Was she really going to pretend as if she had done nothing?

"Did you move pieces on any of these boards?"

She looked up and blinked her ridiculously green eyes in the cool, dismissive manner that brought to mind a cat. "Any? No." She looked down and plucked something out of her bag. "I moved pieces on *all* four of them."

The throbbing in his temples intensified. His body trembled with fury and some tiny corner of his mind still untouched by all-consuming rage suggested his reaction was excessive.

But for once, logic was the loser.

"Other people do not really matter to you, do they? Or, I should say, what other people value does not matter. Everything in life is just a lark and your role is to do whatever you want, to be as reckless, feckless, and selfish as strikes your fancy."

Her eyes slowly widened. "I beg your pardon?"

"You heard me, but I will repeat myself regardless. I said everything is a lark to you. Or at least everything that does not bore you. You trifle with me for sport, disturbing the order I have already told you is necessary to—"

"You think my life is a lark?" She aside her tambour with what seemed like excessive care. "You think I enjoy being the wife of a man who cannot *wait* to put me aside? Who can hardly bear to be in my presence and who has not taken even five minutes to tell me what he does all day, every day. A man who refuses to introduce me to my own tenants and neighbors." She stood and strode toward him until she was close enough that he could feel the heat of her body.

The scent of lavender and warm female invaded his nostrils and began laying waste to his wits like a scythe through ripe wheat. Gerrit swallowed down the blast of lust her familiar fragrance elicited and forced himself to recall what she had just said. "There is no point introducing—"

"Do *not* say that again," she hissed in a remarkably menacing tone. She raised one of her hands and he thought she might slap him. Instead, she pointed a finger at him and then, shockingly, *poked* him in the chest. "You have already made it perfectly clear there is no point in giving me so much as an inch of space in your life." *Poke.* "You do not need to tell me yet again that my only use to you is as a w-womb." *Poke.* "Nor do you need to reiterate that I will soon be shunted off to one of your distant estates to live a solitary existence." *Poke.* "Oh, and I must not forget about your generosity allowing me to take a lover from whatever rural backwater I get to live in once I have fulfilled my duty to you." *Poke.*

Jealousy uncoiled in his belly like a startled asp at her last words, and Gerrit opened his mouth to say what, he did not know.

But she was not finished. "I am so unimportant to you that I don't merit being told what it is you do all day or where it is you go" *Poke.* "You eat one meal with me on sufferance but leave me alone for the other two." She gave a bitter laugh and poked him one last time before dropping her hand. "As I list everything out like this, I can see why you believe my life is a lark." She pushed past him and strode toward the boards. "Let me address the catastrophe of these games I destroyed. Hmmm, let me see," she said, tapping her chin with a finger in an exaggerated matter before reaching for a piece on the first board.

"What are you doing?" he demanded.

She spun on him, her green eyes spitting sparks. "Unless you want to make a bigger fool of yourself than you already have, I advise you to hold your tongue, Your

Grace." And then she turned back around, leaving him standing there with his jaw hanging.

At first, it was her venomous glare and hostile words that stunned him into silence. Nobody had spoken to Gerrit in such a way since he'd been a boy at school.

But his shock at her ill-mannered command was nothing to what happened next.

Her hand was like a blur on the chessboard, move after move—white and black and white and black—until the first game fell to black.

She moved to the second board and once again played the game with flawless precision, the pieces flying across the board so quickly it was all Gerrit could do to keep up.

His jaw was all but scraping the floor by the time she finished the last board and then whirled on him. "Oh dear me! What have I done?" She slapped her hands over her cheeks in a mockery of surprise, her movements jerky with anger. "I have been thoughtless, careless, and brainless and have ruined it all."

And then she whipped back toward the games and one by one put the pieces back.

"There," she said, once she had finished. "They are back the way they were before I defiled them."

Everything Gerrit had just witnessed convinced him that if he consulted his chess notebook—in which he'd scrupulously recorded his games for years—he would discover the pieces were in the exact same positions they'd been last night.

"How on earth did you do that?" he asked dazedly.

"What does it matter?" Her lovely features contorted into a sneer. "Do not fret, Your Grace. I will *never, ever* touch anything of yours again." She swept his body with a scathing look, as if she included his person in her threat. "I will not do anything that is not my wifely duty." She turned on her heel and stalked toward the door in a flurry of emerald silk skirts.

Gerrit had to sprint to get there before her. He blocked the door. "How did you do that?"

She crossed her arms and glowered. "Why do you care?"

"It was one of the most impressive things I have ever seen." And, bizarrely, one of the most arousing.

Her eyes narrowed and then her exquisite features rearranged themselves into a mocking wide-eyed look that managed to be both vapid and vicious. "I cannot tell you how delighted I am that I have managed to do something that is not reckless, thoughtless, or selfish, Your Grace." She uncrossed her arms, her green eyes blazing up at him. "Do not be alarmed; I will not allow it to go to my mostly empty head. I won't expect anything more from you than you have already shown willing to give—which is nothing. I will do my duty and give you your heir and spare and then I will disappear from your life so you can return to your mistress and happy family."

Gerrit blinked. "*What?*"

"Do not treat me like a fool," she shouted.

"I am not treating you like a fool. I genuinely do not know what you are talking about," he retorted icily.

"I know *Miss* Wilson is your lover and those three children are yours."

Gerrit stared, too flabbergasted for words.

"Why are you looking at me like that? No, never mind," she said, although he had made no move to speak. "I do not care what you think. You can—you can just go to the devil for all I care!"

She was always lovely, but never had Gerrit seen her so magnificent, so…*alive.*

A voice somewhere at the back of his head pointed out his admiration was unwise given that her fury was directed at him.

But he could not bring himself to care.

Rather than put a safe distance between them, as a wise man would do, Gerrit reached for her, fully expecting a slap. Instead, his lips had scarcely touched hers when she shoved her fingers into his hair and yanked his head down.

***

Katie was so confused she could hardly see straight. One moment she wanted to club Dulverton over his thick, rock-hard head; the next, she wanted his big, clever hands all over her body and those arrogant lips of his put to more a pleasurable purpose than railing about a blasted chess game.

She nearly wept with joy when his lips met hers. She had missed him so much! "I need you, Dulverton," she shamelessly murmured in between deep, drugging kisses. She yelped when he suddenly scooped her up, strode across the room, and sank down on the settee, where he commenced positioning her as easily as a doll.

"Wh-what are you doing?" she gasped.

"Giving you just what you asked for. Up on your knees," he muttered, lifting her by the waist until she was straddling his lap, her skirts riding up to her thighs. He gave a satisfied grunt. "Lean forward," he ordered, his hands busy with the buttons at the back of her gown. But he abruptly stopped and pushed her out to arm's length. "And is it too much to ask that you call me by my name when we are alone?"

His affronted expression made her laugh; why did she like his anger so much?

182

*Because you are touched in the head.*

"How could I do otherwise when you ask so nicely, *Gerrit?*" she retorted.

He gave a startled snort, but his glower returned. "How could you think I would father three bastards on a woman who relies on me for her livelihood?"

"Are you saying—"

"I am saying that Anna Wilson is not my lover and those are not my children."

"Truly?" she asked—or squeaked, rather.

"Damnation, woman! I don't have any children."

She blinked at his raised voice and exasperated tone. Dulverton showing emotion was… fascinating.

He pulled her forward and finished with the buttons before pushing down her bodice while Katie wordlessly extricated her arms, until the top of her gown was bunched around her waist. He moved his hands to the back of her stays and added, "Nor would I victimize a woman who is dependent on me for the roof over her head."

Katie saw genuine revulsion in his gaze and suddenly recalled just how disgusted he'd been when she lied about bedding her aunt's footman.

"I am sorry for maligning you, but I was—" She broke off.

"You were what?" he prodded, his hands going still, his gray eyes dark and bruised as they looked up at her. "What were you, Kathryn?" he demanded with his usual arrogance, cupping her jaw in his warm palm while his eyes flickered over her face.

*Show him you care.*

"I was jealous thinking of you with another woman," she whispered.

His expression of shock was almost comical "You were—"

Katie leaned down and pressed her mouth against his. She might be willing to admit her jealousy, but she hardly wanted to discuss it.

He resisted a fraction of a second before responding, his kisses gentle, almost…sweet. When he finally pulled away, he didn't go far, his lips drifting to her throat, forcing her head up as he kissed and nibbled the sensitive skin beneath her chin.

When his hands returned to her laces, Katie blindly reached for his coat and unfastened the buttons by touch, making equally speedy work of his waistcoat, until the only thing between her palms and the taut musculature of his chest was the whisper-soft muslin of his shirt.

His body was deliciously hard and hot, but she wanted to feel his flesh not fabric, no matter how fine. Her fingers found their way to his cravat and tugged on one end to loosen it before pulling it off with a soft *hiss*.

Before she could overthink her daring, she laid her palm over hot, satiny skin.

Dulverton—*Gerrit,* she mentally corrected—gave a low rumble of approval and pressed his chest against her hand.

The rare show of emotion emboldened her, and Katie grabbed handfuls of muslin and yanked.

Her husband's head whipped up at the loud *riiiiip.*

"I—I wanted to touch you," she explained as she met his darkened gaze.

"Raise your arms," he said in a husky voice.

She did so and he lifted her stays over her head and then dropped the garment behind the settee. Katie gave a soft, snorting laugh at his uncharacteristically cavalier gesture.

She stopped laughing when he slid his hands under the straps of her chemise and pushed it off her shoulders and down her arms, baring her.

His breathing roughened as he cupped one of her breasts in each hand. "My God, you are beautiful."

Katie should have been embarrassed to be naked from the waist up, straddling his thighs, but she preened beneath his carnal stare. He stroked his thumb over her nipples. She gasped and arched her back, her body begging for more.

Her hands had been lying limply on his chest since he'd pushed down her chemise, but Katie moved them now and lightly thumbed his nipples the way he was touching hers, teasing the little disks into taut nubs.

His eyelids fluttered and his jaw flexed.

"Does that feel good?" she asked breathlessly.

"Yes, it does. Too good. You will make me spend in my breeches."

She laughed, joyful that they were, once again, doing the only thing they seemed to do well together.

"You like the thought of making me shame myself, do you?"

"Yes," she admitted.

He growled and lifted his hips off the settee, raising them both in the process. He held her steady with one hand and tore open his fall with the other. When his erection sprang free, he wrapped his hand around his thick shaft and stroked himself as he lowered them both to the settee. "Up higher," he ordered.

Katie rose up onto her knees and he pushed his hand under the bunched fabric of her gown and cupped her sex, sliding his middle finger inside her while his other hand continued to stroke.

She moaned at the sudden invasion, tipping forward and gripping his shoulders to keep from sliding off his lap into a boneless heap.

"So tight for me," he murmured, working her in slow, rhythmic thrusts. "Yes, like that," he said a moment later, making her realize she was moving her hips, meeting his thrusts.

Her eyelids fluttered shut and she gave herself up to the erotic stretch of his fingers and almost too-sensitive rasp of his thumb as he teased her bud. Need ran rampant through her body, knotting her muscles tighter and tighter, until Katie cried out.

His hand stilled as her climax gripped her, her inner muscles spasming around his fingers with each wave of pleasure, over and over, until she was sapped of strength and slumped limply toward him.

His hand gripped her waist while his mouth pressed against her temple and his free hand pressed his thick crown against her entrance. "I need to be inside you."

Katie nodded weakly and hissed as he slowly pushed inside her, the carnal stretch intensifying the echoes of her orgasm.

She clung to his bare chest with a contented sigh as he held her still and full. There was a tiny nipple right in front of her nose, so she closed her lips around it without thinking.

Gerrit shuddered. "God, yes. Suck me, Kathryn."

His crude command sliced through the haze of pleasure like a razor, and she sucked, nipped, and nibbled one rough pebble and then the other while his muscular torso tensed beneath her. Who would have believed his rock-hard body was so sensitive?

"Are you trying to kill me?" he groaned, making her smile against the damp, sensitive skin.

He slid his arms around her and held her upright as his hips rolled and bucked, lifting them both off the settee, the fierce power of his thrusts making the erotic act all the more arousing.

*Tell him you like it,* a voice whispered.

Katie did not require much convincing. After all, it stood to reason that if she enjoyed the sensual—occasionally crude—things he said, maybe he would, too.

"So big and strong and… hard," she whispered in his ear, and then sank her teeth into his lobe.

His body jolted. "You drive me mad, Kathryn. But you already know that, don't you?" He made a sound deep in his throat and lifted her high before pulling her down, filling her so deeply the line between pleasure and pain was obliterated.

And still he was not inside her deeply enough. "More," Katie ordered. "Harder."

Her words ignited something inside him, and his body flexed and rippled as he worked her with a savagery that thrilled her. "Is this what you want?" he demanded, his voice raw and harsh.

"Yes… yes…*yes!*" she chanted, the words growing more ragged as she sped toward the edge of bliss.

His hips drummed harder and faster and wilder until he hilted himself. "Kathryn!" he shouted, shuddering as he found his release.

Katie collapsed against him, their slick torsos skin to skin, her body on fire as she tucked her face between his shoulder and neck.

She must have briefly dozed, only coming back to consciousness when he shifted beneath her.

"Kathryn?"

"Please, Gerrit," she begged. "Not—not yet. Hold me." *Love me—or at least pretend for a little while.*

He was rigid for a moment before the tension drained out of him and he sank back down, his powerful biceps tightening around her, hugging her to his body as he pressed his lips against her temple.

Almost as if he had heard her.

***

*"Love me—or at least pretend for a little while."*

The shocking words were scarcely a whisper, but her mouth was right beneath Gerrit's ear and so there was no mistaking them. His body responded reflexively, his arms tightening around her slender body as she burrowed into his chest, her hot, damp breath warming the sensitive skin of his neck.

He swallowed down the flutter of panic that surged from his belly to his throat and kissed the top of her head before he knew what he had done.

*Love her?*

She had agreed with him that day in Chatham's library. It was a marriage of convenience first, last, and always.

*Wasn't it?*

Thinking about it hurt his head.

But Gerrit could happily sit here all night feeling her smooth, taut thighs straddling him, her soft breasts pressed against his chest, and her hot, wet pussy squeezing his cock, which had not completely softened.

*Love her?*

Thinking of Kathryn and *love* in the same sentence instantly made him recall his last conversation with Amelia, when she had harangued him until he'd snapped at her, something he had never done before. But then Amelia had never nagged him before, either. And yet now, every time he paid a call on her, desperate for the calming influence she'd exerted on him all these years, the only subject she was interested in discussing was his wife. Or, more specifically, how Gerrit needed to go about mending the breach between himself and Kathryn so they would have a *real* marriage.

That had been Amelia's word: real. As if Gerrit was not *really* caught in parson's mousetrap with no chance of escape. Well, not unless his wife eloped with another man as his last one had done.

His arms tightened reflexively around the slender body pressed against him at the thought, as if he could keep Kathryn from running away with physical restraint alone. She mumbled something against his throat, snuggling closer, her soft, pliant form somehow heavier in sleep.

The sheer vulnerability of the situation—the trust she showed by sleeping in his arms—made his throat constricted with *something*, but he didn't know what. What was wrong with him? Why the hell was he so bloody emotional?

It had to be a result of not just Amelia's nagging, but his mother's as well. He could not recall ever being subjected to so much nagging in such a short time.

Thinking about his mother jerked him back from his maudlin musing. Gerrit's eyes narrowed at her utter gall in offering him unsolicited advice, especially about his marriage. He buried his nose in Kathryn's disheveled curls, the lavender scent pleasing rather than overpowering.

Gerrit reveled in her botanical, feminine smell. Or at least he tried to revel. But a tendril of unease that he'd been suppressing for a while began to grow stronger. Although he couldn't see the clothing he'd cavalierly tossed behind the settee when he'd been in the grip of passion, he could *feel* it. He gritted his teeth against the growing pressure, trying to ignore it.

He could stop the unease by standing up, laying Kathryn on the settee, and tidying up the messy garments. But if he did so, he risked waking her. And Gerrit was not ready to let her go—to let *this* go.

*Chaos, disorder…* the insatiable demon inside him whispered and hissed.

*I don't care.*

But the unease did not diminish in the least. Gerrit needed something stronger to fight off the building pressure, so he buried his nose in Kathryn's curls and inhaled deeply, filling his lungs with her scent. Again and again, he breathed in the intoxicating smell of his wife.

*My wife. Mine.*

The first touch on his neck was so faint he thought he'd imagined it. But then it happened again, soft lips pressing against his sensitive skin. Kathryn was kissing his throat.

Gerrit's eyes fluttered shut at the butterfly touches, the racket behind the settee muted, as if somebody had thrown a bucket of chilly water over a noisy crowd.

She kissed him again and again, and then she buried her nose in his neck and whispered, "I'm happy now."

Later that night—after Gerrit had held his wife a delicious half-hour longer before finally capitulating and folding the bloody clothing—he carried Kathryn's sleeping form up to her bed, tucked her in, and retired to his own room. His mind was more disordered than usual but—interestingly—the lack of mental order didn't make him miserable. Instead, the thoughts bombarding him were pleasurable ones and most of them centered on Kathryn. His thoughts kept returning to his wife's last words to him earlier: *I'm happy now.* Even in her half-conscious state he'd heard the wonder in her voice and understood that happiness was not a normal state for his wife. It wasn't for Gerrit, either.

The last thought he had that night, as he surrendered to sleep was that—astonishingly—he was happy, too.

# Chapter Twenty-Two

Katie might be a fool, but she was not a *complete* fool. She knew that an evening of torrid passion in the library with Dulverton would not miraculously transform how he behaved towards her. And so she was not terribly surprised when she went down to breakfast the following morning and discovered that, as usual, her husband had already left and it was just another day.

No, she was not surprised, but she was more than a little disappointed. And frustrated. How was he able to remain so unmoved by last night? Perhaps he was this way with every woman he'd made love to? Katie had not felt this wonderful with Jasper. And she did not think that just because she now hated him, either. No, she recalled all too well how she had tolerated those uncomfortable couplings with Jasper to keep him happy rather than out of any real desire for him.

But as much as this passion with Dulverton was well and good—actually, it was lovely and wonderful!—it still left her feeling hollow and needy for more. Somehow Katie needed to make him *talk* to her.

Before meeting Mrs. St. Clare, Katie would not have believed her reserved, taciturn, and uncommunicative husband was even capable of confiding in another person. Katie had been consumed by jealousy when she'd believed Anna Wilson was Dulverton's mistress, but that feeling was nothing to the roiling emotions that assaulted her when she thought about Dulverton sharing his thoughts with Mrs. St. Clare.

Before she could become too despondent, she reminded herself that last night had been a step in the right direction. Dulverton had finally seen her. Not just her face, but the person who occupied her body. Even if it had only been her skill at chess that had impressed him, at least it was more than what he'd seen in her before.

Of course, he had noticed her face and body as well…

Katie smirked to herself. Indeed, last night would provide her with erotic memories for months to come, although she hoped not to have to rely on just memories. He would come to her again tonight, wouldn't he?

Katie cursed herself for falling asleep last night before she could somehow find a way to retract her foolish claim about not wanting passion in the bedchamber.

But surely, after last night he would realize all that had changed, now?

And yet, three mornings later—after two nights of perfunctory coupling—Katie was beginning to realize that what had been crystal clear to her had not been apparent to her husband *at all.* If they were ever to return to the way they'd been before her foolish declaration, then she would have to be the one to take steps.

Katie was heading to breakfast and dwelling on just how she would achieve her goal when she heard Dulverton's voice drift up from the foyer and her heart sped. He hadn't left, yet. What was he doing at home?

Instead of turning left on the landing, she hurried down the stairs.

Her husband was pulling on his gloves as she reached the bottom step and glanced up. "Good morning, Your Grace," he said in his abrupt way.

"Good morning, Dulverton. Are you going somewhere?" she stupidly asked.

"I have to go to town," he muttered, his mind obviously elsewhere. But then he appeared to recall himself and say, "Do you have any commissions for me?"

"Might I go with you?"

A notch appeared between his eyebrows, which began to draw down.

"I can be ready to leave in ten minutes," she promised when he hesitated.

"You have not broken your fast," he said after a long, awkward moment.

"I do not need anything. I can be—"

"Eat something before you change your clothing," he said, speaking over her. "I have several matters I can attend to while I wait. I will see you in an hour."

"I don't need a whole—"

But he had already turned on his heel and was headed up the stairs she had just descended, likely bound for the library.

She didn't *need* an hour! Katie pulled a face at his back but followed him up the stairs, turning left for the breakfast room. She was too excited to linger over breakfast and hurriedly ate two pieces of toast and a boiled egg before hastening back to her chambers, where she found Becky fussing about in her dressing room.

"I need to change, Becks. You and I are going to town."

"Ooh, to town! Will you wear the new peridot walking costume?" Becky asked hopefully.

"That seems a bit much for a visit to Lyme"—Katie glanced out the window—"especially when the sky is threatening rain. How about the emerald green and I can wear my new boots."

Katie and Becky were ready a full ten minutes before it was time to leave. "Let us go down and wait. My husband does not believe women can be punctual," she explained at her maid's puzzled look. "I am going to prove we can actually be early."

Naturally Dulverton was already in the foyer talking to one of the twin footmen—either Jeremy or Jacob, she was ashamed that she could never tell them apart—when they came down the stairs.

His eyebrows lifted slightly at the sight of her. "The carriage is ready," he said without preamble, gesturing for Katie to precede him out the door the footman was holding open.

Only when she and Becky were settled in the luxurious coach, both of them sharing a seat, did she realize her husband had no intention of joining them.

"Oh, you are riding," she said rather stupidly as a groom led Dulverton's gorgeous stallion, Centurion, toward the carriage.

"I will escort you to Lyme and see to my business, but on the way back I will go straight to the dig rather than come all the way back here." It was clear from the flicker of annoyance that crossed his face that he did not like having to explain himself to a mere wife.

Fuming, Katie sat back, leaving him to shut the door, which he was obviously so eager to do.

"Don't be angry at him, Katie," Becky said quietly once the carriage was moving.

Katie looked up from her hands, which she was purposely keeping unclenched in her lap when what she wanted to do was ball them into fists and pummel something. "Why shouldn't I be angry at him?" she snapped. "If there is a more awkward man alive, I have yet to meet him."

"He is just shy—"

"*Shy?*" Kaite barked a laugh. "That must be more drivel from Court, the fount of all knowledge when it comes to Dulverton."

Becky scowled. "Mock all you like, *Your Grace*. But the truth is that you are of a prickly and combative temperament, and His Grace is excessively reserved and brusque—"

"*Brusque?* I think the word you are looking for is *rude*."

Becky ignored her comment. "Your differences lead to misunderstandings and bruised feelings. If the two of you keep on this way, you will be living at opposite ends of the country just as the old duke and duchess did."

Katie hadn't had the courage to tell her friend about the bargain she'd made the day Dulverton had offered for her. She found that she did not have the courage today, either. "That might be for the best. I am clearly nothing but a burden—a boring one—to him and he could be left to his own devices, his tidy house, and his bloody dig."

Becky pursed her lips and deliberately turned to look out the window.

"I'm sorry," Katie said after a few moments of silence. She smiled ruefully at her friend. "I should not be snappish with you. You are not the reason I am peeved."

Becky took Katie's hand and laced their fingers together just as she'd done when they were girls and she had tried to talk Katie out of one of her *moods*. "One of you will have to make the effort, Katie. You *know* that."

"Why should it be me?" she demanded petulantly.

"Because you are a woman, and it is our lot in life to be peacemakers while men are the ones who make war. Because you have so much more to lose if you do *not* find common ground with him. And—most importantly—because it is a chance to be happy."

"Happy? With that man?"

"Mr. Court said—"

"Good Lord, Becky! Every third sentence of yours seems to begin with those three words."

Becky gave Katie an irksomely superior look. "If you don't want to hear what he told me about the duke then I will not bore you."

Katie gritted her teeth and forced herself to say, "I'm sorry. I want to hear." And she did want to know, so much that it infuriated and terrified her.

Becky made her stew a moment or two before saying, "Mr. Court said that His Grace was a different person before his first marriage."

"I should think so. He was only ten-and-seven, a mere child."

"Mr. Court said it was more than just his youth. He said His Grace was... romantic."

Katie's eyes bulged. "*Romantic*? I will believe many things, but that is not one of them."

"Why would he lie?"

"Perhaps he is not lying, just mistaken."

"I do not think so. He said His Grace was hopeful about his marriage even though he had never met his bride."

Katie could imagine exactly what the adolescent Dulverton had hoped: that he'd have a woman to warm his bed whenever he wanted. But she knew that comment would not please her maid, who *was* romantic, so she said, "You spend a great deal of time chatting with Mr. Court. And not just about laundry." Becky tried to tug her hand away but Katie held on. "Now, now, don't become all prickly when

I poke my nose into your business. After all, is that not what you were just doing to me?"

"I was not engaging in teasing gossip for the sake of it," Becky snapped. "*Somebody* needs to help you save your marriage before it is beyond your power to do so.

Katie did not tell her friend that she was a member of a quickly growing club.

***

The carriage dropped them off at the Red Lion, which was evidently the nicest posting Lyme Regis had to offer.

Dulverton had already dismounted by the time the carriage rolled to a stop and was speaking to a man who must be the innkeeper because he kept bowing at the duke, obviously delighted to have his custom.

Her husband waved away the footman and opened the carriage door, flipped down the steps, and assisted Katie and a pleased but flustered Becky down from the carriage.

"I have business that will keep me for several hours, but I have reserved the inn's private parlor for the afternoon so that you may return here at any time to rest. I will be back at two o'clock if you wish to share a meal."

Katie was nonplussed at the unprecedented offer of his company.

Becky poked her in the back when she didn't respond.

"Er, yes," Katie mumbled. "That would be pleasant."

He inclined his head, pivoted on his heel, and marched off with one of his red-headed footmen sprinting after him, lugging a heavy satchel of some sort.

"Wasn't that nice?" Becky asked.

Katie grunted.

Becky sighed at her lack of enthusiasm and pulled a folded piece of paper from her oversized reticule. "I have a few things I need."

"I am at your service," Katie said, her gaze lingering on the only reason she had come to town before he disappeared around a corner. She turned to her friend and forced a smile. "Let us see what delights Lyme has to offer."

It turned out that Lyme had a number of stylish dress shops as well as an entire lane filled with the sort of vendors one found at the Western Exchange in London. Becky was in her element, and Katie soon realized they would spend the entire day on clothing, hats, and other frippery if her maid had her way.

"I want to pop into that bookshop we passed on the last street," she said as Becky gazed at a number of muslin samples that all looked the same to Katie.

"Oh." Becky frowned. "I suppose I could—"

"I can go on my own. You here stay and finish whatever you are doing," she added when the other woman looked ready to argue. Becky—as much as Katie loved her—was not bookish in the least and always made Katie feel like she had to rush whenever they were in a bookshop. "I will be fine walking one street over. I'm not an infant, Becky."

Becky gave her an agonized look. "If His Grace heard that I left you alone he'd be beside himself."

Katie doubted that. But she said, "He'll never know."

Before Becky could assemble any more arguments, Katie strode off in the direction of the bookshop. Although she had two entire trunks filled with new books, one could, in her opinion, never have too many. But before she reached the bookstore another shop caught her attention. A plain black and white sign saying only, *Fossils*, hung over the door. A young woman sat in the narrow bow window and appeared to be working on something. Behind her were several other people milling around.

Katie told herself that she wasn't interested just because Dulverton was mad for fossils. Fossil hunting was currently all the rage not only in Lyme, but all over Britain. Why shouldn't she have a look?

The shop was even smaller than it appeared from the outside. Shelves lined walls and shrank the space even more. Six people, four men and two women, were chatting with an older woman—who must be the proprietress—near the back.

"Is there something I can assist you with?" the woman seated at the table asked.

"I was just curious about what has drawn so many people."

The other woman was perhaps a few years older than Katie and dressed in a serviceable gray gown that had obviously been made for utility rather than fashion. She set down the tool she was using and gestured to what she had been working on. "Have you seen one of these?"

Katie approached the table. "Yes, as a matter of fact. My husband has dozens and dozens of them in shadow boxes in his library."

The woman's eyebrows rose. "Ah, then you are married to a collector."

Katie opened her mouth to say she did not know what she was married to but thought better of it. Instead, she said, "We are very newly married, and I have yet to learn much about his interest in fossils."

The woman's eyes widened. "Er, newly married? Would it be—is it too bold to ask if you are the new Duchess of Dulverton?"

"How did you guess? Are newlyweds so rare in Lyme?"

"Well, there is only one man hereabouts who possesses a collection of dozens of ammonites arranged as you've described." She smiled shyly. "If you will forgive my impertinence, I was the one who assisted His Grace in finding a framer for his collection."

"Ah, I see." Katie said, more than a little irked that here was yet another stranger who appeared to know more about her husband than she did.

*And whose fault is that?* a voice in her head that sounded a great deal like Becky asked.

"I'm afraid I do not know your name," Katie said.

"Mary Anning, Your Grace." She dipped a curtsey.

"Is this your shop?"

"It was my father's, but he passed on and now my mother, brother, and I operate it."

Katie gestured to the shelves. "And you have found all of these on the beach? Or do you possess a parcel of land where you er, harvest the fossils?"

"We have been fortunate to fill our shelves with the shoreline's bounty."

"What were you doing to that piece on the table?"

"I was preparing it for sale." She gestured to the tool with a flat scraper end and a pointy end. "I use that to clean away the debris."

Katie lightly stroked the spiral-shaped fossil with one gloved finger. "What a curious creature."

"Indeed, ammonites are fascinating."

*Ammonites.* Katie stored that word away for later. "Have your finds diminished now that so many tourists come to comb the shore?"

"Most of them will only find what washes up. You have to look a bit to find the truly good specimens." She touched the side of her nose with her finger. "But I cannot share all my secrets, Your Grace."

Katie laughed. "No, I suppose not." She turned to look at the shelf closest to her, which held more of the same circular animal as well as something that was long and pointed on both ends.

"Are you curious to try hunting for fossils?" Miss Anning asked.

"I'm curious as to why it has captured so many people's imagination." Not to mention her husband's attention, which seemed to have only enough space in it for these dead creatures. Oh, and chess. "Perhaps I will have to come down one morning and see what is what," she said, smiling.

"Have you gone to your husband's dig?"

"I have not."

"You would be far more likely to find something interesting there," she said, a bit of envy coloring her tone.

Katie had no interest in discussing her husband's *dig* or his unwillingness to share anything about it. "What is this thing?" She pointed to a large fossil that looked to have a round body, head, four legs, and stub of a tail.

"A sea tortoise."

"Is it?" Katie murmured, leaning closer. "It does not look like any tortoise I have seen."

"No, this one is different to the ones alive now."

"Different how?"

Miss Anning glanced around, an almost furtive expression on her face. "Normally I would not say this, but I know His Grace subscribes to the scientific perspective. But none of these creatures"—she waved a hand at the walls of fossils around them— "exist today."

"What happened to them?"

Miss Anning shook her head. "That is a conversation I'm ill-equipped to have, although I do possess my theories, not that I have any proof, mind."

"What are your theories?"

Again, the other woman looked about her before leaning closer. "I think these were animals that could no longer survive, for one reason or another." She shrugged. "Perhaps some other creature came into their realm and provided too much competition. Or maybe the ocean receded and left them on dry land. If you went to your husband's dig you would see how the different layers of earth yield up different finds." She shrugged again. "I am sure His Grace, who has been to Oxford and is a member of the Royal Society, could give you a more cogent explanation."

Andrew had mentioned something about Dulverton going to university at a young age, but she had no idea he belonged to an esteemed club like the Royal Society.

The little bell over the door tinkled and when Katie looked up, she saw Becky wearing a frown and hurrying toward her. "You were not at the bookshop like you said you would be! Fortunately, I saw your emerald silk in the window," Becky said, belatedly adding, "Your Grace," when she saw that Miss Anning was watching them with interest.

"I was on my way to the bookshop but was distracted," Katie said, amused when Miss Anning's eyes bulged to hear a duchess explain herself to a servant.

"We will be late to meet His Grace if we do not make haste." Becky glanced around the somewhat dusty shop with a disapproving look.

Katie turned to Miss Anning. "I very much enjoyed speaking with you."

The other woman's face flushed, and she dipped a low curtsey. "It was an honor, Your Grace. And—and if you should ever wish to accompany me, please let me know."

"Thank you, that is very kind. I will certainly keep your generous offer in mind." She inclined her head and walked to where Becky was already holding open the door.

"What on earth were you doing in that dusty, dirty place?" Becky demanded the instant they were out on the street.

"Looking at fossils."

"I should think you'd get enough of those at home."

"One would think," Katie agreed mildly.

Becky cut her a suspicious look. "What are you scheming about now?"

"Nothing." Katie laughed and bumped Becky's shoulder with her own, although she had to lean down to do so.

"*Your Grace!*" Becky hissed. "People will see."

Katie just smiled.

Becky chattered on about her purchases as they walked the five minutes to the Red Lion. "I need to find Jeremy and have him go fetch the parcels from the drapery warehouse," Becky said, glancing around the foyer as if the footman might be lurking there.

The innkeeper Katie had seen earlier hurried toward them. "Ah, Your Grace—your parlor awaits."

"If you will just point the way," Katie said. "Then you can assist my maid in locating our footman."

He blinked. "Oh. Er, of course. The parlor is just up these stairs and the first door on the right. Are you certain I cannot—"

"I will be fine," she assured him, and then smiled. "If I do not open my own doors on occasion, I will forget how it is done."

The publican's jaw sagged.

Becky clucked her tongue and cut Katie an admonishing look.

Smirking to herself, Katie climbed the stairs. She was just opening the door to the parlor when a male voice boomed from the end of the corridor. "Lady Kathryn?"

She wanted to groan when she saw the Earl of Ampthill striding toward her, his unsteady progress telling her the notorious peer was, as always, the worse for drink.

"Lord Ampthill," she said, making the words as repressive as possible.

Ampthill grinned, unrepressed. "It really is you, Kitty Cat!"

She gritted her teeth at the annoying nickname some wag had applied to her in her very first Season. "As you see," she murmured coolly.

"Lord! You just get more beautiful all the time—although it has been a few years, eh? I just returned from Paris," he said, even though she'd not asked. "I was in Brighton not long ago and heard the maddest story about you."

Katie sighed.

"Don't you want to hear it?"

"No."

He threw back his head and guffawed, as if she had said something uproarious.

Katie turned toward the parlor. "If was a pleasure to see you again," she lied. "But you must excuse—"

Ampthill's meaty arm shot out, his hand landing on the door frame and blocking her entrance into the parlor. "I heard you masterminded a kissing contest at the Earl of Sutton's ball."

"Please remove your arm," Katie said frostily.

Ampthill's brainless grin grew, and he leaned so close that Katie worried she might become intoxicated from the fumes alone. "Not so fast, my kitten. I never had a chance to play your game. I think I'd like to have my kiss now if you don't—"

"What the hell do you think you are doing?" a voice roared right before Ampthill's body disappeared from the doorway.

Katie heard a thud behind her and spun around. Dulverton had Ampthill by the throat and pinned to the wall.

"That is my *wife* you were mauling," Dulverton thundered, his hand squeezing.

Ampthill gurgled.

"Er, Dulverton?" Katie said, glancing worriedly up at her husband and tugging lightly on his sleeve.

Dulverton glared down at her through eyes that looked like chips of ice. "*What?*"

"I think you have cut off his air."

"That is not all I will cut off," he retorted savagely. "Did you arrange to meet him here?"

"Are you quite mad, Dulverton?" Katie sputtered. "Ampthill is drunk—as always—and he accosted me on my way into the parlor."

Dulverton whipped around to his captive. "Is that true, Ampthill? Did you accost my *wife*?"

Again, Ampthill gurgled, but more weakly this time, his eyes rolling back in their sockets.

A startled yelp came from behind them and both Katie and Dulverton turned to find Becky at the head of the stairs.

"Where the hell were you?" Dulverton barked at the stunned maid. "Why weren't you with your mistress as you are supposed to be? That is your purpose, and if you cannot—"

"Do not yell at her!" Katie snapped. "I am the one who sent her away. Now, release Ampthill immediately—unless you want to have an unconscious body on your hands."

Dulverton's lip twitched into a snarl and an actual growl rumbled in his chest. He released the earl as swiftly as he'd grabbed him and Ampthill slid to the patterned carpet like a stunned fish, gasping for air.

Feet pounded up the stairs and the innkeeper appeared beside Becky. "Your Grace? Is something amiss?" He gawked at the floundering earl. "Goodness! What happened?"

Dulverton gave Ampthill an ungentle nudge with his booted foot. "This bounder was attempting to molest my wife. He is drunk."

The innkeeper stared aghast, his eyes bouncing like marbles from peer to peer.

Katie took pity on him when Dulverton continued to glare. "Please help the earl to his feet and take him somewhere… else."

"Oh, yes." The innkeeper darted forward. "Excellent notion. Thank you, Your Grace."

Katie made her way into the parlor on unsteady legs.

"Your Grace?"

She turned to find that Becky had followed her and was peering anxiously up at her. "Did that man hurt you? Is there—"

"You!" Dulverton roared, standing in the doorway, pointing at Becky. "*Out!*"

Becky made a squeaking sound and immediately scurried toward the door, needing to squeeze past the duke's big body.

Dulverton slammed the door behind her so hard the windows on the opposite wall rattled. "If your maid cannot manage to stay by your side while you are in public then I will discharge her and find somebody who will." He strode to the table and yanked out a chair. "Sit."

"I will *not* sit! How dare you order my servant about in such a rude, draconian manner?"

Dulverton closed the short distance between them and loomed over her. "I dare because I am your husband. You would be wise to obey me, or you will discover that I am capable of far more *draconian* behavior."

Katie opened her mouth.

His icy eyes narrowed. "Have a care what you say, madam. I am not in a mood to be trifled with."

Katie was so angry her vision blurred.

Fortunately, the parlor door opened and prevented her from spewing bile. Two servants hesitated on the threshold, bearing loaded trays yet obviously repelled by the atmosphere in the room, which was thicker than the slices of bread piled on one of the trays.

"Get on with it," Dulverton barked, setting the frozen tableau into motion.

Katie ground her teeth together so hard they should have been powder. She looked from the bustling servants to the duke, who was regarding her grimly.

*You are foolish to taunt and infuriate him when he has every right to be angry at me for allowing you to wander alone through an inn,* phantom Becky chided.

Katie suspected she would get an almost identical scolding from the real Becky on the way home.

Once the food had been arranged one of the maids turned to Dulverton. "Will there be anyth—"

"Go," he ordered. "And do not disturb us again. If I want you, I will ring for you," he said, his eyes never leaving Katie.

The women hurried from the room.

"*Must* you be rude to everyone?"

He looked genuinely confused. "Rude?"

Katie snorted. "You really don't know what I mean, do you?" Before he could speak, she held up a hand. "Never mind. Just—just forget I said anything."

"Consider it done." He cast a speaking look at the chair he'd pulled out for her, and Katie dropped into it with an irritated huff.

Dulverton sat opposite her and commenced to cut a slab off the rare roast beef. When he moved to put it on her plate she said, "I am not hungry."

He ignored her and Katie seethed as he proceeded to put portions of all the dishes on her plate. Once he was finished, he turned to his food and commenced to eat with the same single-minded determination he did every night at dinner.

Katie flung down her napkin and stood and then gasped when Dulverton's hand closed around her wrist.

"Where do you think you are going?" he growled, getting to his feet. Still holding her arm, he wiped his mouth with the napkin in his other hand before dropping it to the table.

"Somewhere else. Now, unhand me."

"What did I just say about you wandering alone?"

"I'm sorry, I was not listening—did you say something about wandering alone?"

His pale blond eyebrows drew down and his nostrils flared. "Perhaps you regret that I interrupted that sordid little scene in the corridor?"

Katie was momentarily nonplussed by his offensive question.

"Or were you *trying* to make me jealous, Kathryn?"

"Jealous," she repeated faintly, her heart pounding faster. What was wrong with her that she liked the sound of that so much?

His hand tightened. "That would be a very dangerous game to play," he said, his voice low and menacing.

"I would never do anything so reckless!"

He raised one eyebrow.

Before Katie could tell him to go to the devil, he gave a negligent tug on her wrist and she stumbled toward him, slamming into his chest.

"Dulverton! What do you—"

His lips sealed over hers and one of his big hands slid around her waist and snugged her tightly against the unyielding wall of his chest while he ravaged her mouth.

His actions were so unexpected that Katie forgave herself for freezing with shock. But she could *not* forgive her body for melting against him and kissing him back.

*Have some dignity!*

It took every bit of strength she could muster to pull away from him. Rather than fight her, he instantly loosened his hold, a gesture that, inexplicably, angered her more.

"What do you think you are doing?" she demanded huffily.

"Giving you what you need." His coldly appraising eyes flickered over her flushed face before sliding down her throat and coming to a halt on her heaving bosom. "What you want."

"You do not have the first clue about what I need or want," she retorted, incensed at the quaver of excitement in her voice.

"Lift up your skirt."

"Wh-what?"

"You heard me," he rumbled, closing his hands around her upper arms, and walking her backward.

"What are you doing?" she squeaked when her bottom bumped up against something hard.

"Turn around."

"Dulverton—I demand—"

He easily spun her to face a heavy cabinet of the sort that usually held crockery. "Bend over."

Katie's entire body shook with lust and she could not seem to move.

Dulverton's hand, large, warm, and rough, slid around her neck and cupped her jaw, turning her head to the side just enough that she could see him out of one eye. "Tell me you don't want it and I will stop right now, Kathryn."

Katie swallowed but did not make a sound. *Oh God. Please don't stop.*

His lips twitched and he gave a smug, approving grunt. "Just as I thought. Now, lift up your skirt."

# Chapter Twenty-Three

Gerrit did not truly believe that his proud, hellcat of a wife would allow him to bend her over a cabinet and fuck her in a public inn parlor, but—by God—her hands moved with all haste to pull up her walking costume, a pretty, frilly thing the color of emeralds that turned her eyes an even brighter shade of green.

He knew he was behaving like a savage brute but could not bring himself to step away. If he were a decent man, he would release her and tell her to stop. She wasn't a common whore; she was his duchess. But his hunger for her had turned him into an unprincipled beast and he could not make himself say the words.

Besides which, something told him his prickly, haughty wife would be angry and ashamed if he called an end to this game right after she had capitulated.

The thought gave him pause, and Gerrit was more than a little impressed that her possible reaction had occurred to him. When did he ever notice somebody else's feelings or give a damn what they thought?

And why did he suddenly care now?

Hell! A man could go mad thinking about such things. He was already at least half-mad with jealousy even though he knew damned well that Ampthill was always cup-shot and out of control. He also knew his wife had done nothing to attract the man's attention, but that didn't make him feel any more reasonable. No. It just made his urge to claim her all the fiercer.

Why the hell did he want her so damned badly? Who would have guessed that his Achilles heel was an argumentative red-headed shrew?

With the body of a goddess and the brain of a military commander, if her skill on the chessboard was anything to go by.

Gerrit had to bite his lip to keep from moaning like a fatuous fool when the hem of her skirt reached her knees, exposing the pretty green and blue garters that held up her stockings. Stockings which had lines up the back and—he leaned forward and squinted—butterflies embroidered around the top edge, as if they were holding the garters.

It was bloody adorable.

*Adorable?* Damnation! He'd turned into a blithering idiot.

Gerrit could not bring himself to care, his thoughts firmly riveted to her delectable thighs. Did she wear garments this sensual every day? Perhaps he should have her remain clothed when he came to her at night so that he could undress her.

*Has it slipped your mind what she wants from you in the bedchamber?*

Gerrit gritted his teeth as reality crashed down on him, crushing the pleasurable fantasy he'd just constructed. No, it bloody well hadn't slipped his mind, although he constantly *tried* to forget it. He was working on a way to address that issue and he would do so, in his own damned time.

*Right now* was not that time.

The hem of her gown drifted farther up, over the bare flesh of her slender thighs, pulling her chemise up along with it and exposing her bottom.

Gerrit groaned. "Just like a peach." The terribly trite words came out in a choked voice that sounded like it had been dragged behind a carriage for twenty miles. When he reached out to stroke her generous arse, he half feared she was a gorgeous mirage that would disappear before he could touch her. But the warm, smooth globe that trembled beneath his hand was satisfyingly real, as was her muted half-whimper, half-grunt, a sensual sound that he adored eliciting from his proud, haughty duchess.

*Adorable? Adored?*

He did not want to ponder just how bewitched he was becoming. Not now.

"Lift it higher," he ordered gruffly.

She hesitated a moment, as if she wanted to deny him. But his little sensualist wanted a good fucking just as badly as Gerrit wanted to give her one. And so she raised the gown and petticoats all the way up to the base of her spine.

Gerrit nudged the heel of her emerald-green ankle boot. "Spread your legs."

Her back stiffened at his abrupt command, and she parted her thighs a miserly few inches.

He shoved a foot between hers, his black leather top boot grotesquely large next to her dainty little ankle boots. "Wider," he growled, sliding his hand from her bare buttock up over the bunched skirt to her slender shoulders. "And lean forward." He pressed down. "Yes, like that," he praised when she immediately bowed over the cabinet.

He fumbled with his buckskins with one hand, freeing his prick while sliding the fingers of his other hand between her spread thighs. "Good God," he muttered when he encountered her slippery pussy. "You're soaking wet."

She made a muffled sound in the back of her throat and began to push up.

"Do you want me to stop?" he asked, his fingers stilling in her slit, the pad of his middle digit just shy of her clitoris. "This is the third and last time I will ask, Kathryn."

She turned her head and glared at him from the corner of one eye, anger—as well as something else, lust, perhaps?—radiating off her like heat from a bonfire.

"Well?" he demanded, giving her slick bud a tauntingly light caress.

She snarled like a feral cat. "Just get on with it, you—you lout!"

A startled snort slipped out of him, and she twisted around more to get a better look at him. "Are you *laughing* at me?"

Gerrit bit back his smirk and dredged up the most loutish words he could think of. "Hush, woman!"

Kathryn opened her mouth, no doubt to deliver a proper raking, but Gerrit distracted her by thrusting a finger inside her. She made a most unladylike sound and squeezed him like a vise.

"God, you're tight," he groaned, earning another squeeze. Gerrit stroked her slowly, reveling in the hot satiny feel of her before easing in a second digit.

She lifted her hips and spread her thighs to take his fingers deeper, all but begging to be mounted.

Gerrit was so lust-maddened that it took all his self-control not to dispense with readying her and simply bury himself inside her and pump her full of seed to wipe the stench of Ampthill off her, even though he knew the smell was only in his head.

Instead of mounting her like a selfish beast, he worked her carefully and rigorously, until her desire coated his hand. When he could bear it no longer, he leaned low and covered her back with his chest. "Are you ready to take me?"

She pushed her bottom against him, which he decided was a good enough answer, even though the temptation to make her beg for it was strong.

Gerrit withdrew his fingers and rubbed the head of his cock through her drenched sex, stroking her with his crown until she was writhing beneath him.

"*Gerrit*, please."

"Please what?"

"I need you ins—"

He entered her in one long slide, not stopping until he was hilted. She squirmed when he kept her fully impaled, and Gerrit snaked a hand beneath her hips and lightly stroked a finger where they were joined. He kept her tightly pinned as he caressed her slick flesh, touching her everywhere but where she needed it most.

She bucked beneath him, or tried to, but she couldn't move an inch between the weight of his body and the wooden cabinet.

"*Please*," she whispered so softly he could barely hear it, her body clenched with need.

"I enjoy hearing you beg, Kathryn," he said, leaning lower to kiss the back of her slender neck while his slick finger worked the sensitive bundle of nerves. "Is this what you need?"

"Yes," she sighed, her hips moving in counterpoint to his increasingly hard thrusts.

Gerrit felt the telltale tightening of her sheath right before she exploded. As much as he wanted to make it last and last, he could not entirely forget he was balls deep in his wife in a public inn and so he found his own release a scant moment later. He gave in to sensation and briefly lost track of time, reveling in his orgasm.

When he finally found enough strength to lift his head, he saw he'd fucked the cabinet halfway across the small room. He was also still pressed against his wife, likely crushing her.

Gerrit straightened up before reluctantly withdrawing from her body, tucking himself away as he admired the sight of her reddened, spread buttocks and the slickness coating her thighs. It was a view he could have enjoyed for hours. Instead, he pulled his handkerchief from his pocket and gently cleaned between her thighs.

She jolted at his touch but did not stop him.

Once he was done, he folded the cloth neatly and tucked it into his pocket. "Let go of your skirts," he said when he saw her hands were still bunched into fists.

He gave the material a few twitches to pull it down over her truly magnificent arse and then helped her upright before turning away to give her some privacy, the frenzy of the last few moments falling away and making him realize that he had just fucked his wife in a posting house parlor as if she were a doxy.

And he could not bring himself to regret it, although he was flabbergasted about the reason for his loss of control.

He'd let that fool Ampthill's idiot behavior turn him into a jealous, ravening beast.

There was a timid tap on the door.

"Hold a moment," he ordered loudly, turning back to make sure Kathryn was decent. "Ready?"

She nodded, her cheeks still passion-flushed but her expression cool and collected.

"Come in," he called out.

The innkeeper hovered on the threshold and glanced at the table. "Was the food not to your liking, Your Grace?"

"It was fine. Have my carriage brought round."

The man dropped a low bow before backing out of the room as if Gerrit was a member of the royal family.

Gerrit turned back to his wife, who was looking at him with an unreadable expression. "What?" he demanded.

"Did you need to be so rude to him?"

Gerrit scowled. "You mistake directness for rudeness. What should I have said to the man? I apologize for not eating your meal because I was far more interested in tupping my wife?"

Streaks of color slashed across her delicate cheekbones, and she opened her mouth.

There was another damned knock on the door before he could hear what she had to say. "What is it now?" he asked loudly enough to be heard through the slab of wood.

The door opened slowly, and Stone peered inside the room. Her gaze slid to the almost untouched food and then back to Gerrit. "I beg your pardon, Your Grace. I did not mean to interrupt, but Mr. Stevens said you were finished and—"

"Wait outside until I summon you," Gerrit barked.

"We are leaving," Kathryn said as if Gerrit had not spoken, and then brushed past him on her way to the door.

Gerrit watched in silence as they hurried from the room and left him standing by himself, still wondering what her answer to his question would have been.

***

Katie glared into the darkness and squeezed the bedcovers, as if she were squeezing Dulverton's neck. She had not expected her husband to behave differently during dinner. Nor had she expected him to ravish her in the library. No matter how much she might have enjoyed it.

But after their torrid coupling at the Red Lion that afternoon she *had* expected him to come to her bedchamber and behave normally. Well, not *normally*, but the way he'd been before she had stupidly told him she wanted only a marriage of convenience from him.

Katie snorted and shook her head. Dulverton must be the thickest man in Britain because he had, yet again, snuffed the candles when he'd strode into her room, lifted her nightgown, climbed on top of her, and done his business in a scant five minutes before bidding her goodnight.

For the first time since the night when she'd told him she did not want his passion, Katie pondered the possibility that Dulverton was not merely being stubborn or thoughtless, but that her request might have hurt his feelings. It was impossible to believe he had any feelings—not to mention tender ones—beneath his granite façade, but what else could explain his behavior?

It was increasingly clear that if they were ever to go back to the way things were *before* then Katie would have to instigate things.

*And apologize.*

"Blast and damnation," she hissed through clenched teeth, her hands actually hurting from abusing the poor blanket. Just thinking about dredging up the subject and apologizing was painful. Surely there was some other way?

*Challenge him*, both Betje and Mrs. St. Clare had said, or something to that effect.

Hit him over the head with a club would probably be more useful.

Snarling, she punched the unoffending pillow and then flopped onto her back, still glaring.

She didn't mind challenging him—she actually enjoyed locking horns with him, not to mention how much she loved the way they had resolved their last two disagreements.

But as much as she enjoyed the passion they shared, she needed more. She wanted more. *They* needed more or she would be living alone in Spenwood for the rest of her life.

How could she ever get through to him?

Just… how?

# Chapter Twenty-Four

"—looking for you, Your Grace."

The voice slowly penetrated the dense fog of Gerrit's concentration, and he looked up from the ammonite—which filled one entire table in the tent—to find Jessop, his assistant, hovering on the threshold to the tent, his forehead deeply furrowed.

"What was that, Jessop?" Gerrit said, wincing as he stood up and straightened his back. He should have been sitting instead of bending over, but he often forgot about things like posture when his mind was engaged.

"The duchess is here, Your Grace."

"My mother has returned?" he blurted, his pulse racing. And not in a good way.

Jessop cleared his throat and glanced away, as if embarrassed. "Er, not the dowager, but your wife."

Gerrit felt like an idiot. He opened his mouth to ask what she wanted and luckily realized that would only make him look like a bigger idiot. Instead, he strode out of the tent.

Kathryn's gelding, Robin, was grazing not far from Centurion but he could not see her. "Where is she?"

"She is at the dig, Your Grace."

Gerrit strode toward the well-trodden path that led to the terraced hillside everyone referred to as *the dig*.

He spotted Kathyrn immediately, her emerald riding habit vivid against the dun background. She was talking to Leopold Scott and Albert Everett, both junior lecturers at Oxford who'd spent several months here for the last two summers.

Albert, the more sociable of the two, was gesturing with his arms and whatever he said made Kathryn laugh.

Jealousy boiled in his belly at the younger man's apparent ease when it came to chatting with women. Gerrit had never made a woman laugh—at least not intentionally.

By the time he reached the trio he was seething, more at his own consuming jealousy than anything else.

"You should have told me you were coming today, Your Grace."

Kathryn, who'd been speaking, stopped at his harsh announcement, her pleasant smile fading at whatever she saw on his face. "Hello, Dulverton."

"I would have arranged a tour for you," he said, biting back the urge to tell Scott and Everett to sod off and get on with their bloody work.

"You needn't put yourself out. Alby was just showing me what he was working on."

"Alby?" he repeated, probably more loudly than necessary.

Everett cleared his throat. "Er, yes, Your Grace. Um, Her Grace and I had the pleasure of becoming acquainted several years ago at a house party," he said, reminding Gerrit that Albert Everett was the younger son of Viscount Everett.

A house party? Although Gerrit had never actually been to one, he knew country house parties were, if not outright orgies, certainly notorious for the amount of bed hopping that occurred. Had Everett fucked Kathryn?

*You are allowing your jealousy to run away with your sense. Kathryn already told you she's had only one lover.*

Gerrit was stunned that he heard the tiny voice over the sudden roaring in his head.

"Er, Your Grace? Is aught amiss?" Everett asked, anxiously peering up at Gerrit.

Gerrit's eyes slid from Everett to his wife. "A house party," he repeated, sounding demented to his own ears.

"Chatham's house party," Kathryn said, cutting him an odd look. "They host one every summer."

Gerrit grunted, his gaze moving back to Everett. The man was handsome in that golden-haired, blue-eyed vapid sort of way that women seemed to like.

Did Kathryn admire such a man?

Everett swallowed, his cheeks turning darker the longer Gerrit stared.

"Oh, those are fascinating," Kathryn said.

Gerrit wrenched his gaze off Everett and saw that his wife was pointing at the partially excavated piece that Mr. Scott had been working on, prior to fraternizing with Gerrit's wife.

Kathryn looked up at Gerrit, her green eyes especially vivid today. "They are like the ones you have in those shadowboxes, but enormous."

He felt a twinge of pleasure at her observation. "People have been unearthing ammonites for centuries in this part of England, but the size of this particular specimen is remarkable."

"His Grace has donated spectacular samples to dozens of museums both here and abroad," Everett said, making Gerrit feel a twinge of guilt for wanting to thrash him only moments earlier.

"That is very generous of you," Kathryn said.

It was tempting to bask in her approval, but…

"Specimens of such size and clarity should be available to the masses," he said. "It would be wrong to hide them away in a private collection or profit by selling them." Good God, he sounded like a pompous arse!

"I saw them for sale in Lyme Regis in a shop operated by a woman who—"

Mr. Scott guffawed. "Ah, you mean Mary Anning. She's something of a moneygrubbing nutter who—"

"Miss Anning happens to be one of the foremost authorities on marine fossils in Britain. I daresay she has forgotten more about the specimens found in this part of the country than most of us will ever know," Gerrit said coolly.

Both men's jaws sagged at Gerrit's rebuke, and Kathryn's lips curled up. No doubt she viewed Gerrit's scolding as *rude*. Too bad.

"As for Miss Anning selling what she finds," Gerrit went on, "she does so to support not only herself, but also her widowed mother. Scarcely *moneygrubbing* behavior."

Mr. Scott's face was bright scarlet. "Er, just so, Your Grace."

Kathryn set her hand on Gerrit's arm. "Will you show me what you have been working on, husband?"

A muscle in Gerrit's eyelid twitched at the word *husband*. Her lips were curled up slightly at the corners and she was regarding him with the oddest look. A look that made his collar feel too tight.

"Er, yes," he stammered, sounding like an idiot. He cleared his throat. "This way."

***

As Katie followed Dulverton, she pondered his reaction to her visit. Although he had glared at poor Alby and Mr. Scott with a rather violent glint in his pale gaze, she did not think he was displeased that she had paid a visit to his dig.

Katie's foot slipped as they ascended the terraced slope.

"Allow me," Dulverton said, taking her elbow and slowing his pace to help her up the hill.

"Thank you," she said, flustered by the slight touch. "I wouldn't be so clumsy if I did not have this heavy skirt."

"Mind your step," he said, leading her around a deep depression and stopping before a large, level area.

"Oh, my," she exclaimed when she realized there was a pattern to what had been unearthed. "What *is* that?"

"It is a belemnite, a rather large one."

Katie dropped to her haunches to have a closer look and reached out a hand before stopping and glancing up. "May I touch it?"

"You won't hurt it."

She lightly traced a finger along one of many long swirling ribbons. "It looks a bit like a squid's tentacle." She squinted. "But… are those hooks at the end?"

"That is very observant of you. Yes, they are hooks. And there is likely some relation between this animal and the squid swimming in the ocean today."

Katie preened at his praise and then wanted to slap herself. Why did she always have to be so desperate?

She pushed away the unhappy thought and instead looked from the belemnite to the hillside. "Is that slide recent?"

"Yes, this spring."

Katie saw three young men and one woman working together in an area, all four garbed more simply. "They work for you, too?"

"Correct." She thought that was all he would say, but then he went on. "They are from town and spend much of the year fossil hunting along the shore. I pay them during the summer months to work for me, and they are allowed to sell anything they find that I do not donate or keep."

"That is generous of you."

He shrugged.

She gestured to the huge fossil. "Is it difficult to dig these out?"

"No, it just takes time and patience."

"I would like to help," she said, getting to her feet and brushing off her habit.

His eyes widened comically.

"Why do you look so thunderstruck?" she asked, more amused than annoyed.

"I never imagined you would be interested in such a thing."

"Why not?"

He seemed to undergo some sort of internal struggle and then gestured to her habit and his own dusty clothing. "It is dirty work."

"Believe it or not, I used to love being out-of-doors and climbing trees and looking for birds' nests, exploring, and even hunting fossils. Not that we ever found much of anything."

"We?"

"My brother and I. Doddy and I spent most of every day together until I was sixteen. And when he was off with the curate taking lessons I wandered my father's estate by myself." Katie pulled a face. "So much so that my mother despaired of me."

"Why?"

"She said I was more animal than female." She smiled wryly. "Looking back, I cannot gainsay that."

"What happened when you were sixteen?" he asked.

"Everything changed when my sister Phoebe married. My brother went off to school and my mother sent me to my aunt to make me into a lady."

His brow furrowed. "What did that entail?"

"Staying clean, dressing properly at all times. And if I *did* go outside, I was only allowed to wander in the confines of the garden with a hat and gloves and parasol and—" Katie broke off and glanced away from his penetrating gaze. "And I became a lady," she finished softly. Being a lady was something she had always believed she'd wanted. But then she had discovered the price of fine gowns and fancy parties.

She forced her gaze back to his and saw that he looked uncomfortable and bemused. Doubtless it was a bit too much personal information for such a private man, so she returned to the point. "I would like hunting for fossils. At least—" She bit her lip.

"At least?" he prodded.

"I would like to do so here, unless you think I might ruin something. I can always go where everyone else goes to hunt for them."

"You mean the shore?"

Katie nodded. "Miss Anning offered to take me with her one morning if I cared to go. I—I talked to her the day I went into Lyme Regis with you." Katie's cheeks heated at the memory of that day, and she could see by the sudden swelling of his pupils that he was remembering too.

She swallowed and lowered her gaze. "Miss Anning said she walks the beach after each tide, rather than digging. I thought I might go to Lyme Regis one morning when the tide is not terribly early."

"There are safe places here you can dig."

Katie's head whipped up and she tried not to grin like an idiot at his offer. "Er, safe?"

"Often the best fossils are exposed by slides like that one." He gestured to the hillside. "To a fossil hunter the temptation to dig in a freshly uncovered area is difficult to resist. But it's dangerous and people are frequently hurt or even killed."

"Oh, I see."

"You will not need to worry about that here," he assured her. "There are plenty of safe places to dig where you can still find something interesting."

"Miss Anning said your dig was far better than the shoreline for fossil hunting."

"Correct." He glanced at her emerald-green habit, with its sweeping train, and a notch formed between his stunning eyes. "Do you have something—"

"I have a more practical habit."

He nodded.

She gestured to the large fossil. "If you don't mind, could you tell me more about this—what was it called again?"

"It is a belemnite." His eyes met hers, and the expression in them was one she had never seen before. It was far too slight to be called a smile, but the harsh lines of his face seemed to relax. "I do not mind. In fact, it would be my pleasure to tell you about them, Kathryn."

***

By the time Gerrit finished showing his wife around the dig and introduced her to his other workers it was past noon and Jeremy arrived with two large hampers of food.

"Would you care to join me for my midday meal?" Gerrit asked, wishing he didn't sound so bloody stiff.

"Will there be enough?" Kathryn asked.

"Yes. Cook always packs plenty," he assured her.

"Then I would like to join you." She followed him into the work tent. "This is nice," she said, glancing around.

"It is functional and convenient," he said, pouring some water into the basin for her.

While they washed their hands, Jeremy set out their meal of roasted fowl and crusty bread, both still warm.

"I think I will bring my sketchbook when I come back tomorrow," Kathryn said.

Gerrit finished chewing his mouthful of food and washed it down with some ale before saying, "Are you any good?"

She blinked, and her mouth pulled down at the corners.

Damnation! "I did not mean that to sound rude," Gerrit admitted. "I was just curious."

It must have been the correct thing to say because her lips relaxed.

"I am not bad at sketching, but my watercolors are barely adequate. Of course I am not nearly as good as my sister Aurelia, who was a professional illustrator before she married the Earl of Crewe."

Gerrit was momentarily speechless; her sister had *worked*. "Indeed? A female illustrator?"

Kathryn's forehead furrowed and her eyes narrowed.

He identified her sudden change in mood with an ease that startled him. Why was it so difficult to converse with her? Why did he keep saying the wrong things? "I am not being critical," he assured. "I only meant that I have never met a woman who does such work. Especially not a peer's daughter."

After a moment, her face relaxed and she nodded. "Before my sister Phoebe married Viscount Needham, our family was in danger of losing our home, so Aurelia decided it would be prudent to learn how to support herself."

"I knew of Addiscombe's, er, fascination with cards," Dulverton admitted.

Kathryn snorted, her expression bitter. "There are very few among the *ton* who *don't* know about my father's gambling."

"I had no idea matters were so dire," he added.

"They were," she said grimly, her gaze distant. "But thanks to the generosity of my brothers-in-law—especially Needham—our family estate is no longer in danger."

Gerrit could only nod. What could a person say about such a thing? Addiscombe's behavior was criminal, in Gerrit's opinion. But Kathryn hardly needed to hear that.

Thankfully, she changed the subject. "Do you hire people to sketch your specimens?" she asked, taking a piece of bread he had sliced and slathering it with butter.

"I make drawings for myself, but for anything I want to use in a presentation or article I employ a professional."

She gestured to Gerrit's specimen journal, which sat on the other side of the table. "Are those your sketches?"

"It is a newer book and contains only the most recent ones.

"May I see?"

He slid the book toward her and ate while she untied the leather thong that bound it and flipped through the pages. Once she'd finished, she looked up. "You are very good."

"Merely adequate," he demurred, quartering a pear and handing her a section.

"Thank you. Do you paint your drawings?"

"I have not done so in the past."

She bit into the pear and a drop of juice escaped and clung to her full lower lip.

Gerrit stared, transfixed.

"What is it?" she asked.

"There is a bit of juice."

"Where?"

He wordlessly pointed to a place on his own lip that mirrored the spot.

She hastily dabbed at it with her napkin. "Did I get it?"

He grunted, wrenched his gaze from her mouth, and adjusted himself beneath the table.

"Thank you for showing me around today."

"You are welcome."

"I—are you sure you don't mind if I come to the dig?"

"I am sure," he said, perplexed by just how much he liked the thought of her joining him.

Kathryn opened her mouth, hesitated, and then smiled and stood. "Well, I should go so you can return to your work."

Gerrit tossed down his napkin. "I will ride back with you."

"You do not need to do that. You said I was safe as long as I stayed on the estate."

"You are safe, but I want to ride back with you," he said, realizing as he said it that it was true. For some reason, he was not yet ready to end this pleasurable interlude.

Gerrit felt a pang at the way her face lit up; it took such a small thing—his company—to make her happy and yet he had brought her so little joy during their brief marriage.

# Kathryn

He lifted her onto her mount, and they rode toward Briarly, Kathryn chattering about the dig, her excitement about tomorrow—her first day—causing a cascade of emotions that left Gerrit both terrified and hopeful. Terrified because he could not recall ever wanting to please a person this much, and he had very little idea how to do that.

And hopeful at the thought of a future that did not contain a bloodless marriage of convenience, but something fulfilling and meaningful.

The words she'd murmured two nights before in the library—*I'm happy now*—had come back to him several times over the intervening hours.

If Gerrit had made her happy once, surely he could do so again?

***

Gerrit stared at the blank wall opposite his bed, his thoughts in an unaccustomed jumble. Actually, the jumbled feeling was not so unaccustomed since his marriage.

Half his mind was on the delightful afternoon he had spent with Kathryn at the dig and the other half was still back in his wife's bedchamber half an hour ago where he had, in a perfunctory fashion, carried out his nightly duty.

After their enjoyable day Gerrit had been tempted to disregard her demand for workmanlike coupling, but there had been nothing in her demeanor to suggest that she had changed her mind about his visits to her bed. She was an intelligent woman; if she had changed her mind, she would tell him.

He told himself that just because she had visited the dig today did not mean she wanted more from him. Fossils were fascinating; he could understand why she was interested in them. Gerrit, however, was the Duke of Dullness. He had never denied the validity of that nickname as little as he had liked it. She might have evinced an interest in fossils, but that did not mean she wanted more of *him*. After Christina, there was nothing more repulsive to him than the thought of foisting his company on another person.

Kathryn had asked for so little in their marriage that Gerrit could not bring himself to ignore her one request, no matter how much he yearned to return to the way things had been at the beginning of their marriage.

When he'd gone to her tonight, she had not said a word to him. Not when he'd been in her bed or when he'd slipped on his robe, thanked her, and left.

Opening the connecting door and leaving her room had been almost painful, which was odd because he had always left afterward, even when their couplings had been passionate and enjoyable.

The urge to share her bed grew stronger every night he went to her, regardless of how little pleasure their intercourse now brought him. For a moment earlier tonight Gerrit had wondered what Kathryn would do if he simply crawled back under the covers beside her and went to sleep. The yearning had been so powerful that it had actually frightened him.

Thankfully, he'd gained control of himself and suppressed the impulse, which would have been a horrific invasion of her privacy.

Gerrit had accidentally fallen asleep in her bed one night early in their marriage and had been ashamed by his lapse afterward, vowing to never to encroach on her in such a way again.

It bothered him that he would even want to sleep with her. He'd never wanted such a thing before. What was happening to—

"Gerrit?"

He jolted and turned to find his wife lurking in the shadows near the connecting door. "Is something amiss, Kathryn?" He began to push back the blankets.

"No, nothing is wrong." She hurried toward him, her green silk dressing gown fluttering around her. "Please, do not get up." She swallowed, fidgeted, and then said, "May I get in with you?"

"In?" he repeated stupidly.

"In your bed." Uncertainty began to rearrange her features.

Gerrit shifted over and wordlessly pulled back the bedding, his heart squeezing in his chest when a smile banished her uncertainty and she hurriedly mounted the steps and crawled in beside him.

"*Mmm*, nice and warm." She scooted so close their hips and shoulders touched.

Thankfully, Gerrit had already steeled himself for her touch so he didn't stiffen and jerk away, which even he knew would have been bad.

Instead, he steeled himself yet again and, as if in a trance, laid his arm around her shoulders, earning a satisfied humming sound as she wiggled closer.

His pulse thudded and his gaze flickered over his bedchamber and the comforting order that Court imposed on it, drawing a sense of calm before he turned his attention to his wife's disheveled curls. They were the sullen red of a banked fire in the low light of the single candle. Red was the color of passion and indulgence, meant to whet one's appetite. He had never before considered just how much the color suited her. Everything about her teased his appetite.

She turned to him, her catlike eyes dark and mysterious with the light behind her. "I want to ask you something, but you must promise you will answer me with complete honesty."

"I would never do otherwise."

She chuckled wryly. "No, you wouldn't, would you? Do you like having me here in your bed?"

Gerrit opened his mouth to say *no*, but thankfully caught himself. Instead, he considered her question. It was undeniable that she felt nice—wonderful, in fact—and he'd begun to harden just sitting beside her.

But—

She started to move away and Gerrit tightened his arm around her, holding her in place easily. "Where are you going?"

"Clearly your answer is *no*, so I thought I would spare you having to say it," she said tightly, staring straight ahead rather than at Gerrit.

"Have you ever known me to refrain from speaking my mind, even when it offended you?"

Her lips parted in surprise and then twisted into a wry smile. "No."

"Look at me, Kathryn." She turned toward him with grudging slowness. "I am not like you—" He paused when she made a soft scoffing sound. "By that I mean I need time to ponder matters. I was giving your question the consideration it deserves. It does make me uncomfortable to have you in my bed, but most of my discomfort is probably due to the fact that I've never had a woman in my bed before."

"Not—not even your first wife?"

*God no!* he was tempted to retort.

"No," he said. "Not even her."

"What—what about your mistresses?"

Gerrit was amused. "What is this fascination you have about my mistresses?"

"It is not a fascination, I just—well, you said you did not take lovers from the *ton* nor from your estate. Do you keep a mistress?"

Her voice was scarcely a whisper by the time she reached the last word, and her eyes, which had been fixed on his face, dropped, her blush fiery.

Just what the devil was he supposed to say to that? Well-bred men did not discuss their bits of muslin with their wives, but she had asked. To tell her it was not her concern would, he was certain, bring an end to this delicate détente between them.

"You do not need to tell me," she said, her expression one of mortification and misery.

"I have always kept a mistress." Her face fell, and it was like a punch to the chest. Did she really care that much?

*Would* you *care if the situation were reversed?* a snide voice asked.

A caustic blend of jealousy and rage boiled up inside him, his hands fisting at the thought of Kathryn so much as *looking* at another man.

"G-Gerrit?" she asked, her brow pinched with worry.

He forced his hands to unclench. "I have not had a mistress since we married. You are my only lover, Kathryn."

Something indecipherable flared in her gaze and her lips slowly curved into a shaky smile. "I am—that is a relief." Almost as quickly as her smile had arrived, it faded.

"What is it?" Gerrit asked.

"It is just that I do not understand how men… do that. Keep a woman just for physical satisfaction with no future objective."

Gerrit eyed her warily. "Objective?"

She rolled her eyes at him. "Yes, objective. I was raised with the *objective* of marriage."

"You are a peer's daughter; that is entirely natural."

"My maid, who is not the daughter of an earl, was also raised with the objective of marriage."

Gerrit considered her comments and question, his mind flickering back to the mistresses he had kept over the years. There had only been four of them, which was a lot fewer than most men of his class. How did one explain to a gently brought up lady the arrangement with one's mistress. And *why* was he expected to explain such a thing?

"I can already see you are closing up," she said.

"Closing up?" he repeated, although he knew exactly what she meant. What was he supposed to do? Tell her all the explicit details? Explain that fucking had always been about physical release to him and never about intimacy.

Until now.

"Did you never become emotionally attached to any of them?"

Gerrit opened his mouth to scoff at the thought of becoming emotionally attached to a mistress when suddenly Amelia leapt to mind. As uncomfortable as it always was to think of her in those terms, there was no denying she had been his father's mistress for longer than the duke had been married to Gerrit's own mother. For the first time he wondered what that must have been like not only for his father, but for Amelia. For his mother.

Christ. He was truly dull not to have considered any of that before.

"Did you become attached to somebody?" Kathryn asked, misreading the reason for his silence.

"No, I never have," he said truthfully. "As to why men can do such a thing, I can only answer for myself: It is a matter of convenience, nothing more."

"Like our marriage," she said blankly.

Gerrit wanted to deny that, but really, wasn't it the same thing in a way? Hadn't he taken the coward's way out when he'd proposed? If you foreclosed on love—or even affection—then you couldn't be hurt when it never came.

But that was not something he wanted to talk about. Or even consider too deeply. At least not right now.

Instead, he said, "I know it could not have been easy to come to me tonight."

Kathryn looked startled, and Gerrit had to admit he'd stunned himself with the rare burst of perspicacity.

"No, it wasn't."

"I am grateful you made the effort."

"I—I had to come because I wanted to explain."

"Explain what?" he asked, suddenly wary.

"I wish I'd never said what I said. I mean about wanting to, er, get our nightly, uh…" She shook her head, her face scarlet.

Gerrit wanted her—he *craved* her—but his pride was hungry, demanding to be fed. *He* had not been the one to reject *her*, after all.

*You are an arse, and a grudge-bearing one, at that.*

The accusation struck its target dead center and Gerrit felt ashamed that he could be so petty.

"Are you talking about your request that I only come to your bed for procreative purposes rather than pleasure?" he asked.

Her face was almost as red as her hair, but her shoulders sagged with relief. "Yes. I—I regret saying that. Deeply." She pleated the top of the sheet over and over again before looking up. "I want to renegotiate the terms of our marriage."

"What do you mean?" he asked sharply, his guts roiling as he watched her gnaw her lower lip.

"I mean I don't want to occupy a small corner of your life. I don't want to tuck myself away in the country—alone—when I am with child." Her jaw flexed, her expression determined. "I don't want to live separate lives once our child is born."

He could not seem to draw enough air into his lungs.

"Gerrit?"

She sounded so vulnerable that it shook him from his daze. He looked at her beautiful face and struggled to leash the joy leaping inside him like an exuberant puppy. "You want to remain at Briarly?" he asked, sounding harsh and cold to his own ears.

"It's not Briarly, Gerrit. I want to be where you are." The last three words were scarcely a whisper.

He knew his jaw had sagged and he probably looked even uglier than usual with such a stupefied look on his face, but he suddenly didn't care. He nodded slowly, holding her gaze. "Yes, I would like that. A great deal."

"Truly?" she squealed.

Gerrit almost laughed. "Truly."

"Good. Good—that's, I'm—" She gave a breathy chuckle. "Thank God." She lowered her gaze before him, the submissive gesture arrowing straight to his cock.

Gerrit took her chin and turned her to meet his gaze. The dominating, controlling bastard that lived inside him gorged on her squirming and blushing. "As to your question from earlier—about having you in my bed."

"Oh, yes?"

"The pleasure of feeling you next to me, and of talking to you, far outweighs any discomfort engendered by a new situation. That is my honest answer." He released her chin, but she did not turn away.

Instead, she caught his hand and held it. "Thank you."

He nodded, too disoriented by the pleasurable press of her slender fingers on his beastly paw to speak.

"Will you tell me something?" she asked, lightly stroking his palm.

He would never have believed there was a direct connection between his palm and cock.

"Gerrit?"

"Er, I beg your pardon—what did you want me to tell you?"

"Just… something. Something about you."

He frowned. "I don't understand."

She gave him an exasperated look. "I am trying to get to know you."

For the first time he could remember, his mind was blank. A complete and utter blank.

Kathryn laughed. "Come now! It cannot be that difficult to tell me something about yourself?"

"I am glad you came to the dig today."

Her face softened. "Thank you."

"And I am glad we are married," he said, surprising both of them.

Her eyes became dangerously glassy. "Oh. That's—that's lovely." She gave a watery laugh. "But it is not really something about *you*, is it? But I like it, all the same. I like it very much."

Gerrit allowed himself to revel a bit in her approval. "I will try to think of something interesting to tell you, er, tomorrow night."

She laughed again and squeezed his hand.

He plucked at her dressing gown, which was, he suspected, all she wore. "I want to take this off you," he said, done with talking.

Thankfully, she nodded, and he slid the garment from her shoulders and then tugged it from beneath her, hesitating a moment before dropping it off the bed.

Kathryn pulled the sheet up to cover her chest. "It bothers you to leave that on the floor, doesn't it?"

Were his thoughts really so transparent? That should worry him more than it did. "Bother is too strong—but I do get a queasy twinge when there is disorganization or clutter."

"Even if you can't see it?"

"Not so much," he said, which was not really a lie. Or at least a very small one. But the last thing he wanted to do while he had his beautiful, naked wife in his bed was scurry around his bedchamber folding clothing.

Gerrit gently pulled down the soft sheet and she released it. He gave a rumble of approval and cupped one of her breasts, the pink tip already hard.

She hissed and her head tipped back, her chest thrusting toward him.

He teased each nipple in turn, until she was trembling, and then lifted her leg and draped her thigh over his hip before using his cock to stroke and caress her to climax. She was still shuddering when he entered her, rolling his hips in slow, gentle waves as he had wanted to do times beyond counting but was always too eager to wait. When the last echoes of her orgasm faded, he reached between their bodies and employed gentle but firm pressure to draw out a second orgasm, or perhaps just a continuation of the first.

Gerrit stilled his thrusting, keeping himself buried deep inside her as the spasms gradually diminished. Her eyelids lifted lazily, a satisfied smile curving her lips as he flexed his erection in the tight clasp of her body.

"Where did you learn such a clever trick?" she murmured.

"What—this?" Again he flexed his cock.

She chortled. "That is pretty clever, too. But no, I meant the other—the way you draw out my pleasure."

It had been his first lover, the mistress his father had engaged for him on his fifteenth birthday, who'd taught him most of what he knew when it came to women's bodies, but—for once—he did not tell the truth, which he strongly suspected she might not like.

"Trick?" he repeated, raising his eyebrows in a purposely arrogant fashion. "I don't know what you mean."

She allowed herself to be diverted, laughing softly as she lifted a hand and rubbed his chest, teasing one of his nipples with her palm before moving lower and lower.

Gerrit gave a muffled groan, and his hips began to move. He worked her with deep, leisurely thrusts as she stroked his abdomen, her fingers strumming the taut striations.

Her eyes danced with mischief as she lifted them to his. "You like that." It was not a question.

Gerrit had to grit his teeth to hold back another moan as she dug into a particularly sensitive spot, her strong fingers stroking him in an odd sort of rhythm.

It took him a moment or two to decide what it felt like. Gerrit lifted one eyebrow. "Are you playing me like a harp, Kathryn?"

She gave an intoxicating, joyous laugh. "Yes, I am, Gerrit."

"I didn't know you played," he said, his voice thick with pleasure.

"I don't."

"I beg to differ; you are a virtuosa." His voice broke on the last word, and he thrust deep and hard, losing himself in his release.

Gerrit forced his heavy eyelids up once he'd floated back to consciousness. He was vaguely aware that Kathryn was caressing his back.

"Rest, Gerrit."

*Just for a moment,* he thought.

But he must have fallen asleep because when he opened his eyes the candle was guttering in the socket. Amazingly, his cock was still inside his sleeping wife and once again hard.

He rolled his hips, slowly rousing her from her slumber, amused when she did not wake fully until her climax was upon her.

The next time he woke there was no light from the candle and none seeping from between the drapes.

It took him a moment to realize what had wakened him was his wife's hand, lightly stroking the taut skin of his belly.

"I want you again," she whispered in the darkness.

Heat roared through his body as Gerrit flipped her onto her back and gave her what she asked for, their lovemaking wild and hungry.

When Court came to wake him just after dawn Gerrit saw that his bed was empty. Only the faint scent of lavender and a spiral of red hair on his pillow proved that it had not all been a dream.

# Chapter Twenty-Five

The following morning when Katie went down to breakfast, the room was not empty. Gerrit was already seated at the table, garbed for riding in buckskins and a dark blue clawhammer, a heaping plate of food in front of him.

He stood when she entered. "Good morning, Your Grace."

"Good morning, Dulverton," she said, unable to completely mask her surprise at finding him breaking his fast at almost ten o'clock. She glanced at Thomas, whose eyes quickly slid in the other direction. So, she wasn't the only one surprised to find the duke in the room.

"Coffee please, Thomas," she said, and then turned to the buffet and put far too much food on her plate while she pondered her husband's presence.

She had fallen asleep with a smile on her face when she'd returned to her room just before dawn. Evidently, she'd still been grinning like an idiot when Becky woke her at nine.

"Don't you look happy this morning, Your Grace," her saucy servant had observed, smirking to herself.

Katie realized her lips had again curled up at the corners as she'd stared unseeingly down at her plate.

She snatched glances at Dulverton from beneath her eyelashes as he poured himself a glass of ale from the pitcher, evidently eschewing coffee and tea. Katie realized at that moment that she had no idea what he liked to eat or drink for breakfast.

She commanded herself to act normally and took a bite of eggs. Why did breaking her fast with him seem more intimate than what they'd done all night?

Dulverton's plate was heaped with an astonishing amount of food. He glanced up, saw her looking, and—to her amusement—the skin over his axe blade cheekbones reddened, but he did not speak.

"I dressed for work," she blurted when the silence stretched.

His eyes briefly flickered over her habit, which was a sturdy navy nankeen with a more modest train than most of her others. There were ties on the skirt that could be used to shorten it so that she would not be dragging it through the dirt.

"Would you care to join me on a ride before we go to the dig?" he asked. "I have to call on two of my tenants," he explained before she could answer. "I want to check on some work being done."

He was going to introduce her to his tenants?

"It will only take an hour or two," he went on. "We should get to the dig in plenty of time to help with the big belemnite."

Katie nodded, entranced by his red cheeks. Was he embarrassed? Why did that cause a joyous leaping in her chest?

"Yes, I would like that," she said.

He gave an abrupt nod, cut off a large piece of beefsteak and pushed it into his mouth, chewing determinedly. He lifted up his glass of ale and then seemed to notice Thomas, who was staring at them with rapt interest, and frowned.

The footman quickly looked down, but not before she'd noticed that his lips were curved in a faint smile.

So were hers.

And hope, as tiny as a snowdrop sprouting in winter, thrust through the ice inside her. Going to his chambers last night had been the right thing to do. She had finally done something *right* in this marriage!

Once they'd finished breakfast, Katie said, "I just need to fetch my gloves and whip. Shall I meet you at the stables?"

"Yes, but you needn't rush," he said, glancing at his watch. "I've got one piece of business to see to first. Shall we say half an hour?"

That was far more time than she needed, but she nodded. "Yes, half an hour."

Katie took the stairs two at a time, smiling ruefully at a housemaid who paused to watch her hasty behavior with a look of surprise.

She was so happy it was almost frightening. How could things have changed so quickly? She'd been a fool not to go to him before now. He'd not made her grovel or feel ashamed. Instead, he'd been grateful and welcoming.

And very, very amorous.

Katie laughed and opened the door to her chambers.

Becky, who was seated in the chair she favored to do her mending, looked up.

"I'm just here for a few moments and then I'm going to inspect two of the tenant houses with His Grace."

A smile spread across Becky's face.

"What?" Katie demanded, not that she could not guess.

"I am *so* happy to see you like this. Mr. Court said—" She broke off, her cheeks looking as red as Katie's felt.

"What did he say?"

"He said he's never seen the master the way he is now."

Katie pulled a face. "That could either be a good thing, or a—"

"He said it was a very good thing."

"Thank you for telling me that," Katie said. "I suspect there are few people who know Dulverton better."

"I suspect you are right. Oh, I forgot that this came for you," Becky said, picking up at letter from the table and handing it to Katie.

She squinted at the spidery script on the envelope, her pulse speeding. "It is from Lady Grimsby." She unfolded the heavy cream paper and frowned at the half-page of difficult to decipher writing.

"What is it?" Becky asked.

A name leapt of the page at her: Lord Jasper Staines.

Her knees buckled and she clutched the back of the settee to steady herself.

"Katie?" Becky's voice seemed to come from a long way off. A hand grasped her shoulder. "*Katie*! What is wrong?"

Katie could not look away from the name. "N-nothing is wrong. I just became lightheaded for a moment."

"You are as pale as milk. Here, sit down while I get you some water."

Rather than argue, Katie sat on the narrow settee and forced herself to read the rest of the letter. Lady Grimsby was inviting Katie to a tea in honor of her great-granddaughter, the daughter of Lord Jasper Staines, who was coming to live with her at the end of the month.

The message said nothing about Jasper visiting, but surely he would be the one escorting his daughter to the old lady's house?

Good God.

Katie could *not* face the man.

"What is wrong?" Becky sat down beside her, a glass in her hand.

Katie took the glass and dutifully drained it before handing it back.

"Katie?"

Katie opened her mouth to lie but then met her best friend's eyes. For years she had been tempted to tell Becky about Jasper, but it had seemed more painful than worthwhile. After all, it happened and there was nothing she could do about it. But now… Now she would have to face him again.

Bile rose in her throat at the thought of seeing him and she pressed a hand over her mouth.

Becky leapt up and fetched a basin which she shoved into Katie's limp hands. For a moment, she thought she might have to use it but she closed her eyes and breathed deeply until the feeling passed.

"What is wrong?" Becky squeezed her shoulder. "Tell me."

Katie looked at her friend's worried face. Becky couldn't help her avoid Jasper, but it would be nice, just for once, to have somebody who cared about her in her confidence. Her mother and aunt—and her aunt's maid, of course—knew her awful secret but the three of them had been revolted and ashamed.

Was she willing to risk her best friend's love and respect? "I'm worried that if I tell you what I've done that you will despise me, Becks."

Becky's sandy brows drew together, her expression fierce. "How could you ever think that? Would you cast me aside if I did something you did not approve of?"

"No, of course not. But this is—"

"You are closer to me than my own sisters, Katie. I will always—*always*—be on your side."

Katie almost wept at the thought of confiding in somebody. She swallowed down another surge of nausea and nodded. "It is not that I don't trust you, Becky. It's that I'm ashamed. But you are right; it is time I tell you the truth." She had to swallow three more times before she could get the next words out. "It is about the summer I spent at my aunt's house."

# Chapter Twenty-Six

D o come back soon," Mrs. St. Clare said as she escorted Katie to the foyer. "I have enjoyed your visits greatly."

"I have enjoyed them, too," Katie said. This was her fourth visit to the older woman's house, and each and every time she came away with a better understanding of her husband. It wasn't that Mrs. St. Clare told her Gerrit's secrets but rather shared recollections about him—mainly from his boyhood—as well as her memories of his father, a man who sounded even more reserved than his son.

"I wish I could come by more often, but now that Gerrit and I ride to the dig together it is difficult to find an excuse to get away," Katie admitted as she pulled on her riding gauntlets, put on her hat, and collected her whip from the console table where she'd left her things an hour earlier.

Mrs. St. Clare looked pleased. "I am sorry that you cannot visit as often, but I am delighted about the reason, my dear."

Katie could not help grinning like a fool; she, too, was thrilled by how much time she was spending with her husband in the weeks since she had first visited him at the dig.

St. Clare suddenly grimaced. "I regret that I asked you to keep our friendship a secret from Gerrit," she said as she walked Katie out to the small carriage house and stable block where Robin stayed while Katie visited. "But I fear he might put a stop to them if he knew. I realize that is a terrible admission for—"

"If you are terrible then so am I. Who knows what sort of flight of fancy he might take against me visiting?" Katie said, giving the other woman a sheepish smile. "It is better this way; he cannot forbid what he does not know about, can he?" She could see her words did not make the older woman feel better, but she did not want to risk losing this unorthodox friendship. And something told Katie that Gerrit would not approve of her friendship with his father's mistress.

A wife should probably feel guilty about concealing things from her husband, but really, what could it hurt to visit Mrs. St. Clare for an hour here and there? After all, if not for the older woman's urging—and Betje's too, of course—Katie's marriage would be doomed to failure. In truth, Gerrit should be *grateful* that she'd befriended Mrs. St. Clare.

But somehow, she did not think he would see it that way.

Katie waved goodbye and guided Robin back through Echo Forrest toward the path that would take her to the dig. She cut a worried glance at the sky. There was thick cloud cover, but the air did not feel especially humid, so hopefully the rain would hold off until tonight.

It was already past one o'clock, which meant she'd only have a few hours at the dig. Katie had missed her ride with Gerrit that morning and the first half of the day with him because she'd felt so guilty about allowing her domestic duties to slide that she'd decided to spend the morning with her housekeeper. After she'd finished at Briarly it had seemed a perfect opportunity to sneak in a visit to Mrs. St. Clare before heading to the dig.

Now that she'd developed an interest in fossil hunting, everything else seemed like a chore. Well, not her needlework. It was nice to enjoy plying her needle again. But as for the rest of the activities that *ladies* were supposed to enjoy—paying calls and attending neighborhood gatherings—Katie was grateful that Dulverton did not seem to care if she did any of those things.

Thinking of her husband made her smile. They were getting along swimmingly, and not only in the bedchamber. Having fossils to talk about had opened the door to other subjects, from estate matters to current events. Dinners had become almost lively affairs and their evenings in the library were no longer conducted in monastic silence.

The best times, however, were those nights when he stayed in her bed. While she had not gathered the courage to invade his domain again, Dulverton had slept with her at least one night in three. Not only was their lovemaking gloriously satisfying, but her husband was at his most approachable after they had eased each other's carnal appetites.

The only subjects they seemed to have any difficulty discussing were each other.

Twice Katie had attempted to lure him out of his shell by asking personal questions, but his eyes had shuttered and that had been enough to keep her from probing.

For some reason it did not worry her over much. Especially when she remembered what he'd said the night she went to his bedchamber—that he was glad he had married her. Katie knew lots of men might have said that merely to please her, but Dulverton was not lots of men. If he said something, he meant it.

As far as she was concerned, the important matter was that they were talking, which was miraculous considering how their marriage had begun. Katie felt sure they would grow closer as time passed and they felt more comfortable with one another.

If only she did not have the matter of Jasper hanging over her head.

Her smile dropped away at his unwanted intrusion into her happy thoughts.

The only reason she was not consumed with terror at the thought of Jasper visiting his grandmother was because of Becky. Telling her friend the truth about that summer was one of the wisest decisions she had ever made. Becky, who was stricter about matters of social protocol than most dowagers, had strongly advised Katie to send her regrets to the Countess of Grimsby's garden party.

"You are newly wedded," Becky had reasoned when Katie asked how she could possibly avoid the countess's function. "You can claim a prior engagement that cannot be avoided. She will understand. Later in the summer—after you are certain Lord Jasper is not coming—then you can pay her a visit."

Katie had been pathetically grateful for Becky's advice because it had been exactly what she wanted to hear.

"With any hope Lord Jasper will deposit his daughter with his grandmother and disappear back to wherever he came from," Becky had added, echoing Katie's thoughts. "We are fortunate that Cook's daughter—who is an insatiable gossip—works in Lady Grimsby's kitchen." Becky had smirked. "Cook will probably know about Lord Jasper's arrival before he does."

Katie had laughed, although it had been tinged with hysteria. And then she'd written to the countess to express her regrets.

The event was only three days away and thus far Cook's daughter had made no mention of Lord Jasper. Evidently Lady Grimsby's granddaughter had arrived at her house in the company of the countess's own groom, housekeeper, and the baby's nanny.

She felt a slight twinge of remorse that she had rejected Lady Grimsby's invitation when—

"Katie!" a voice yelled behind her.

Katie shrieked and jerked the reins causing Robin to whicker nervously and dance sideways. Once she'd settled him, she twisted in the saddle, her heart almost pounding out of her chest at the man currently guiding his horse out of the woods onto the path.

"Sorry about that, darling," Jasper said, not sounding sorry at all.

"*You,*" she said flatly.

He grinned. "In the flesh."

"What are you doing here?" she demanded, returning his smile with a scowl.

"Looking for you." He brought his horse to a halt beside her. "I was beginning to believe it was impossible to catch you without Dulverton."

"Why are you looking for me? And why does it matter if I am alone?"

His blue eyes, still as brilliant as she recalled, widened in mock surprise. "You are an old, dear friend. Why wouldn't I look for you? As for wanting to talk to you privately? Well, I have things to say. Things that are for your ears alone."

She ignored his ominous comment. "I'd heard that Lady Grimsby's servants brought your daughter here."

His lips twisted into a bitter smile. "Yes, that's true. Grandmama did not know I was coming and is not best pleased. She has tucked me away in a cottage on her estate until she decides what to do with me." He made a moue of disgust. "While it is a relief not to be under her roof and forced to endure her dour looks and constant carping, I have only my valet to do for me at the moment and am living quite rough."

"Why are you here? I was given to understand that your grandmother is raising your daughter while you mourn the loss of your wife by indulging your appetites in Naples." Yet another piece of information Becky had gathered. Nothing Becky had heard about Jasper was good. It appeared his reputation in the neighborhood was less than sterling, although Becky had not been able to discern any specifics.

Rather than be offended, he laughed. "Ah, little Katie has claws, does she?"

"I am almost three-and-twenty, not so little anymore."

His eyes flickered over her in a way that had once sped her pulse but now made her want to slap him. "No, not so little. As for my wife?" He shrugged. "Well, you and I both know that Judith was my grandmother's choice—not the choice of my heart." He gave her such a calculated look of longing that it was all she could do not to laugh. Or vomit. Had he always been so transparent? Katie feared that he had. And that she had been a little fool, looking for acceptance and love and too oblivious to notice his true colors.

When she did not respond, he relinquished his brokenhearted lover expression and changed tack. "So here we are! I am widowed and you are now a grand married lady." He suddenly laughed. "I stopped in London for a few days on my way here and heard how you ended up with Dullness."

"I do not care for that name."

Jasper ignored her. "Kissing games?" He clucked his tongue. "Poor Katie, hoist by your own petard."

She opened her mouth to tell him that marrying Dulverton was the best thing that had ever happened to her but then shut it again. He didn't deserve to know anything about her, especially nothing important.

Jasper, self-absorbed as he was, assumed her hesitation had to do with him. "I am sorry, Katie. Truly, I am," he added when she merely stared. "I am afraid that jealousy has given me a forked tongue."

"Jealousy?" she repeated, morbidly curious about what he would say.

"I am consumed with jealousy for Dulverton—or is it envy I am feeling?" He shrugged. "Probably both. It eats at me that he was fortunate enough to win you, even if it was through no effort of his own."

Katie stared for a long moment, and then laughed. "As entertaining as this little *tête-à-tête* has been, I really must be going."

For a moment he looked truly befuddled. And then thwarted. But his ebullient nature took control after only a few seconds. "I will ride with you."

"I wish you wouldn't."

His smile slid away, and this time it was not so fast to rebound. "You are still angry with me?"

Was she? Katie gave his question more consideration than he deserved, but then it wasn't really for him, but for her. And she deserved an answer, didn't she?

"I am still angry at myself for believing you." The relief she felt after speaking left her a bit lightheaded. How had she not realized who'd borne the blame for his duplicity until now? *Five years* she had punished herself.

His too-perfect features shifted into an almost convincing expression of remorse. Almost. "I never wanted to break your heart, Katie. You have no idea how much I regret what happened. I wanted to believe that we could live on the scant allowance my father grudgingly gives me—and when I was with you anything seemed possible—but when I sat confronted by the bills I could not pay, and those just for modest bachelor rooms in London, I knew I could not marry you." He pulled a face. "Tragically, if I had waited just a few weeks I would have heard about the generous sum your brother-in-law, Needham, settled on you." He frowned, visibly thwarted.

Katie thought this last expression was a great deal more authentic than his broken-hearted swain look.

"Needham was very generous, as were all my brothers-in-law. Thanks to them, I could have married a street sweeper if I'd wanted," Katie said, unable to resist twisting the knife a little.

He looked almost excited—no doubt at the thought of all that money. "I wouldn't have needed great wealth, darling, just your love and enough money to keep body and soul together. I will always regret I was forced to do my grandmother's bidding."

Katie believed that he regretted getting his hands on her dowry. "It is all long behind us now, Jasper."

"Yes, a lifetime ago."

She allowed him to hold her gaze for longer than she should have, looking for… *something* in his robin-egg blue eyes.

Once again, she experienced only relief. Relief that she felt nothing for him. And even more relief that he had abandoned her five years ago, regardless of how much it had hurt and terrified her at the time. Had he broken her heart? Until a few moments ago Katie would have said *yes*, but now she was not so sure. She had certainly nursed her wounds as if he had.

But none of that mattered any longer.

*He* didn't matter.

"Goodbye, Jasper." Katie hoped the finality in her voice would be a gentle but firm hint that she wanted this to be the last time he sought her out. Judging by the soulful and—she believed—smug look he cast her, she suspected she should have employed a more direct message. Perhaps a large club over his head.

"I vastly prefer to say *au revoir*, Katie," he said, confirming her suspicions. He lifted his hand and set it over his heart. "I refuse to believe we have been thrown together again by fate for no reason. Not when we once meant so very, very much to each other."

Katie held her tongue, inclined her head, and urged Robin into a walk. She felt his gaze on her back until she rounded a corner. Only then did she let out the breath she'd not been aware she'd been holding.

*Please let this be the only time I see him,* she prayed.

But the grim feeling that settled over her like an unpleasant London fog told Katie that she would not be so lucky.

***

Three days later Katie had just arrived home from the dig and was changing out of her habit when Becky flung open the door and hurried into the room, moving so abruptly that the steaming ewer she held in one hand slopped water over the side.

"Lord Jasper is *here!*" Becky hissed, slamming down the water with a sloshing *thud* and pushing aside Katie's fingers to take over the task of undressing her.

Katie had hoped Jasper would come and go without anyone but her being the wiser. She should have known better "Yes, I know."

Becky's hands froze. "You know? Surely he did not seek you out?"

"Yes, he did."

"Oh, *Katie!* When? And why did you not tell me?"

"I did not tell you because I just wanted to forget about it." It was mostly the truth, if not all of it.

"When?"

"Three days ago. It was the day I rode to the dig alone and he was waiting for me in the woods." Katie could not help wondering how he'd known her schedule.

"You did not stop and talk to him, did you?" Becky asked.

"What was I supposed to do? Ride him down?"

Becky's mouth pursed tightly at her sarcasm, and she yanked on Katie's riding coat.

"Ow! You just about pulled my arm off," Katie groused.

Becky ignored her complaint and forcibly spun her around to access the back of her habit.

"I thought dressers were supposed to do the moving, not manhandle their employers?"

Becky did not take the bait to bicker. "Lord Jasper is in disgrace with the countess and has been banished to a cottage on her estate. Evidently, he has run through all his money and came back to beg for more."

"Perhaps Lady Grimsby did not leave him much to begin with," Katie said, not that she believed it.

Becky shook her head. "That is not what I heard. He might not be inheriting the title, but he is her heir when it comes to everything else."

Katie's eyes widened at that. "Are you sure?"

"He boasted of it at The Sleeping Boar."

Katie knew that was the village pub.

"He is supposed to live on an allowance until the countess dies. She is evidently extremely wealthy in her own right and owns not only Elm Hall but two other estates. The Earl of Grimsby—who is Lord Jasper's cousin—inherited Grimsby Park and very little else. In any case, this afternoon dunners showed up from London looking for Lord Jasper, and Lady Grimsby was furious. That is when all the servants learned that Lord Jasper was on the estate. The countess paid off the bill collector but told Lord Jasper that was the last one. Can you guess what he said?"

Katie was astounded, and a little horrified, by the sheer amount of detailed gossip. "I can guess that somebody has been listening at keyholes at Lady Grimsby's house." She stepped out of her skirts and turned around to face her servant. "I certainly hope our own household affairs are not so widely or accurately broadcast."

"Of course not!" Becky said, affronted.

"I know, Becks. I was just teasing." But not entirely. After all, *somebody* had told Jasper where to find her three days ago.

Becky grunted and disappeared into the dressing room. A moment later her voice drifted out. "Lord Jasper said he would take his daughter away if the countess did not give him what he wants."

"Take her where?" Katie asked, pouring hot water into the basin and washing her face, neck, and arms.

Becky reappeared holding one of Katie's favorite gowns, an antique gold silk with green and gold beaded embroidery around the hem and puffed sleeves.

"Does it matter where he would take the little girl?" Becky asked.

"No, I suppose not."

Poor Lady Grimsby dotes on the child. Besides, what would a widower know about taking care of a baby girl?"

"I suspect the countess will give him what he wants rather than risk his threat."

"As do I." Becky cast a worried glance toward the connecting door, as if Gerrit might have his ear pressed against the door. "What did Lord Jasper want from you?" she whispered.

Katie pondered lying but dismissed it. There were already enough lies for her to clear up; it was time to stop adding to the problem. "Although he did not come out and say it, I believe he wants to resume our *association*."

Becky gasped. "Why, that *devil!*"

That was one word for Jasper, and far kinder than the ones Katie could think of. The man was a pathetic, greedy, manipulative, shallow cad. She liked to believe that if she had met him for the first time three days ago, she would not be taken in, but his act was quite convincing. Probably because he believed in it himself. He saw himself as a thwarted lover, his choices stolen from him by cruel fate. If what Becky had just said about him was true, then he'd frittered away the money he'd been given—at cards, horses, women it hardly mattered—and was now using his daughter as a weapon to extort more out of his grandmother.

Becky slipped the gown over Katie's head. "What did you say to him?" she asked, meeting Katie's gaze in the looking glass while she tugged the gown this way and that before commencing to fasten the numerous tiny buttons that ran up the back.

"I told him to leave me alone."

Becky looked gratified. "Did you now?"

"Well, not in those exact words, but close enough."

"What are you going to do if he accosts you again?"

"I'm going to do my best to make sure that does not happen until he leaves."

"You think he will leave?"

"I think he will be off like a shot the moment he has money."

Becky grunted. "You do not think you should tell His Grace about all this?"

"No! You must have heard what Dulverton did to his last wife's lover."

Becky's sudden blush told her that piece of gossip had indeed come her way.

"Dulverton does not know, and I want to keep it that way. The last thing I want to do is give him a reason to shoot the man."

"No, no of course not," Becky murmured, fastening Katie's pearls around her throat. "Do you really believe Lord Jasper will stay away from you?"

*No.*

But if he *did* bother her again, Katie just might have to make him regret his temerity. An idea—a very bad, dangerous one—had been slowly growing in her head over the days since their meeting. It was the sort of nasty, punitive plan that would leave his arrogant pride in tatters.

*Do you never learn?*

Katie grimaced. *Somebody should teach him a lesson.*

*Why does it have to be you?*

"Your Grace?"

Katie looked up. "Did you say something?"

"I asked if you thought he would leave you alone as you asked?"

"I don't know. If he is wise, then he will."

"Wise men do not throw all their money at horses and cards and—and other things."

Katie smiled at the other woman's inability to say *whores*. "Having lived through my father's depredations, I heartily agree."

Becky set a hand on Katie's shoulder. "Are you sure keeping the truth from the master is the right decision?"

"I hope so." Because telling Dulverton about Jasper at this point was something she could not bring herself to do. Not now. Not when things were finally going well between them. Telling him that she'd lied about Jasper was something he'd never forgive. She just knew it. This was one secret she would have to keep to herself.

# Chapter Twenty-Seven

Katie was so happy it was frightening. As day followed day with no further word from Jasper, she found herself feeling lighter and freer than she had in years. Relations between her and Gerrit—not just in the bedchamber—seemed to get better with each hour that passed.

She should have known that such happiness could not last.

Katie was riding alone to the dig that morning as Gerrit had to spend the day ensconced with his man of business, who had traveled all the way down from London.

When Jasper emerged from the woods not far from where he'd met her the first time, Katie wasn't especially surprised.

"I'd hoped I would see you today," Jasper said, falling into step beside her.

Katie's heart leapt, and it was not the good sort of leaping, either. The plan that had begun to grow in her fertile imagination—a plan she had tried to ignore, but which tantalized her with fantasies of humiliating Jasper as thoroughly as he had once humiliated her—pulsed in her head like a living thing demanding to be fed.

Katie had asked him at least once to let her be, and yet here he was. So, really, he deserved her worst, didn't he?

"Here you are, despite what I said the last time." Katie arched one eyebrow, allowing the faintest of smiles to curve her lips.

It was like hooking a fish in a barrel.

Jasper's smile, which had been a bit strained, immediately grew—not so obvious that it would annoy her, just enough to charm her. Or so he believed.

"I had no other choice, darling."

Katie held in her snort of disgust—barely. "If you keep waylaying me somebody is bound to notice."

He came close enough to stroke Robin's neck. "That is a magnificent horse," he said, the envy in his tone the first genuine thing to come out of him.

"Dulverton bought him for me."

Jasper's mouth tightened and he pulled back his hand. His handsome face was remarkably easy to read, and Katie was amused to watch as he slowly but surely conquered his anger and gave her a caressing look. "Circumstances have forced me to be brash because it is the only time I can get you to myself. By all accounts Dulverton keeps you on a very short leash. There are already stories circulating about how possessive he is of you."

Katie was tempted to mention the stories circulating about Jasper, but managed to bite her tongue.

Jasper gave a derisive laugh when she did not respond. "I suppose he is determined not to lose a second wife."

Katie's hand twitched to cuff him, but instead she slyly chided him. "Dulverton is not a man to be trifled with, Jasper. At least not without taking your life in your hands."

Jasper bristled at her imputation that Dulverton was the more masculine, dangerous man. "The days of dueling are over—even for dukes, Katie. The law no longer looks the other way, and Dulverton should know that." He leaned over in his saddle far enough to set his hand on her leather-clad ankle and give it a gentle squeeze. It was all she could do not to kick him. "Besides, he can hardly call me out for talking to you, can he?"

She eased Robin away enough to break Jasper's hold. "As interesting as this conversation is, I don't have time for idle chatter today."

His mouth tightened briefly before smoothing back into a smile. "Say you'll meet me tomorrow—there is a cottage not far from here. A pretty little place that is abandoned since the old lady who lived there moved away."

"How well versed you are in neighborhood matters for a man who is only visiting. Unfortunately, I am engaged all day tomorrow." She clucked her tongue, and Robin broke into a trot.

"Then the next day. Or the one after. Please," he begged, trotting after her. "I will come to the cottage every day at three o'clock just in case you can get away."

Katie urged Robin into a canter. "How nice to be a man of leisure," she threw over her shoulder.

"I will wait every day!" he called after her.

Katie forced herself to laugh as she rode away. But inside, she seethed at his temerity.

Such towering conceit deserved punishment.

And Katie would be the one to deliver it.

***

"You want me to do *what?*" Becky shrieked.

"*Shhh.* Lower your voice, Becks. I want you to spread some gossip for me—just say a few things in Cook's hearing. Nothing too egregious, just mention my trust fund and how it is *mine,* no matter that I am married or—or what I do."

Becky turned pale. "*No matter what you do?* Good Lord, Katie! What do you mean by that?"

"I will tell you, but only if you swear to keep my confidence."

Becky drew herself up to her full five feet nothing inches. "I have never in my life—"

"I'm sorry." Katie hurriedly cut in. "I know you wouldn't gossip."

"What are you up to, Katie?"

"I am going to teach Lord Jasper a lesson."

"*What?*"

Katie winced. "Would you please keep your voice down?"

"*What?*" Becky managed to shriek in a whisper.

"I am going to make him sorry for what he did. I am going to make him think twice before ever using a woman again."

"How?"

"By making him believe that I still care for him. By making him think that I would run away with him"—she scowled at Becky's ear-piercing yelp— "and by making him believe that he will get his hands on my vast riches. And then…" She paused and narrowed her eyes, visualizing the scene. "Just when he is secure in his newfound wealth and imagining himself wasting my money all over the Continent, I will *wrench* the rug out from under his feet and leave him humiliated and poor." She grinned and knew the expression was not a nice one.

Becky stared for a moment in open-mouthed horror before slumping into a nearby chair and covering her face with both hands. "That is the worst idea you have ever had! We are doomed. His Grace will find out and banish you to the north of Scotland. I will never see my family again. I will never—"

"Will you quit exaggerating?" Katie demanded. "I will not get caught."

"Yes, you will."

"I won't. But if I *do* get caught then I can explain this to Dulverton. He is not an irrational man, he—"

"He is irrational where you are concerned, Katie. And you know it. Everyone knows it. He almost choked that foolish earl to death at the Red Lion just for talking to you."

Was it wrong to enjoy the warm feeling of satisfaction that spread through her body at her friend's words?

"Fine," Katie said. "I will allow he can be a little possessive"—Becky snorted—"but I feel certain that he will listen to me before doing anything rash." She didn't, really, but what else could she say to convince the other woman?

Becky shook her head, unconvinced. "If he will be so understanding then you should tell him *now*. Because this—what you are talking about—is madness. Lord Jasper is viewed as a scoundrel in the neighborhood. His Grace would be most disple—"

"That is for me to worry about," Katie said firmly. "Now, will you spread the gossip or do I need to find another way?" Katie suspected that Jasper was already in hot pursuit and didn't really need more encouragement, but it couldn't hurt to set the hook a little deeper. She had no real idea whether she could get her hands on the money her brothers-in-law had settled on her, or not, but suspected it was all under Gerrit's control, just like everything else. But Jasper was so greedy he would probably believe anything.

"Oh, Lord," Becky mumbled, shaking her head. "If I do what you ask then I am abetting you to ruin. If I do not, who knows what you will do to spread your—your gossip. So, *yes*, I will do it. But I will say this one last time, Katie. I am your friend and love you, but you are wrong-headed in this. Just as wrong-headed as you were with your kissing contest. Worse, even."

"Thank you," Katie said, and then squinted at her reflection in the mirror and changed the subject. "I think I am getting a freckle on my chin."

Becky just groaned.

Despite what she asked her maid to do, Katie behaved herself for five whole days. She told herself that she stayed away from the cottage to give Jasper the chance to do the decent thing and stop pestering her. After all, she wasn't really angry at him anymore. She saw him for the vain, shallow, grasping man he was. He truly had no idea what he'd done to her that summer. It simply would not occur to a man like him that there could be repercussions from lying with a woman half a dozen times.

But the real reason she stayed away was because of Gerrit. She was happy for the first time in years, and it was thanks to him. Katie did not want to hurt her husband. Not just because Gerrit angry was a terrifying sight, but because she cared about him. She thought she might even love him, although she was such a stranger to that emotion that she wasn't sure how a person could tell. Oh, she loved her sisters and brother, of course, but that was not the same thing. At least she did not believe it was.

But whenever she ran all these reasons to stay away through her mind, at the end was always the sheer, unmitigated gall that Jasper possessed to believe for even a second that she would have anything to do with him at this point.

And so on the sixth day, after the vague rumors of her great wealth had time to circulate, she stayed home on the pretext of tending to some genuinely overdue correspondence—she owed all her sisters at least one letter and Phoebe had written a stunning *four*—and kept herself busy until a quarter to three, at which time she donned her work habit and had the stables saddle up Robin.

It was just a few minutes past the hour when she turned onto the narrow path that led to the cottage, riding for perhaps one hundred yards or so before the trees cleared, and the tiny house came into view. A horse was tethered at the hitching post.

Katie paused, uncertain. Meeting him here for a few minutes was one thing, but going into a cottage with him? No. That was one step too far, even for her.

The door opened. "Katie! I knew you'd come." Jasper's grin was triumphant, and his blue eyes shone as he hurried toward her.

"I was just passing by and was curious if you *really* came here every day at three."

He laughed. "Putting me through my paces, are you?"

She shrugged.

"Let me help you down. I've brought a few delicacies in the house and—"

"I am not going into the cottage with you Jasper."

He frowned. "Whyever not?"

"The reason I came to see you—other than curiosity—was because you are correct, we can't talk in the middle of the path. But now that I am here why don't you tell me why you are so keen to see me?"

For a few seconds, he was flummoxed, and Katie could almost hear the clanking of gears as his brain shifted directions. But Jasper would always come about when it came to getting what he wanted.

"I cannot stop thinking about you—even though I know it is… wicked. The truth is, Katie, that my heart has never gotten over you."

Katie suspected that was about as far from the truth as a person could get, but she maintained a straight face and continued to listen although he looked expectant—as if he anticipated a similar declaration from her. Katie wanted to shame him—to string him along and build his hopes—but she could not lie about loving him back—that would shame her worse than him.

When it became clear that she would not speak, he went on. "When I heard you had married Dulverton and were so close to Elm Hall, I could not resist coming to see you." As he had the other day, he wrapped a hand around her ankle.

When she did not pull away, his expression grew bolder. "I *know* you cannot be happy with him. He is a cold-hearted man—inhumanly so—and it makes me ill to think of him putting his cold, emotionless hands on you."

Katie burned to tell him that Dulverton was anything *but* passionless and cold but—once again—she kept that to herself. Jasper did not deserve to know anything important about her.

He took her silence as approval. "I know what it is like to live with somebody you don't love. You have no idea how liberating it is to live on the Continent—away from the crushing, cloying rules we of the *ton* impose upon ourselves. How you would flourish in a city like Naples, Katie!"

Katie couldn't stop staring, repelled but morbidly fascinated. Was he really asking her to run away with him?

"Won't you come inside and sit with me for a while?" He began rubbing up her calf and she jerked away. He chuckled, but it sounded strained. "So skittish. I won't hurt you, sweetling. Don't you recall how much fun we had together? Those wonderful afternoons in our cozy little bower?" He gestured to the cottage behind him. "That old musty gamekeeper lodge was not nearly so pleasant as this private nest. Remember the pleasure we shared in that cramped little bed? We could have that again, my darling."

That long-ago summer came rushing back as clearly as if it had been last week. The choking, overwhelming sickness of both body and soul as she'd waited for Jasper to come back and make good on his promise. And then the crushing humiliation when she saw Jasper standing beside his new wife. She had run and run and run but still could not get free of the horrible sight. She'd gone to her aunt's small stable and saddled the poor old gig horse her aunt kept. The horse had sensed her wildness and had galloped with the hectic speed she had not been able to achieve with her two legs.

She hadn't been nearly as experienced a rider back then, and when the stone wall loomed up in front of her the poor, terrified horse had twisted and reared, throwing Katie to the ground.

And in the blink of an eye one of her problems had been solved.

"Katie, my dear?" Jasper said. "What is wrong? You have gone as white as a—"

Katie jerked the reins causing Robin to shove Jasper to one side as he leapt forward.

The moment she broke contact with his hand the suffocating sensation ceased. She turned her startled mount and held him in check, the poor creature dancing side to side wondering what madness had come over his mistress.

Jasper was glaring up at her. "What the hell is wrong with you? You almost knocked me off my feet!"

"I cannot do this." She felt as if she were waking from a fever dream. What had she been thinking? What a mad, reckless, and foolish and—and *dangerous* notion she'd been nurturing!

"What's that?" Jasper demanded, striding toward her, his movements angry and aggressive.

"Just leave me alone, Jasper. I don't want to see you again!" She urged Robin down the path.

"Wait—stop!" He waved his arms, as if to block her way.

Katie did not stop Robin, and Jasper had to leap out of the way at the last moment as she thundered past.

"You bitch! You almost—"

A low-hanging branch tore her hat from her head, and she cried out. But not even the pain could stop her.

Katie fled not just from Jasper and his rage, but from the disaster she had almost made of her life.

***

Gerrit crouched down to admire the massive accretion of belemnites. "I do not think you'll be able to get much more out," he said to Mr. Scott, who had been painstakingly working on the fossils for several weeks.

Mr. Scott grimaced. "If I could just move that boulder, I'm sure there is more beneath that could be salvaged."

"Perhaps, but already this is going to prove problematic to transport." Gerrit stood up and fixed the younger man with an approving look. "You have unearthed a spectacular sample, Mr. Scott."

"Do you think we'll be able to remove what I've exposed in one piece?" the younger man asked, pushing back his hat to scratch his head, his worried gaze on the fossil.

"As to that, we will certainly give it—" Gerrit turned at the sound of horse hooves, a smile pulling at his lips when he saw who it was. "I will make arrangements to organize a group of men to lift it," he said absently, his gaze still on Kathryn, whose face was excessively red. Where on earth was her hat? "Excuse me," he said, not waiting to hear the other man's response before striding to the shaded area where they generally picketed the horses to allow them to graze.

He reached Kathryn just as she was unhooking her knee from the saddle. "Here, let me help you," he said, reaching up and taking her by the waist and then letting her slide down his torso. It was a blatant way to enjoy her body, even if she was still clothed, and she usually gave one of her charming gurgles of laughter when he behaved so naughtily.

But not today.

"Thank you," she said in a breathy voice. Her face, he noticed now that he was closer, looked flushed rather than burnt by the sun.

"Is something wrong?"

"No, no, I just wanted to get here. I've already wasted so much of the day."

Was her smile… forced? Gerrit wished like hell he was better at reading emotions. "You forgot your hat, Kathryn."

She lifted a hand to the top of her head. "Oh. How thoughtless of me. I was so eager to get here, you see—"

"You have plenty of time. I've arranged with Cranston to eat here again tonight so we can work until it is almost dark."

She brightened. "Oh, good."

"I keep a spare hat in the tent," he said. "It is old and not pretty—"

"It will be fine, thank you."

He nodded and she followed him to the tent where he located the hat and set it on her head, where it promptly fell down to her nose.

"Oh," he said stupidly. "I should have thought—"

She laughed and lifted it up. "I can make it fit," she assured him.

Gerrit watched dubiously as she shifted her hair around, removing a pin here and adding one there until the hat was no longer covering her eyes. Somehow, she managed to make even an ill-fitting man's hat look fetching.

"How is that?" she asked, her cat eyes sliding up to meet his.

"Good," he said, sounding like a dolt to his own ears.

She tucked some loose hair beneath the brim while her green eyes slid toward where Mr. Scott was now pacing around his find. "Is he still—"

"He is finished. Although he would like to move that boulder."

"Why doesn't he?"

"The piece is already too large to transport. If there is more, as we suspect, it will have to come out separately."

"You said this would go to the British Museum?"

"Correct. They are one of the few establishments that can do justice to such a piece."

"It will make a stunning display."

Gerrit thought so, too.

"Oh, did you look at that section I mentioned last night at dinner?"

"I did look at it, first thing this morning."

"What do you think it is? It is terribly damaged, but I did not think it was an ammonite."

"You are correct. I believe it is a nautiloid fragment. That piece is extremely small, and most people would have mistaken it for an ammonite fragment. You have a good eye for this work," he said, not exaggerating.

She gave him a shy smile. "Thank you… Gerrit."

Hearing his name on her lips in the middle of the day pleased but unnerved him, and he could only nod and offer her his arm. "Come and I will show you how I made that deduction."

***

They rode home in the moonlight.

"What a beautiful sky," Katie said, trying not to recall her frantic ride down this very path earlier that day.

"Yes. Very beautiful."

Katie turned at her husband's odd tone and found him looking at her.

"You aren't even looking at the sky," she chided in a foolishly breathless voice.

He merely regarded her with an intense, almost brooding, stare.

"You are making me shy," she said a moment later.

He turned away. "I apologize for staring."

"What?" Katie shook her head. "No—you don't have to apologize. It is true that I feel shy, but I—I like it."

He turned back to her. "You *like* it when I stare at you?"

"Yes," she said, her face hot in the cool night air. "I like it a great deal. I only mentioned it to explain why I was becoming so red and fidgeting like a child."

"You look silver in the moonlight, not red."

"I am relieved to hear it," she said, flustered by his caressing tone. "Tell me, why do you sound so surprised that I would enjoy your eyes on me? Gaining a man's attention is the entire point of a London Season, after all."

He turned away, his lips tightening and his jaw firming in a way that usually presaged a cool silence. But this time, he surprised her. "My first wife disliked it when I stared at her. She said it was freakish."

Katie flinched at the word *freakish*. "Surely she did not use that word?"

"She used precisely that word."

"Oh, Gerrit—" Katie stopped, biting her lip.

"*Oh, Gerrit?*" he repeated. "That sounded like a prelude to something more."

"It was," Katie admitted. "But I—I don't know how to put it in words. Not yet."

"I will wait patiently until you do." His stern mouth curved up slightly and he turned to face her. "And enjoy looking at you in the meantime."

She gave a startled laugh, his compliment and smile all the more intoxicating for how rare they were.

"I am very fond of your laugh, Kathryn."

"It is nice to have things to laugh about."

"Why have you not had reason to laugh? I am not the most perceptive of men, but I believe I've noticed a—a sadness, for lack of a better word—in your eyes at times."

Katie's chest tightened at the dangerous turn in the conversation. Talking about the shadows in her eyes would lead to that wretched summer five years ago. And until she told Gerrit the truth about that—

"You do not need to confide in me, Kathryn. I did not mean to sour the mood."

"The mood isn't sour," she hastened to assure him. "You are right that I am sometimes melancholic. Although far less so these past few weeks."

Did she imagine the dark stain on his cheeks at her words?

Katie cleared her throat. "As for my *oh, Gerrit*," she said, moving the conversation toward safer ground. "I was lamenting that people often say the most hurtful things to those they are the closest to." Hy's face rose up in her mind, but Katie shook it away. This was about Gerrit, not about her. Besides, Katie deserved what Hy said to her. Gerrit did not deserve being called a freak. "Your first wife said something that shaped the way you perceive yourself. If she'd said something pleasant, that would be one thing. But to say your attention was *freakish*? That is not only cruel, but also *wrong*."

"I am glad to hear you do not mind my attention, Kathryn." She was about to correct him—to remind him that she'd said she *liked* it—but he was not finished. "Because I find it difficult to look at anyone or anything else when you are near."

"That—that is a lovely thing to say," Katie said, stunned by how good his words made her feel.

He was watching her again, wearing the look she'd once thought of as critical and arrogant, but which she now knew meant he was thinking deeply about something. How glad she was that she'd never thrown angry words at him about his expression during those early days.

*Tell him that. This was what you wanted—to talk—so talk.*

"During the early weeks of our marriage, I mistook your resting expression for arrogance and conceit and thought your gaze held only censure," Katie blurted. "But I now realize your face is sternest when you are pondering something."

His eyebrows rose. "I am glad you no longer think that. It is true that I take pride in myself, but I hoped it stopped short of arrogance." His lips twisted slightly. "But perhaps I am wrong."

"No. No, I don't think so."

"Good. Because your opinion is the only one that matters."

Katie laughed. "Now *that* just might be a bit arrogant."

He chuckled and Katie almost fell off her horse. "I like the sound of *your* laugh."

Once again, he looked startled. Katie was beginning to think that nobody had ever given Gerrit even the mildest of compliments. At least no lover.

"Thank you," he said a bit stiffly. "I, too, have not had much in my life to make me laugh." He paused and gave her one of those heavy-lidded looks that felt like a physical caress. "Until lately."

# Chapter Twenty-Eight

The following morning Katie was puzzling over the letter she'd just received from Doddy. Getting any correspondence from her brother was a miracle. Deciphering it required an even greater miracle.

"Becky?" Katie called out, looking up from the chicken scratch.

"Yes, Your Grace?" her maid said, her voice as cool as it had been for days—ever since Katie had asked her to spread the gossip.

Katie set down the letter and sighed. "Come and sit here." She patted the settee beside her.

Becky's eyes narrowed in suspicion. "What have I done?"

"Just come here," Katie said with an exasperated eyeroll.

Becky put down the garment and ungraciously stomped over to the settee. "Yes, Your Grace?"

"I meant to tell you last night, but we got home so late I did not have time. I changed my mind about Jasper, so you needn't treat me as if I were a plague carrier any longer."

"You mean you aren't going to see him again? Or—or get your revenge?"

"Correct," Katie said, amused that Gerrit's word came so easily to her tongue.

Becky threw her arms around her. "Thank God you came to your senses, Katie!"

Katie laughed. Her arms were trapped against her sides, or she would have returned her friend's embrace. As it was, she kissed Becky's cheek and whispered, "I should have listened to you to begin with. Thank you for being the voice of reason."

Becky released her and sat back. "Will you tell the master now?"

Katie thought about their magical ride home in the moonlight and the evening of lovemaking afterward and hesitated. "I want to… but—"

"You do not want to ruin things between you," Becky finished.

Katie nodded. "I will tell him once Jasper is gone."

"Given how possessive His Grace is that is probably for the best," Becky said with obvious reluctance. "I think you will feel relieved after you confide in him."

So did Katie. She wanted to tell him *right* now, but she needed to wait until Jasper was far away from Briarly. She changed the subject. "Can you tell me what this sentence says?" she asked, holding up Doddy's letter and pointing to the line in question.

Becky squinted at the cramped writing. "He is—that cannot be *harm;* it must be *home.*" Her lips moved slightly as she worked out the rest. "There is a termite— no, a tenant—at Queen's Bower?" She looked up.

"That is what I read, as well," Katie said. "Although I cannot make out the name he gives."

"I daresay my mother will mention it in her next letter."

"Yes. I expect Phoebe will have some news, too." Her older sister and her husband Paul lived less than five miles away from Doddy.

"Well, it's good to have somebody in the old place," Becky said before returning to the dressing room. "Houses aren't made to sit empty," she called from the other room.

Katie stared at the letter and tried to imagine somebody else living in the only home she had really ever known. It was a little painful to think of strangers in Queen's Bower, although she knew her regret was foolish. For years Katie had thought she might occupy the house herself one day. The unmarried aunt who would spoil the half-dozen children Doddy would likely have.

Now she had a different vision of the future—one that brought a tentative smile to her face—and a home of her own.

Katie set Doddy's confusing missive aside and reached for the other piece of mail she'd received that morning, a rare letter from Hy. They had exchanged several letters since Katie's marriage, although neither of them was a prolific writer like Phoebe, Selina, or Aurelia.

Hy's letters were polite and filled with news of her sons and life at Chatham Park. They held no hint of the disappointment she had expressed that grim day Dulverton had come to make his offer of marriage.

Katie had relieved her sister's pointed words often, especially during the first unhappy weeks of her marriage, when she had wanted, like a grudging child, to write and let Hy know that she was miserable and paying penance for her behavior.

She was exceedingly grateful that she had suppressed that vindictive, embarrassing urge. Everything Hy had said had been right. Who knows what would have become of Katie if Hy had not given her that talk? She'd been angry at Hy for far too long.

She went to her writing desk and took out not one, but two pieces of paper. It was past time she wrote to Hy to apologize for her behavior and, more importantly, to thank her for putting Katie on the path to happiness.

***

251

Gerrit stole a glance at his wife as their coach rolled down the hill into Lyme Regis. Whatever had been bothering Kathryn for days seemed to have finally dissipated. He wished he knew how to ask her what was weighing on her mind, but he had no clue how to even word such an inquiry. If somebody asked him that question, he would feel they were impinging on his privacy and tell them so directly.

Although, to be honest, Gerrit did not mind when Kathryn asked him personal questions. Indeed, he was beginning to if not exactly *like* it, at least recognize it for what it was: her way of getting to know him because he was somebody she valued. The thought that she wanted *him*... Well, that was something he tried not to look at too closely.

In any event, the shadows that had darkened her green eyes had lifted and their time together at the dig had been some of the best days of his life. Her enthusiasm for her new hobby had breathed new life into his own interest and made him realize that it had been far too long since he'd gone fossil hunting just for the joy of it.

At first, he'd wondered if she would grow tired of it. After all, it wasn't just hard, dirty work, but often a person would dig for days only to discover that significant portions of the find had been destroyed.

But her enthusiasm seemed to be growing, rather than fading. In fact, it had been Kathryn who'd asked if he would like to accompany her today on her visit to Mary Anning's shop.

"If you do not care to go, I will understand," she'd said last night in the library when she'd mentioned making a trip into Lyme. "I do not wish to pull you away from the dig—"

"I would like to go with you. Miss Anning is a fascinating woman with a great deal of experience and knowledge about the fossils in this area." Gerrit pulled a face. "It is unjust how many of her discoveries have been claimed by others, some of them men I know and once respected before learning they have no compunction about stealing another's work if that *other* is a female."

Kathryn had given him a look of surprise mingled with approval. "I am so pleased you feel that way. It quite annoys me whenever Mr. Everett or Mr. Scott diminish her contributions. Miss Cates said the Annings are barely getting by now that Miss Anning's brother has gone to apprentice for an upholsterer and Mrs. Anning is too ill to assist at the shop.

Miss Cates was one of the young people from town who put in time at the dig. She was a hard-working, careful woman who did a far better job than most of the men Gerrit employed.

"When we are in London next time, I will take you to see Miss Anning's most famous find," Gerrit said.

# Kathryn

Kathryn had clapped her hands with delight. "I am dying to see it. One of the other workers saw the ic—icky—oh dear," she'd laughed. "What is it called again?"

"A man named Koenig—who purchased it for the British Museum—has called it an *ichthyosaurus*."

"And what does that mean?"

"*Fish lizard.* What did you want to see in Miss Anning's shop?"

"I'd thought to buy some of her fossils to give to my sisters and brother."

"You do not wish to send your own to them?"

"I would like to support Miss Anning."

"That is very thoughtful of you."

"I just wish I could do more. She is the one who first got me interested in fossils."

Yes, because Gerrit had been too bloody stupid to do so. He owed Miss Anning a great deal—very likely his marriage. Or at least the happy version of it.

Perhaps he might contrive some way to help the woman as a *thank you*.

***

Kathryn was contentedly stitching and re-living their lovely day in Lyme Regis. She was proud of Gerrit, who'd thought of a surprisingly subtle approach to helping poor Miss Anning supplement her income by offering her access to the dig and allowing her to keep anything that Gerrit did not donate.

"Kathryn?"

Katie looked up from the tambour to find Dulverton standing beside the settee.

"I am sorry to interrupt you."

"The interruption is a welcome one. I quite forget to move," she said, stretching her neck and setting aside her work.

"You were deep in concentration." He looked from Katie to the tambour, and his eyes widened. "You are stitching an ammonite."

Katie smiled. "I am relieved you can recognize it."

"May I take a closer look?"

"Of course." She handed him the large tambour.

He held it close to the candles, his pale gaze flickering over it, his expression rapt.

"It is from a sketch I made of that huge—"

"I recognize it," he said, still not looking away. "It is truly astounding work and incredibly intricate." He lightly brushed a finger over the threads. "How astonishing there are so many different shades of brown."

"Actually, I couldn't find them, so I had to dye my own."

He looked up. "Indeed? What sort of dye?"

"Tea."

He blinked. "Tea?"

"I put a dozen hanks of floss into a bowl of tea I'd steeped for a long time and then withdrew one every few minutes as they reached the color I needed. The one that is darkest was in the longest."

"Ingenious," he said, his gaze back on the ammonite. "I never would have thought such realism was possible with needlework." He paused, his forehead furrowing. "Although now that I think on the matter there are several tapestries at Spenwood that are quite detailed." He handed her the tambour. "Fascinating work, Kathryn."

Katie warmed at his obvious admiration. "Thank you."

He clasped his hands behind him and rocked back on his heels, looking almost…nervous?

No, surely not!

"Er, did you need something?"

He cleared his throat. "I wondered if you would play me a game of chess."

Katie's heart sank. "I do not think that wise."

"Whyever not?"

She could not blame him for sounding bewildered. But how could she ever explain—

"There is no need to weigh your words with me, Kathryn. Give them to me with the bark still on them."

She chewed her lip. "I will beat you."

His eyebrows shot up. "You sound quite confident."

"I am."

"And that is somehow a bad thing?"

"You will get angry. People always do."

Rather than refute her claim—another thing people usually did—he pondered her words. After a few moments, he said, "Play me one game. If you beat me and I get angry, we will not play another. But if you beat me—or, lo and behold, I beat *you*—and I do not get angry then we can play another. Until one of us becomes angry."

"I don't get angry."

He cocked an eyebrow. "Is that so?"

Katie snorted. "I meant I don't get angry about *chess*."

"Are you so sure?"

"I have never been angry after a chess game." She paused and then added, "At least not since I was fourteen." Probably because she had won most of them since then.

"Neither have I," he said.

Katie stared up into his eerily pale but beautiful eyes and tried to suppress the anxiety blooming in her belly. Life had been good since she had gone to his room that night. Better than good. She loved working at the dig and being outside and not worrying about smudges on her hands or dirt on her hem. She loved the camaraderie at the dig and she adored talking to Dulverton about the curious finds that every day brought. She liked sitting in companionable silence with him in the library every evening.

And she especially loved their nights together.

She did not want all of that to disappear just because she beat him.

*You could always lose.*

No, she refused to do that—not again.

*Or you could try trusting him.*

She inhaled deeply, exhaled, and nodded. "Fine. One game."

# Chapter Twenty-Nine

Gerrit had the oddest impulse to grin like a maniac as he led Kathryn over to the chessboard, but he wisely suppressed it. He had wanted to ask her to play for weeks. Clearly somebody in her past had reacted poorly when they had lost to her. Like anyone else, Gerrit did not like to lose—at anything—but he had done his share of it in chess as well as other competitive endeavors and liked to think he had always behaved in a sportsmanlike manner.

"Have a seat." Gerrit gestured to the chair where the white pieces had been set up.

"No, we choose for it." She picked up a white and black pawn and put her hands behind her back for a moment before holding out her closed fists.

Rather than argue Gerrit tapped her right hand: it was white.

"You first," she said, taking a seat behind the black.

Gerrit sat and then moved his queen pawn forward two spaces.

She moved her king's knight to bishop three.

Gerrit moved the queen's knight to queen's two.

Pawn to king's four.

Pawn takes pawn.

Black knight to knight five.

White pawn to king's rook three.

Black knight to king's six.

Gerrit's gaze slid from his queen—currently being menaced by her knight—to his king. If he didn't capture the knight, his queen was gone.

He picked up his king's bishop's pawn and moved to take her knight.

But then he saw it and froze.

"Good Lord," he muttered, breathless at what he had almost done. He hastily replaced the pawn and mentally moved pieces before accepting the truth of his situation. Bloody hell… he'd have to lose his queen! But at least he could liberate his bishop. He gritted his teeth, prepared to move his pawn, and then it hit him.

There *was* no move for him. At least nothing that did not lead to mate in two.

He looked up to find her watching him, dread in her eyes. Gerrit swallowed down his disbelief and—yes, his anger, but at himself, not her—and laid his king on his side. "I concede." He cleared his throat, twice, and then forced the words out,

"Excellent game." He began to set up the pieces. "Let us have another. God knows you beat me quickly enough that we've plenty of time for it," he muttered beneath his breath.

**_Three-quarters of an hour later…_**

"Hell and damnation," Gerrit muttered softly as he stared at yet another imminent loss. He choked down his disbelief and for the third time that night laid down his king.

When he looked up, his wife had the same anxious expression on her face that she'd worn the other times she won.

"Yet another excellent game," he said, proud that he managed to conceal his profound irritation—fine, his fury—at three thorough trouncings.

"Thank you," she said colorlessly.

"How—er, how are you so very good at this?" He barked a laugh. "Perhaps that is the wrong question. Maybe I should be asking how I am so very _bad_ after all the years I have spent studying the game."

Her smile looked a bit twisted. "I suppose everyone has one talent and this one is mine. For all the good it's done me."

"You have a good many more talents than just one, Kathryn."

She looked unconvinced.

"You possess a knack for making others feel at ease in your presence."

"Do I?" she asked, her forehead deeply furrowed.

"Assuredly." He kept to himself the fact that he was often proud—and yes, a little jealous—of her ability to chatter easily with the others at the dig, regardless of their social station.

"Your needlework is nothing short of miraculous," he went on. _And you are bloody well astounding in the bedchamber_, he wanted to add but did not.

"Oh. Yes, I am good at needlework."

Gerrit frowned, trying to understand why she wore such a melancholic expression. "You sound unhappy about that. Do you not enjoy needlework?"

"I used to love it when I was younger, and we were poor." She colored slightly at the word. "Back then I used my skills to refurbish our rather threadbare clothing or to make something new. But…" She stopped, her green eyes looking past him to something not in the room. He had the oddest feeling she was about to tell him something important. But then her vague gaze sharpened, and she gave him a faintly dismissive smile. "For a long time, I took little enjoyment in it."

"But you have engaged in needlework every night since coming to Briarly," he persisted.

"I first picked up a needle again to help your mother. But I have come to enjoy it again after years away from it."

Gerrit snorted. "I saw my mother's work. I am surprised you did not merely start over rather than rescue her dismal projects."

She opened her mouth but then closed it.

"What is it?" he asked, even though he suspected he should not.

"I am curious as to why you dislike the dowager so much."

Gerrit's eyebrows shot up. That was direct indeed.

She sighed. "I apologize. You needn't answer that."

He really did not wish to, but he had asked her to be direct, hadn't he?

"It is not a story I enjoy telling, but I daresay you will hear about it eventually. It has to do with my mother's lover." Her cheeks flared to life, and his own warmed, as well. "I apologize for raising such an indelicate—"

"I asked the question, Dulverton. Like you, I would have plain speaking."

"Her lover was one of my father's servants."

Her eyes widened. "I see."

Gerrit wondered if she was recalling her footman lover but quickly banished the unhappy thought and went on. "The man came to England with her." He cleared his throat, which had constricted at sharing the next part. "His name is Helmut Berg and he is the illegitimate offspring of my paternal grandfather. My father's half-brother, in other words."

"Ah," was all she said. But then what else could a person say to such a sordid tale?

He grimaced. "I am ashamed to admit that my grandfather fathered numerous children outside of wedlock. In any case, he sent this woman back to Utrecht to have her child. When Berg was old enough, he found a position in my mother's family's household. My father did not know of the man's existence until he arrived as part of my mother's bridal retinue."

Gerrit rubbed the back of his neck, squeezing the tendons until they hurt to distract himself from this next part of the story. "My father and Berg bore a striking resemblance to one another. I did not know the nature of their relationship until I was much older, but I daresay every adult in the area was aware they were related." The rife speculation he saw in everyone's gaze was one of the reasons Gerrit loathed going to Spenwood.

"My father rarely spent time at Spenwood, and until I was eight years of age I only visited him here at Briarly once a year. That meant it fell to somebody else to see to my instruction in riding, hunting, and so forth." He moved his jaw back and forth to loosen it. "I spent a great deal of time with Berg and he taught me all those things a father would normally teach his son. He was the stablemaster at Spenwood by the time I was born. As such, he had his own cottage on the estate, and I grew up treating it as a second home." Gerrit swallowed. "Until the day I inadvertently came upon Berg and my mother in bed together."

Gerrit looked up. Her face was a fiery red, but he saw the sympathy beneath her embarrassment. He shrugged away the unpleasant memory, which was still vivid even after all these years. "I ran away and came to Briarly. My father allowed me to spend my school holidays here and I did not see my mother for some years afterward. Berg still lives at Spenwood and it is he my mother went to see when she left here so hastily. Evidently, he suddenly took ill. I was very fond of Berg when I was a lad, but naturally after that day—" He stopped, vaguely nauseated at having to recount the sordid tale after all these years.

He shook away the past and looked at his wife. "So that is part of why I do not enjoy her company. And then there is her interference in household matters that do not concern her." She nodded at him, but Gerrit could see a glint of *something* in her gaze. "You do not think those two reasons are sufficient?" he could not resist asking.

She gave a humorless laugh. "I am not one to point fingers when it comes to filial relations. My own mother is currently barred from visiting any of my sisters' homes and I have no intention of allowing her to darken my door, either. I am not sure if my brother has forbidden her to visit Wych House. But if he is wise, he will do so. I know that sounds cruel," she said, although Gerrit had not made a sound. "But my mother is… Well, she is not a kind or pleasant person. To be honest, I think she is far more content living away from us. All of her children are, in various ways, disappointments to her."

Gerrit frowned. "I know our betrothal began in scandal, but surely she cannot be displeased by our marriage?"

"You do not know my mother," she said, her gaze grim and distant.

"You mentioned your brother was on the Continent," he said, wanting to keep her talking about her family, but perhaps not her parents.

"He went to see my father, who fled to Naples last year. I am sure you have heard of the earl's… affliction." She snorted. "Indeed, who has not?"

"I know he has an unfortunate weakness for cards, which is not unusual among our class."

"It is more than unfortunate; it is catastrophic. By the time I was ten-and-five he'd gambled away everything—including his children's futures."

Gerrit had not known it was so bad. "You say your father *fled* to Naples. Is he evading his creditors?"

"Yes. All my sisters' husbands have been franking his habits for years. Two Christmases ago the six of us discussed the matter and decided it was time to put an end to his allowance. It may seem like a ruthless decision, but he ran through all the money my brothers-in-law gave him within *weeks* of receiving his quarterly allowance. They paid for his lodgings and necessary expenses themselves. He even had a generous clothing allowance. Having no money did not deter him and he lived on his expectations for a year. Only when it became known that Needham, Crewe, Chatham, and Shaftsbury would no longer pay his debts did his situation become desperate."

This was the first Gerrit had heard of this, but then he was not fond of gossip. "Are the debts still outstanding?"

"Yes. I would ask that you do not pay them. Because if you do, he will return and—"

"And run up new ones. Even so, it seems rather unjust to his creditors." It went against all Gerrit's principles to leave unpaid debts.

"Perhaps at Christmas you can speak to my, er, *our* brothers-in-law and discuss if there is anything to be done."

He nodded slowly. "You wish to spend Christmas at Wych House? I take it that is where you gather?"

"This year Christmas is at Wych House. My sisters and brother take turns hosting it and the last time it was there was five years ago."

"Was that the last time you went home?"

"Yes. Although in truth I do not really consider Wych House my home because we moved into a small manor on the property when I was very young. My father had to lease Wych to pay for our expenses, but even that was not enough," she added, darkness once again seeping into her eyes.

Clearly her parents were a sore subject. Gerrit felt a pang of sympathy for her. His mother was impossible, but at least he'd had his father. The duke had been a reserved man, but Gerrit had never doubted that he'd loved him.

"Can we go to Wych House for Christmas?" she suddenly asked.

She looked so hopeful that even a man as thick as a plank could see it was important. Doubtless the visit would be excruciating for him—not just spending days and weeks in a chaotic environment, but meeting new people always left him exhausted—but he would gladly bear it to make her happy. "If you like," he said.

She smiled. No, she *glowed.* "I would like very much for you to meet the rest of my family."

*The rest.*

He blinked at the wording. Why did it take him by surprise so to hear himself referred to as her family?

Perhaps because it was only in the past week or so that he had begun to truly behave like a husband.

***

"You were very late tonight," Becky said as she brushed out Katie's hair.

"Yes," Katie agreed, her thoughts on the evening. Playing chess again had been… fun. Yes, it had definitely been fun. She played with her family when they all gathered at Christmas, but she always curbed herself during the holidays and often let people win. Tonight, she had not held back, and Dulverton had simply become more grimly determined with each game. But not once had he looked at her with the open dislike she recalled seeing in Jasper's eyes.

Instead, his gaze had been respectful, if thwarted.

And then there had been their conversation afterward. She'd been shocked by what she'd learned about the dowager. She could also understand now why Gerrit had been so very disgusted when she'd told him her lover had been one of her aunt's footmen.

"Your Grace?"

Katie looked up to see Becky holding up two nightgowns. "Which do you prefer?"

She was tempted to tell her neither, but she knew her rather prim maid would be shocked by such a disclosure.

"The green," she said, and then stood and removed her undressing gown so Becky could slip the pale green muslin over her head.

Green was her best color; Gerrit would like this, she was sure.

*He would like you better naked.*

Katie gave a choked laugh at the shocking thought.

"What's that, Your Grace?" Becky said absently as she cleared off the dressing table and prepared to leave for the night.

"Oh, nothing," Katie lied.

The moment the door shut behind Becky, Katie pulled the nightgown over her head before she could lose her courage. She was going to throw it over the foot bench but then thought about Gerrit and hurried to the dressing room and tossed the garment over the clothes horse before scampering back to bed. Something about running naked, even in her own chambers, felt indescribably wicked.

Smirking to herself, she dove beneath the sheets and had just pulled them up above her breasts when the connecting door opened, and Dulverton entered.

He stopped a few feet from the bed, his pale gaze lingering on her bare shoulders before lifting to her hot face and regarding her with the intense, inscrutable expression that always made her squirm.

He came close enough to lightly stroke the back of her hand. Katie dropped her gaze to his teasing finger, which was far easier to look at than his eyes. But she should have known it would not be so easy.

"Look at me, Kathryn."

She made herself look up.

"Is this for me?" he asked, his distracting touch sliding up her arm and causing her entire body to break out in gooseflesh.

"Yes," she said, aiming for saucy but sounding squeaky, instead.

His lips curled up at the edges. But rather than stopping at their usual twitch, they kept going up and up, until he was smiling a real smile.

"That is a first," she said, breathless with astonishment at how *young* he suddenly looked.

"*Hmm?*" His attention was focused on his finger, which was gently but inexorably pulling down the sheet that covered her breasts.

"Your smile."

"What of it?"

"That is the first time I've seen it."

"Surely not."

"Oh, yes."

"I smile when I am happy. Let go," he said, gently tugging the sheet.

Katie lowered her arms, and he exposed her breasts, not stopping until he'd brought the sheet to her hips.

A low rumble emanated from his chest. "Kathryn," he said, his voice harsh and his pale eyes turning dark.

The effect on him was so mesmerizing that she hardly noticed when he removed the sheet entirely, baring her to his consuming gaze.

"So beautiful." He swiftly tugged on his sash and shrugged out of his robe, letting it puddle on the floor at his feet.

Katie gestured to the robe. "Should I—"

"Leave it."

*Hmmm. That was interesting…*

Her eyes immediately lowered to that most masculine part of him, and her mouth flooded at the sight of his thick, ruddy shaft jutting straight up from the nest of straw-colored curls. She wanted to touch him—desperately—and had done for weeks, but the fear of what he might think of her, of how he would wonder about her experience and how she had gained it held her back.

*Be bold.*

Katie somehow doubted this was what Betje had meant, but she was so tired of second guessing herself. And of hiding what she wanted.

And so she reached for him but then hesitated an inch away, looking up to find his gaze locked on her. He gave a slight nod, and she curled her fingers around his thickness, earning another of those intoxicating animal growls.

She had stroked Jasper before and knew what to do. She made a tight fist of her hand and focused her attention on the area below the crown.

Dulverton hissed and his hips flexed to thrust into her hand, the action causing a truly fascinating cascade of muscles in his thighs, abdomen, and chest. "That feels so good, Kathryn."

She loved the feel of him hot and hard and throbbing against her palm. She cut a glance up at him, entranced by his hooded gaze. *Do it*, her inner devil urged.

Katie swallowed down both her nervousness and the copious moisture in her mouth and leaned closer, watching him the entire time. His eyelids slowly lifted, and his nostrils flared as she shifted on the mattress until she could kiss his swollen crown.

He groaned, his expression one of desire rather than disgust or judgment. He slid a hand around her jaw and slowly pushed his hips toward her. "Suck me, Kathryn."

It was her turn to groan at his crude command, and her hand shook as she positioned him at a better angle and opened her mouth and took him inside.

***

Part of Gerrit's brain was loudly shouting that one did not use one's wife as if she were a harlot. But the rest of his mind, which reveled in the sight of his beautiful wife valiantly attempting to swallow him whole, kicked the complaining voice into a distant corner.

"Lovely," he rasped, lightheaded with lust at the sight of her pale pink lips stretched around his disappearing length. He caressed the slick, taut skin with his thumb, their eyes locked as she slowly lowered to take more. This was not her first time engaging in such an act, but her watering eyes and the scrape of her teeth told him it was not far off. That she had offered such a gift to Gerrit was almost more arousing than the act itself—not that she didn't work him toward release with impressive speed.

But he did not want things to end so quickly.

"Kathryn," he murmured, placing a hand on her shoulder and carefully withdrawing.

Her brow pleated as she looked up at him. "Was it bad?"

He gave a brief, incredulous laugh. "No, quite the reverse. I am on the verge of shaming myself like an overeager schoolboy."

She grinned.

"Ah, that makes you proud," he accused. She laughed and did not deny it. "I need to be inside you," he said, climbing onto the bed. "Lie down for me, darling." Gerrit did not know who was more surprised by the endearment. Had he ever called a woman darling—or sweetheart or my love or any pet name—before? Not that he could remember.

She lay back, her long, slender body so enticing that Gerrit forgot about burying himself inside her and instead satisfied his hunger by tonguing her delicious breasts, sucking and nipping and laving.

Only when she was a mess of twitches and gasps and moans did he nudge apart her thighs and lower his hips. "Put me inside, Kathryn."

Her long, slender fingers were hot when they closed around him, and she'd scarcely positioned him at her entrance when he sank inside her, filling her with one long, hard thrust that left them both gasping.

"So hot and tight," he murmured, having to bite his tongue to keep from shouting when she contracted around him. Yes, she liked it when he spoke. And he liked it when she liked it.

"Can you do that again for me?" he asked, rolling his hips slowly.

Her expression was one of intense concentration before she shook her head. "I cannot seem to control it unless—"

"Unless I say something vulgar?"

She gave a breathy laugh. "Yes, that seems to—"

"How should I fuck you, Kathryn? Hard and fast?" He demonstrated with a powerful thrust that pinioned her to the mattress. "Or slow and deep?" Once again, he matched deed to words, gritting his teeth when her slick passage contracted around him.

"Do I have to choose?" she asked, her eyes sensual slits as her hands stroked from his shoulders to his waist before resting on his arse, one palm on each cheek.

"My greedy girl," he said approvingly, lowering to one elbow and then reaching between their bodies. "I like to feel where we are joined." He stroked the slick, taut flesh of her sex.

"Gerrit," she breathed as he slid his wet finger to the swollen nub at the apex and lightly pinched it between his thumb and forefinger. She bucked as passion swamped her, her sheath clenching like a vise and sending him hurtling toward his own release.

Her limp arms tightened around him when he would have moved off her, so he laid his full weight on her, enjoying the press of her small body beneath his for a few seconds before rolling them both onto their sides. "I do not want to crush you," he explained when she made a noise of dissent.

She burrowed her face between his neck and shoulder. "Don't go…Gerrit." Her words were muffled and hot against the skin of his throat.

Rather than answer her, he slowly withdrew from her body and then turned her until her back was to him. He tucked his softening cock between her buttocks as he pulled her tight to his chest. She fit so perfectly. Why had he held out against this intimacy for so damned long?

"Gerrit?"

"*Hmm?*"

"I am looking forward to bringing you home for Christmas."

Well. What could he say to that?

*Why not say what you feel? You do it often enough when something displeases you, after all.*

Gerrit pulled her closer. "So am I, Kathryn." He burrowed his face into the wiry mass of curls and pressed a kiss to her head. "Now go to sleep."

But judging by the soft snore that met his command, she already had.

# Chapter Thirty

Several mornings later Gerrit surprised Katie.

"Where are we going?" she asked when he led her past the large open excavation where the fossil hunters from town worked and where Katie had spent her days helping them.

"You will see," he said mysteriously. About fifteen feet before they reached the area where he was working, he stopped and gestured to an undisturbed section. "This area is yours."

Katie's head whipped up. "Mine?"

He nodded, a faint curl at the corners of his mouth.

"All mine?"

"All yours. Miss Frampton and Mr. Nelson have both spoken highly of your care and patience, so it seemed time to give you your own patch."

"They are just being kind," she said, but flushed with pleasure regardless.

"They are not just being kind," he demurred. "You have an instinct for this, and I believe you possess the patience necessary for the bigger finds." He gestured to the area he'd just given her. "Who knows what you might unearth here?"

It was tempting—or habit, rather—to shrug off his praise, but then she thought about the past weeks and realized he was right. Not only did she enjoy the excitement of hunting fossils, but she did not mind the hours of painstaking labor required to extract something without destroying it.

"Thank you. I find that I have caught the fossil fever," she confessed.

Although Dulverton merely nodded, Katie could see her words pleased him. When she had first begun to accompany him, it had been his approval she'd sought. But it had not taken many days before she looked forward to their daily digs for her own reasons. It was no surprise to her that fossil hunting had become all the rage. It was like solving a mystery and digging for buried treasure rolled into one. Yes, it was dirty work, but that did not bother her in the least. Indeed, it reminded her of the best time of her life: her childhood, when every day had felt like summer and had been spent running free and exploring with her siblings.

Even Becky had noticed the change in her. And, aside from chiding her to wear a hat with a larger brim and netting when she was out in the sun, her maid had been delighted.

"You remind me of young Katie," she'd said just last night as she'd brushed Katie's hair and readied her for bed. "Full of life and excitement and optimism."

# Kathryn

Katie had scoffed at her friend's embarrassing declaration, but the truth was that she felt better than she had in ages—in years.

As she looked from her very own section of the dig to where Dulverton had settled down to his work, she could not believe how happy she was.

Indeed, she would be almost *completely* happy if not for the matter of Jasper, who was still lurking in the area although he had not again accosted her.

Katie wanted to tell Dulverton the truth—to truly clear the air between them—in the worst way. She chewed her lip and pensively regarded her husband. Would it be the wise thing to do?

He was kneeling on one of the thick canvas pads everyone used to spare their knees. His hat was pulled low, his hands bare as he exposed the delicate tracery of the long-dead creature's tentacles. When he turned his mind to something, as he was doing now, his focus was total, and he looked almost fierce.

He wore the same expression at the chess table.

And in bed.

They had gone from spending only an hour or so in each other's company to spending most of their days and nights together. They broke their fast together, traveled to the dig together, ate a midday meal and tea in the tent, rode home together, discussing the finds of the day, they were apart a few hours before dinner but back together, and alone, after dinner in the library where they played a few games of chess every evening and then worked on their own projects until bedtime.

Ah, bedtime… the best time of the day in Katie's opinion, especially since Dulverton had begun to spend the night in her bed. True, he was always up and gone before she woke, but he was there all night. Sometimes they made love; sometimes he just held her.

"Is aught amiss?"

Katie blinked and saw that Dulverton had stood up and was approaching her.

"No, nothing is wrong. I am just… happy."

The stern Duke of Dulverton smiled. It was not a half-smile or a wry smile or a cool smile, but a slow-growing full-blown grin. Who would believe the man had teeth?

Katie found herself grinning in return, vaguely aware the two of them were standing in the middle of a churned-up hillside like a pair of fools just…smiling.

***

"That is twenty-two games you have won," Gerrit said, replacing the pieces on the board.

"You have won some, too," Kathryn generously pointed out, replacing far fewer pieces on her side of the board.

"Four. I have won *four*. And what is worse than losing all those games is the fact that you trounced me using only fifteen pieces three times." It had been his wife's idea to give up a piece of his choosing—other than her king or queen—and she had still beaten him.

She bit her lower lip.

"Ah, you find that amusing, do you?" he demanded.

She pulled her lips between her teeth, but the corners of her mouth curled up all the same.

"Go on—laugh. I find it amusing, too." He did. In a painful sort of way.

Kathryn laughed and then all the pain was worth it, just to hear her joyful gurgle.

*You are a fool for her.*

He was, but he didn't care. In fact, he was grateful to learn that his father had been wrong about him. Gerrit *could* feel strongly about a woman. He'd known filial love, of course, but it was nothing like the powerful roiling sensation that seized control of him whenever he looked at—or even thought about—Kathryn.

*Tell her.*

Before he could over-analyze his impulse, Gerrit held out his hand. Eyes wide and lips parted in surprise, Kathryn set her slender fingers in his palm. "These past weeks have shown me how pleasurable and fulfilling life is with you. I am grateful every single day that you came to my bed that night to bridge the gap between us." Gerrit enjoyed her blushing before continuing. "Were you aware that Chatham spoke to me the day I made my offer to you?"

"I knew you had a meeting with him, although I do not know what was said."

"He wanted to make sure I was not going to take revenge on you for being trapped into marriage. I assured him that I would not. I wasn't lying—I truly believed I could be fair. But right from the first day I was very *un*fair to you. I was so hidebound by my first marriage that I could not see anything but protecting my own pride. Will you forgive me for behaving in such a selfish manner?"

Her green eyes glowed and she squeezed his hand. "I already have. And will you forgive me for behaving so combatively?"

Gerrit cocked his head. "Were you combative?"

She opened her mouth but then must have noticed the amusement in his eyes. She laughed. "Ah, you are teasing. Now *that* will take some getting used to."

He lifted her hand to his lips and kissed her palm. "I will give you all the time you need to become accustomed to me."

"I think you enjoy making me blush."

"I do," he said simply, and then gestured to the chessboard. "If you are quite finished thrashing me for the night, I propose we go to bed."

"I cannot promise I won't thrash you there, too."

Gerrit laughed. "That is a challenge I cannot resist. Are you ready to go up?"

"I am."

Gerrit stopped outside her bedroom door as he always did but took her chin between his thumb and forefinger and tilted her face up to his. "Come to my chambers tonight."

Her delicate nostrils flared, and her pupils swelled. "Very well. When should—"

"Just give me enough time to shave and wash—ten minutes." And then he gave her lower lip a light caress with his thumb before opening her door and gently pushing her unresisting body over the threshold. "No more than ten," he said, and then shut the door.

***

Dulverton was lying in his massive bed, the sheets and blankets pulled up to his waist, his chest and mountainous shoulders bare when Katie entered his chamber ten minutes later.

She closed the door and then leaned back against it, finding it hard to breathe for some reason. Well, not *some* reason, but because her gorgeous husband was naked and staring at her, eyes blazing.

And he *was* gorgeous. Katie could not think why she had ever found him ugly. Is that what *beauty is in the eye of the beholder* meant? She could not believe that every woman didn't find him irresistible. He might not possess the lissome elegance so prized by tulips of the *ton*, but his powerful body, keen intelligence, and generous nature made him the masculine ideal as far as she was concerned.

It suddenly struck her that Dulverton, with his raw sensuality and complex personality was a man for an adult woman. Jasper, with his unthreatening angelic beauty, flirtatious manner, and frivolous self-indulgence, was the sort of man a young girl would find attractive.

"Come here." Dulverton pointed to a spot beside the bed.

Katie tried for a sophisticated saunter but was so eager that she doubtless resembled an exuberant puppy.

But if her husband was amused by her enthusiasm, there was no sign of it on his stern face or in his darkened gaze.

"Take off your clothes—slowly."

She swallowed hard and lowered her eyes to his thickly muscled forearms and broad-palmed hands which rested on the blankets covering him to his hips. "Um—"

"Look at me, Kathryn."

Her eyes jerkily skittered up his taut abdomen with its narrow trail of pale, downy hair, to his broad chest, her breathing roughening when she finally met his eyes.

The muscles in his jaws were even more pronounced than usual, as if he was gritting his teeth. So, Katie was not the only one finding this encounter stirring.

Once she'd removed her dressing gown, she set it neatly over the bench at the foot of his bed.

"That is a lovely nightgown," he rumbled. "Turn around."

She turned in a clumsy circle, her face continuing to flame.

"Is that a new gown?" he asked, the bedding around his hips shifting and drawing her gaze to the thick ridge.

His hand curled around his erection and her eyes jumped to meet his.

"Answer my question."

"Er, no, it is not new. It is part of my wedding trousseau."

His arm moved slowly, his thick biceps bulging as he grasped himself over the blanket. "You look lovely in it. But you look even lovelier wearing nothing. Remove your gown."

Katie's fingers trembled so badly that it was a challenge to unfasten the tiny buttons at her throat. He had seen her naked before, of course, but usually it was in the throes of passion rather than blatantly disrobing before him.

She reached the last button far sooner than she would have liked. When she hesitated, he cocked one eyebrow.

Katie was grateful for the very-Dulverton reaction, which sent a jolt of defiance through her and made her want to wipe that smug look off his face. She pulled the gown over her head, stopping to stare challengingly at him before letting it fall to the floor.

His chest rose and fell faster; his stunning irises were mere slices of silvery gray. He pointed to the bed. "Up here. *Now.*"

Katie climbed the steps up to the high mattress with as much grace as possible.

"No," he said when she would have laid down beside him. "Here"—he patted the bed by his hips, one hand on each side. "Straddle me."

She considered the view she'd be affording him. "But—"

"Yes?"

She huffed a sigh, firmed her jaw, and shuffled from his ankles to his calves slowly.

He pulled the blanket off his hips, exposing his thick erection. "Right here," he said, his eyes hooded.

Heart pounding, Katie inched forward, stopping only when she was above his bobbing member. She sucked in a harsh breath when his warm palms closed over her breasts and stroked lightly, her thighs trembling as she lowered herself onto his hard shaft, which nudged between her nether lips.

"You're so wet," he hissed as he rolled his hips, his slick crown rubbing her in exactly the right place.

"Yes, please," she murmured, grinding against him as he took her nipples between his thumbs and forefingers and pinched and tugged until she was half-mad with sensation. And when his hips lifted to pulse against her cleft a bolt of raw sensation shot from her breasts to her womb, and—shockingly—she climaxed.

Even in the throes of her bliss she heard Gerrit's smug-sounding grunt as his hands slid around her waist and he lifted her until he could line himself up and then thrust inside her, the feel of him intensifying her contractions.

Rather than move inside her, he held still, his gaze pinioning her when she emerged from her erotic torpor, his thumbs tracing light circles on the tender skin of her pelvis as she came back to herself. "I love watching you come apart."

Naturally, she blushed.

He cupped her hips with both hands and lifted her bodily with a show of strength that would have made her swoon if she had not already been boneless.

Katie frowned when he withdrew from her. "But you haven't—"

"I know. Come up here. All the way," he said, inching down the mattress.

"Gerrit?"

"Take hold of the headboard," he said, not stopping until his head was between her knees. "Good. Now lower yourself over me."

The comfortable fog of bliss that had surrounded her burnt away as she imagined how she would appear to him in such a position "Oh. Are you… certain?"

He made a sound that might have been a muffled laugh. "I am certain."

Katie swallowed convulsively and lowered her hips. "Like this?"

"Just like that." He looped his arms around her thighs and brought her down to his waiting mouth. His tongue, which seemed longer than normal, snaked out and lapped at her. When he closed his lips around her bud and sucked, her hips bucked and he gave a rumble of approval that vibrated through her entire body.

Her self-consciousness dissipated so quickly she knew she would be mortified later when she thought about it. But that was later. Right now Katie ground against him, her hands clutching the headboard as she used him for her own pleasure. She came apart with a loud, ragged cry, only vaguely aware when Gerrit lifted her up and then laid her down beside him.

"What are you doing?" she asked, a yawn distorting her words.

"Go to sleep, Kathryn," he murmured, pulling the bedding up over her.

"But—you still haven't—"

"*Shhh.*" He tucked her against his chest, the gesture so sweet and tender her eyes teared even though they were closed.

*I love you*, she thought, wishing she were bold enough to say the words.

# Chapter Thirty-One

Katie sat back in her chair and studied the ammonite, blowing away some of the dirt she had just loosened. The fossil was the size of a serving platter and by far the largest intact sample she'd unearthed in her part of the dig. Most of the pieces she'd found had been damaged in some way, all of them smaller than this one.

The tent had piles of samples awaiting their final cleaning. Mr. Everett and Mr. Scott disliked the painstaking task, but Katie found it soothing and rewarding to gradually expose the full beauty of a fossil. Sometimes unexpected, and disappointing, fractures became clear as the cleaning progressed, but this time the ammonite was stunningly intact.

Katie smiled when she imagined Gerrit's reaction to the beauty of the ammonite. A month ago, she might never have noticed the subtle signs that meant her husband was happy. But now, she found herself eager for the tantalizingly slight curve of his lips and narrowing of his eyes that meant something had pleased him.

Thinking about pleasing him naturally made her think about the past three nights, all of which she'd spent in Gerrit's bed. Although she was alone, her face still heated at how boldly she had behaved last night, when she'd pushed him onto his back, climbed on top of him, and taken him inside her without speaking a word, posting him until they'd both exploded within moments of each other.

"You're so beautiful, Kathryn," he'd murmured just before he'd pulled her body tightly against his and they'd both fallen asleep.

She'd woken before dusk to find that he still held her tightly. He'd stirred when she'd tried to ease out of bed without waking him.

"Where are you going?" he asked in a sleep-roughened voice, his hand closing around her arm.

"It is morning."

He'd opened his eyes, looking so adorably rumpled that she'd climbed back in bed and made them an hour late this morning. Grinning at the memory, she stood and brushed off her skirt before putting her tools in the metal bucket where she kept them. She'd just turned toward the tent entrance when a familiar, unwanted voice froze her in her tracks.

"The duchess mentioned your dig the last time I spoke to her so I thought I would come by and see what all the fuss is about, Dulverton," Jasper said, his voice rich with mocking bonhomie.

Katie's breath froze in her lungs as she glanced out the tent opening. They always rolled the flap back to allow in the maximum amount of light while still having some protection against the sun's glare. Katie briefly considered untying the flap and hiding in the darkened tent, but she could see the shadows of the two men approaching and knew it was too late.

"I was not aware you knew my wife, Lord Jasper."

The last time Katie had heard Dulverton's voice so frigid he'd had his fist around the Earl of Ampthill's throat. Jasper, the fool, had no idea how much physical danger he was in.

"Oh yes, we are old friends," Jasper said, oozing a slimy sort of charm.

Katie winced at the suggestive way he said *old friends*.

"Is Her Grace here today? I swear that is her mount."

Katie hurried from her shelter before Jasper could do any more damage.

"Ah—there she is!" Jasper cried when she almost barreled into the two men. "Hallo, Katie darling."

"What a surprise, Lord Jasper," she said coolly, risking a glance at her husband and then wishing she hadn't. The white-hot fury in his arctic eyes said he wanted to hurt something. Or someone. "You have come to see our work, have you?" she added.

"How could I resist after you spoke of the dig with such enthusiasm, Ka—er, Your Grace?"

Katie's hands itched to slap the mocking, sneering smirk from his lying face but instead forced herself to meet Dulverton's predatory stare. "Have you given him the tour, Your Grace?"

"I am too busy. Mr. Scott can—"

"I will do it," Katie interrupted. "I was just taking a break from my work inside the tent. It will be no bother."

Dulverton's jaw flexed dangerously but he pivoted on his heel and stalked away.

Katie grabbed Jasper's upper arm and jerked him toward the tent. "I would be happy to show you what I have been working on, my lord," she said in a loud voice. And then added beneath her breath, "What are you *doing* here?"

"If the mountain will not come—"

"I *told* you I did not wish to see you again," she hissed when they reached the flimsy privacy of the tent.

"I just wanted to see you, darling. Our last conversation ended on such a sour note that I've not been able to get a good night's sleep since. Do not be angry with me, Katie. Please." He stuck out his lower lip in a pout she remembered from five years ago. She was such an idiot. She'd thought it adorable then; now she saw it for what it was: grotesque and pathetic for a man his age to behave like a coy schoolgirl.

"I have nothing to say to you, Jasper. I'm not sure how many different ways I have to explain that before you comprehend my meaning." Her eyes flickered over his shoulder, to where Dulverton was standing and—ostensibly—talking to one of the workers, his eyes riveted to Katie and Jasper.

Katie pointed to the table, as if she were showing something to Jasper, and snarled beneath her breath, "There is nothing between us and there never will be. *Nothing.* And I want nothing to do with you. You are putting my marriage in jeopardy, and I do not appreciate it."

Jasper smirked. "Dulverton guards you like a dog with a bone. I thought he'd take my head off just for saying *hello.*"

"Can you really be so stupid?" she demanded. "My husband is not a man to be trifled with. You will find yourself facing pistols at dawn if you do not stop pestering me and leave."

"I am not frightened of Dulverton." He gave a dismissive flick of his hand and then his eyes narrowed. "Because you will never tell him about me, will you?" His smile turned ugly. "How much is it worth for him to continue in blissful ignorance, *hmm?*"

"What are you saying, Jasper?"

"I think you know what I'm saying."

"You want money, is that it?"

"I know you are well larded—I've heard all about the money your generous brothers-in-law bestowed on you."

*Ah, the chickens are coming home to roost.*

They certainly were. Impotent rage boiled within her. She wanted to throttle Jasper, but she wanted to throttle herself even more. This whole mess was *her* fault.

"I do not know what gossip you have heard," she lied. "I have no money of my own. Everything I had now belongs to my husband.

"*Tsk, tsk,* no point in trying to hide your golden egg from me, sweetheart."

Oh, God. He was blinded by greed and would never give up.

*And whose fault is that?*

Her eyes darted again over his shoulder. Dulverton was headed toward the tent, his jaw set and his eyes blazing.

"Look at this," Katie snapped.

"Look at what?"

"At the fossil, you idiot! Dulverton is almost upon us."

Jasper scowled but dropped his gaze. "This isn't over, sweetheart," he hissed. He might like to behave as if he did not fear the duke, but he quickly played along. "Quite fascinating—and you say you dug it out yourself?" he asked loudly.

"We all help each other here."

"Well, I can see I am keeping—ah, Dulverton, old chap!" Jasper said, edging away from Katie. "I was just taking my leave of your duchess. Thank you for being so generous with your time." He hesitated a moment, clearly waiting for some kind of acknowledgement from the other man, but Dulverton was ignoring him so utterly that Katie suspected he truly did not notice that Jasper was standing there.

Jasper snorted, rammed his hat on his head, and sauntered off.

Dulverton stepped closer, until Katie could feel the heat of his body. She had to force herself to hold his gaze rather than look away guiltily.

"I do not like his sort coming around the dig. Or anywhere near my property, Kathryn."

The way he glared at her made it clear he was not referring to only his land when he said the word *property*.

Rather than irk her, as it should have, his possessive stare caused heat to flare in her belly. "I never invited him. He took it upon himself to come."

"Why did you not tell me you had seen him? Or that you knew him?"

Katie lowered her gaze, unable to bear the weight of his scrutiny when she lied. "I suppose it just slipped my mind."

Gerrit took her chin and forced her to meet his eyes. He did not speak but gave her a searching look, his nostrils flaring slightly at whatever he saw.

Katie's heart pounded beneath his icy regard, and she was grateful that her high collar hid the pulse she felt fluttering at the base of her throat.

"Lord Jasper has been gone from England for several years, running from his debts," Dulverton said in a toneless voice.

"That is what I have heard."

"That means you would not have encountered him in London these past Seasons."

"My aunt lives near Lord Jasper's family's country house. We attended many of the same functions one summer." All true, but not even close to all of the truth.

He remained so motionless he hardly seemed human.

A throat cleared behind him, and Katie startled when Mr. Scott's head peered around her husband's shoulder.

"Er, Your Grace?"

Dulverton finally blinked but his eyes never left her face. "Yes?"

"The men with the wagon are here." Mr. Scott paused and then said, "Er, you asked that I—"

"I will be right there."

"Very good, sir," Mr. Scott said, and then quickly darted off.

When he'd gone, Dulverton did the oddest thing. He leaned down, still holding her chin, and placed a feather-light kiss on her lips. And then he dropped his hand and turned away without saying another word.

Katie watched his large form as he confidently strode across the broken ground. When she raised her fingers to her lips, she discovered her hand was shaking. Badly.

What had that been about?

# Chapter Thirty-Two

Gerrit knew he was behaving like a jealous, sullen beast and had done so all through dinner, rarely deigning to speak even though Scott and Everett were guests at their table tonight. He'd continued to brood and sulk after dinner in the library, when it had just been him and Kathryn.

When she set aside her needlework to play chess, Gerrit had begged off, claiming he had too much work. He *did* have a mountain of correspondence and bills, but he did very little of it. Instead, he'd unobtrusively observed his wife. Or at least he hoped he'd been unobtrusive.

Gerrit had long ago accepted that he was clueless when it came to reading other people's emotions. But he would have wagered a pony—if he were the wagering sort—that something was amiss with Kathryn. And he could trace the change in her demeanor to Lord Jasper's impromptu visit today.

Gerrit knew very little about Lord Jasper, but what he knew, he did not like.

Part of his dislike was, he admitted, because Lord Jasper so effortlessly did what Gerrit had never been able to do: he was charming.

But charming is as charming does.

To Gerrit's knowledge Lord Jasper had impregnated at least one young woman in the neighborhood. The girl had been hastily shunted off to family in a nearby village to have her child.

Gerrit's grandfather had fathered children on women on every one of his estates. But one of the main differences between his grandfather and Lord Jasper— not that it excused his grandfather's behavior—was that the old duke had always supported his offspring and their mothers.

Lord Jasper had not paid any expenses for the young mother or his own child, so it had been left to Gerrit and Sir John Staniforth, the local squire, to see that the girl had ample money to live on. That had been five or six years ago, the last time Lord Jasper had come to his grandmother's house. Gerrit knew the man had come to visit the Countess of Grimsby and meet the woman he was to marry. What sort of man impregnated one woman while becoming betrothed to another?

Not an honorable one, that was certain.

And now Lord Jasper's wife was dead, and he had returned—probably to bleed more money out of Lady Grimsby—and he was entertaining himself not with the baker's daughter but by sniffing around Gerrit's wife.

Kathryn had appeared less than delighted to see the man, but it irked Gerrit that she had never told him of their connection. And it irked him even more that she'd said nothing of their meeting.

# Kathryn

*Perhaps she kept it to herself because you have been so unreasonable when it comes to other men so much as speaking to your wife…*

Gerrit refused to feel guilty about his behavior. It was true he was jealous where Kathryn was concerned. She was *his*, dammit. He had been unforgivably stupid at the beginning of their marriage, and it made him feel ill when he thought how easily he could have lost her if she had not been brave and brought them both to their senses.

He would not make the mistake of pretending to be a detached husband again. Not to spare his pride and not to avoid conflict. Not for anyone or any reason.

The clock on the mantel chimed eleven o'clock and Kathryn looked up, meeting his gaze. The notch between her brilliant eyes told him she could sense his anger and was confused.

Gerrit folded the letter he'd had in front of him for the last half-hour and replaced it neatly on the pile before standing. "It is time for bed."

She put her work away in the large basket she kept tucked beneath the end table.

Not a word was exchanged until he stopped in front of her door. He grasped the door handle but paused and looked down at her, his eyes lingering hungrily on the snug bodice of her gown which was a dark rose shade that he would have not expected to look so good on a ginger. But then he was beginning to suspect she could make sackcloth look good. "What are you wearing beneath that gown?"

She sucked in a breath, doing interesting things to her bodice. "Er, what do you mean?"

"I mean tell me about your underclothing."

Her jaw sagged and she glanced about, as if somebody might be lurking in the corridor.

Gerrit raised an eyebrow and waited.

"A p-petticoat, chemise, stays, and stockings."

"What color?"

"P—" Her voice broke, and she cleared her throat. "Pink."

"Leave them on for me. Only remove your gown." He opened the door and nudged her inside before she could speak, not that she appeared to be very talkative, for a change.

He strode to his room, already tugging his cravat before he opened the door.

Court was waiting for him as always. If he thought it unusual that Gerrit had already removed his neckcloth, he kept the thought to himself but drew the correct inference: Gerrit was in a hurry.

He disrobed Gerrit with slightly more haste than usual, managing to have him washed, shaved, and garbed in his banyan in less than a quarter of an hour.

As always, Gerrit used the connecting door. His wife was still seated at her dressing table, wearing a dressing gown, and brushing her hair.

Her cheeks bore twin bright spots of color, and she was breathing more rapidly than brushing of one's hair required.

His wife was excited.

So was he.

The pale column of her throat flexed, and her pearl-handled hairbrush rattled against the wood as she set it on her dressing table.

Gerrit placed his hands on her shoulders when she would have risen. "Stay a moment," he said, his voice harsh with need as he stared at their reflection in the mirror. "*La Belle et la Bête*," he murmured, taking a handful of her hair, the dark red spirals twisting around his fingers like living things.

"What did you say?" she asked, drawing his gaze to hers in the looking glass.

"Beauty and the Beast—it is a French story."

The pulse at the base of her throat beat against her skin hard enough that he could see it.

"You are hardly a beast."

That made him smile, a contortion of his ugly features that did nothing to improve his brutal appearance.

Her eyes widened at his expression, a rare one, he knew. Gerrit wrapped her hair around his fist and exerted pressure on her head until her back was pressed against his cock. "Open your dressing gown and show me what you are wearing." His gaze dropped to her hands as they fumbled with the sash and then pulled the edges wide, exposing the pale pink half-stays and matching pink chemise beneath it.

He had always disliked the color pink, associating it with his mother. But right now, he could see the appeal.

"Raise your chemise."

Her eyelids fluttered slightly, but she reached for the bottom edge of the garment and drew it above her knees, exposing the pink stockings and the darker pink garters that held them up.

"Higher," he ordered, looking up to watch her face.

Her lips parted and she inhaled deeply as her hands lifted the garment until he could see the dark red curls of her sex.

"Part your legs."

"Gerrit," she said, making his name a plea.

"You know that you want me to see you," he said, daring her to deny it.

A dozen emotions galloped across her expressive face: pride, arousal, and, finally, the headstrong, challenging glare she excelled in hurling his way like a gauntlet of old.

And then she spread her legs for him.

***

Katie had no idea what had got into Gerrit tonight.

*Whatever it is, you like it...*

She did like it. Because she was a wanton, hedonistic trollop. And she didn't care about anything other than keeping that hungry expression on her husband's face.

"Look at yourself," he rasped, his eyes riveted to the part of her that a decent woman would never look at.

But Katie looked, and not for the first time, either. She did not personally see the appeal—men had a far more interesting reproductive organ in her opinion—but she liked the effect it had on Gerrit.

"So pretty and pink," he muttered, his words causing even more waves of heat to surge through her. He flexed his hips, hissing in a harsh breath when his hard shaft stroked her back, not once, but again and again.

"Do you touch yourself, Kathryn?"

Her head whipped up at the filthy question, her eyes running straight into his. "Wh-what?"

"You know what I mean."

"No!"

He grinned, the expression even more unexpected than his earlier smile had been. He looked wolfish, his teeth remarkably white against his darkly tanned skin, one side of his mouth pulled up higher than the other. His pale eyes gleamed, mischievous and carnal.

"You are fibbing, aren't you, Kathryn?"

"I don't—that is—oh fine, *yes,* for pity's sake!" she snapped, flustered and annoyed and aroused all at once.

His grin just grew. "Some night you will show me," he said, resuming his distracting grinding against her back. "I will spread you out on the bed and you will demonstrate how you give yourself an orgasm."

Katie could not believe how erotic his threat sounded. Embarrassing, but erotic.

"But not tonight," he said, and then abruptly leaned down and pulled her robe from her shoulders. "Get on the bed."

The order reminded her of their very first night and Katie got to her feet, just as eager to comply as she had been then. But she paused and gestured to her clothing. "Should I—"

"No. I want to take you this way." He shrugged out of his banyan, his own body naked from his toes all the way up. The most intriguing part of him was thick, rigid, and glistening. "On the bed," he repeated, punctuating his command with a swat on her bottom.

Katie jumped and made the mortifying yelping sound that she seemed to make only in her husband's presence.

She glared at him, and he raised both eyebrows as if to ask what she was going to do about it.

Katie wanted to shove him or climb him or kiss him or do all three. Instead, she gave him what she hoped was a seductive smile and sauntered slowly to the bed, earning a low chuckle for her efforts.

"No, not on your back," he said. "Hands and knees."

She turned to him, shocked. "Like beasts?"

"You've seen that, have you?"

"I grew up in the country. Of course, I have—" She broke off when she saw he was grinning. Again. Three times in one night!

Katie scowled at him for teasing her even though she liked it and then climbed up onto the mattress, briefly turning to give him a challenging look over her shoulder before settling on her hands and knees.

"My God, Kathryn." His voice throbbed with desire. One of his big hands landed gently on her lower back, making her jolt.

"*Shhh*," he murmured, as if soothing a nervous filly. "Look at you," he said, the words low and worshipful as he stroked first one buttock and then the other. "Yes, like that," he said, making her realize she was thrusting against his hand. "No, don't stop." He slowly pulled up her chemise, until his rough skin was caressing her bare buttocks. She felt movement and then was startled to feel the press of his lips against her hip. "Spread your knees so I can see how wet you are," he ordered gruffly. He gave an approving rumble when she complied. "Such a good, obedient wife." His thick fingers slipped into the slick folds of her sex, the pads caressing her in exactly the right spot. "So hot and wet and eager."

She made a mewling—yes, a *mewling*—sound but could not have cared less. He worked her like a musician with a favorite instrument, and she gave herself up to his virtuosic mastery, bucking and grinding and, finally, calling out his name, her inner muscles rippling with the force of her climax. She rode the waves of pleasure until they faded to warm, when she felt the pressure of his thighs against hers.

"Down," he said, his hand splaying across her shoulders and lightly pressing her toward the mattress.

Katie went gratefully, not sure how her arms, shaky and weak, had not collapsed already. She had some vague notion of what he must see from his vantage point above her, but rather than shame her, it made her feel desirable and she pushed her bottom up toward him, begging for whatever he might deign to give her.

"Ah, sweetheart," he said thickly. "I would like to do this all night long, but I am nearly at the end of myself." He slid all the way inside her.

Katie squirmed and let out a muffled whimper. "You—it feels—"

"Bigger?"

Katie grunted out a *yes*.

He chuckled and slid in a bit more.

Who was this man who smiled and laughed?

He reached a hand beneath her and circled the source of her pleasure, his hips commencing to move. She closed her eyes and luxuriated in the slow, deep plunge and the immensely stimulating friction.

His hips moved faster, and his finger kept time. She could feel by the increasing wildness of his thrusts that he was close.

He leaned low, until his muscular chest molded to her back and making her wish that her stays and chemise did not separate them.

"Are you close?" he whispered, his hips pumping so savagely that he pushed her up the mattress.

His question had scarcely left his lips when the spiral that had been building inside her snapped. He thrust only a few times more before he buried himself and they flew over the edge together.

Katie must have dozed, because when she opened her eyes, she saw the candles were no longer burning. She lifted her head, as if she could see anything in the pitch darkness. Gerrit's chest was still pressed against her back, but now there was no clothing between them. He had undressed her, and she'd slept through it? *Pity, that.*

"Close your eyes," he murmured, drawing her closer and pressing a kiss against the back of her head.

Her lips curled into a smile as her heavy lids lowered.

Katie was still smiling as she drifted off to sleep.

# Chapter Thirty-Three

Katie was aggrieved, but not surprised, when not long after Jasper's visit to the dig she received another invitation from Lady Grimsby. This one for a picnic that would also double as a going-away party for her grandson.

That was certainly something Katie could celebrate.

The invitation had been hand-delivered after dinner, so naturally Gerrit was there when she opened it.

"Do I need to attend?" he asked, radiating preemptive displeasure at the prospect.

"No, I shouldn't think so," she said. Just thinking about Gerrit in the same vicinity as Jasper made her stomach roil. "But I shall have to make an appearance, although I shan't stay long," she added.

Gerrit had nodded with obvious reluctance and frowned with equally obvious displeasure.

Katie hadn't been pleased about it, either.

Now, as Becky dressed and primped her for the wretched event, Katie wished she'd done the socially unthinkable thing and declined a second invitation from the countess.

"Are you sure about this?" Becky asked as she set Katie's sage-green hat on her head and stood back to examine the placement.

"What possible excuse could I give for not going at this point?" Katie asked, pulling on her sage-green kid gloves. "Besides, this is his *going away* party and that is something I truly am jubilant about." She had not told Becky about the extortion threat, because... Well, because she didn't want the other woman to voice all her own fears. Jasper was leaving, and soon. All Katie had to do was get through the next few days without doing something dangerous or foolish. Or dangerously foolish.

The carriage ride to Elm Hall felt like a trip in a tumbril to the guillotine, and Katie's nerves were stretched aggravatingly thin by the time the miserable fifteen-minute journey was at an end.

*No, your miserable journey is just beginning,* an unhelpful voice pointed out.

Judging by the number of servants and carriages dotting the drive, Katie was among the last to arrive.

"The Duchess of Dulverton!" a tall, gaunt butler bellowed after opening the door to an old-fashioned drawing room in shades of dark green and with plenty of gilt. It felt like stepping into the past—circa 1760s, or thereabouts—and Katie surmised the décor was that of the countess's youth.

All conversation ceased when Katie appeared. There were perhaps thirty people milling about on the terrace that overlooked Lady Grimsby's back garden. Katie's shoulders stiffened when she recognized her tormentor's profile. Jasper was surrounded by a bevy of local girls, no doubt all charmed by his handsome person and smooth manners.

A slender woman with silvery white hair held court from a dark wood Bath chair. "Good afternoon, duchess," she called out in a firm, strong voice at odds with her fragile appearance. "I hope you will forgive me for not rising to greet you."

Wearing a polite smile, Katie opened her mouth, but the countess was not finished.

"I was beginning to think you were a figment of our neighbors' imagination."

Katie blushed at the well-deserved chiding. Once again, she opened her mouth, this time to apologize for failing to pay a call.

But again, the countess was not finished. "I understand you are already acquainted with the guest of honor, my grandson Lord Jasper."

"We are old friends," Jasper said, smiling broadly as he came toward her. "Aren't we, Katie?"

The dowager clucked her tongue. "Such a casual attitude young people take today. In my day, one would never greet a married lady so informally."

"I may call you Katie, mayn't I?" Jasper said, his caressing tone scraping like needles on her skin. "I hope we will not stand on ceremony now that you are a married lady."

Before she could contrive an answer, Lady Grimsby resumed the monologue that Jasper had interrupted. "I'm sure you are aware that my poor Judith—Jasper's wife and my dearest friend Lady Tinsley's granddaughter—passed away last year."

"I'm sorry for your loss," Katie said.

It wasn't clear if the countess heard her, but Jasper inclined his head. "Thank you," he said, assuming the sorrowful expression of a bereaved widower.

"What are you saying, Jasper?" the countess bellowed, raising an ear horn to her head.

"Her Grace was offering her condolences," Jasper said in a raised voice.

The countess waved a dismissive hand. "Yes, yes. Sit here, Your Grace. This is the seat of honor."

Katie found herself seated right beside the old lady, who preferred to make a long string of declarations rather than engage in conversation. That was just as well as Katie's brain was addled, so she gratefully settled in to listen.

While the rest of the guests played croquet, rowed on the tiny lake, and mingled with each other, Katie listened to the countess tell her, at exhausting length, about Jasper's marriage. "The match was arranged when Lord Jasper was just a boy and Judith was still in her cradle."

Katie knew that Jasper had married to please his grandmother and ensure his inheritance, but Jasper had never confessed that the union had been of such long-standing. The lying, manipulative swine.

According to the countess, Judith had given birth a scant eight months after their marriage. So, Katie had not been the only one Jasper had seduced that summer.

By the time an hour and a half had passed, Katie was ready to scream.

When the garrulous squire's wife, Lady Staniforth, came to take her leave of the countess, Katie leapt up from her seat. "Yes, I'm afraid I must be going as well, my lady."

The countess frowned and opened her mouth. Katie knew she was going to come up with an excuse to keep her longer, but then Jasper—of all people—came to her rescue.

"Lady Grimsby and I are grateful for your company today, Your Grace," he said, insinuating his body between Katie and his gaping grandmother. "Allow me to walk you two ladies to your carriages."

"My, my! What an honor to have such an escort," Lady Staniforth burbled, giddy with pleasure.

The two chattered as Katie followed along silently, willing the nightmare afternoon to be over.

Lady Staniforth's carriage was the only one out front.

"Oh, dear me, Duchess. Where is your carriage?" Lady Staniforth dithered. "Do you need a ride home?"

"No, no. It will be along presently," Jasper assured her as he handed her into her carriage. "Good day to you, Lady Staniforth." He firmly shut the door on further conversation and the squire's ancient coach rumbled off down the drive.

Thankfully, the sound of more wheels came from the drive leading to the stables.

"That will be me," Katie said, relieved. "Thank you for your escort, Jasper, but you should get back to your party."

But it was not the Dulverton barouche that came around the corner but some other vehicle. She turned back to Jasper. "Where is my carriage?"

"I sent it home earlier."

"You did *what?*"

"I will take you in mine."

Katie was so angry she could barely speak. "Jasper, what—"

"Hush, now, Katie, darling. You don't want the servants to stare, do you?" He gestured to where two of the countess's footmen stood a few feet away.

"I do not want to ride with you—especially not in an enclosed carriage!"

He gave an insufferable chuckle. "You don't want any servants hearing our conversation, my dear."

Gritting her teeth, Katie allowed him to help her into the old-fashioned carriage, which she could not help noticing had the Grimsby escutcheon emblazoned on the side, so *not* Jasper's carriage, as he had claimed.

"Do not be angry with me, Katie," Jasper crooned as the carriage moved down the long driveway. "I wanted to talk to you, but it is impossible to get you alone— and god knows I have tried."

"We have nothing to say to one another."

He pushed to his feet, as if to cross the space that separated them and sit beside her.

"Stay on your side of the carriage, please."

His eyebrows shot up at her harsh tone, but he sank back down into worn chocolate-brown velvet. "You are angry."

Katie gave a disbelieving laugh. "Now, I wonder why that could be? Because you tried to extort money from me?"

His good humor wavered, exposing something darker, only for a second, but she saw it.

"By dismissing my carriage and taking me home—*alone*—you risk creating a scandal," she added, not that he cared.

"Why, we are old friends, Katie; even your husband knows of our friendship. Surely nobody could cavil about me joining you on a fifteen-minute carriage ride?"

Katie sighed wearily. "Why won't you just leave me be? What little feeling there once was between us is long dead. You are only making an embarrassing nuisance of yourself."

His smile twisted but hung on by a thread, displeasure flashing in his blue eyes. "My, my, what a little shrew you have become. Is it age? Or your newly elevated status?"

"Whatever it is, it is none of your concern," she retorted. "And you could have spared yourself the rough side of my tongue had you simply left me alone."

"Oh, Katie darling. When will you stop fighting it?"

"It?"

"The attraction between us. I know you can feel it just as I can. It is not too late, you know. I realize you have just been punishing me for my behavior five years ago. But it would be a crime to throw everything we had away."

Her jaw dropped. "Did you hit your head?"

"Pardon?"

"Your head. Have you injured it? Even if I were willing to put aside your recent abominable behavior, my recollection of what happened five years ago is a good deal different than yours. I recall you promising me marriage to get beneath my skirts, which I was stupid enough to allow. I also recall you running off to your grandmother when she snapped her fingers. I recall you marrying another woman after telling me we were betrothed. *That* is what I recall."

"Good God, Katie! You behave as if you did not know that I was as poor as a church mouse," he snapped, finally showing his ire. "How the devil did you think we could marry? I had nothing but my meager allowance and you had nothing at all—or so I believed at the time. Surely you must have known that I was just voicing my dreams rather than promising you anything."

"I was six-and-ten—a child—how was I to know that when a gentleman tumbled a woman and then gave his word of honor, it meant nothing? Less than nothing as you could not even tell me face-to-face that you had married. Do you know how I felt at that ball your father gave to celebrate your wedding *to another woman*? Can you imagine how devastating it was to see you—a man who'd pledged himself to *me*—dancing and laughing and smiling with your new wife?"

He flinched at the heat in her words, but his expression was petulant. "I have repeatedly apologized for that. What else do you want?"

"If you think your empty apologies mean anything to me, then you cannot be nearly as smart as you think you are. I have told you *repeatedly* that I do not want to be seen with you, not to mention indulge in—in, well, whatever you seem to be suggesting. You must have a maggot in your head if you think—"

"*Enough.*" A dull red flush slashed his cheeks and his stunned expression turned unpleasant. He leaned forward so suddenly she recoiled, hitting her head against the worn bolster. "So high and mighty you've become." His handsome face turned even uglier. "As you've been such a little bitch to me, I have changed my mind about offering you a bit of fun."

"Let me guess," she retorted. "We are back to extortion, now. Well, you can go to the devil because I will not give you a penny!"

"That is what you say now. But what will happen when your husband receives a letter that tells him—in graphic detail—about your deflowering."

"Dulverton already *knows* I did not come to his bed a virgin, you odious fool."

"But does he know all the lurid details such as how often, what positions?"

Katie was momentarily rendered speechless. "You really are a disgusting worm, aren't you?"

"Please, keep talking, darling. Every vicious word out of your shrewish mouth only sends the figure I will demand higher."

"Why are you so desperate for money? I thought you were headed off to Naples again with your grandmother's money bulging in your pockets. Lady Grimsby also mentioned—in excruciating detail—how Judith's grandmother left all *her* wealth to you."

"The amount she is giving me is insulting. I'm only taking it to get away from her incessant hectoring. As for the money Judith's grandmother—that mad old cunt—left for my poor dead wife?" He smirked when Katie gasped at his vulgar language. "The old crone didn't even leave enough for poor darling Judith's laudanum overdose." His smile turned sour. "So, yes: I need money."

"Laudanum? Lady Grimsby said your wife died from some fever."

He laughed bitterly. "Not hardly. I might like a flutter at the gaming tables, but Jude had a taste for laudanum that had been years in the making—so do not think that I drove her to it."

"I doubt you helped matters."

His eyes narrowed. "I believe three thousand pounds is what I will require to forget what a bitch you are."

"I repeat—since you didn't appear to hear me the last time—you will not get a penny from me."

"Then I shall commence scribbling my epic."

"Do your worst."

He eyed her thoughtfully, and Katie did not like the malicious gleam that entered his gaze. "I cannot tell whether you are bluffing or not. You are much more interesting now than you were five years ago." His expression softened so suddenly that the shift left her dizzy. "Come, Katie, let us not argue and fight. Put aside your hurt feelings. We were so *good* together. You would love it on the Continent. It is the perfect place for free spirits. Don't you recall how we used to talk about the journeys we would take together? You cannot really wish to remain here and scrabble in the dirt with Dulverton. Run away with me and we can live without any of the tiresome constraints that society imposes. Come *with* me, my love."

Katie could only stare in horrified disbelief. "You expect me to believe you care about me after you've been threatening me with extortion?"

He gave a dismissive wave of his hand. "You and I are passionate people, darling. We say things in anger without thinking. Come now, you know that I didn't really mean any of that nastiness. I am positively *wild* about you, and it eats me up thinking about you wasted on old Dullness. You fill my thoughts all day and my dreams at night. Just think how happy we would be together!"

Katie could not imagine a worse future. "How happy we would be," she repeated, dazed.

Hope lit his eyes. "Yes! Now you are—"

"—just you, me, and my money."

The dreamy, cozening smile on his plush lips fled in an instant. "Now, that wasn't a very nice thing to say, was it?"

"It doesn't make it any less true."

"Fine. Have it your way," he snarled, his eyes glittering with malice. "Three thousand pounds by Friday or I will deliver an epic to Dulverton the likes of which has never been seen. And if he is too dull to find it stimulating reading, I'm sure I can find a few newspapermen in London who will. I'll wager I could sell our juicy story for a handsome price."

Katie felt a stab of real fear. "You would be muddying your own name in the process, Jasper. Lady Grimsby would cut you out of—"

"No. She would not cut me out of her will. Not if she wishes to keep my daughter. As to shaming my name?" He laughed. "Rakes never take any harm from raking, do they? In fact, it would just enhance my reputation."

The worst part about his words was that there was more than a grain of truth in them. "You are revolting."

He grinned nastily. "I will send word to you about when to bring the money—but we both know the place, don't we, darling?"

"Just where do you think I will get so much money?"

"Where there is a will, there is a way. Or so I've heard."

The carriage jolted to a stop and Jasper leaned toward the door. "Ah, here we are. Allow me—"

"Don't bother," she snapped, yanking on the door latch, and tumbling out of the carriage without either steps or assistance. She left the door hanging open and strode toward the house without a backward glance.

Cranston opened the door before she even reached it. "Ah, Your Grace—"

"Not now," she barked, knowing even as she spoke that she would have to apologize to the ancient butler later for her abruptness. But not now. Not when she barely made it up the stairs before the tears began to flow.

Katie prayed her chambers would be empty. Of course, that was too much to ask, and when she flung open the door, she almost ran poor Becky down.

"What is it?" Becky demanded, grabbing Katie's arms, her small hands surprisingly strong.

"I—I just shut my foot in the door and it hurts."

Becky scowled. "I saw Lord Jasper in the carriage with you." She led Katie to the settee in front of the dormant fireplace. "Sit here a moment and I will ring for a tray."

"If I eat or drink anything I will just cast it all up."

Becky dropped down beside her. "I was downstairs in the kitchen when your carriage returned without you. John Coachman said Lord Jasper sent it back. What happened?"

"If you can believe it, he once again tried to *rekindle* what we had."

"He must be mad."

"No, just desperate for money." Katie yanked off one glove and then the other and flung them onto a nearby table where they landed with a very unsatisfying *floof*. "That isn't the worst of it. When he realized I was not afraid of him telling Dulverton—"

"*What?* How can you not be afr—"

"Because *I* am going to tell him everything, that is how."

Becky gave Katie an annoyingly self-righteous look. "That is what I have said all along. If that is the case, then you need not fear Lord Jasper at all."

"Unfortunately, he had another, more awful threat in reserve."

"What could be more awful than telling tales to His Grace?"

"Telling them to a newspaperman."

Becky's jaw dropped. "Oh, Lord. What—what are you going to do?"

"He wants three thousand pounds."

"Are you—do you have such a sum?" Becky sputtered, her eyes round.

"Of course I don't." She did not tell her friend that she had at least that much in jewels. Nor did she admit she was considering giving some of them to Jasper in lieu of money. The pearls from Selina and Gaius were worth a fortune alone. It would be agonizing to use her sister and brother-in-law's generous gift to bribe a man, but getting Jasper away from Gerrit, and out of her life, was worth even more.

"Perhaps His Grace can talk sense to—"

"Do you honestly believe Dulverton would *talk* to a man trying to blackmail me?" Katie snapped. "This is *my* problem; *I* will deal with it."

"But I thought you said you would tell His Grace everything?"

"After that *cad* is gone."

Becky covered her face with her hands. "Why must you be so *willful?*" Her words were muffled, but Katie still heard the frustration and fear in them.

She patted her friend's back. "I do not know why," she answered honestly. "But it is too late for me to change now, even if I could. I made this mess, and I will clean it up."

"*How?*" Becky wailed.

"I don't know," Katie admitted, rubbing soothing circles on her agitated friend's back as she thought about giving Jasper what he wanted. "But I will think of something."

And she would have to think of it in a hurry because he was leaving in a mere five days.

# Chapter Thirty-Four

The evening after Lady Grimsby's party had been one of the longest of her life as Katie waited for Gerrit to confront her about the carriage ride with Jasper. But the servants must have held their tongues because her husband never mentioned it. Indeed, he had been more affectionate than usual last night. He'd stayed in her bed after their passionate coupling, but—for once—Katie had not slept. Instead, her mind had raced, her thoughts churning endlessly about Jasper and what to do.

Thanks to her sleepless night Katie was heavy-eyed this morning and grateful that Dulverton—who was busy with his bailiff—had postponed going to the dig until two o'clock.

Katie had ordered a pot of tea rather than her usual chocolate because she'd needed something to wake her up. Something to help her think.

She finished her last cup of tea an hour ago and now she was staring at the product of her morning's labor: two sheets filled with her cramped handwriting. Did she dare give this to Jasper when she met him? Or should she bring the jewels?

"Your Grace, it is here!"

Katie jolted and swung around, ready to chide Becky about sneaking up behind her. But her maid held out a letter with familiar handwriting.

"Already?" she stupidly said, taking the message she'd hoped would not come for at least another day. She sighed and unfolded the letter, her eyes flickering over the few sentences.

"Well, what does it say?" Becky asked, radiating impatience.

It amused and comforted her when Becky forgot Katie was now a duchess and hectored her just as she had when they'd been girls.

"He wants to meet at that cottage… tonight."

"*Tonight?* That is impossible!" When Katie did not immediately agree, Becky groaned. "Please tell me you are not considering it."

"I am considering it."

Becky cast her eyes ceilingward. "Why, why, why, why?"

"Do you think I am enjoying this, Becky? I have to end this, and it is not as if he is giving me any choice."

"But tonight? How on earth could you get away?"

"I don't know."

"What time?"

"Midnight."

"Midnight!"

Katie winced and cut Becky a quelling look.

Becky crossed her arms and shook her head, unquelled. "It will be full dark and too dangerous,"

"There is a half-moon." Katie tore the message into tiny pieces before throwing it away. "It is as good a time as any and the path is well-trodden. There will be plenty of light." At Becky's skeptical glare she added, "I promise to be careful; will that satisfy you?"

"None of this satisfies me. Whatever will you tell His Grace? He is either in your chambers every night or you are in his." She bit her lip, her face flaming.

Her friend's mortification amused her and lightened her grim mood. Becky was scandalized by how often the duke came to his wife's bed, not to mention being outraged that he did not just do his *duty* but stayed in Katie's bed for part of the night. She had pondered telling the other woman that one's wifely duty could be pleasurable, but decided to leave that conversation until Becky became betrothed. Judging by how much she idolized Mr. Court, hung on his every word, and spent all her free time with the taciturn valet, that would not be long.

"I don't know what you're smirking about," Becky snapped.

"You will," Katie said.

Becky narrowed her eyes.

"As for His Grace, I will just tell him I do not feel well. Or I will tell him—" Katie frowned and pulled open the overstuffed drawer on her secretaire desk, pawing the contents until she found her appointments diary. She'd hardly consulted the little book since she had no balls, parties, or other social engagements that required scheduling. She skimmed over the prior months, tracking the dates that marked the beginning and end of her flux.

And then she read them again. And again.

She closed the slim book and looked at Becky.

Becky nodded, even though Katie hadn't said a word. "Yes, you completely forgot about it, didn't you?"

"Why didn't you say something?"

"I thought it was better if I did not mention it. I didn't want you to think too much about it until some time had passed."

"Do you think I am—" Katie could not make herself say the words.

"I think it highly likely," Becky said with the certitude of a woman who had seven younger siblings. Becky might be shy about the subject of coupling, but when it came to childbirth, she spoke with the dry practicality of a matron in her eighth decade.

Katie placed her hands over her midriff, which felt the same as always, which was to say soft and relatively flat. "You will tell Court that my time of the month is here."

"What? But then how will you tell His Grace you were wrong afterward?"

"I will confess when I tell him everything else and admit that I lied so I could finish this business with Jasper."

Becky pursed her lips and shook her head in disgust.

"Oh, don't look at me that way. He will be so happy about the prospect of a child that he will forgive me the lie."

"Something tells me he will be even angrier that you are risking your child meeting with such a villain."

"Jasper is hardly going to attack me." Katie dropped the diary into the overstuffed drawer and shoved it hard to close it.

"I think His Grace will beat you when he discovers you've gone to meet a man alone. At midnight. And he *should* beat you." Becky glared at her.

"Probably," Katie agreed. Not that all the slapping and pinching and verbal abusing her mother had subjected her to had ever made her obey. She had just been sneakier about disobeying.

"I am your maid and should attend you. It isn't proper for you to go alone."

Katie seriously considered the other woman's offer. She did not want to go alone, and having her maid along might help soothe Dulverton once this was all over. But then she groaned. "You do not ride, Becky. I can hardly put you up before me on Robin."

"There must be some way—"

"How? Do you propose to run behind me in the darkness?"

"We could walk."

"That would take three-quarters of an hour each way. No," she said before Becky could argue. "I shall go alone. I will be fine."

"But what about your horse?"

"I am no fragile flower, Becky. I can saddle my own mount."

Becky looked unconvinced. "You have been lucky before, but if you press your—"

"This is the last time, Becks. And then he will be gone."

"Aye, but not forever. There is nothing to say he can't come back and ask for more."

"That is certainly true, but—"

"And where are you going to get that much money?" she interrupted.

"I'm not giving him any money."

"*Katie!*"

"*Shhhh,*" Katie hissed, glancing toward the connecting door. "I can hear Court moving about in there—perhaps even Dulverton—do you *want* to get me caught?"

Becky ignored her question, but she did lower her voice, "Why on earth are you meeting him if not to pay him?"

"Because I am going to tell him I will send my *own* letter to the newspapers." Katie was ashamed it had taken her so long to come up with a response to his threats. How could she be so good at chess and yet have neglected to see the best move against him?

Becky's perplexed expression was comical. "*What?*"

"It's a gambit. A bluff," she explained when her friend continued to look confused. She gestured to the missive she'd worked on all morning. It had been painful, but she'd laid out the general circumstances of their liaison—including his false promise to marry her—and then gone on to describe their physical relations in excruciating detail, depicting Jasper as a selfish and inept lover. Katie hadn't even needed to exaggerate much. Jasper was an appallingly selfish lover compared to Dulverton. Katie was relying on Jasper's towering conceit and pride to work in her favor. What man would enjoy having his lack of amorous skills broadcast to the world?

Becky snatched the letter Katie had written off the desk. Her cheeks turned brighter and brighter as she read. "I do not even know what half of this means," she admitted with obvious mortification. "But the half I *do* understand?" She shook her head. "You are just as mad as he is, Katie—madder, for you actually have something to lose."

"What are my other options? Tell me, what do you think Dulverton would do if I told him right now that Jasper was threatening to expose me if I did not pay him?"

Becky opened her mouth, but then closed it, furrows marring her forehead. Katie knew the other woman was recalling Dulverton's rage toward Ampthill for merely *talking* to her. She finally sighed. "His Grace would probably kill him."

"Precisely. And if I pay Jasper now, he will just come back again in a few years—or maybe even less time—when he is pockets-to-let. I have no other choice, Becky. He needs to leave here knowing that I cannot be bullied or threatened into doing his bidding. I need to show him I am willing to tell my side of the story if he tells his. It is fighting fire with fire."

Becky's expression was grimmer than Katie had ever seen. "I hope it will be enough, Katie. I surely do."

So did Katie.

***

Getting through dinner and two chess games afterward was difficult. Not because of anything Dulverton did, but because of Katy's own guilt.

And then there was the fact that he was so uncharacteristically sweet when he stopped outside her door. "I will miss you tonight," he said, and then kissed her palm, opened the door, and left her with a pounding pulse and equally pounding conscience at lying about her flux.

"Are you sure about this?" Becky asked half an hour later, her cornflower-blue eyes flickering over the buckskin breeches and clawhammer coat that Hy had given Katie several years back so they could ride astride around the grounds of Chatham Park.

"Yes. I am sure." Katie pulled the hood of her dark gray cloak over her hair and then tugged on her black gloves. "I should only be gone an hour. If I am gone longer than… let's say two hours, then tell His Grace where I went."

Becky pursed her lips but, to Katie's relief, did not argue.

They tiptoed down to the sunroom, which had a door that was closer to the stables than the main entrance. When Becky began to follow her, Katie shook her head. "I don't need help saddling a horse, but I do need the key to the tack room."

Becky handed over the key she'd taken from somewhere—Katie hadn't wanted to ask since her friend had looked so angry about it. "Here. Make sure you bring it back—along with yourself. Be careful, Katie."

"I will." Katie gave her a quick, hard hug, opened the door, and then hurried across the lawn toward the stables. This would be the trickiest part, but Becky assured her that the stablemaster, Mr. Bickle, always went to bed not long after dark unless he knew that Dulverton would require him. Once Mr. Bickle shut down the stables none of the other servants loitered in his domain.

Katie took the lantern from the hook in the brick-lined courtyard and carried it into the utter darkness of the building, stopping first at the tack room, where the key slid into the lock like a knife through butter. She located Robin's saddle and blanket and set it outside the room before slinging his bridle over her shoulder and re-locking the door.

It was far warmer in the bowels of the stable than it was outside, and the smell of horse was strong. The sound of hooves shifting uneasily in their boxes and a few low nickers greeted her as she counted stalls to the seventh one, which is where Becky said Robin was kept.

"Robin?" she whispered, amused when the horse gave what sounded like a puzzled but happy whicker.

She hung the lantern on the hook, quickly bridled him, and then hurried back to fetch his saddle and blanket. Once she'd cinched his girth, she led him to the courtyard, quickly rehung the lantern, and then stepped up onto the heavy mounting block and lowered herself on his back. It was much easier situating herself on the side-saddle without a heavy train getting in her way.

"Good boy," she murmured, taking a moment to stroke the side of his neck. "Let's go, shall we?" He sprang forward and Katie cringed at the sound of his hooves on the cobbles, expecting to hear shouts and raised voices any minute, but she reached the path in blessed silence.

The moonlight was bright enough until she reached Echo Forest, where it was almost pitch black beneath the heavy tree canopy. Katie sorely missed the lantern, and even though Robin knew the path well, he picked his way slowly, giving her far too much time to ponder what she was about to do.

She breathed a sigh of relief once they'd made their way out of the forest, but her relief was short-lived because she reached the path that led to the empty cottage a scant five minutes after that.

"Wish me luck, boy," she said to Robin as they turned onto the narrow driveway that led to the cottage. The tree canopy was thinner here than in Echo Forest, and the moonlight danced eerily. She ruthlessly suppressed the nasty tendril of fear in her belly. "There is nothing to be afraid of, is there, boy?" She stroked Robin's neck as they came out of the tunnel of trees into the clearing that surrounded the cottage.

Katie reined in, frowning. There was no horse and no lights in the house. Was she too early, or—

A hand closed around her ankle, and she shrieked. Robin reared, but a huge man appeared at his head and caught the reins.

"*Shhh*, lad," the man mumbled, easily holding the skittish horse.

"What's this? Breeches?" Jasper asked, laughing raucously. "You are a spirited wench and will make a most invigorating traveling companion."

"I am not going anywhere with you," she said, pulling on her leg.

Jasper's grip tightened. "Ah, I beg to differ, darling."

"Why would you want a woman who hates you?"

"Because it's not you I want, you fool; it's your money."

"I have no money—it all belongs to Dulverton."

"Keep lying if it makes you happy."

Katie wanted to scream. "Even if I *did* have a fortune, I would die before signing so much as a ha'penny over to you."

He gave an ugly laugh. "That is what you say *now*." He tugged on her ankle, almost pulling her to the ground. "Get down or I'll drag you off."

Katie heard the barely restrained violence in his voice and scrambled down. "There. Now what do you want?" she demanded, trying to sound brave but failing.

"Here is something I've wanted to do for weeks." He struck her across the face so hard it knocked her back a step.

Katie cried out and clutched her cheek while Jasper grabbed her other arm and yanked her against him.

"I have put up with your nonsense for far too long, you little bitch." His fingers ground her bones together. "If you give me any more trouble it won't be a slap next time." He turned to his huge companion. "You! Get over here and hold her."

"I dunno 'bout this, me lor. I din't sign up for no rough and tumble. You said as 'ow 'Er Grace would go willing like." The giant absently stroked Robin's neck while the horse danced nervously.

"You idiot! What sort of business did you honestly *think* you were hired to do at this time of night? Now come here and hold her while I mount and then you can lift her up." He turned to Katie and hissed, "Unless you are going to misbehave and I need to tie you up, my dear?"

"I do not think that will be happening," a low voice said behind them.

It was Jasper's turn to yelp as he spun them both around.

Dulverton rode out of the dark shadows into a beam of moonlight, his harsh features as hard as a cliff face. "Unhand my wife or I will tear your arm off your body, Staines."

# Chapter Thirty-Five

Whatever you think is happening here, Dulverton, you are probably wrong," Jasper yelled shrilly, gripping Katie's arm even harder.

Dulverton dismounted with the fluid grace that always left Katie feeling a bit breathless and strode toward them. "Unhand her," he snarled.

Jasper stumbled back a step and yanked on Katie's arm, but she dug in her heels. "Grab him, you fool!" Jasper shouted over his shoulder. But there was no answer and when Jasper twisted them both around, she saw that Robin was alone.

"I think your minion decided that discretion was the better part of valor, Staines." The duke's quiet, toneless voice was more terrifying than a shout.

Jasper whirled them around. "You want her?" He shoved Katie so hard she stumbled. "*Here* she is!"

Dulverton caught Katie before she could fall and steadied her, seemingly unconcerned as Jasper's footsteps receded into the darkness. He lifted her chin and his pale eyes turned to ice when he saw her cheek. "He struck you."

"It—it doesn't hurt," she lied. "I'm so sorry about all this, Dulverton. I never thought he would—"

"*Shhh,*" he murmured as he leaned down and lightly kissed the offended cheek.

A scream shattered the night. "*Aaargh!* What the hell do you think you are doing?" Jasper demanded in a high-pitched voice.

Katie heard an answer voice—low and masculine—right before a dull *thud,* which was immediately followed by the sound of branches snapping and something being dragged.

"Stay here, Kathryn." Dulverton held her chin until she nodded. He released her and they both turned as Mr. Court emerged from the gloom, effortlessly dragging Jasper by one foot.

Katie had never thought Court an especially large man—certainly not when compared to her husband—but he was obviously wiry and strong. "I caught him trying to reach his carriage," he said, shoving his normally impeccable hair off his brow with the hand not gripping Jasper's boot. His bland features twisted into a scowl. "His minion was nowhere in sight. Shall I go after him, Your Grace?"

"Thank you, Court. That won't be necessary," Dulverton said when the valet yanked Jasper the last few feet and then dropped his leg, leaving him belly up in front of the duke.

Jasper whimpered and began to push himself up. Dulverton put his huge, booted foot in the middle of the other man's chest. "You struck my wife."

Even ten feet away Katie shivered at the frost in her husband's voice.

"I—I—she incited me," Jasper said in a choked voice.

Dulverton struck like a serpent, grabbing Jasper by the front of his coat, and yanking him to his feet in a move that demonstrated his massive strength. Even though Jasper was not as husky as her husband, he was still a tall, well-proportioned man.

"It is unfair to beat on those who are weaker, but that did not stop you from hitting my wife, so—" Dulverton backhanded Jasper so hard it was a wonder his head did not fly off his neck.

Katie gasped and then winced at the pain in her cheek, lifting a hand to hold the swollen, pulsing flesh, as if that would somehow ease the pain.

Dulverton looked up at the sound, his murderous expression kindling when he noticed she was cupping her cheek.

Jasper was just lifting his head when the duke hit him again.

And again.

And again.

"Dulverton!" she cried.

Her husband stopped in mid-swing and turned to her, Jasper dangling from his other hand like a ragdoll. Katie recoiled at the naked rage on his face. *Never* had she seen so much anger—on his face or anyone else's—and it sent an icy shiver down her spine, even though it was not aimed in her direction.

"What?" he growled when she did not speak.

"You—you might kill him."

His blond brows drew down sharply. "You care for this piece of filth?"

"No! Of course I don't. But I care for you—and I do not wish to flee England and live on the Continent. I—I like it here at Briarly." She paused and added, "With you."

He stared at her for what felt like years but could only have been a few seconds. And without speaking, he turned back to Jasper, whose body was limp, his head lolling. "You threatened to go to the newspapers to discredit and shame my wife?"

Katie's jaw dropped. How did he know that?

When Jasper only moaned, the duke shook him like a terrier shaking a rat. "Answer me, you piece of dog refuse."

"Yeth! Yeth! *Pleath, thtop*!" Jasper lisped, as though he was missing a tooth.

"Yes, what?"

"Yeth, I threatened her," Jasper whined. "But I wathen't going to do it," he moaned. "I thwear."

"You are a man without any honor. Why should I take your word?"

"I—I thwear on my daughter."

Dulverton's eyes narrowed.

"I thwear on my life," Jasper amended.

Dulverton grunted. "I would be more inclined to believe that." When Jasper's eyes drifted shut, the duke shook him again.

"What?" Jasper whined piteously.

"You are vermin and deserve to be exterminated."

Katie gasped and Dulverton cut her a quick look, his face twisting as some strong emotion wracked him.

"But I cannot kill you."

Jasper started sobbing and babbling what sounded like *thank yous*.

Grim-faced, Dulverton turned to Court. "Did his horse run off?"

"Yes, but his carriage is only a few minutes away."

Dulverton turned to Jasper and hit him again.

"*Aaargh!* What wath that for? I promithed you!"

"Shut up or I will change my mind about letting you go."

Jasper cringed and Dulverton thrust him toward Court. "Get him out of my sight before I come to my senses and kill him."

Jasper whimpered.

Court shoved his shoulder beneath Jasper's armpit. "I'll not carry you. You can walk, or I can drag you again, the choice is yours."

"Walk—I can walk."

He could, but just barely. Despite his words to the contrary, Court all but carried him into the darkness.

Dulverton turned to her. "Come. You will ride with me."

"But—Robin?"

"Court will take him back." Dulverton swung himself up on Centurion's back, held out a hand and extended his foot.

Katie took his hand and set her foot on his and he effortlessly lifted her up. "Swing your leg over." Once she'd complied, he held her with one arm and turned the horse.

"How did you know where to find me?" she asked, even though she could guess. But anything was better than silence.

"Your maid went to Court, who brought her to me."

Thank God Becky was every bit as willful as Katie. What had she told him? Everything? Somehow Katie could not believe that. Becky would have left most of the story to Katie.

"I need to tell you some things—things you might not know," Katie said when they entered Echo Forest, whose darkness felt soothing rather than scary now that she was safe with her husband.

"We will be home in less than—"

"I want to tell you now so I don't have to look you in the eyes."

A long pause, and then, "Very well."

"There was no footman."

"Yes, I gathered that," he said dryly.

"I—I didn't tell you about Jasper because I didn't want you to challenge him to a duel."

He gave a mirthless laugh. "Lord Jasper owes his life to your maid. She extracted a promise from me before she would tell me your whereabouts." Although he sounded like a man thwarted of his due, Katie could not help thinking there was a certain—if grudging—respect in his voice when he mentioned Becky. "He would not have gotten off so easily if I had not given my word."

Katie thought about Jasper's misshapen face and bloody mouth. If that was Dulverton's notion of getting off *easily*, she did not want to see *hard*.

In any case, she owed her friend even more than she'd believed. And she owed her husband the truth. "I came here tonight to tell Jasper that I would not give him money even though he was threatening to expose every detail of our long-ago affair—as well as creating a few of his own. He said he would sell the story to a newspaper."

"He would never have done so."

Katie twisted until she could see just one side of her husband's face. "What do you mean?"

"Lady Grimsby would cut him off if he did such a thing—even if she did not realize he was the source of the rumor."

"He said she would never cut him off because he would take his daughter back."

"He signed away his rights to his daughter months ago."

"*What?*"

"Yes. In exchange for money, of course."

"I never heard anything about that."

"It is not common knowledge; I know his solicitor."

"And he told you?"

"Yes."

"Isn't that—er, illegal?"

"Under the circumstances, no."

"What circumstances?"

"I will tell you later. Finish your story."

Before she could lose her nerve, she blurted, "I became pregnant that summer five years ago."

His big body jolted, telling Katie that was not something he had expected. "I see," he said a moment later.

"We had been, um, meeting each other for several weeks when he was called away by Lady Grimsby. He promised he was going to tell her that he was marrying me." She snorted. "I was so stupid that I—"

"You were but six-and-ten and Staines must be a good decade older."

"There are twelve years between us."

He made a noise of disgust. "You were not to blame, Kathryn. He was. You were a child."

"Many women marry at that age."

"We are talking about manipulation and deflowering, not a marriage."

"I suppose so. But I was not entirely without blame."

"What did he say when you told him about the child?" he asked, ignoring her claim.

"I did not get a chance to tell him because he brought a wife with him when he returned to his father's house."

Dulverton muttered something under his breath.

"I beg your pardon?" Katie said.

"Nothing," he said. "Go on."

"His father hosted a ball for him and his new bride. I did not want to go, but my aunt insisted. I thought he would just ignore me," she confessed, loath to tell him just how petty Jasper had been. "But he—he taunted me that night, taking pleasure in baiting me in front of our neighbors. It was—it was one of the worst nights of my life and my aunt would not allow me to leave."

His arm tightened around her, but he did not speak.

"The ball was awful, but it was not much better when I was in bed that night. I was terrified of the future and was awake all night but still unable to think. I went for a ride at first light hoping to clear my head. I was upset and stupid and reckless and tried to jump—" Her voice broke, and she choked back a sob before she could finish. "I was thrown and lost the child."

He held her so tightly she could scarcely breathe. "Oh, Kathryn, my poor darling."

Katie had been hanging by a thread and his tender words and gentle tone—one she'd never heard from him before—snapped her control and she sobbed. Once she started, she could not seem to stop, crying uncontrollably just as she'd done all those years ago when she'd woken up on the ground, the skirt of her habit soaked in blood.

Dulverton stopped Centurion and wrapped both arms around her, holding her silently in his strong arms while she poured her grief out into the night.

Katie cried until there was nothing left, until she felt empty, the old pain burnt away. She realized when she emerged from her weeping that Dulverton was not only holding her, but was pressing light kisses on her head, temple, and cheek, carefully avoiding the swollen part of her face.

"Th-thank you," she said hoarsely. "I can continue now."

He answered with a firm kiss on her crown and a gentle squeeze around her waist. "There is no need to hurry," he murmured into her hair. "I can let you down and we can walk or sit, if you would rather?"

Katie eyes burned with fresh tears at his thoughtful, generous offer. "Thank you, but I am fine."

One last kiss before he took up the reins and they moved on.

Katie cleared her throat, feeling a sudden urgency to tell the rest of the story and be done with the painful subject. "My aunt found out the truth when I went to her terrified by all the bl-blood. She told my mother, of course. The countess was furious, disgusted, and ashamed. She forbade me to tell my sisters or—or anyone else. I obeyed her until a few weeks ago when I told Becky—er, Stone."

Dulverton's hand, which still rested on her belly, tightened and he pulled her even closer, a low rumbling emanating from his chest. "If I had known all of this back there, I would have killed Staines," he seethed.

"That is why I could not tell you. Everyone says you are a capital shot and lethal with a blade. I—I did not want you to be punished for killing a peer's son."

"*A capital shot?*" he repeated in an amused voice. "I think you have been listening to gossip, my love." He pressed more kisses against her hair, his breath hot on her scalp.

*My love?*

Katie did not dare to hope he meant it as anything more than a casual endearment. "So that is why I had to come alone tonight to—to end this. You see that, don't you?"

"No."

Katie bit her lip at his curt response, recalling Becky's words from earlier. "Are—are you going to beat me?"

Dulverton snorted. "Something tells me that you would not respond well to a beating, Kathryn." Before she could agree, he added, "And I am not the sort of man who beats women. However, if you *ever* keep an important matter from me again, I—"

"I won't! I promise. And this—this was all of it."

"All?" he asked, sounding skeptical.

"I give you my word. It was all." But then Katie recalled one more thing.

"What?" he demanded.

"I did not say anything."

"No. But your body tensed. What is it, Kathryn?"

"It is nothing bad," she hastened to assure him.

"If it is not bad, then why won't—"

"It is possible that I am with child."

Dulverton reined in sharply. "*What* did you say?"

"I—I suspect I am with child."

After a long, worrisome silence, she felt his thighs flex and Centurion resumed walking.

"You are angry with me for risking our child tonight."

"I am angry—no, furious—with you for risking *yourself* tonight, Kathryn. I have been since the moment your maid told me of your reckless plan. And I am furious that you did not trust me enough to ask me for help. Have I really been so awful that you—"

"No! You have not been awful at all." She gave a watery laugh. "Not for a long time. I should have trusted you, Gerrit." She felt his body tighten at the sound of his name and knew herself for the shameless manipulator she was. "I am so sorry—for all of it. For lying to you to begin with, for withholding the truth for so long, for not asking for help. Can—can you forgive me?"

His voice, when he finally answered her, was quiet and filled with pain. "It will take time, Kathryn."

Silent tears slid down Katie's face as they rode the rest of the way home without exchanging another word.

# Chapter Thirty-Six

The Briarly stables were lit up like Vauxhall Gardens and at least five servants scurried about the courtyard when they rode up.

Knowing their master well, nobody chattered or asked questions when Katie and the duke arrived on only one horse.

Dulverton swung down first and then lifted her down. Rather than slowly sliding her down his body, an activity she heartily enjoyed, he set her on her feet and gestured to Thomas.

"Escort your mistress back to the house and see that a bath is brought up to her chambers."

"Mrs. Cranston has already got water on the boil, Your Grace," the footman said.

"Go with him," Dulverton said to Katie.

"But… aren't you—"

"I have several matters to attend to."

Katie nodded, her heart leaden as she walked the short distance back to the house. She did not even reach the door to her chambers before it flew open.

"I am *so* sorry, Your Grace! I had to tell him! I had to," Becky cried, her eyes red and swollen. "I have packed my things and can leave in—"

"*Shhh*, Becky. I will never be able to thank you enough," Katie said, briefly embracing her stunned servant before turning away.

"Dear God, your poor face!" Becky reached out and cupped Katie's cheek. "Did His Grace—"

"Of course not!"

There was a knock on the door.

"Come in," Katie said wearily.

The door opened and Jeremy entered with a large steaming cannister of water. "For Her Grace's bath," he murmured, looking anxiously from woman to woman.

Katie nodded and gestured for him to fill the tub, waiting until he'd gone into the other room before turning to her friend. "I will tell you the whole of it tomorrow," Katie said, struggling to keep back her tears. "But I am too tired now."

Becky gave her a concerned look but squeezed Katie's shoulder. "I will see to your bath."

"Thank you."

Katie found herself in steaming, chin-deep water less than ten minutes later. The tub had been built for her husband, which meant she could stretch out and wallow in her misery in comfort. She closed her eyes and tried to forget about Dulverton's pained, betrayed words. She deserved his anger and more. What if Becky had not told him about tonight? Katie would be tied up in a carriage on the way to Dover right now.

God! She was such a fool.

She heard a footstep behind her and dashed away her tears. "You can go to bed, Becky. I will wash my own hair and see to—"

"It is not Becky."

Katie jolted, sending water sloshing, and twisted while sinking lower in the water.

Dulverton stood in the doorway in his shirtsleeves and buckskins, his coats and cravat gone, a large V of muscular chest exposed. In one hand he held the short stool Becky used when she washed Katie's hair. He set it down near the head of the tub and then lowered himself onto it, looking huge on the tiny stool.

He glared as he reached out and lightly touched her cheek. "This is swollen. You should have a beefsteak on it."

"That is what Bec—er, Stone said. But I do not want to hold meat on my face."

"*Hmm.*" He looked as if he wanted to argue but dropped his hand and proceeded to roll up his sleeves, which she saw had already been freed of cufflinks. Once he'd exposed his thick, muscular forearms he reached for the bar of soap. "I will wash your hair."

"But—" She broke off.

"But?"

"I thought you were angry with me?"

"I am no longer angry."

"You said it would take time!"

He shrugged. "Time has now passed."

Katie gave a slightly hysterical laugh. "I thought you meant *months* or maybe even years."

"I have already wasted enough of our marriage being a stubborn fool. I am not about to waste another minute." He hiked an eyebrow. "Why? Did you wish me to be angry longer?"

"No, of course not, but—"

"Good. Now, dip your head—"

"I don't use that soap for my hair. There is a bottle over there"—she pointed to the collection of glass stoppered crystal. "The tallest one."

He replaced the soap and fetched the decanter, setting it on the marble floor before moving the footstool behind her head until she could no longer see him.

She heard some clinking and a sniff.

"*Mmm*, this is why your hair smells so good. What is it?"

"Chamomile and some other herbs. Stone makes it for me."

"Dip your hair in the tub." One of his palms settled on top of her head. He did not push hard, but she slipped under fast and came up sputtering. A fistful of toweling appeared in front of her.

She snatched it from him and wiped off her face. "A little warning would have been nice."

He made a sound that might have been a chuckle and began to massage her scalp with strong fingers.

Katie closed her eyes and reveled in his firm, caressing touch, speedily forgiving him for almost drowning her. He slowly moved from her head to her neck. Katie bit back the first few moans of pleasure but stopped caring when his strong fingers began to knead her aching shoulders.

Katie must have dozed because she startled when his hands disappeared. "That was nice," she said sleepily, yawning hugely.

"I am about to rinse; so there is your warning."

She closed her eyes and mouth just as warm water streamed over her head.

Once he'd rinsed away the soap, he caught her hair up in his fist and squeezed most of the water from it.

Katie began to stand, but his hand curved around the back of her neck, stopping her. "Where do you think you are going?" he asked.

"I, er, thought you were done."

The loud *scritch* of the stool answered her, and Gerrit appeared at her side. "The washcloth is dry, so you did not yet wash your body. I will clean you."

"Oh. You don't need to—"

"Hush."

To Katie's utter astonishment, she *hushed. But only because I am so tired*, she assured herself.

Dulverton dipped the cloth in the water and then worked up a lather. "Give me your arm."

She lifted the arm closest to him, and he cleaned from her shoulder to the meaty part of her upper arm and then down to her forearms, massaging her as he went.

Katie groaned. "Why does that feel so good?"

"You do a great deal of work with this arm," he answered gruffly, his strong fingers moving to her hand, which he proceeded to rub in lovely ways.

"Where did you learn to do this?" she asked, forcing her eyes open.

He raised one eyebrow.

The happy, lazy feeling that had filled her vaporized like a drop of water on a hot stove. "Oh. I see. From one of your m-mistresses," she snarled, infuriated at herself for stammering.

One corner of his mouth lifted slightly, and he took her other arm, now stiff with anger, and began to wash it. "I am almost eight-and-thirty, Kathryn. Of course I have had other lovers."

*Lovers.* The word scraped on her nerves like a razor. Katie hated how curious she was about his mistresses—even more so than about his first wife. After all, he had chosen his mistresses while his wife had been foisted upon him.

*You are an idiot. Asking questions will only lead to pain.*

She knew that. And yet she burned to know every detail about her reserved husband's past.

The irony that *she* had been the one meeting a former lover tonight and yet *she* was the one boiling with jealousy did not escape her. Nor did it escape her that she had just as much control over her husband's past lovers as she did over his future ones.

Her mother had told her, and her sisters, over and over again that all aristocratic men engaged mistresses. The countess had been adamant that a well-bred woman should pretend they knew nothing about such matters. Her eyes had glittered viciously whenever she'd spoken about the subject, her white-lipped fury telling her daughters far more than her words had done.

Five Seasons in London had taught Katie her mother's warning was *almost* always true. The only exceptions she'd met were her sisters' husbands.

But those marriages had all been love matches.

Unwanted, her mother's voice pushed into her thoughts.

*You will be grateful when your husband takes his base, vulgar needs elsewhere.*

But Katie *would not* be grateful. Just thinking of Dulverton with another woman made her want to hit him with a brick. It also made her want to crawl on top of him and tear off his clothing and mark him as *hers*. And it made her want—

"What is going on inside your head, Kathryn?" Gerrit asked, pausing his ablutions to tuck an escaped curl behind her ear.

Katie shrugged and glared down at the water. The bubbles had mostly disappeared and the soap-clouded water did a poor job of concealing her body.

"Kathryn."

She refused to look up.

Dulverton lifted her chin.

Katie closed her eyes.

"Look at me."

The only reason she opened her eyes was because she heard a rare hint of humor in his voice. But she saw no evidence of a smile on his stern mouth, and his pale eyes looked strangely dark in the low light as he absently stroked her chin with his thumb, his jaw flexing.

"What?" she demanded rudely.

His penetrating eyes lifted to hers. "Why are you so angry?"

"I am not angry," she snarled.

He leaned forward and kissed her, the hand holding her chin sliding around to the back of her neck. It was a deep, drugging kiss that left not just her eyelids but the rest of her body feeling heavy. By the time he released her and sat back on his ridiculous milking stool, Katie was weak and breathless.

"Why are you angry?" he asked again.

"How can you do it?"

He frowned. "Kiss you?"

"How can you just p-pay a woman to be your—to do the same things you and I do together?" she finished miserably, wishing she had never opened her mouth.

He regarded her silently for what felt like hours. Katie had given up on any answer when he said, "Nothing I've ever done with anyone else is anything like what you and I do together. And that is because there is nobody else like you, Kathryn."

Katie realized her mouth was open and shut it.

"Now, will you let me finish bathing you?"

Katie was stunned into silence by his declaration and all she could manage was a nod.

By the time he finished her second foot, Katie's body was limp and her mind was no longer spinning but hazed with sensual pleasure.

And then he reached into the water and slid both hands around her thighs.

Katie's eyes sprang open. "Oh! You—you don't need to do up—up there."

He met her gaze with a serious look. "I am very thorough, Kathryn."

Her heart was back to pounding at her ribs like a fist on a cell door when he finished soaping and stroking the inside of her thigh.

When he reached for her other leg, his hand grazed her mound and she jumped.

"Don't worry, Kathryn. I'll get to that part next. I'm saving the best for last." And then he *smirked* and proceeded to shred her few remaining wits.

Instead of leaving her leg in the tub when he'd finished with it, he draped her knee over the side.

"Gerrit?"

Without speaking, he did the same with her other leg.

"What—what are you—"

"You are so beautiful," he said while both his hands sank below the water, one landing on her breast while the other stroked her wickedly exposed sex.

Katie shuddered as he circled her swollen, aching bud, his other hand teasing and pinching and caressing her nipples until she felt ready to burst.

Gerrit leaned low enough to suckle the tip of her breast, one thick finger sliding inside her slick passage while his clever thumb nudged her over the edge. "Come apart for me, darling."

***

Kathryn could scarcely keep her eyes open as Gerrit dried off her wet, sex-flushed body. She was so lovely that it hurt to look at her. That was not hyperbole; he felt an actual ache in his groin as he carefully ran the soft flannel over her skin. His cock had been hard for the last half hour and the front of his breeches was obscenely tented. He desperately wanted to spread her out on his bed and bury himself inside her—claim her and wipe any association with Staines from her mind and body. But the night had been a difficult one for her, and the swollen side of her face had to be paining her, so he restrained his savage desire and gave her the tender care she needed and deserved.

"Time for bed," he said once he'd finished.

She sat on the short stool and yawned and blinked up at him. "I need to comb out my hair and plait it or it will be a knotted mess." She blew a damp spiral of hair out of her eyes.

"I will do it for you when you are in bed." Gerrit leaned down to slide his arms around her and lift her.

She made a startled noise in her throat, one of her slim arms snaking around his neck. "Oh, you needn't carry me. I can—"

"Kathryn."

"Yes?"

"Let me take care of you."

"Thank you," she mumbled, her uncharacteristically obedient response a good indicator of just how tired she was.

Gerrit set her down on the high mattress and fetched his banyan from the dressing room, draping it over her shoulders.

"Thank you," she said, pulling it around her body.

Gerrit took his comb off the tray where Court kept it and climbed up on the bed. He pulled her into the V of his legs, put a pillow between her back and his chest so she could recline, and began carefully teasing out the snarls that had formed already.

"*Mmmm*," she hummed, snuggling against him. "You are much gentler than Stone."

Gerrit grunted, somewhat stunned by the enormity of the task. Good Lord she had a lot of hair.

By the time he finally worked his way through the last tangle Kathryn's head was listing to one side. "Still awake?" he asked, setting the comb on his nightstand, and shaking out his cramping hand.

"You must p"—she gave a great yawn. "Sorry, you must plait it." She turned just enough that her heavy-lidded gaze met his. "Do you know how?"

Gerrit nodded and painstakingly divided her hair into three thick ropes and commenced to braid it. Once he'd worked all the way down to the ends he frowned when he saw the results of his labors. Despite his careful efforts, one of the strands was thicker than the others and the thick plait was not quite centered on her back.

"Damnation," he muttered quietly. He gritted his teeth and was about to undo it and start again when she yawned.

"So tired," she murmured.

Gerrit dropped his hands, his fingers twitching and an oily sense of unease spreading in his belly at the unsymmetrical plait.

Kathryn twisted in his arms, her head lolling back on his shoulder as she gazed up at him. "Your eyes look just like the moon."

Gerrit blinked. "Er, thank you?"

"They are the most beautiful eyes I've ever seen," she added, smiling drowsily.

He opened his mouth but did not know what to say. She liked his eyes?

*You have eyes like a corpse!* Christina had shouted at him the night Gerrit had told her he was taking her back to Spenwood and leaving her there. That he would no longer tolerate her fucking her way through the *ton*.

Kathryn gave a little shiver and pulled him out of his unhappy memory.

He turned back the blankets on the other side of the bed. "Let go of the robe and get beneath the covers," he murmured, kissing her damp head.

She shrugged out of the robe and began to crawl across the bed. Gerrit knew the exact moment she realized the view she was affording him because her body stiffened. But fatigue was stronger than embarrassment and she quickly burrowed beneath the blankets, asleep before her head hit the pillow.

Gerrit reluctantly left the bed long enough to return his comb and robe to their proper places and then he finished undressing, his gaze lingering on his wife's sleeping face. Her *swollen* face.

He was *furious* that he'd let Staines go free. If he left Briarly right now, he could easily catch the man and exact the appropriate retribution.

Gerrit's eyes narrowed as he imagined his hands around the other man's throat. He had never been so close to breaking his vow in his life.

He looked down at his fisted hands and sighed. It did not matter that he'd given his word to Kathryn's servant; he *always* honored his promises. Staines had been lucky tonight. But his sort could not stop their scheming and manipulation. His vile deeds would catch up with him sooner than later.

He twitched the heavy drapes closer together. It was already three-thirty; he did not want dawn's light disturbing Kathryn in the morning.

He snuffed the remaining candles and climbed under the blankets beside his wife. Having her in his bed, naked, was painfully arousing and his hand closed around his cock.

Gerrit gave himself a brief squeeze, sighed, and dropped his hand. The thought of bringing himself off was less than satisfying. If he could not have Kathryn, then he would rather do without.

Kathryn

# Chapter Thirty-Seven

I am sorry I've been neglecting you," Gerrit said to Amelia. In the five days since the fracas with Staines, he had been too caught up in several new discoveries at the dig to pay his usual visits.

*Too besotted with your wife, is more like.*

Gerrit did not bother to deny the accusation. The business with Staines had been nasty, but it had drawn Kathryn closer to him. It had also rid her eyes of the shadows he'd seen far too often. She seemed almost jubilant now that she no longer had secrets to keep.

*Unlike you.*

He gritted his teeth against the thought.

Amelia gave him the calm smile that had always soothed him. "I think you've been missing visits for a good reason."

"What do you mean?" he demanded warily. Had somebody talked? Surely not Court or—

A strange expression crossed Amelia's face. "I like your wife, Gerrit."

Gerrit frowned. "You don't know her—only what I've told you." But he had been thinking that perhaps he should introduce them, as unorthodox as it was. Now that Kathryn would be living at Briarly she could hardly go on in ignorance of who was living in the dower house.

*Yet more secrets…*

He would ponder the matter before acting. Right now, however, he could tell Amelia his news. "Kathryn is with child."

"Congratulations, Gerrit. You must be very happy."

He was happy, although several unpleasant issues continued to plague him, throwing an unpleasant pall over his happiness.

But that was another matter entirely.

"Yes, I am pleased," he said when he saw she was waiting.

Amelia's smile faded and something else replaced it; something that looked like… guilt?

"Is something amiss, Amelia?"

"I *do* know your wife, Gerrit."

Gerrit frowned when her pale cheeks flushed. "Explain."

Ten minutes later Gerrit was shaking his head at her duplicity. "She visited you this past Wednesday?"

Amelia pulled a face. "Yes."

So, his wife had not yet told him *all* her secrets.

"I made her promise not to tell you," Amelia said, clearly reading his thoughts. "Please do not blame her."

Gerrit was too annoyed to speak.

Amelia cleared her throat. "There is something else, too."

"What?" he barked.

Amelia went to her writing desk and took out two pieces of lavender paper that Gerrit recognized all too well.

"I received this from your mother."

"She *writes* to you?" He shook his head in disbelief. "Does every female in my life secretly communicate with each other?"

Amelia chose to ignore his second question, which was not entirely rhetorical. "The dowager wrote only twice." She handed the letters to him.

"I do not want them."

"You need to read them. Especially the newer one." She held his gaze.

He scowled and rudely snatched them away. "*Faugh*," he coughed when the overwhelming floral scent assaulted his nostrils. "It even smells like her."

"Gerrit!"

His head whipped up at the unprecedented sound of Amelia's raised voice. "What?"

"She is your *mother*. She gave life to you. And you owe her respect. And love. And—and more than you—" To his utter horror, Amelia choked on a sob. "Oh, just read them. I will come back." She all but ran from the room and Gerrit stared, shocked. In all the years he'd known Amelia she had never lost her composure. Not even at his father's funeral.

Gerrit turned slowly to the letters. Is this what upset her so? He stared at them as if they were venomous.

Something told him their contents would sting in ways he could not imagine.

He looked from letter to letter and sighed.

And then he unfolded the older more faded missive and commenced to read.

***

Two hours later Gerrit tracked Kathryn down in one of the two succession houses. No surprisingly, it was the one that held mostly ornamental plants.

He paused in the entrance and regarded her for a moment, savoring the breathtaking beauty of his wife among thousands of blooms.

Gerrit wished he could simply approach her and kiss her rather than share the shocking news he had just learned. But there was no sense in putting off the inevitable. After all, hadn't he been the one to say no secrets? Now he had one so mortifying that—

"Dulverton! Have you been there long?" she asked, nudging back an escaped red spiral with the back of one gloved hand and leaving a smudge on her cheek.

"What are you doing?" Only after he'd asked did he realize that he'd ignored her question—a habit he was determined to break, at least with her. He took out his watch. "I have been here less than a minute," he said, replacing it in his pocket.

For some reason she was grinning. Gerrit raised his eyebrows; was something amusing?

But she merely smirked and gestured to the freshly churned dirt. "My sister Phoebe sent me some cuttings. I am no gardener, but I wanted to grow these myself, so I asked Mr. Norland and he gave me detailed instructions."

"I am pleased he was helpful." His ancient head gardener was as fiendishly obsessive about plants as Gerrit was about fossils.

"Did you need something?" she asked.

"I can wait until you are finished."

"I'm actually finished. I was just standing here… thinking."

"About?"

She laughed. "My, my, how times have changed."

Gerrit scowled. "I have always asked questions when I am interested in something."

"So, I have joined the company of fossils, have I?"

"There is worse company to be in."

She smiled. "That is true. I was thinking I'd like to do a bit more gardening. I find it restful."

"I'm sure Norland will be delighted."

She cocked her head at him. "Are you well?" she asked, tugging off gardening gloves that were far too large for her. Gerrit made a mental note to have proper pair made for her. She had her work gloves, of course, but those needed to stay out at the dig and—

"Gerrit?"

He looked up from her hands. "I have to tell you something."

"Is it—did something bad happen to one of my sisters or brothers?"

He blinked. "What? No, no, nothing like that. This is about me." *Unfortunately.*

"Do you want to talk here?" she asked,

"I would rather go for a walk."

"Of course. Let me fetch my hat and return these gloves to Mr. Norland."

A short time later they were strolling through a part of the gardens he almost never visited. He liked flowers, of course, but he did not go out of his way to observe them. Especially when they were wild, these were. His preference was for the precision one found in the parterre garden his father had created.

*His father.*

The utter shock of his mother's letters crashed over him yet again like a brutal, chilling wave.

Good God. Soon he would have to share his shame with Kathryn.

"Gerrit? My slippers are not the best for this slick slope."

Out of habit Gerrit had led her toward the long, gently sloping expanse of lawn that led to the hedge maze. He had no need for a maze today, not when it felt as if there was one in his head with him trapped inside it.

"Apologies," he murmured, taking her arm and slowing his pace. When they reached the bench outside the maze entrance, he stopped. "Let us sit."

Once they were both as comfortable as they would get on cool stone, he turned to her and took her hand, his need for physical contact with her almost overwhelming.

"You are worrying me, Gerrit," she said, setting her other hand on both of theirs.

"I just left Amelia St. Clare's house."

Her lips parted and a guilty, wary look flickered across her face as she opened and closed her mouth, no words emerging.

"I know you have been visiting her."

"Oh. I see. Are you angry?"

"No, I am not angry. It was my intention to introduce you both, but—"

"But it was awkward," she finished for him.

He nodded.

"I like her a great deal," she said after a moment.

"As do I." He reached into his coat and withdrew the letters. "Amelia gave me these a few hours ago. I would like you to read them aloud and I will answer your questions when you've finished."

Her forehead pleated with confusion, and she hesitatingly took the two letters.

"Read the one on top first."

She unfolded the missive and darted a startled look at Gerrit. "It is from your mother."

"Correct."

"And—and it is from decades ago."

Gerrit inclined his head. "Please read it."

She turned back to the letter. "*It pains me that I am reduced to writing to you, but Dulverton is as unyielding as a block of granite. I beg of you, Mrs. St. Clare, if you have any influence over him, use it to good purpose and convince my husband to send my son back to me.*

*I know Dulverton will have told you the truth about Gerrit. I also hope that given your own situation as the lover of a married man that you will not judge what I did harshly. And always remember that everything I've done has been at Dulverton's behest.*

*My marriage was a lie from beginning to end and you are a large part of that lie. You stood as wife to my husband in everything but name and position before I left my home and family and friends behind and came to this country. My son visits you at your house with Dulverton's permission. And yet I am excoriated for living the only life my husband allowed me to have.*

*It is unjust, madam, that you should have both my husband and my child.*

*If you possess any shred of decency, send Gerrit back to me.*

*Lijsbeth Van Draak*"

Kathryn slowly folded up the letter before turning to him. "She must have sent this right after you ran away."

"Yes. Amelia told me today—when she gave me these letters—that she implored my father to send me to my mother on alternate school holidays. But he refused to insist that I visit her and left it for me—a child—to decide. I did not see her for almost a decade." He turned and stared unseeingly at the high foliage walls of the maze. "Read the other letter."

"*Mrs. St. Clare,*

*I am doing what I told myself I would never do again. I am writing to beg you. This time, I want you to tell my son the truth before it is too late. Before his father dies and—"*

Kathryn looked up. "Your father? But this letter is dated only a few days ago."

"Keep reading," he said through gritted teeth.

*"Before his father dies and he does not have the chance to acknowledge him. The silence Dulverton demanded of us was cruel. Certainly, it was unnecessary after Gerrit grew old enough to understand what the duke had done and why. I asked you for decency once before and received nothing. This is an opportunity for you to redeem yourself. You owe me this. And you owe Gerrit, too. If you care anything for my son, you will tell him who his real father is and you will do it before it is too late.*

*Lijsbeth Van Draak"*

Kathryn stared up at him with incomprehension on her beautiful face. "What on earth does she mean, *real father?*"

"She means that I am not the fourth Duke of Dulverton's son. I am the son of Helmut Berg, the last duke's stablemaster."

***

Katie clamped her jaws shut just in time to catch her shocked gasp. Not that Gerrit would have noticed at this point. He was staring at nothing, and his face, usually so healthy and tan, was a sickly gray.

"Evidently my father—the last duke, that is—lied to me when he said that he'd not known Helmut Berg was his brother." He stared down at his hands, which were balled into fists and resting on his knees. "He brought Berg to England along with my mother—his new, innocent seventeen-year-old bride—because he had realized he was impotent and he wanted a child of Van Draak blood—regardless of what he had to do for one. Helmut was the best way for him to get what he wanted." He snorted softly. "That was what he told my mother on their wedding night. *On their wedding night.* Can you imagine how she must have felt? She was just a *girl.*"

He shook his head, his expression one of disbelief and disgust. "Berg was not her lover then. There was nothing between the two of them other than a regular mistress-servant relationship. It was my fath—the *duke*—who orchestrated everything that happened. For the rest of his life he allowed me to blame her—and my real father—when *he* was the one who threw them together. All these years I believed my mother drove my father out of his house." He gave a mirthless laugh. "And now I find it was the other way around. All these years," he said again, his voice tight with pain. "I have ignored my real father and shunned my mother." His eyes were like raw wounds when he finally turned to her. "Good God. I am so ashamed of myself, Kathryn."

Unable to keep her distance any longer, Katie set her hand over one of his clenched fists. He jolted at her touch but did not pull away. "How can you be ashamed for what you did not know? If anyone should be ashamed, it is them."

The skin between his eyes puckered. "Them?"

"Yes, *them*. Not just the duke—although he bears the brunt of the blame—but your mother, Berg, *and* Mrs. St. Clare. All four owed you the truth. I do not care if the duke demanded their silence. Some things are too important to hide. And there was no excuse to keep the truth from you when you came of age." She shook her head, dismissing the issue for the moment. "There is a more important matter now—Mr. Berg's health. Have you heard anything? Is he—"

"I received a letter from my mother this morning. She wrote to tell me that he is not at death's door as he was when she arrived to care for him."

Katie gave a sigh of relief.

Gerrit laced their fingers together. "I must go to Spenwood and repair what I can, Kathryn."

"Of course you must!"

He kissed the back of her hand. "And I must apologize to both my mother and—and my father for what I have done and hope they will forgive me."

Katie suspected neither of his parents needed an apology, but she knew her husband needed to give one. "Of course we must go—immediately."

"I do not feel right asking you to embroil yourself in this sordid matter."

She squeezed his big fingers so hard she felt her own bones grinding painfully. "You mean after you stood by me during *my* sordid matter? Besides, you did nothing wrong, Gerrit. *Nothing*. All this"—she gestured to the letters— "happened before you were even born. It is time to leave the past behind and mend your relationships with both your mother and father. You cared greatly for him at one time."

"I cared greatly for both of them." He grimaced. "I know my mother's nature is frivolous, but I cannot deny she loves me. As for Helmut…. He spent hours teaching me everything he knew. He is the reason I can shoot and fence and box. My father"—he pulled a pained face. "Lord. How bloody confusing. *The duke* was not interested in such physical pursuits. He could shoot adequately and handle a sword as well as any gentleman, of course, but he took no pleasure in either activity. It was Helmut who saw that I was able to defend myself against bullies at Eton. Helmut, my mother, and I spent so much time together we were just like a real family, I realize now. He accompanied us when we went riding or when we had picnics or went fishing." He smiled faintly. "My mother loves to fish—at least she used to—but could never bring herself to bait a hook. Helmut told me that was a man's job." His smile faded. "After I caught them together so many of my childhood memories became tainted and ruined."

"I cannot imagine any child wishes to see such a thing, so it is not to be wondered at." Katie did not add what she was thinking—that the old duke's behavior had callously destroyed what must have been a very close mother-son relationship, not to mention Gerrit's love for his real father.

Gerrit stared at her without speaking, his face the inscrutable mask it often was. Would she ever be able to read him more clearly or know what he was feeling?

And then he opened his mouth and said the last thing she would have expected. "You are the best thing that ever happened to me, Kathryn."

Katie's jaw sagged and she had to blink rapidly to keep the tears at bay. "I— you—" she sputtered and then gave a watery chuckle and tried again. "Even better than excavating the largest intact belemnite?"

He gave a startled laugh. "Yes, Kathryn, even better than that." He released her hand and then, with strength that delighted and aroused her, lifted her bodily onto his lap.

Katie smiled down at him and draped an arm around his shoulders before lightly kissing the tip of his beaky and much beloved nose. "When do we leave for Spenwood, my love?"

# Epilogue

*Spenwood*

*Three Months Later*

Katie quietly closed the book she'd been reading aloud and set it on the table next to Helmut Berg's large, overstuffed wingchair. She tiptoed from his private sitting room and closed the door noiselessly behind her. She'd just turned toward the stairs when her mother-in-law's voice came from behind her.

"Katie!" the older woman chirped. "I was just coming to relieve you."

Katie raised a finger to her lips. "He is asleep," she whispered, leading the dowager away from the door before speaking in a normal tone. "He seems much better today, but I thought it best to let him rest whenever he needs it."

Betje nodded vigorously enough to set the pink bows in her hair—which matched her pink gown—dancing. "That is wise. I'm afraid my reading voice is not nearly so restful as yours."

It wasn't the tone of the older woman's voice that kept poor Helmut's eyes open but her non-stop chatter; not that he didn't love it. "Your presence is always a balm to him," Katie said, which was no more than the truth.

"Oh, you are so kind, my dear. Were you looking for Gerrit? He is in the library with Mr. Turner but should be free within the hour." Betje looped her arm through Katie's. "Come and walk with me inside as we cannot enjoy our usual walk in the garden today." She pulled a face as they strolled past a window that showed a snowy, blustery day outside. "I hate the winters here. I always have." She smiled. "I am a frivolous creature of spring and summer."

"Then you should come to Wych House with us when we leave tomorrow—it is not too late to change your mind," Katie said, issuing the invitation not for the first, or even fifth, time. "Although I cannot guarantee it will not snow there, too," she added.

"No, no. I could not do that—although I appreciate your invitation to spend Christmas at your family home." She sighed and gave Katie a beatific smile. "I never even imagined that Helmut and I could go anywhere together as guests rather than mistress and servant."

"You would both be welcome at any of my sisters' or brother's gatherings." Indeed, several of the Bellamy sisters had some rather unconventional friendships with their husband's ex-lovers and had invited them to Christmases in the past. None of her siblings or their spouses would judge Betje and Helmut for their love.

"Perhaps next year, if Helmut continues to mend as he has," Betje said. And then her eyes widened. "Oh, I almost forgot. You will never believe what the vicar said to Mr. Benson!" The dowager proceeded to regale Katie with gossip about her neighbors, most of whom Katie had met over the past three months.

They strolled companionably through the corridors of Spenwood as Betje chattered, but when they entered the gallery, the older woman's feet stopped in front of the portrait of the last Duke of Dulverton. She wore a fond but sad smile as she regarded her long-dead husband. "They are so alike—all three of them."

That was an understatement. Katie had seen a painting of the last duke at Briarly, of course, but he had been quite old in that one. *This* one had been painted when Boon was Gerrit's age and the resemblance between the two was startling. She'd also seen a miniature of Helmut that Betje kept in her chambers. It had been painted not long after Gerrit was born, when Helmut was five-and-thirty. He bore an almost eerie resemblance to his half-brother and, as Gerrit had said, everyone who saw him would know he was related to the old duke.

"How often did Helmut and the duke see each other after, er—" Katie broke off, at a loss how to phrase her question more politely.

"After Boon told me that he wanted me to have a child with another man?" Betje suggested, uncharacteristic bitterness creeping into her normally happy voice.

Heat rose in Katie's cheeks. "I'm so sorry, Mama. I never should not have asked you that."

"Nonsense! You can ask me whatever you like, Katie. Quite honestly, it is a relief that somebody else knows the truth after so many years." Betje's smile slid away, and she gestured to the ancient gilt bench across from the portrait and they sat. "After Boon spoke to me on our wedding night, I told him I needed some time to consider what he proposed. Naturally, I was… shattered. I thought I could never agree to such a thing, but—as matters turned out—I had my answer for Boon in less than a week." She cut Katie a wry look. "Perhaps that reflects poorly on me, I don't know. In my defense, I was young, in a foreign country, and I'd just married a man who did not want me. I had known Helmut since I was a girl and was comfortable with him. Of course I had never considered him in a romantic light, but after Boon's rejection I just—I just needed somebody to want me." She gave Katie a watery smile. "After I gave Boon my answer he spoke to Helmut."

"That must have been an interesting conversation."

"Helmut told me about it later, once we—well, once we knew each other better. He said Boon had been aloof but respectful and oddly humble. That he had made a request rather than issuing an ultimatum." She paused, a mischievous smile curving her lips. "Helmut said to me that he had wanted me for as long as he could remember but had always accepted that I was too far above him to ever hope. He said his heart leapt at the duke's offer, but that he had a condition of his own: if he took me, he would want to keep me." She paused, coloring prettily. "He told Boon he would not share me."

Katie already liked Gerrit's quiet, gentle father a great deal, but now she was a little bit in awe of him, too. Helmut was so soft-spoken that it was hard to imagine him confronting a man like the last duke, who was said to have been every bit as daunting as Gerrit.

"It was no hardship for Boon to agree as his heart had long been engaged elsewhere." She sighed. "I have hated Amelia St. Clare for so long. Not because Boon loved her, but because I believed she had taken Gerrit. I should have defied Boon and gone to Briarly and brought Gerrit back. But I allowed myself to be intimidated by him." She shook herself, her naturally ebullient nature quickly rising again. "It is a long time ago and there is no point in wishing I'd done differently. Besides, everything has worked out well in the end. I am so delighted that you came to Spenwood with Gerrit, Katie. I believe he would have visited Helmut, regardless, but he would not have stayed nearly so long if you'd not accompanied him."

"These past months have been wonderful," Katie said. That was no lie. It had warmed her heart to watch as Gerrit became close to both his parents.

Betje looked pleased, her gaze lowering to the very slight swell of Katie's midriff. "I wish you were not leaving tomorrow, but you will come back here to have the child, yes? The Dukes of Dulverton have always been born at Spenwood."

"We will come back, Mama," Katie promised. "And you and Helmut will come and stay with us at Briarly often. I want my son or daughter to grow up knowing their wonderful grandparents." And Amelia, too, of course, but Katie wisely kept that thought to herself.

Betje gave a sigh of pure happiness. "Isn't life wonderful, my dear?"

Katie slid her arm around her mother-in-law and squeezed her tight, her lips curving into a smile as her thoughts drifted back to that unhappy day all those months ago in Chatham's library, when her reckless behavior forced a proud, aloof man to coldly offer her a marriage of convenience.

"Yes," Katie murmured. "Life is wonderful—wonderfully surprising."

***

Gerrit watched his mother's diminutive form become smaller and smaller as his coach pulled away from Spenwood. When she disappeared entirely, he realized that his throat was tight with emotion and was stunned by the ferocity of his feelings.

"I will miss her," Kathryn said, echoing his thoughts. "I will miss both of them, but I will dearly miss your mother."

Gerrit met her green, cat-eyed gaze and the swell of emotion inside him grew more powerful, more insistent.

*I love you.*

The thought should not have surprised him as much as it did. Deep down, for months, he had known that *love* was the name for the singular emotion he had been feeling. Love. Who would have believed he was capable of feeling such a powerful, moving emotion?

"What is it, Gerrit? You are looking at me in the oddest way."

He opened his mouth, but Kathryn suddenly leaned forward and took his hand. "You will miss them too, won't you? You have come to care for them deeply. That is what you want to say? It is alright to admit to such a thing, you know."

*And now the moment has passed…*

Gerrit swallowed his regret. "Yes, I will miss them." He moved onto her bench, his body crowding hers. "Is this uncomfortable?" he asked, angling himself to give her more room and also to see her better.

"I like it very much." She gestured to the traveling chess set they had brought along with them to while away the time. "But it will be difficult to play chess if we are both on this side."

"For some reason, I would rather sit beside you than play a game just now."

"Coward!"

"Guilty as charged." Gerrit took her slightly thickened waist in his hands and easily lifted her onto his lap.

She immediately snuggled closer. "*Mmm.* You are so warm."

He adjusted her green velvet cloak so that it sat evenly on her shoulders. "You are cold?"

"Not anymore." She glanced out the window, to where snow was swirling. "Do you think we will make it to Wych House in time in this weather?"

It amused Gerrit that she had been asking this question for days.

"We will arrive on time. The journey would normally take three days and I have allotted six just in case we are delayed by weather or for any other reason," he reminded her, shrugging aside the anxious twinge he felt every time he imagined spending three entire weeks in somebody else's house. At least Kathryn would be with him.

She eyed the storm doubtfully. "It is coming down *really* heavily."

"There are many inns on this road. If the snow makes travel hazardous then we will find someplace warm to stay and bundle up and entertain ourselves however we can."

"Do you have answers for everything?"

"When you ask such easy questions." He tucked a bright corkscrew of hair behind her ear and kissed her. He'd intended it to be a peck, but she slid her arms around his neck and deepened the kiss. When he finally pulled away, she was flushed and breathless, her green eyes sparkling and her hair glowing like burnished copper even in the low light of the carriage.

"I hope our child has your coloring." He paused and then added, "But perhaps not your temper."

She laughed, as he'd hoped she would, and gave him a playful shove. "I am not the only one with a temper."

Gerrit knew she was remembering him thrashing Staines. And grabbing Ampthill. And perhaps he *had* become a bit tetchy with that obnoxious young buck who'd approached their table when they'd been dining in a posting inn and—

"As for my hair," she said, pulling Gerrit from his musings. "I wouldn't wish it on my worst enemy. Do you know how often I was mocked for it?"

"Did you not have anyone to protect you?"

"My sisters would leap to my defense whenever they overheard any teasing. Even Doddy would protect me, although he reserved the right to tease me when there was nobody else around."

"If anyone mocks you now, I shall thrash them."

"My own personal knight."

"God no. I know how cruelly you sacrifice your knights."

She gave an enchanting gurgle.

Gerrit cleared his throat and met her merry gaze. "There is something I have been wondering about for quite some time now."

***

"Oh dear. That sounds ominous," Katie teased, wriggling a bit on his lap and smirking when her bottom rubbed against something hard that was not his thigh.

He winced. "You little witch."

"Gerrit!" Katie yelped when he lifted her again, this time positioning her so that she was straddling his thighs.

"Hush," he muttered, and then fussed with her cloak so that she was covered before reaching beneath it and pulling up the hem of her gown until she was naked to her waist. And then he drew her down on his lap so that Katie felt the cool buckskin of his breeches against the heated folds of her sex.

She moaned. "Gerrit."

"Much better," he said, a faint smirk on his lips. "Now, I want to know who else was on that list."

Katie's eyes, which had been drifting shut as she shamelessly reveled in her wicked position and the friction it afforded her, flew open. "List?" she said, although she was afraid that she knew exactly what he meant.

His eyes narrowed. "Kathryn."

"Oh, *that* list. Erm, I don't really recall."

"I know you remember."

"How do you know that?"

He cocked his head.

How did he manage to be more intimidating when he *didn't* speak?

"Why are you asking me this *now*, Gerrit?"

"Fowler will be at Wych House for Christmas, won't he?"

"Yes, along with Letty, his new wife. You have nothing to—"

"Did you kiss him, Kathryn?"

She swallowed down her teasing response—judging by the glitter in his pale gaze now was *not* the time—and shook her head. "I did not kiss Angus."

"Will there be anyone else at your family's party who was on the list?"

"No."

He made a rumbling sound deep in his chest. "Good."

Katie reached out and carded her fingers through his hair. He'd let it grow for her and it was just as gorgeously curly as she'd suspected. She pulled as she stroked, and his eyelids became heavy, the suspicion and anger that had been there only seconds before draining away.

"Are you trying to distract me?" he demanded.

"Correct."

He barked a laugh and then slid both his hands around her face and drew her closer, until they were scarcely an inch apart, and he kissed her nose, the warm, no-longer-so-rare smile on his face.

"I need to work on my subtle manipulating techniques, do I?"

"No. You are quite skilled enough as it is—as you are well aware." He kissed her. "You are a very wicked girl."

"I think you like that about me."

"I do like that. I like everything about you," he murmured.

*"Everything?"* she teased.

"Everything except the way you use your knights to humiliate and destroy me."

Katie laughed.

He rubbed their noses together before releasing her.

Katie straightened up, biting back a grimace at the twinge in her back. She was no longer as flexible as she'd been even a month ago. She looked down at her husband, lightly stroking her palm over his sharp cheekbone. "I'm sure there are plenty of things you dislike about me—or at least things that you don't care for."

"No."

"Why do I think you are fibbing?"

"I do not *fib*." He gave her a stern look, but the slight curve of his lips gave him away. "Now, about your list—"

She covered her eyes with one hand and groaned. "I don't want to think about that dreadful list or who was on it. I which everyone could just forget that night and—"

"I won't forget it."

"Oh, Gerrit! Please can't we—"

"Why would I want to forget the night I met the woman I love?"

Katie caught her breath and then spread her fingers and peeked out between them. "Love?" she squeaked.

He removed her hand from her eyes, kissed her palm, and then placed her hand on his chest. "You've stolen my heart, Kathryn." His lips twitched. "And I didn't even know I had one."

Katie blinked rapidly but a tear still escaped and slid down her cheek. She quickly brushed it aside.

Gerrit grimaced. "Please don't cry. I—"

"They are tears of happiness. I never thought to hear you say those words, Gerrit. I was not sure you even believed in love."

"I didn't until I met you. When I look at you, or when I'm with you, or even when I am thinking about you, I feel a rush of pleasure more intense than anything else I've ever experienced. I've never felt this way before, Kathryn. I am not sure you can imagine how—"

"I can imagine it because I have been feeling the same thing for months and months." She dashed away another tear, smiling. "I am sorry for being a watering pot. It is just that I did not think you felt the same way."

"I didn't either." He pulled a face. "I do not mean that *I didn't think I felt the same way*, but that I did not believe that *you* did. Listen to me, babbling like a fool."

"I rather like it."

He snorted. "Proud of yourself for reducing me to this state?"

"Very."

He chuckled and his usually formidable gaze suddenly softened, and a vulnerable expression settled on his face, something Katie had never thought to see on his aloof features.

"What is it, Gerrit?" she asked after a moment.

"I often think about how you came to my bedchamber that night."

She felt herself blush to her roots. How could she be so silly after everything they had shared?

Gerrit saw her blush and looked amused. "I did not mean *that* part of your visit. Although of course I am thinking about it now." He pulsed his hips, making her groan, but then grew serious. "No, what I think about is that we would be living separate lives right now if not for your wisdom and bravery in coming to me."

"As much as I would love to take all the credit for my behavior, I have to remind you that I did not come to that decision without plenty of encouragement from your mother, Amelia, and Stone."

"Perhaps. But *you* were wise enough and brave enough to listen to their advice. You will not convince me that you are not largely responsible for my happiness, Kathryn. And for teaching me how to love."

If he hadn't already melted Katie's heart half-a-dozen times already, *that* declaration would have done it. "You already knew how to love—you show it in dozens of ways for the people you care about. As for loving you? You are very loveable, Gerrit." She placed a finger across his lips when it looked like he might argue that point. "I think we were both just waiting for each other," she said, leaning low to give him a kiss. When she released him, she cupped his face. "I want to hear it again."

He cocked his head, as if confused. "I know how cruelly you sacrifice your knights?"

Katie laughed. "You know what I mean."

He tightened his arms until she was pressed snugly against him. "I love you, my duchess, my seductress, my darling wife."

Katie sighed happily. "I will never get tired of hearing that."

"Good," Gerrit said, covering her face with light kisses. "Because I will never get tired of saying I love you."

"And showing it?" Kathryn cocked a taunting eyebrow and then reached between their bodies and quickly unhooked his fall before tugging open his soft, well-worn leathers.

Gerrit laughed as she freed him from his garments. "And showing that I love you," he agreed.

And then he took her in his arms and did exactly that.


The end

# Dearest Reader:

Firstly, I hope you enjoyed Gerrit and Katie's love story!

Secondly, Microsoft did a "middle of the night" update and trashed my Dearest Reader letter! Yes, that happened because I had written it but not saved it. Don't be like me—save your documents IMMEDIATELY!

Anyhow, that means this letter is being written in a hurry! So it will not sparkle with brilliance as my other one did…

Katie is definitely one of my pricklier heroines. She reminds me a lot of my heroine in INFAMOUS—Celia—who was a "bad girl" who behaved in truly unlikeable ways (of course she redeems herself by the end). Although I don't think Katie is especially mean spirited like Celia was.

One of the historical romance authors who read and blurbed my book, INFAMOUS told me she admired me for being brave and creating such a bitch for a heroine. It was her contention that readers will forgive a hero just about anything, but they don't like it when their heroines behave like assholes. I don't know if I believe that. I certainly hope we women give heroines as much latitude as we give to men.

Anyhow, it doesn't matter if being difficult makes Katie less marketable or not because she—like all my characters—came to my brain fully formed. It's pretty much impossible for me to try and change a character once they've arrived in my head. I've tried and tried and tried and it never works. Personally, I wanted to slap Katie several times and stop her from doing something ill-advised, but she was gonna do what she was gonna do.

She certainly got her comeuppance in Gerrit, a man who is not about to be led around by the nose or engage in games (well, except chess, of course).

Gerrit was not an easy hero to get to know. He doesn't like to talk very much, which makes him a mystery not only to his heroine, but also to his author, lol. I just needed to learn patience and listen, and he finally trusted me enough to open up. I have to admit I'm a sucker for the strong, silent type. And of course I love a bossy, masterful man and he was all that and more.

One of my four beta readers wanted me to go into more detail on the page about Gerrit's' "condition" but it feels terribly anachronistic to me to discuss Obsessive Compulsive Disorder in a Regency Era romance. He certainly wouldn't have received much sympathy (or acknowledgement) for his condition back then. Even now many people think OCD is just fodder for jokes rather than a debilitating condition.

As for whether he inherited his condition, or it was learned behavior? I don't know and the jury is still out on how much nature vs. nurture matters when it comes to OCD. I'm not a licensed mental health professional, so my apologies to those of you who are if I've oversimplified.

When I started this book, I wanted to make it a double romance (just like INFAMOUS, which I mentioned above) and have an upstairs/downstairs thing going on.

I wrote about five chapters of Becky & Court's romance, interspersing it with Katie and Gerrit's chapters, and then realized that including two romances would make the book too long. So, I pulled the chapters and maybe I'll write a novella at some point.

People weren't widely calling paleontology by that name during the timeframe in this book, I just used the term to make it more accessible to the modern reader.

Also, chess notation would probably have been different back then, but I decided to use the system that I know best to describe the games.

So, what am I working on next? Well, I kind of booked myself into a corner— pardon the pun!—by putting 2 books up for preorder a month apart next year. I'm working like crazy on both DAUNTRY and THE SPIRIT OF LOVE and hope I can meet those deadlines.

Of course, you might have noticed that I dropped Fowler into this book? Heh. That means he and Letty will need their own story, too! Not sure yet if he will get his story before Lucy.

So, the good news is that I have lots of new books in my head, I just seem to be writing them more slowly these days, lol. Please be patient with me, I'm writing as fast as I can.

As always, I love hearing from readers, and you can reach me at minerva@minervaspencer.com. I'm not on social media these days, so email really is the best way to get in touch.

I wish you a safe and happy autumn fill with great books!

Xo

Minerva

# Who are Minerva Spencer & S.M. LaViolette?

Here I am with Mr. Spencer and Lucille (on my lap) trying to wrangle Eva and Winston for a Christmas photo.

Minerva is S.M.'s pen name (that's short for Shantal Marie) S.M. has been a criminal prosecutor, college history teacher, B&B operator, dock worker, ice cream manufacturer, reader for the blind, motel maid, and bounty hunter. Okay, so the part about being a bounty hunter is a lie. S.M. does, however, know how to hypnotize a Dungeness crab, sew her own Regency Era clothing, knit a frog hat, juggle, rebuild a 1959 American Rambler, and gain control of Asia (and hold on to it) in the game of RISK.

Read more about S.M. at: www.MinervaSpencer.com

Follow 'us' on Bookbub:

Minerva's BookBub

S.M.'s Bookbub

On Goodreads

Minerva Spencer & S.M. LaViolette

Minerva's OUTCASTS SERIES

<u>DANGEROUS</u>

<u>BARBAROUS</u>

<u>SCANDALOUS</u>

THE REBELS OF THE *TON:*

<u>NOTORIOUS</u>

<u>OUTRAGEOUS</u>

<u>INFAMOUS</u>

<u>AUDACIOUS (NOVELLA)</u>

THE SEDUCERS:

<u>MELISSA AND THE VICAR</u>

<u>JOSS AND THE COUNTESS</u>

<u>HUGO AND THE MAIDEN</u>

VICTORIAN DECADENCE: (HISTORICAL EROTIC ROMANCE—
SUPER STEAMY!)

<u>HIS HARLOT</u>

<u>HIS VALET</u>

<u>HIS COUNTESS</u>

<u>HER BEAST</u>

<u>THEIR MASTER</u>

<u>HER VILLAIN</u>

THE ACADEMY OF LOVE:

www.ingramcontent.com/pod-product-compliance
Lightning Source LLC
Chambersburg PA
CBHW011148190726
48288CB00010B/3221